BLACKOUT

Chris Ryan

WINDSOR
PARAGON

First published 2005
by
Century
This Large Print edition published 2005
by
BBC Audiobooks Ltd by arrangement with
Random House Group Ltd

ISBN 1 4056 1192 8   (Windsor Hardcover)
ISBN 1 4056 2179 6   (Paragon Softcover)

British Library Cataloguing in Publication Data available

Printed and bound in Great Britain by
Antony Rowe Ltd., Chippenham, Wiltshire

BLACKOUT

London. Paris. New York. One by one the power systems get switched off in three of the world's major cities, plunging them into darkness and chaos. Is this the greatest terrorist spectacular since 9/11?

Josh Harding, a battle-hardened SAS soldier, is working undercover on anti-terrorist operations, tracking the leaders of al-Qaeda. He wakes up in a ditch in the wilderness of Arizona. Two bullets have shot up his leg and his neck. His memory is gone. And the police are hunting him for murder.

As Josh struggles to recover his memory, and to stay one step ahead of the police, he finds himself drawn into a deadly conspiracy. To stay alive, he must find out who he is, and why he was shot and who is turning off the power around the world.

ACKNOWLEDGEMENTS

To my agent Barbara Levy, editor Mark Booth, Kate Watkins, Charlotte Bush and all the rest of the team at Century.

PROLOGUE

April 20th. Night.

The air was warm and humid, with the faint smell of the wild irises that dotted the hillside drifting through the night air. Josh Harding paused. He lifted the Russian-built AN-30 rifle to his shoulder, the butt nestling into the thin linen shawl wrapped across his shoulder. His eyes narrowed, the skin of his face creasing as he focused all his concentration into the thin cross-hairs of the gunsight.

The man in those sights was about thirty, with a black, wispy beard and the slow, ponderous movements of someone preparing for bed after a long hard day. The flickering embers of a fire were illuminating the darkness, sending pale shafts of light out across the tiny encampment. Josh could see various people moving in and out of the shadows. Ignore them, he told himself. He narrowed his gaze still further. Stay focused. Wait until the weapon and the target are perfectly aligned. Then squeeze the trigger.

One bullet, thought Josh. That's all it takes to shatter a man's skull.

There were only a tiny handful of people in the world whom you could assassinate with total peace of mind. With no doubts, no regrets. And Khalid Azim—one of the top five al-Qaeda leaders in the world, and the man charged with delivering a terrorist atrocity in Britain—was one of them.

A movement. A woman slipped across the camp, blocking Josh's line of fire. Josh hesitated. The bullet he had loaded into the AN-30 was made of

1

hardened tungsten, a lethal alloy designed for the battlefield: it was said that it could kill one person, move straight through a body, and still have enough strength to kill the next person it hit. That was in the manufacturer's manual, thought Josh. Every soldier knew that the kit never did what it said on the box. There was a *chance* that the bullet *could* slice straight through the woman, and then take out Azim. But it was risky. A bone or even a thick artery could deflect it from its path, sending it harmlessly into the ground. And once Josh fired, the whole camp would know he was up here in the hills.

If I ever set up an assassination school, Josh told himself, I know what my first lesson will be. *You only get one shot. Make sure it's the right one.*

Azim moved away. The woman was still in front of him, blocking Josh's line of fire. Two other men stepped forward, both heavily armed, shadowing Azim's steps as he went back inside the tent. 'Fuck it,' muttered Josh to himself. 'I've lost him.'

He rested his forearm, letting the gun drop to his side and looked down towards the camp with disappointment. Ashfaq Dasmunshi moved across to where Josh was standing. 'We'll still get him,' he said.

Josh nodded. For three months he had been tracking both Azim and Osama bin Laden through the border region where al-Qaeda still had its most loyal supporters, and where its leaders still returned to retrain and re-equip themselves while they planned their next atrocity. Since joining the Regiment five years ago, he had been on some tough assignments: first in Bosnia, then in the Afghan invasion, then in Gulf Two. But this was

2

the toughest of the lot. Placed on secondment to The Firm's specialist anti-terrorist unit, he had been sent out here to the Afghanistan-Pakistan borders with a mission that was as simple to define as it was difficult to accomplish: to track down and execute any al-Qaeda leaders he could find, spending whatever money it took, running whatever risks he had to.

'We need help,' said Josh. 'I'll speak to base.'

Ashfaq nodded. The pair of them had been together for three months now. They worked their way through the region on foot and by motorbike, bribing and cajoling local villages into giving them any information that might lead them towards their target.

Josh knew that Ashfaq was a mercenary: he was only doing this for the five hundred dollars a day he was being paid, and he would go back to his village and live like a king on the money he had made in the past few weeks.

Still, a decade of soldiering had taught Josh that mercenaries were as good as any other men on the battlefield. It didn't matter whether a man was fighting for the security of his country or the security of his wallet—as long as he knew how to hold his weapon, and how to play for the team, Josh was never going to question his motives.

'We'll have to be quick,' said Ashfaq. 'They won't be at that camp for more than three hours. Four hours maximum.'

Josh glanced back down at the camp. He had counted a dozen people, at least two of them women. A squadron of about thirty-six men would be enough for an assault, so long as they were properly armed and properly led. He picked up the

3

satellite phone, checked the area to make sure that they were still hidden from view, then punched through the call.

'What do you want, Harding?' said Mark Bruton.

The base camp was at Khost, about eighty miles back along the border. It served as the headquarters for the British and American soldiers who had been in the country since it had been invaded two years ago. Although it was three months now since Josh had been back there, it was the place he reported back to for orders.

'We've found Azim,' said Josh. 'I need back-up to take him out.'

'What's your position?' barked Bruton.

Over the satellite phone, the voice was transmitted as clearly as if the man was sitting right next to him. It doesn't matter where the Rupert is, reflected Josh as the tone of the commanding office grated on his nerves. Smug, self-satisfied, and dead wrong—they all sound the same.

Josh read out the GPS coordinates. They were nestling high in the mountains, just on the Afghan side of the border, among tribesmen and warlords who recognised no law or government other than their own. Borders didn't mean anything out here: every tribe was a government all to itself.

'Stay where you are, Harding,' said Bruton. 'I'll send in a cruise to blow the camp. I'll put a couple of drones into the mix to clear up any stragglers, then send along a Black Hawk to pick you up. Got that?'

Josh gripped the side of the Motorola 9500 sat phone. It was hooked up to an Iridium satellite a couple of miles up in the sky and he could feel the slim black plastic casing of the machine vibrating in

4

his tight grip. 'I've spent three months tracking this man,' snapped Josh. 'I can't wait for a missile strike. All I need are some guys in a chopper and we can go in and get him.'

There was a pause. Even at a distance of three thousand miles, Josh could feel Bruton's annoyance. 'Nobody's going to win a bloody medal on this one, Harding. We're using missiles. Now hold your sodding ground, and wait for the big boys.'

'But . . .'

The single word struggled from Josh's lips, but the rest of the sentence was never born.

'That's a bloody order, Harding. Got it?'

'I'll guide the fireworks home, sir,' he replied stiffly.

He put the phone down, flicking off its power. Ten years in the Army, five in the Parachute Regiment before he moved up to Hereford, had taught Josh about anger management. A girl he had knocked around with once had even given him a book on it: take deep breaths, find a still spot somewhere inside yourself, accentuate the positive, and some other rubbish he couldn't remember. The girl had chucked him after he'd lost his rag once too often, and he'd never finished the book.

Whoever wrote it had never had to deal with a quarter-brained Rupert like Mark Bruton. He'd get a whole chapter all to himself.

'The tosser,' said Josh contemptuously, looking towards Ashfaq. 'He's sending some cruises in, then a chopper to bring us out.'

'That could take hours,' said Ashfaq.

Josh nodded.

A look of disappointment flashed across Ashfaq's

5

face. Josh knew that the other man was as anxious as he was to get the fighting over and done with. There was a thousand-dollar bonus for every al-Qaeda operative they captured and killed.

'Azim never sleeps in the same place two nights running, and he never sleeps for more than a few hours. He's constantly on the move, that's how he stays alive,' said Ashfaq. He swatted away a mosquito that had landed on his thick, trimmed beard. 'Maybe we'll be lucky, maybe not. We'll see.'

Josh glanced at his watch. It was just after eleven at night. Dawn would start breaking about five tomorrow morning. The chances were that Azim would be gone by three. That gave them less than four hours.

Josh fed the coordinates of the position back to base, then lay down on the pebbled ground. In the past three months, he had grown used to sleeping on the open ground, his body hardened to the roughness of the surface. The dusty perfume of the mountain flowers even made sleeping easy. You woke after an hour or two as alive and fresh as if you'd just come out of the gym.

Josh glanced up at the stars. Missile strikes weren't the answer to this war, he reflected to himself. That was just robot wars, not proper soldiering. You had to be willing to take the same risks the enemy were. *That meant putting your life on the line*.

Josh started to close his eyes. The Motorola phone strapped to his belt was switched to vibrate: a call a few minutes before the missile strike would wake him. Take the sleep when you can get it, he told himself. You never know when the chance will come again.

6

Waking, he turned over, looking at his watch. It was one-fifteen in the morning. Josh sat bolt upright. He placed the AN-30 to his shoulder, using its telescopic sights to scan the camp. Apart from a single guard patrolling the perimeter, there was no sign of movement.

Where the hell are they? Josh thought.

He scanned the night sky, looking for a vapour trail among the twinkling stars. He'd seen enough cruise missiles to be able to spot them: they flew gently through the sky, like ducks skimming the surface of the water. A low, throaty hum was the only sound they made. They are a familiar enough sight in Afghanistan, he told himself. *Even the kids recognise them.*

He picked up the Motorola and punched out the number. 'What's happening?' he said into the phone.

'Hold your position, Harding,' said Bruton. 'The missiles are being got ready.'

Josh glanced down at the camp. 'It won't wait much longer.'

'Just sit tight, man,' snapped Bruton. 'The fireworks will start soon enough.'

Josh snapped the phone shut. He lay back down on the ground. Cruise missiles are no way to fight a war, he said to himself. *We'd be better off with swords and sabres.*

Josh checked his watch. Two-fifteen. He felt certain that he could see a man moving in the camp. Were they preparing to leave? he wondered. Or were they just changing the night guard?

He punched the same number into the Motorola. 'Where are they?' he demanded.

'Couple of glitches on the cruises,' said Bruton.

7

'For two million dollars a pop, you'd think they'd give you a bugger with a proper starter motor on it. We're having to send one in from one of the American subs in the Indian Ocean. Might be a bit of a delay.'

Josh lay back down on the ground and tried to sleep some more. His eyes closed, but sleep wouldn't come. He was burning with anger. Three months I've spent tracking these bastards through this wilderness. Three months of crap food, no washing, and only a sodding cave to sleep in. *And now that I've finally tracked one of the bastards down, they're going to let him slip from my grasp.*

Another hour. It was three twenty-five now. More movement in the camp. The guard was drawing some water from the barrels strapped onto one of the trucks. For washing, thought Josh. That meant they would be leaving soon.

'There isn't much longer left,' he snapped into the phone.

'Relax,' said Bruton. 'The missiles are airborne, and the chopper is on its way. Get ready to evacuate. You're coming home for a shower.'

Josh stood on the hillside. He could see the guard preparing a basin and boiling a kettle, taking them towards the tent. Leaving, he thought. A quick wash and a cup of tea, and they'll be on their way.

He looked up to the sky. If it was coming from one of the American subs, they'd be sending a Raytheon Tomahawk cruise missile. They were subsonic, travelling at around five hundred miles an hour, about the same speed as a commercial passenger aircraft. If it was being fired from a sub in the Indian Ocean it could still be another ten minutes or so before the strike.

8

Josh started pacing, walking around in smaller and smaller circles. A breeze was starting to blow across the mountain, rustling through the white robes that hung loosely on his body. After three months without anything except a stream to wash in, or a cave to sleep in, he could feel the dirt clinging to his body. Good to get back to base, he told himself. *But I don't want to go back without a notch or two on my belt.*

He fingered the trigger on the AN-30. There was just a chance he could take them himself. To risk Ashfaq's life would be unfair. The other guy was just a hired hand. Yet one man with a machine gun could do a lot of damage against a camp that was waking up. Take the guard with a single shot from here. Put down some grenades to distract them. Then go in quick, dressed like a local, and hope to get them all before they realise what's hit them.

No, he told himself. You can't bank on that kind of luck. It's suicide. And there's no glory in that.

'Did you hear something?' he whispered towards Ashfaq.

The Afghan nodded. 'A starter motor,' he replied. 'The white truck. It's leaving.'

Josh strained his eyes. He could see a man climbing into the passenger side, another climbing into the driver's seat, firing up the engine. It started to pull away, moving down the mountainside.

The bastard is escaping.

He peered through the AN-30's telescopic sights again. One bullet, he told himself. Blow a tyre out, and hope that sends the car crashing down the mountain. Behind him, he could hear the distant drone of the Tomahawk, like an aeroplane, except quieter, and lower in the sky. He squeezed the

9

trigger.

The bullet smashed into empty scrubland. The truck kept on moving.

In the next instant, a blinding flash lit up the sky. A BGM 109, the Tomahawk could either be equipped with a thousand-pound high-explosive bomb, for destroying big targets or penetrating deep bunkers, or it could be equipped with a thousand pounds of cluster bomblets, which showered a camp with dozens of tiny, lethal explosives. Now Josh saw that this one had a deadly pack of cluster bombs built into its nose. The bombs were spinning out of the missile like confetti. A rain of fire drenched the camp, sucking up everything within it as the fireball gathered force. Josh could hear the pop, pop, pop of the charges exploding down in the valley, the echoes bouncing off the sides of the mountains to build a murderous wave of noise.

Josh turned his gaze back to the white truck. It was disappearing along the single-track road that led away from the valley. It's him, thought Josh grimly. *They can send across as many clouds of fire as they want. It's useless unless the target is standing right beneath them.*

Now Josh could hear the roar from the helicopter blades slicing through the air above him. A smell of avgas filled the air as the machine dropped out of the sky. The Black Hawk hovered a few feet above the ground. A soldier was leaning out, waving him on board.

Josh looked towards the truck. A trail of dust had been kicked up as it turned the corner and vanished from view. *Just as I thought. The bastard has escaped.*

* * *

Dawn was starting to break as the helicopter dropped down at the centre of the compound. Josh hopped from its side hatch, walking out across the thin strip of tarmac that led away from the landing circle. Three months, he thought to himself, looking across to the low, prefabricated row of huts that made up the mess room, the barracks, and the debriefing centres. A long time to be out in the wilderness, with only your own wits to live on.

Some beer, some food, a shower and then some sleep. In that order, Josh thought.

'Harding?' said a young soldier, standing by the side of the road.

Josh nodded. The man was maybe nineteen or twenty, a signaller on his first proper tour of duty by the looks of him. I'm only thirty myself, reflected Josh. But already the raw recruits are starting to seem like boys to me.

'That's me,' he replied.

He could see the signaller running his gaze over him. Dressed in a long white robe, with sandals on his feet, a black beard, and with his rifle slung across his back, Josh knew that he was starting to look more like an Afghan tribesman than a British soldier. His face was tanned to a dark shade of brown, and the sweat and dirt had seeped into his skin, giving it the appearance of raw leather.

'Bruton will see you in an hour,' said the soldier. 'Room C.' He paused. 'You might want to have a bit of a wash before you go in.'

'Too much of a pong for you?' said Josh.

'*Diabolical.*'

11

Josh grinned. 'There's worse smells than me in the field. You'll find that out soon enough.'

He smiled as he walked towards the mess. Khost had been an Allied base since soon after the invasion of Afghanistan. Of all the bases established by the Allied forces, this was the roughest: up closer to Kabul, the invaders had been welcomed, or at least tolerated, but down here the American and British soldiers were hated with an intensity that only religion could inspire. They weren't just the invader. They were the infidel.

Step outside, and the chances were that you'd find one of the local kids lobbing a petrol bomb at you. It was, Josh told himself, like Ulster. *But with snakes and curry.*

'Hey, it's Osama,' shouted a man from across the room.

Josh smiled again. He recognised Peter Boshell at once. Same age, and one of five Regiment men stationed at Khost. But he could well be the only other British soldier on the base right now, because Khost was mainly an American set-up and the Regiment guys were spending most of the time out on patrol. That was the way it had to be. You weren't going to catch any terrorists sitting around the base playing computer games—whatever the Americans thought.

'Nab him, boys,' continued Boshell. 'We let the fucker get away at Tora Bora. Don't want to do that again.'

Josh walked across to the bar. Boshell was sitting with a group of tough-looking American marines, their heads shaved and the tattoos bright on the huge muscles of their biceps. 'What's happening?' asked Josh.

'World War Three, by the looks of it,' said Boshell.

Josh grabbed himself a Coke and a packet of crisps and sat down. The television was tuned to Fox News, and the dozen soldiers sitting around the mess were gripped by what they were watching.

Josh turned his gaze towards the screen. 'The most dramatic day in the War on Terror since 9–11,' said the newsreader.

Josh took a swig of the Coke, and threw some of the crisps into his mouth: it was three months now since he'd had anything apart from the local curries.

'In a day of mayhem that has already been dubbed the Three Cities Attack, power supplies were today switched off in three of the world's major cities: London, Paris and New York,' continued the newsreader.

Christ, thought Josh. *What's happened now?*

Up on the screen, Josh could see a familiar backdrop: Trafalgar Square at twilight, the road turned into a mess of snarling traffic, and the square thronging with more people than on New Year's Eve. 'The day's events started in Paris, at noon local time precisely. Power systems throughout the city shut down, leaving millions of people stranded in subways and on roads, and shutting schools and offices. One hour later, at noon local time, the power went out in London, closing the city completely. The police reported widespread incidents of panic, looting and total confusion as the transport networks ground to a halt. Troops were deployed around Whitehall and Parliament Square as speculation grew of a major terrorist incident. London Mayor Ken Livingstone

13

and Prime Minister Tony Blair appealed for calm, but to little avail. Then, in the most dramatic development of the day, precisely five hours later, again at noon local time, the power shut down in New York. Mayor Bloomberg was appealing for calm as panic-stricken New Yorkers feared another devastating strike on their city. Police had to try to restore order at several skyscrapers as workers emptied buildings that could become targets.'

Josh looked at the faces of the other men in the mess. They were watching the screen intently, talking among themselves. Their tone was hushed, whispering to one another, as if they were both exhilarated and appalled by the events being played out in front of them. Just as I am, Josh thought.

'Already people are speculating that the Three Cities Attack must be the work of al-Qaeda terrorists,' continued the newsreader. 'If so, it would be the most audacious coup by the organisation since 9–11.' Josh watched as the screen switched to a reporter standing outside the Pentagon, his hair disturbed in the strong gusts of wind blowing past the building. 'Military sources are denying that this is necessarily a co-ordinated terrorist attack,' said the reporter. 'They are insisting that it is possible for the power to fail accidentally in all three cities at precisely the same time. But so far, no information is available on what caused the power failures, or how it can be prevented from happening again.' The reporter paused to deliver the emphasis on the final sentence. 'Outside the government, some experts are saying this is likely to be the work of al-Qaeda.'

'So is it a terrorist attack, or isn't it?' said the newsreader, looking towards the reporter.

'Right now, we just don't have enough information to say,' answered the reporter. 'The world may now have to get used to the terrifying possibility that somebody, somewhere, can get control of the world's power systems. And can turn off the electricity at will.'

Josh put down his Coke. Now there was silence in the room. An ad break had interrupted the news, and nobody was saying anything. 'Think it's al-Qaeda?' said Josh finally, looking towards Boshell.

Boshell shrugged. 'Who else?'

'Has to be,' said one of the Americans. 'Nobody else could pull a stunt like that.'

'The Pentagon is saying that it doesn't think so,' said Josh.

The soldier smiled, revealing a huge set of white teeth. 'Hell, I've been on missions myself that those sons of bitches were denying before we got back to base.'

'Al-Qaeda taking control of power systems for cities around the world?' said Boshell. 'Of course they're not going to own up to something like that. There'd be panic.'

'Looks like we've got work to do, then,' said Josh.

He could see himself being summoned across the room by the young signaller. Josh finished his Coke and started walking towards the corridor. The walk was a short one, but he suddenly felt the energy drain out of him. It was months since he'd slept in a proper bed, or eaten a decent meal. Soldiering was like that sometimes. Your nerves held up fine while the battle was still on. But once it was all over, the exhaustion hit you: the adrenalin drained away, and every wound, knock and bruise suddenly

15

started screaming out in pain.

'Back to your cave, Osama,' shouted Boshell.

Josh looked back and grinned. During the last three months he had missed the camaraderie of the Regiment.

'I'll get you a razor,' said Bruton as soon as Josh stepped into the room. 'You look like crap.'

'The whole country looks like crap, sir,' said Josh. 'I blend in.'

Bruton was a tall man, with dark hair cropped close to his skull, a thick, round nose, and ears that stuck out from the side of his head like the handles on a jug. In the six months that he'd been under his command, Josh had not warmed to him: there were plenty of Ruperts who made stupid decisions, but few of them could do it as consistently as Bruton.

'Well, good to see you again,' continued Bruton. 'And congratulations.'

Josh looked around the room. There was a detailed map of the Afghanistan-Pakistan border on the wall, and next to it a series of thirty pictures: the most wanted al-Qaeda terrorists believed to be operating in the area. Azim, the man The Firm reckoned was charged with delivering a major attack on Britain, was among them.

There was a water cooler in the corner. Josh helped himself to a plastic beaker, then sat down on the single chair facing the desk. Bruton sat opposite him, a pad of paper spread out in front of him. He was swivelling a biro between his fingers, tapping its end against his mouth.

'We'll do a full debrief in the morning,' he said. 'But the good news is that the strike was a success. Azim is dead. The boys in Vauxhall are going to be pleased with that one.'

Josh looked at him, scrutinising his face. He could see no trace of hesitation or doubt there. 'Azim's not dead.' He paused, his eyes flicking upwards. 'Sir.'

Bruton leant forward. 'The Tomahawk went into the precise location you gave us,' he said firmly. 'A drone flew overhead and took some pictures. Everything in that camp was burned to a cinder.'

'There was a truck,' said Josh. 'A white one. It left the camp a few minutes before the missile came in. Azim was in it. He escaped.'

Bruton shook his head. 'The mission was a success, Harding. That's what it's going to say in the files.'

Josh took a deep breath. Anger management, he told himself. 'It took too long,' he said, his voice steely. 'If we'd got the missile in sooner, we'd have got him. But I'm telling you, he escaped.'

'Listen to me, Harding,' said Bruton. He stood up and walked across the room, standing in front of Azim's picture and tearing it from the wall. 'When I say a man's dead, he's dead. And he stays dead. Got it?'

Josh stood up. 'Then we'll just have to wait until the bugger comes back with a different name. And then kill him again.'

ONE

Monday, June 1st. Morning.
The smell drifted past Josh's nostrils. His senses twitched, coming slowly back to life as he struggled to regain consciousness. A faint musty smell mixing lavender with some kind of spice. I know it, thought Josh. I know that perfume. It's on the tip of my tongue.
If only I could remember the name.
For a moment, Josh struggled, annoyed with himself for not being able to dredge up the name from his memory. Sod it, he told himself finally. I never was any good at remembering perfumes.

Slowly, Josh tried to open his eyes. But the skin on his lids felt heavy and unyielding. He was starting to become aware of a pain, throbbing slowly yet still intense, starting at the side of his neck and running down deep into his spine. Another pain was rippling up from his calf. Then his left eye sprang open first, a flash of light flooding his senses as a fierce sun shone into his face. He closed the eye quickly, succumbed to another wave of pain, then opened it again.

A woman. A bright lock of red hair.

Josh closed the eye.

Where the hell am I? *What the fuck has happened to me?*

He tried the right eye this time. The same heavy sensation as the lids were reluctantly prised open, and the same blinding effect as sunlight overwhelmed the retina. He shut it hard, let a fresh wave of pain roll down from his neck into his back,

19

then opened both eyes.

The woman was leaning over him.

She was in her late twenties, maybe just thirty, but no older. Her skin was tanned and freckly, and still moist and clear. Her eyes were bright blue, shaped like almonds, set above her nose and full red lips. But it was the hair that held Josh's attention. A thick red wave of curls, it tumbled playfully across him, growing away from the woman's face like a lion's mane.

He started to speak. The words started somewhere in his brain, then travelled down towards his throat. 'I . . . I . . .' he started.

Suddenly Josh was aware of another terrible pain shooting through his neck. He stopped, choking on the rest of the sentence, unable to deliver it.

A finger came to rest on his lips, thin and elegant, and without any ring on it. 'Don't speak,' she said. 'You're hurt.'

'I . . . I . . .' Josh started again.

'You're hurt,' she repeated, her tone firmer this time. 'I'll put you in the truck.'

It was too painful for Josh to speak. The jabbing in his neck was growing worse, and his leg was feeling numb: it was a pain that he knew he had felt before, although he couldn't now remember where. He started to turn on his shoulders. He was lying in a ditch of baked, cracked earth. Ahead of him he could see a thin strip of tarmac: a one-lane road, nothing more. Behind it, a giant rock loomed, its pitted surface made of red and yellow stone, and beneath the rock flaked and chipped slices of the mountain lay in a jumbled heap. The air was dry and dusty, without even the murmur of a breeze to soften the fierce heat of the sun beating down on them.

Josh looked out across the bleak landscape. Somewhere in the distance, he could see some dust rising up from a ridge. The place was completely empty.

Where am I? he wondered.

He swivelled quickly, staring at the ditch into which he had fallen. A crimson stain had spread out into the sand.

Blood. My blood, Josh thought.

He started to run a hand across his body, making a rough reckoning of the extent of his wounds. He had been shot in the neck, he guessed: there was a gaping flesh wound, and the bullet must have missed his windpipe only narrowly. He was lucky to be alive. The calf of his left leg had taken a hit as well. A chunk of flesh the size of his index finger had been blown away: he could still see pulpy, messy fragments of the torn tissue lying in the dirt. At least a pint of blood, maybe two, had been spilled already.

What in the name of Christ happened to me here?

'Quick,' said the woman. 'You need treatment.'

Her hand was wrapping itself around Josh's wrist, taking his pulse. He could just see her lips moving as she silently counted out the beating of his heart. 'We need to get some drugs into you,' she said. 'Right away.'

Josh let her arms slip around his waist. She didn't have the strength to lift a man of his size but she could help him balance himself as he used the strength left in his legs to push himself upwards. He felt dizzy, and his vision was clouding up as he started to move his feet. The left leg, where the bullet had struck, was screaming with pain: every

21

nerve seemed to have been set on fire, sending burning jabs of pain up through his body. His breathing was ragged and the loss of blood had sapped his energy, making it hard for him to hold onto consciousness for more than a few minutes straight. He was already suffering from palpitations and his lips were sweaty, enough to suggest that he'd maybe lost more than a couple of pints.

'Hold me,' he muttered, some blood spitting from his mouth as he pronounced the words.

The woman was strong, he could tell that. She was five-nine, maybe five-ten. She couldn't have weighed more than a hundred and ten pounds: she was thin, not in an anorexic fashion-model way, but thin as in wiry, muscly, and tough. She was dressed in blue denim shorts, with a pale pink T-shirt: a deeper pink heart was stencilled on the cotton, just below the delicate curve of her small breasts. A country girl, thought Josh suddenly. Good with horses and dogs, and she probably knows how to handle herself in a fight pretty well.

That perfume, thought Josh, as he leaned into her, using the strength of her shoulders to help keep his balance. What's its name again? *I just can't remember.*

He stepped forward. His left leg was in the worst pain, so he was using his right one to carry his weight. About ten yards ahead of him he could see the pick-up truck: a black Ford Ranger, at least five years old, with a thick layer of mud and dust coating its wheels and some thick scratches to its bodywork. Not far to walk, he told himself. Even on a shot-up leg, I should be able to manage ten yards.

'Careful,' said the woman, steering him to the

left.

Josh looked down. He was fighting to straighten out his vision, taking deep gulps of air to try to calm the spinning in his head that was clouding up his eyes. Suddenly he was able to focus. At his feet there lay a body.

A corpse.

Josh stopped. He had moved sideways to avoid stepping on it. It was a boy, no more than fifteen. He had thick black hair, down to the back of his neck, and he was wearing black jeans and a huge pair of Nike trainers. Josh couldn't see his face: he was lying face down in the dirt. But he could see the wounds. One bullet had torn into the centre of his neck, taking out his throat. Another had ripped into the centre of his skull, entering from the back and blowing his brains out through his forehead. A pool of blood was still seeping from both the wounds.

'Wh—' Josh started to say.

'No, quiet,' hissed the woman, her tone turning sterner now. 'You want to end up like him?'

Josh hobbled forwards. No time to think, he told himself. Don't worry now about who you are, what you are doing here, or why there is a corpse lying in front of you. In a fight you don't look for explanations. You just try to survive.

Another three yards. The pain in his left leg was terrible, and he could feel the pressure of hobbling forward crunching the nerve endings, the tendons and the muscles. Every step, he knew, was only making the injury worse. He had to find somewhere where he could lie up for a few days, assess the extent of his injuries, and start to recover his strength.

23

Not here. *Not surrounded by corpses.*

The door of the pick-up was open. Josh threw himself inside, using his forearms to lever himself up onto the battered cloth seats. There the glass had magnified the fierce sunlight, and if it was thirty degrees outside, here in the scrublands, it must have been closer to forty inside the truck. Sweat started to pour from Josh's skin, mixing with the blood already caked to the surface of his body. His breath stabbed against his chest as the hot, humid air filled his lungs.

The woman handed him a bottle of water. 'Try to drink something.'

Josh took the plastic container in his hand. It could have been thirty degrees as well. I could use it to brew up a nice cup of tea, he reflected sourly. Wrenching the top free with his teeth, he slung the neck of the bottle into his mouth, pouring the water down his throat, then letting it splash across his face. One tooth was missing, he figured: maybe he'd lost it when the bullets had slammed him onto the ground. There was a dull throbbing pain at the base of his jaw, spreading out from the gums, and the water was making it worse, a sure sign of a broken tooth. Sod it, he told himself. I have to drink. *And right now a trip to the dentist is the least of my worries.*

The Ranger roared into life as the woman slotted the key into its ignition. The Ford had a big, powerful engine, and even though it had overheated in the midday sun it still kicked to life with a snarl. The smell of petrol started to flood through the air, making Josh's stomach churn. He lifted his foot into position, relieved to finally be taking the pressure off it, and looked closely at the

24

woman as she gripped the steering wheel and turned the truck onto the road.

She's afraid, he noted. A trickle of sweat was running down her back, staining the fabric of her T-shirt.

Josh closed his eyes. His brain was still fuzzy, and the blurring in front of his eyes was still severe. Unconsciousness, he knew, was just a breath away. He could feel the truck vibrating as it kicked past the stones on the single-track road and started to pick up speed.

Just try and stay alive until you get there, he told himself. *Wherever 'there' might be.*

Then there was a new sound. It was vicious and sharp, the noise of metal digging into metal. Josh opened his eyes with a start, instantly recognising what he had just heard. A bullet. The truck had been hit by a bullet.

He looked across at the woman. She was gripping the wheel, swerving the truck as the shot winged its side. Her grip was tight and her expression grim. The truck was swaying violently. Another bullet. Amid the deafening noise Josh couldn't be certain where it had come from. Maybe one of the high rocks? A sniper. Maybe another vehicle, already in hot pursuit. He looked across at the woman. 'Evade,' he snapped. 'You have to evade.'

His throat had strained to produce the words, the muscles in his neck screaming with pain as he flexed them.

'Keep still,' she screamed. 'Otherwise you'll die.'

Sod it, thought Josh. I'll die anyway, the way you're driving.

He turned round. He could feel some blood starting to seep down his neck as the scab that had

25

formed across the open wound cracked. A bike was on their trail. A Honda, he judged. Big and powerful, with chrome handlebars that glistened in the sun. He could see nothing of its rider. The man was wrapped in black leather, with shades pulled down over his eyes and a helmet covering the top half of his face. His left hand was gripping the handlebars, and in his right there was a pistol. Josh couldn't tell the make from where he sprawled in the truck. But it was a heavy piece of kit, he could tell that much. The biker was straining to hold the gun steady.

Josh looked straight back. For a moment, he had the sensation that he was looking straight down the barrel of the gun.

Another shot. The biker jerked back slightly as the recoil from the pistol forced him to lose his balance. The bullet winged the side of the truck, opening up a gash in the metal along the driver's side. The vehicle swayed again under the impact, then gripped the road once more.

'You got a gun?' hissed Josh.

The woman shook her head.

'Then I'm driving,' snapped Josh.

She shook her head again, more fiercely this time.

'I said I'm driving.'

The woman turned to face him, her eyes bright with anger. 'No,' she said, her tone harsh. A bead of sweat was rolling down from her forehead onto her face. 'You don't even have the strength to stand up. Don't even think about driving.'

'When I need the strength, I'll find it,' answered Josh.

The truck swerved. Another bullet had hit it, this

time smashing into its back. Its frame vibrated under the force of the impact. Josh moved swiftly across the front seat, pushing the woman with his open palm and taking hold of the wheel. He left some traces of blood smeared across the front of her T-shirt.

'Okay,' she said angrily. 'You drive if you have to.'

They'd have to switch places while they were driving: a tricky move at the best of times, but even harder when you were under fire. 'Just take your foot off the accelerator,' said Josh.

The woman shifted sideways, her foot easing off the pedal. She kept one hand on the wheel. Josh now grabbed it with his left hand. The truck was starting to wobble and swerve. He pushed himself up and over the woman's lap, blood dripping down onto her jeans. The truck started to drift seriously off to the left. Josh gripped the wheel harder as he slipped into the driver's seat. His foot jammed down onto the accelerator, taking the speed back up again.

'I need your help,' he muttered.

She looked across at him.

'I'm losing too much damned blood,' he snapped. 'I have to stop it.'

With his left hand still on the wheel, Josh ripped a strip of cloth from his shirt, handing it across to the woman Leaning down, she gripped it between her hands. Her fingers dug into Josh's thigh. She was searching for the femoral artery he knew. Dig into that hard enough, and it would staunch the bleeding. Next, she took the cloth, and wrapped it tight around his thigh. Josh could feel the bleeding starting to slow immediately. But the amount of blood loss was still worrying him. More than four

27

pints and he'd pass out.

The truck swerved violently as Josh struggled to keep control of the wheel as another bullet flew past them. Get a grip, man, Josh told himself. *Or else we'll both be dead in the next few minutes.*

The road stretched out in front of him. Dazzling sunlight was searing through the high windscreen of the Ranger. Josh flipped the sunshield down, protecting his eyes. He was struggling to focus. From a glance in the mirror, he could see the bike tracking him ten yards to his rear, the rider steadying himself on the machine again, his hand raised high in the air as he tried to line up the next shot.

One of those is going to hit its target, Josh realised. *That's just the law of averages.*

He started to swing the truck from side to side, jerking the wheel to produce an unpredictable, irregular motion. That was the first rule of any kind of evasive action: make yourself a hard target.

I might be a hard target, but I'm still a big one. This truck weighs a ton and half. Hard to miss.

Now the swaying of the truck was starting to make Josh feel sick. Blood loss had already weakened him and, with the violence of the vehicle's motion, he could feel his concentration draining away and his vision starting to blur again. Keep your grip, man, he told himself. *You can do this.*

The bike was holding a steady distance, ten yards to his rear. Another shot. This time the bullet smashed through the window at the back of the Ranger, shattering the glass into a thousand pieces, sending it cascading forward across Josh and the woman like hard confetti. Tiny splinters of glass

28

flicked across Josh's back, peppering the skin of his neck and getting into his hair. He could also feel a pair of wounds opening up, fresh blood streaming from the scabs.

Makes no difference, thought Josh with grim resolve. *I couldn't be in much worse shape than I am already.*

He heard the woman screaming: a long agonised howl of fear. Had the glass shattering broken her nerve? Josh reached across to her with his right hand, while his left held the steering wheel. There was one cut at the top of her neck, and a splinter of glass seemed to have lodged itself underneath the skin. That would be painful to get out. But otherwise she was okay. 'We're all right,' hissed Josh, gasping for air.

The bullet had travelled though the cab of the truck and drilled through the windscreen, one foot to the left of the driver's seat. A fissure had opened up down the centre of the glass, but although it had cracked it hadn't yet broken. Close, realised Josh. The rear window had deflected its path, steering the bullet slightly to the left. Without that deflection, the bullet would have landed a foot to the right. In the centre of my skull, Josh mused.

He glanced in the mirror. The biker was still there, the pistol still raised in his right hand. You're not a bad shot, pal, Josh thought grudgingly.

The rider's tactics weren't hard to figure out. The bike had plenty of power, more than enough to accelerate past the Ranger if he wanted to. He was just holding his position a steady ten yards behind, firing shot after shot after shot. Sooner or later, he was going to land one right into Josh's brain. *And the way he was shooting, it was going to be sooner rather than later.*

Josh jammed his foot hard on the accelerator. The Ranger might have a few years and many more miles on the clock, but there was still plenty of power in its 3.2 litre engine. Now that engine roared and revved, and Josh could feel the truck surging forward. He was up to a hundred miles an hour, skidding across the hot surface of the tarmac. Another glance in the mirror. The bike was still there, a steady ten yards behind him, the pistol already lined up for the next shot.

I haven't the strength for a long chase, realised Josh. If I was fit and healthy, I might be able to out-drive and outwit this opponent. Not in my current state. I stand and fight. *That's my only chance.*

Josh tapped the brake. The truck started to slow. He bunched all his strength into his shoulders, took a second to compose himself, then threw himself into action. I'm getting one chance at this, he told himself. *Screw it up, and it's an early supper for the vultures.*

With his right hand, Josh wrenched hard at the steering wheel, spinning it around. With his left hand, he pulled savagely on the handbrake as his foot jabbed viciously against the footbrake. The combined impact of the sudden deceleration and the violent turning of the wheel yanked the vehicle into a classic bootlegger's turn. The heat of the day had already made the truck's tyres soft and slippery, loosening their grip on the road. The Ranger skidded, hurtling off the track and out onto the scrubland. A huge cloud of dust kicked up, briefly blocking Josh's vision. Beneath him, he could hear the engine roar and the suspension

30

creak under the pressure put upon it by the sudden manoeuvre.

'Hold steady,' Josh rasped to the woman at his side.

She looked back at him, clutching the side of the door as the suddenness of the movement threw her sideways. 'I'm trying.'

Josh swivelled his gaze right, looking up the road. It had worked. The speed of the turn had caught the biker by surprise. In the seconds that it had taken him to assess what was happening and react, he had sped past and was now fifty yards up the road. Already Josh could see that he was slowing, preparing to turn around. Just as I thought you would, Josh exulted inwardly.

My plan owes nothing to brains or cunning, he told himself. *Just guts and adrenalin.*

The trick was to get behind your assailant. In any battle between a pick-up truck and a motorbike, the bike was always going to win on speed and agility. But the truck, like a tank, could win on size and strength. From the right position it could attack.

And that position was from behind.

Josh started driving into the scrub. The wheels of the Ranger kicked up sand in every direction, but its grip was steady. Summoning his strength into his shoulders again, he spun the wheel hard to the left, and yanked again on the handbrake. The truck stopped, its metal frame shuddering, then started to turn. The wheels struggled to get a grip on the sandy surface of the ground and for a moment Josh could sense the vehicle skidding. He was losing control—he could feel the truck starting to slide backwards. Then the tyres found some pebbles

31

they could grip onto. Slowly, the Ranger started to move around, facing directly back at the road.

Turn, Josh told himself. Then drive straight into the bastard. He'll get one shot, straight at me, through the windscreen. And if he doesn't kill me with that shot, then I'll crush him like an insect.

Josh tapped his foot on the accelerator, waiting for the surge of power to carry him forward.

The engine stalled.

Christ, thought Josh. *Prayer time*.

'Duck,' he hissed to the woman. 'Get your bloody head down and keep it down.'

Up ahead he could see the biker turning, could hear the wheels of the Honda screeching. Josh pushed his head down low, taking himself below the level of the windscreen. The truck was still moving forwards, carried by its momentum even after the engine had died, but it was slowing fast. Josh's leg was squeezed up against the pedals, sending terrible pains jabbing upwards through his spine.

Count to five, he told himself. The engine might just be flooded. Give it a moment to cool down, then try it again. *One, two . . .*

A bullet smashed into the windscreen, this time shattering the glass. The shards tumbled downwards, falling on them like solid, sharp-edged rain. The woman gasped, her hand shooting upward to try and protect her head and her face. 'No, no,' she screamed.

Three, four . . .

Josh jabbed the Ranger's key back into the ignition, twisting it viciously. For a brief moment, his action was greeted only by silence. Sod it, Josh muttered to himself. Then the engine spluttered.

Josh jammed his foot on the accelerator, twisting his body to reach it while still taking cover beneath the dashboard and now the engine revved into action, roaring into life, a sudden surge of power shaking the truck's frame. Josh levered himself upwards as the Ranger leaped forwards, skidding across the rough surface of the scrubland. The left tyre collided with a rock, jerking the truck upwards. The force of the impact briefly jolted Josh sideways, making him loosen his grip on the wheel. The truck swerved violently to the right, bouncing a foot into the air.

The pain searing though his body was making it tough for Josh to hold himself at the wheel. He was sweating and shaking from loss of blood. Concentrate, he told himself. Concentrate or die.

He could see the biker sixty yards ahead. The man had completed his turn with military precision and was now riding the bike hard out into the open scrubland. Josh could see nothing of his expression through the shades and helmet that masked the whole of his face, but he could tell from the way he was opening up the throttle and firing up the gas that there was not a flicker of fear or doubt running through the man. He was riding with total confidence, his gun held high in his right fist, certain that his opponent could be eliminated before he could retaliate.

That's your mistake, pal. *Always be a little bit afraid.*

Josh levered himself higher up into the driving seat, pressing hard on the accelerator, then slamming the steering wheel hard right. The bike lay directly in his path—sixty yards of open sand was all that separated the two vehicles.

Still not a flicker of fear from the biker. Nor any sign of him changing direction. You're a brave man, pal, Josh repeated to himself. *Brave, but stupid.*

'You're going to hit him,' said the woman at his side, the words delivered as if she was trying to warn Josh of some terrible, impending catastrophe.

'You bloody bet I am.'

'You're fucking crazy,' she screamed.

'You got a better idea, you've got three seconds to tell me.'

Josh looked back into the open scrubland. The biker had raised his gun again. He was steadying himself, struggling to hold the bike level so that he could aim the pistol accurately. One factor is on my side, reckoned Josh. It's always hard to fire a gun from a moving vehicle and even harder when that vehicle is racing across rough terrain.

He ducked instinctively as the gun was fired: above the noise of the Ranger's engine, it was impossible to hear the gunshot. But he could tell from the way the man's hand jerked backwards that the bullet had already left the chamber giving him time to duck.

Prayer time.

The shot struck the metal frame of the truck. Where it had hit, Josh couldn't tell.

Not me, that's all that counts.

Using all the remaining strength in his leg, Josh pressed even harder on the accelerator, urging every last ounce of power out of the machine. The Ranger sped forward, spitting huge clouds of dust up from its heavy wheels. Thirty yards left. The biker could see that his shot had missed. Decision time, mate, thought Josh. See if you've got time for another shot. Or just turn and try to run.

For just a fraction of a second, he could see the biker struggling with the decision. *Half a second is too long.*

The biker started to turn, swinging the handlebars to the left. There was a downward slope on that side of him, enough to give him some extra speed.

Twenty yards, and closing.

The biker was turning, his engine spluttering and his boots dragging on the ground. Josh adjusted his steering and powered forwards.

Ten yards.

The biker reared back, putting pressure on his machine's back wheel to try to complete the turn.

Five yards.

'Hold on!' Josh shouted at the woman.

Three yards.

He had lost sight of the biker as the man and the machine disappeared from view. Suddenly he could feel the force of the blow. It started with the front wheels. The Ranger was thrust up several feet into the air, Josh's head banging against the roof of the vehicle as the collision threw him up from the driver's seat. The engine stalled, and Josh slammed his feet hard on the brakes. The impact of the front wheels would kill any normal man. *After the back wheels had chewed him up, even the rattlesnakes would think twice about having him for their lunch.*

The truck landed hard on the ground. Josh could feel it swerve sideways as the rear wheels kicked in hard against the fallen bike. He gripped the steering wheel to try to bring the machine back under control. Slowly, the Ranger juddered to a halt. The sand kicked up by its wheels was still falling through the air, making the atmosphere thick and dusty: Josh's lungs were already filling up with the tiny particles that were choking off his breath and clogging up his vision.

Suddenly he could feel the energy draining out of him. In the midst of the battle, the adrenalin had kept his pain under control. Now it was flooding back through him. His leg was numb with agony, and blood was still seeping from the open wound in his neck. He looked behind him. Ten yards to the right, the bike was lying broken and mangled on the ground. The handlebars had been crushed into the front wheel, leaving a messy spaghetti of tubes, tyres, piping and wires. The petrol tank had broken open, but had not burst into flame: instead, the liquid had spilled out over the wreckage, covering it with a thin oily film. Josh looked harder, peering out beyond the bike.

He saw the leg first. The separation must have been relatively clean, he decided. If the boot had caught on the underside of the Ranger while the torso had stayed with the mangled bike, then the leg could have been pulled clean from its socket, the muscles, veins and tendons snapping like a pod being popped open to expose its peas. Six yards further on, the rest of the body lay face down in the dirt. Blood was still pulsing from the socket where the leg had been attached.

No man could have survived that kind of pain. *It would have been unendurable.*

The biker was dead.

Turning the key in the ignition, Josh fired the truck back into life. Wearily he started to reverse, using the rear-view mirror to help him to steer the Ranger back over the broken torso of his opponent. 'Broken into a thousand pieces, pal,'

36

muttered Josh as the debris kicked up by the Ranger's wheels spread a sprinkling of dirt over the bleeding body of the biker.

Josh pulled the truck back up towards the road, then slumped back, leaving the engine still idling. The pain was starting to win now. Josh could feel himself starting to lose concentration. Nothing else mattered except trying to fight back the terrible agony assailing every inch of his body. He could feel himself starting to become afraid.

'I'll drive,' said the woman, leaning across him and starting to pull him away from the driving seat. With difficulty, they swapped seats again. 'I'll get you home. You need treatment.'

Josh had no intention of resisting. He moved back across to the passenger seat, trying to rest his head in the space between it and the driver's place. He could feel the woman brushing her hand across his forehead, gauging his temperature. For the touch alone he was grateful.

There was nothing worse than the thought of dying alone. And right now I feel as if I really might die, Josh thought.

'Who am I?' asked Josh, looking up into the woman's eyes.

She shrugged, tossing back a lock of her red hair that had fallen down over her forehead. 'How the hell should I know? I just found you at the side of the road.'

Josh struggled to keep his eyes open, fighting to hold on to consciousness. Suddenly, he had a sense that if he closed his eyes he might never open them again. Even in the humid, sweaty cabin of the Ranger, he could feel himself growing colder. 'No, I'm serious,' he said, gripping the woman's hand

37

hard. 'I don't know who I am.'

TWO

Tuesday, June 2nd. Afternoon.
The sweat lay thick on Josh's forehead. He opened his eyes reluctantly. The light flooded over him as he glanced towards the window. Through the doorway he could see a yard with two pick-up trucks parked on the gravel, and a barn that looked as if it had been empty for years. Somewhere in the distance he could hear a dog barking, but otherwise it was completely silent. The heat was still stifling.

The woman was leaning across him, a swab of cotton wool in one hand and a bottle of disinfectant in the other. That perfume again, thought Josh, as the fragrance drifted over him. *What was its bloody name?*

The woman dabbed some disinfectant on the cotton wool, then started rubbing it onto Josh's arm.

A jolt of pain shot through his system, running deep into his spine. He pushed her aside. 'No,' he said firmly.

'Let me,' she replied. 'I'm a doctor.'

Josh looked up into her eyes. She was wearing a blue denim skirt, and a white blouse through which Josh could just see the outline of a white lace bra. There was some make-up on her face—a dab of face powder and some pale red lipstick—but she still looked fresh and natural. Her hair was tied up behind her neck and a pair of sunglasses was pushed up over her forehead.

'A doctor?' said Josh, the surprise evident in the tone of his voice.

The woman nodded. 'And you're sick. Very sick. So just lie back and let me treat you.'

Josh's gaze roamed around the room. Wherever it was, it certainly wasn't a hospital. Or a doctor's surgery. The room was about ten foot by five, with a pair of French windows at one end that led out into the yard. It was painted a pale grey-cream, but Josh reckoned that it was at least five years since anyone had run a paintbrush over it. There was nothing on the walls, and the bed he was lying on was a single, with a wooden frame and with only one sheet covering his body. Next to the bed was a jug of iced water and a face flannel. Apart from that, the room was empty.

Josh lay with his head back against the pillow. A thick bandage was strapped to the side of his neck, and beneath it his skin felt burning hot. His head was throbbing with pain, as if someone was chipping away at the inside of his skull with a chisel. The beat of the pain was a dull, steady rhythm that kept time like a jazz drummer. Every three seconds came another beat, making it almost impossible for Josh to hold a straight thought.

First things first, he told himself. Figure out where you are, what's wrong with you. Who attacked you yesterday? *And who the hell are you?*

The woman dabbed some more disinfectant onto his arm, sending another bolt of jabbing pain through him. She paused, as if she was wondering where to start. 'You were shot,' she replied. 'Twice.'

Josh nodded. 'How bad?'

'Once in the neck—that was the worst one,' the woman replied. 'It went in just to the left of the

39

windpipe, nicking the skin and blowing out a chunk of flesh. Another centimetre and you'd be dead. I've cleaned it up and cut away all the infected skin. That bandage stays on your neck for at least two weeks, and I'll need to change it every three days. Keep it clean, though, and you should be okay. You were lucky.'

She *sounded* like a doctor, thought Josh. She could discuss his injuries with a cool, professional detachment, as if she was explaining how to fix a machine.

'The second bullet went into your left calf. Nasty and painful, but not as dangerous. It took out a chunk of flesh but didn't sever any of the main arteries. The bullet was lodged in there but I took it out, and I think the wound's pretty clean. You lost at least two pints of blood, and you're going to have a nasty scar there, but it will heal okay. I'll keep the bandage on for a few days, then go in and take another look.'

The woman looked closely at Josh. 'You're strong,' she said softly. 'A lot of men would have died from these wounds. You know how to take a bullet.'

Josh sighed. The throbbing in his head was still intense. He leaned across the bed, pouring himself a glass of water and raising it to his lips. From the heat of his body, he suspected that he was suffering from a fever as well as from his wounds. 'What am I on?' he asked.

'I've patched up and cleaned your wounds, and given you some painkillers,' the woman replied. 'Trust me, you'd be feeling a lot worse without them. I haven't got any blood here, but if I had, I'd have given you some. What you lost is making you feel a lot weaker. It's going to take a few days in bed, lots of rest, and plenty to eat before you start getting your strength back. And that's before we start worrying about the wounds healing.'

Josh examined her closely, watching how she held herself when she spoke. She certainly seemed to know what she was talking about.

'Who are you?' he asked.

The woman took the sunglasses from her forehead, holding them in her right hand. 'I'm sorry, we haven't been introduced,' she answered, an easy smile playing across her lips. 'My name is Kate. Kate Benessia.'

'How long have I been sleeping?' said Josh.

'Just over a day,' said Kate, putting her shades back on. 'We got here just after one yesterday. It's now three o'clock on Tuesday afternoon. You slept for twenty-six hours, and, believe me, you needed it. That's partly the painkillers. But I gave you some sleeping tablets as well. A man in your state needs a lot of rest.'

Josh paused and drank some more of the water. His throat felt as if it was made of rock, and the throbbing in his head was making it hard to concentrate. Nothing makes any sense, he told himself. Who is she? *What am I doing here?*

'Where are we?' he asked.

'Near Fernwood, in Coconino County,' Kate answered. 'Although it's just a tiny town with a gas station, a diner and a general store, and even that's two miles away. Boisdale is bigger but that's ten miles away. So you might say we're in the middle of nowhere.'

Josh looked out into the yard. The ground was bone dry, the soil caked and cracked. A few weeds

41

had sprouted through the earth, but even they seemed to have dried up and died. 'I'm sorry, I don't even know which country I'm in.'

Kate laughed. 'You really don't know?' She looked towards the window. 'Coconino is in Arizona. That's part of a country called the United States. Big place, just between the Atlantic and Pacific oceans. You've probably heard of it.'

Josh had heard of it. It seemed that the general knowledge was still there. He knew what the capital of France was and how many inches made up a foot. He just didn't know anything about himself or his own history.

If only I could stop my head from hurting, thought Josh. I need to concentrate on who I am, and how I got here. *I need to start remembering things.*

Kate took the shades off, her eyes looking down at him intently. 'What were you doing lying in a ditch with two bullet holes in you?'

'I don't know,' said Josh.

'Okay, we'll worry later about how the wounds got there. Now, who are you?'

A cold sense of fear started in Josh's mind, then began to creep down his spine, slowly spreading through every nerve in his body. 'I told you, I don't know.'

Kate smiled, but her lips tightened as she did so, and her expression was angry. It was the kind of forced smile that doctors use on difficult patients. 'Take a deep breath, relax, then tell me who you are.'

Josh could feel his hand starting to shake.

I don't know, he repeated to himself. *I don't even know my own name.*

'Just try taking it slowly,' said Kate. 'Say it out loud. My name is . . .'

Josh hesitated. 'My name is . . .'

Nothing.

A wound was one thing. A lump of steel could bury itself in your leg, and after a few weeks there would be nothing to remind you that it had ever happened apart from a scar. A soldier could lose his money, even a lot of his blood, and still recover. But without his name he was nothing.

Get a grip, man. Remember. *It's there somewhere, you just have to find it.*

'I . . . I can't remember,' Josh said, looking up at Kate.

Her expression told him that she was suspicious. Her eyes were narrowing, and a frown had started to crease her brow. 'Think,' she said. 'Just relax and think.'

Josh shook his head. 'I can't,' he stammered nervously. 'I don't know.'

'Your age, then,' said Kate.

My age, thought Josh. I feel about a hundred and three right now, but that's not it. He attempted to think, taking a moment to try and bring the throbbing in his head under control. Nothing. The memories just weren't there.

'I don't know,' he replied.

'Okay,' said Kate. 'Your mother's name?'

'Nothing,' answered Josh, shaking his head. 'Is that sort of memory loss possible?' he asked, looking back up at Kate. 'Medically?'

'It's rare, except when it is drug-induced,' she said. 'But it *can* be a consequence of severe injuries. Maybe the bullet wound to your neck has done something to your nervous system.'

43

Josh closed his eyes for a second. He tried again, stretching the muscles of his mind to see if he could recover anything, but it was like pushing your foot on the accelerator of a car that had an empty petrol tank.

'Can it be fixed?' He looked up at her, scrutinising her reaction.

Kate lowered her eyes, then looked back into his. 'Depends,' she said slowly. 'Usually it's just a short-term thing. A few days' rest and recuperation, then it will all start to come flooding back.' A smile suddenly curled her lips. 'A month, and you'll be remembering your second cousin's birthday.'

'And *un*usually?' asked Josh. 'What then?'

'I'm not an expert, so I can't really say,' answered Kate. 'Memory is a very delicate thing. Nobody really understands what memories are, or where they are stored. People forget things all the time, then remember them, then start remembering them slightly differently. Who can say how all of that works?'

'Which means that I might not be okay?'

'Which means that if the memories don't come back naturally in a week or two, then you're into a strange place which doctors don't understand very well.'

Josh lay back on his pillow. He was fighting a desperate urge to rip the bandage from his neck, and start scratching his wound: it was itching, as if pepper had just been rubbed into the raw skin. His leg was aching too, and his eyes were starting to water from the constant throbbing in his head. A fly had come through the window. It flicked past Josh, then landed on the side of his cheek, but he lacked the strength to swat it away. Kate brushed it

44

off for him.

'I know nothing about myself,' he said, speaking as much to himself as to the woman at the side of his bed. 'I don't even know what I do.'

'He's a soldier,' said a man standing in the doorway.

Josh glanced upwards. The man was about sixty, with grey hair combed back over his head, grown long so that it reached the top of his shoulders. He was wearing black jeans and a pale blue linen shirt. His skin was tanned and heavily lined, carved like an old piece of granite. And his nose was long and prominent.

'This is my father,' said Kate. 'Marshall.'

Marshall walked forward, standing next to the bed and examining Josh as though he were a piece of livestock at a cattle market: he was probing Josh's character and worth, without any detectable trace of sympathy.

'You said I was a soldier?' Josh asked.

Marshall nodded. 'Yes,' he replied. 'You have the build and physique of a military man. Seen some action as well, I reckon.' The words were delivered slowly and carefully.

Josh tried to sit up, but the pain in his body was too great: he could command his muscles to move, but right now he could not make them obey. 'What makes you say that?'

'I was a soldier myself, once,' said Marshall. 'Vietnam. Two tours. 1968 to '69. Then 1971 to '72. The worst of it. Saw a lot of men get wounded. So I like to think I can recognise the scars.'

He leaned over, gently removing the cotton sheet that was covering Josh. He pointed towards a scar running across his abdomen. 'See this?' he

45

continued, his voice dropping down to a whisper. 'Knife wound. Whoever gave it to you was clearly aiming for your heart, but you rolled sideways, took it in the stomach instead. That's military training. If the blade is going to cut you, try to make sure it's somewhere it can't do too much damage.'

Marshall moved sideways. 'Then here,' he said, pointing to the top of Josh's leg. 'That's a scar from where a dumdum bullet has gone in. Only on a battlefield are you going to find that kind of ammunition in use.'

Marshall shrugged. 'There has to be some explanation for those scars on your body. You could just be some small-time drug dealer who's got caught up in one too many street fights, but I don't think so. Look, a series of small wounds up the side of your rib cage. Those are frag wounds, the kind you get from a hand grenade. That tells me you're a soldier.'

'What kind of soldier?' asked Josh.

Marshall shrugged. 'A lucky one, I'd say, and that's the best kind. You took a lot of damage yesterday, and you've taken some big hits before. But you're still alive. Be grateful for that. There are plenty who aren't.' He ran his right hand through his long, greying strands of hair. 'Those tattoos. They're military as well.'

At the top of Josh's arm a pair of wings was etched in thick black ink, the design fluttering every time he moved his shoulder muscle. Beneath the wings was the letter 'O', then the word 'Pos'.

'Do you know what that means?' asked Marshall.

Josh shook his head. Wings, he was wondering to himself. *What the hell have I got that for?*

'British Parachute Regiment,' said Marshall. 'An

46

O-pos will be your blood group. A lot of soldiers get that info tattooed onto themselves so that the doctors know what to pump into them if they get dragged off the battlefield and need a lot of blood in a hurry.'

'He needs sleep, dad,' Kate interrupted.

Josh looked up towards Marshall. 'Someone came after us on a bike,' he said. 'He was trying to kill us.'

'Seems like you're an unpopular man,' said Marshall drily.

'Who the hell was it?' snapped Josh.

Kate looked at him fiercely. 'You need to sleep,' she repeated.

'I need to know who was on the bike,' Josh shot back.

'Later. Sleep first,' said Kate quickly.

Josh could see the hypodermic needle in her hand. A shaft of sunlight had caught its tip. He winced as the device approached his leg, inhaling sharply as he felt it pierce his skin. He could feel the liquid starting to flow into his bloodstream.

'What is it?' he snapped, looking up at Kate.

'Easy, boy,' said Marshall. 'She's just trying to help.'

'This will help you sleep,' said Kate softly. 'You need it. You're very weak.'

Josh could feel his eyes starting to close. For a moment he resisted. A sense of dread overcame him. He could feel the sweat trickling off his forehead. Get a grip, he commanded himself, for the second time that afternoon. You'll be okay. You just need to get some sleep, and start getting your strength back. *Then you can figure out who you are and what happened to you.*

47

His mind emptied. Except for a single image that now flashed through his mind. It was briefly as clear and vivid as a picture on a cinema screen. A boy running. And a man falling to the ground.

THREE

Wednesday, June 3rd. Morning.
Josh reached up to feel his forehead. The sweat was still there, but there was less of it than he remembered from yesterday. A light breeze was wafting in from the two open doors: the air was hot but dry, and somehow its movement cooled his face.

Sleep, he told himself. *You must restore your strength.*

Slowly he opened his eyes. The light was fierce, but he couldn't see enough of the sun from his bed to get any fix on the time. Morning, that was all he could tell. He reached across for the water, taking the full glass and throwing its contents down his throat. The skin inside his mouth was parched and dry, the way it would get after a hard drinking session, and even a second glass did nothing to help.

His head was still throbbing but now it was only as if someone was chipping at the inside of his skull with a screwdriver, not a chisel.

Welcome to another day, Josh told himself, a grim smile twisting his lips. *Mr Nobody.*

He tried to lift himself. His bandaged neck was still itching, and the wound in his leg was jabbing at his nerve endings. But his torso was beginning to

48

feel better: the strength was starting to come back to his upper body. He could feel more blood filling up his veins. Using his elbows, he levered himself upwards, taking a deep breath as he did so. He sat on the edge of the bed. Next to the single chair there was an old crutch, made from aluminium and plastic. About a foot away.

I can make it.

Josh started to stand. He winced as his leg rebelled against the movement. Then a blinding flash of pain burst through him. He sat down, closing his eyes, trying to bring it under control. Count, he told himself. Do anything to take your mind off it.

At the count of fifty, he tried again. More carefully this time. He stood on his right leg only, using his arms to balance himself, then took one hop. He could feel himself wobbling, and for a moment he was terrified that he might fall onto the wounded leg. But, steadying himself, he grabbed for the crutch, holding on to it as if it was the last lifeboat leaving a sinking ship.

Steady yourself, man. You can do this.

Holding on to the crutch, Josh started to hobble forwards painfully. He grabbed a blue dressing gown that was hung on a hook on the door, then stepped outside. It felt good to feel sunlight on his face again, and to smell the air. The yard measured twenty feet by fifteen. There was nothing there but scrub, and one slow-dripping tap in the corner. To his right he could see two pick-up trucks: the Ranger, which looked shot to pieces, and a three-year-old Chevy Avalanche which aside from a layer of dust covering its bodywork and one dent above the rear left wheel looked in reasonable shape.

Josh looked up. In the distance, he could see a mountain: a thick slab of reddish rock that looked as if it had dropped straight into the desert from space. About a mile or so down the flat road, he could see another building, but whether it was a barn or a house he couldn't tell from this distance. Aside from that, the landscape was empty: just sand, dust and scrub stretching out as far as the eye could see.

Why the hell would anyone want to live here? he asked himself.

For a moment, Josh lent against the window, trying to compose himself. My memories, he asked himself. *Where are my memories?*

He started searching around in his mind again but it was like walking through a pitch-black maze. There was nothing there to guide him. He ran through the same questions he had tried yesterday—what's my name, how old am I, who was my mother—but no matter how hard he concentrated, there was nothing there.

The main building was ten yards in front of him. A low bungalow, probably prefabricated, it was just one step up the housing ladder from a mobile home. The house was a rectangle, about sixty yards long, divided into different rooms. Next to it was a satellite dish, but otherwise nobody had done any work on its appearance. Not for years.

Josh stepped forward, biting his lip to control the pain in his leg as he did so. He could hear voices from a television. 'Anyone up?' he called, leaning against the aluminium frame of the French windows that led from the kitchen into the yard.

Kate looked up, startled. 'You,' she said. 'You should be in bed.'

50

Josh hobbled towards her, using the crutch to steady himself. The kitchen looked as though it had been put together from a flat-pack at Wal-Mart a decade ago: a slab of Formica ran around its perimeter, interrupted only by a sink, a cooker and a pair of cupboards. Kate was sitting at the small wooden table—cheap pine—eating a bowl of cereal. The television in the corner was tuned to Fox News.

'If I can walk, I'll walk,' said Josh. 'The first thing I need to get back is my will-power.'

Kate nodded. She was wearing pale blue slacks, and a loose blouse with the top two buttons undone, displaying an inch of freckled cleavage. Some powder and lipstick had brightened up her face. 'Sit down,' she commanded, pointing to the spare seat. 'You don't need any weight on that leg.'

Josh placed himself beside the table, relieved to take the weight off his feet. Naturally he couldn't remember whether he'd ever had to walk with a crutch before. But it took practice. And it was more tiring than it looked: all the weight had to be carried in his shoulders and arms. Even travelling a few yards strained the wound in his neck.

He took a sip of the coffee that Kate had placed in front of him. The caffeine hit him like a gale blowing into a tree: he could feel his head swaying as it shot into his bloodstream. It had been at least two days now since he'd had anything to drink but water, and he could feel the coffee-jolt rushing through him, delivering a sudden and unexpected burst of energy.

Josh glanced towards the television. The newsreader was discussing a power cut in Memphis last night: the lights had gone off for a few brief

51

minutes, causing a tremor of panic and alarm throughout the city. 'Could it be a repeat of the Three Cities attack of earlier this year?' asked the newsreader. 'We'll have more after this break.'

Kate looked at Josh. 'So how're you feeling?' she asked.

He paused. It was a difficult question to answer. He was in bad shape, yet, in truth, not as bad as he had been twenty-four hours earlier. Physically, I'm probably starting to get better, although it's still a long road back to full health, he mused. *Mentally, I'm feeling worse.*

'Like a field mouse that's just been dragged backwards through a combine harvester.' Josh smiled. 'But I'm getting better—slowly. I think.'

'We'll need to do a proper check soon,' said Kate. 'Blood pressure, temperature, the works. I'm going to keep those bandages on today because I don't want to disturb the wounds. We'll change them tomorrow.' She stood up, taking down a bowl of cornflakes from the cupboard. 'Now, you need to eat. Get some calories back into the system. You like cereal?'

'Can't remember,' answered Josh, glancing back at her. 'I'll try.'

Kate put the food on the table. Josh dipped his spoon into the cereal, raising it to his lips. His throat was still dry and sore, and it was difficult for him to swallow. The food tasted okay: bland, but he could feel the energy starting to sink into him, restoring his strength. I have my hunger back, he thought, and that's a start.

'Even if I don't know who I am,' said Josh, pushing aside the cereal bowl and taking another sip on the coffee, '*somebody* knows—because they

52

tried to kill me.'

'And they sure came close,' said Marshall.

The older man had just walked into the room. He poured himself a coffee and looked across at Josh. 'What do you think happened?'

'Someone tried to kill me,' Josh repeated. 'That's all I know.'

'Or you tried to kill someone?' Marshall asked.

Josh paused. The thought that he might have killed someone had been lying there somewhere, beneath the conscious surface of his mind. *When you couldn't remember who you were, there was no way of knowing what you were capable of.*

Marshall smiled, the lines on his weather-beaten face creasing up. 'Even out here in Arizona, a man has a couple of bullet holes in him, we reckon he ran into someone who knew who he was and wasn't too well disposed to him. The trouble is, boy, we don't know who the hell you are.'

'What was I wearing?' asked Josh.

'Pair of jeans, and a black T-shirt,' replied Kate. 'They're covered in blood, and the jeans have a hole in them where the bullet went into your leg. I threw them away. Marshall has some spare pairs— you can wear one of 'em when you feel able to walk properly.'

Josh leaned forward on the table. 'Nothing on me?' he asked. 'No wallet, driving licence, credit card?'

Kate shook her head. 'We found three thousand dollars in cash in your back pocket. It's up there on the shelf, in an envelope. Take it when you need it. Apart from that, nothing. No clue to who you might be.' She paused. 'You are clearly a man who travels light.'

'Three thousand dollars,' said Marshall. 'What kind of man carries that amount of money around with him?'

Josh stayed silent.

'A gangster?' persisted Marshall.

Josh started to squeeze his knuckles together. 'We'll find that out when we know who I am,' he said, the statement delivered more to himself than to anyone else. 'Right now I need to know who was trying to kill me and why? What the hell was I doing there?' He looked down at the floor. 'If I can figure that out, I can start to figure out who I am.'

*　　　*　　　*

The sandwich tasted good. A thick slice of turkey breast, with some salad on top and a hefty dollop of mayonnaise, wrapped between two hunks of chewy white bread. Josh bit down on it, tearing off big mouthfuls with his teeth. He sipped on the Coke that he had poured into the tall, thin glass, and looked out onto the surrounding scrubland. It had a harsh beauty to it. The terrain rolled into the distance, dipping towards the far horizon, scarcely disturbed by any living thing, whether animal or human. *If you wanted to hide, this would be a good place.*

I've been here before, he told himself. Mountains. Rugged landscape. Sand and dust. I don't know when or where but I've seen this or something very like it.

My memory is there somewhere.

Kate stepped out onto the porch and sat down next to him. She was holding a hypodermic syringe in her hand. Josh looked down at its needle and

54

winced. There was only one man's skin that needle was going to puncture, he thought. And I'm living in it.

'You're eating,' she said softly. 'Another day or two and you'll be surprised at how strong you are feeling.'

Josh nodded. 'My body will be okay, I can feel it. It's my mind.'

'Any memories yet?'

Josh shook his head. 'Nothing.'

'You're a soldier—we've figured that out.'

Josh nodded. 'If you say so.'

'I reckon you're British as well,' continued Kate. 'From the accent.'

'You recognise it?'

'From films, that kind of stuff. I've never been there.' Kate took her shades from her face and started fidgeting with them. 'You may not sound much like Hugh Grant. But I still reckon you're a Brit.'

'Then what was I doing here?'

'In Arizona?'

Josh nodded. 'A British soldier. Serving or not serving. Lying in a ditch with a bullet through him. That's some puzzle.'

'I'll try some associations,' said Kate. 'I'll say a word. You tell me what it makes you think of. Okay?'

Josh took another bite of his sandwich, chewing vigorously. He felt that if he could just eat enough to get his strength back, maybe he would start to drag some memories out of the back of his brain.

'Army,' said Kate.

Josh stopped eating. 'Nothing,' he said.

'War?'

55

Josh shook his head again.

'Okay, I'll try another track,' said Kate. 'Family.'

'Nothing.'

'Parents?'

Josh shook his head once more.

'Home town?'

The look of sadness was visible on Josh's face as he shook his head yet again.

'Conspiracy,' said Kate.

Josh hesitated. 'Me,' he replied slowly. 'You said conspiracy, and I thought of myself.'

'Maybe we're getting somewhere,' said Kate, a hint of excitement in her tone. 'Mystery?' she went on.

'TV, films,' said Josh, his tone hopeful.

Kate stopped him. 'No, we need real memories. Not just stuff you've seen on TV.'

'Then, nothing,' said Josh.

'If you're British, you must come from somewhere over there. Maybe Liverpool?'

'I don't know.'

'London?'

'I don't know,' Josh repeated.

'How about Manchester?'

Josh shook his head—it was getting to be a habit, he thought.

'Birmingham?'

'Not a sodding Brummie. Maybe it's better not to get my memory back if that's all there is to look forward to.'

'How old do you reckon you are?' said Kate.

Josh shrugged.

'You look about thirty.'

'I could be. I don't know.'

'Married?' she asked.

Josh shrugged again. 'I can't remember.'

Kate laughed, raising her hand to her lips. 'I bet you use that line on all the girls.'

FOUR

Thursday, June 4th. Afternoon.
Josh lifted his head from the pillow. He kept his eyes closed, trying to cling on to the image that had been playing through his mind as he awoke. A man falling. A boy running. A shot. Then a shout.

The shout. What was he saying?

Josh squeezed his eyes tight shut, trying to hold himself in a state where he was half awake, half asleep. The shout, he repeated to himself. *What the hell did it say?*

No good.

The image had gone now, consigned to the dustbin, along with all the rest of his memories.

Josh opened his eyes. He took a long drink of water, looking at the clock. It was just after four in the afternoon. He must have slept for at least twenty-four, maybe twenty-five hours. His body felt lazy and tired still, but the aching in his head was starting to ease, and the itch on his neck underneath the thick layer of bandages was getting weaker.

If there was a shot, was it my finger on the trigger?

Twenty-five hours, thought Josh. Whatever Kate jabbed into me must have been the strongest stuff in her locker.

A fly landed on the sheet. Josh slammed down his fist, squashing it against the white linen. Getting my strength back, reflected Josh. *And my reflexes.*

He levered himself from the bed, using all the strength in his elbows. Carefully, he put his left foot on the floor, pressing it against the cold tiles. The pain was still there, but it didn't scream up through his leg the way it had yesterday. His eyes were still bloodshot, but the red streaks running through his pupils were not quite so thick. And the fever heat on his brow seemed to be lessening. Gently, he reached out for the crutch and started to walk.

A gunshot rang out from the yard.

Instinctively, Josh ducked, his shoulders turning sideways, his hunched posture protecting both his head and his torso from any bullets that might come flying through the window. Looking around, he started searching through the room for something that could be improvised as a weapon. Nothing. The crutch might make a staff, but against a man with a gun it would be useless.

Another shot echoed across the empty landscape. Josh looked through the window. Marshall was standing in the yard, a pistol in his hand. Fifty yards away he had lined up a row of tin cans and was firing at them one by one.

A soldier, Josh thought to himself. They said they thought I was a soldier. And those were a soldier's instinctive reactions to the sound of gunfire. Shield yourself. Stay alive. *And look for a way to fight back.*

He watched Marshall from the window, noticing the ease with which the older man carried the weapon in his hand. A Browning, Josh noticed. A Browning Buck Mark field pistol, with its distinctive black metal barrel and polished walnut grips. Who are these people? he wondered to himself. Why have they taken me into this house?

Why are they looking after me?

What do they want from me?

A tin can had fallen to the ground as one of Marshall's bullets tore through it.

'Nice shot,' said Josh, stepping out from the porch.

The heat of the midday sun was still beating down on the parched ground. It must be at least forty degrees, reckoned Josh. As soon as he stepped outside, he could feel the sun burning into the back of his neck, but the air was so dry and arid that it hardly raised a bead of perspiration on his skin.

'I'm not really any good,' said Marshall. 'I can fire a gun if I have to, but I was never really blessed with a natural aim. Only a few men are.' He looked hard at Josh, his eyes narrowing. 'How about you?'

Josh shrugged. 'I wouldn't know.'

Marshall smiled, walking across the dusty yard towards the back of the main building. Josh hobbled at his side, using the crutch to hold his weight as he moved forwards. He was dressed in just his gown, and the ground felt hot on the soles of his feet. 'Take a shot,' suggested Marshall. 'I think it might be good exercise for you. Get your senses working again.'

Josh just nodded. So far, he was uncertain what he should make of Marshall. Kate was a doctor, although even her motives were hard to figure out. But the old guy, thought Josh—he was a puzzle without any clues.

The door swung open to reveal a storeroom full of guns and ammunition. There must have been a dozen hunting rifles stacked in rows. Josh ran his gaze over them, recognising a Saiga, a Kalashnikov, a Winchester, a Marlin and a Browning. They were all sporty, heavy-duty models with polished wooden stocks, designed to fell a deer or a stag at two hundred yards in the woods. Next to them was a range of pistols.

'Pick one,' said Marshall.

Josh looked at the weapons and let his instincts guide him. He took a Sig-Sauer P228 pistol, cocked it, then uncocked it and activated the firing-pin safety.

'I keep these loaded all the time,' said Marshall. 'Give it a go.'

Marshall held the gun for him while Josh hobbled outside. He walked across to the side of the porch, leaned his crutch against the wall and used the frame of the door to support some of his weight.

'Think you can hit one of those cans?'

'I have no idea,' answered Josh.

He released the safety, lifted the pistol and gripped the weapon in both hands, his feet positioned slightly apart like a boxer's. He raised the gun so that it was level with his eye.

'The weaver position,' said Marshall.

'What?' asked Josh.

Marshall smiled. 'Never mind. It's a police term.'

Josh squinted, concentrating on the tiny sight at the tip of the barrel. The tin can was fifty yards distant, and only just visible. He lined up the pistol's barrel, then took a deep breath to steady the muscles in his shoulders and his forearms.

Is this instinct? he wondered. Like a dog chewing on a bone. *Or have I been trained to do this?*

He squeezed the trigger gently, exerting only as much pressure as was needed to release the bullet. The barrel of the gun slammed backwards with the recoil but Josh had enough strength to control the kickback. Without thinking, he fired again. A double tap: two bullets in quick succession.

The tin can spun into the air, then shot forward as the second bullet punched through it.

'A shot,' said Marshall, standing two yards behind him. 'I thought so.' He paused. 'Try again.'

Josh steadied the pistol, took aim and fired. One shot, then two. The can clattered to the ground.

'Again,' said Marshall.

Josh paused, took a breath, then squeezed the trigger—once, then twice. Another can bit the dust.

Marshall stepped in front of him. He took a swig of the beer bottle gripped in his right hand, emptying its contents down his throat. He glanced across towards Josh. 'Let's see if you can hit a moving target.'

With a swing of his hand, Marshall slung the bottle high up into the air. Josh followed it with his stare, tracking the arc of its movement. Wait until it peaks and starts to fall, he told himself. That is when it will slow down. *That is when it will be easier to hit.*

He squeezed the trigger. The bullet streaked high into the sky, hitting nothing. Almost instantaneously, Josh released the second round. This time he could hear the satisfying crunch of steel smashing into glass, sending a shower of tiny fragments of the bottle down from the sky.

'Like I said, a marksman,' said Marshall, stepping towards him. 'A soldier always fires twice. It's drilled into him.'

'You already said I was a soldier.'

Marshall nodded, his expression turning serious. 'Plenty of soldiers can't shoot straight,' he replied.

'Look at the way you always fire twice. Assault troops do that—it's part of their training. If you want to kill a man, two bullets are always twice as good as one. Squeeze once, then twice, then drop your weapon.'

'Assault troops?' asked Josh.

Marshall shrugged. 'Special forces, maybe.'

Josh looked down at the ground. The shot. The memory he had woken up with. It was still there, struggling to emerge, like a worm trying to wriggle its way out of a hard piece of ground. The noise of it was vivid in his ears now: he could hear the echo of the bullet spreading out across the empty scrubland.

Did I shoot someone?

'A beer,' said Marshall, reaching down into the icebox propped up on the front of the porch. 'You like beer?'

'Maybe. I can't remember,' replied Josh with an easygoing smile.

Marshall handed across a beer, snapping off its cap between his right thumb and forefinger. 'I never met a soldier who didn't like beer,' he said.

Josh put the bottle to his lips. The taste was familiar. The alcohol hit his bloodstream, sending a sudden rush of energy surging through him. He felt light-headed, giddy. But he could also feel the aching in his head starting to ease. 'I like beer, that's for sure,' he said, looking back towards Marshall.

The older man nodded, looking down at the ground, the beer bottle still in his hand. 'What do you want to do?'

Josh turned to look at him. 'I'll stay, if you'll let me.' He took another hit of the beer. 'Just for a few

62

days, until I get myself straightened out. I can pay you from the cash that was in my pocket.'

'The money doesn't matter,' said Marshall. 'You're not costing us anything apart from a few scraps of food.'

'I could go to a hospital,' continued Josh. 'I've thought about it. But I don't know who I am, or what happened to me back there. Like you said, a man doesn't get shot for no reason. Maybe I was mixed up in something illegal.'

'You're worried that if you check into a hospital the cops are going to be looking out for you?'

Josh gripped the beer bottle tightly between his hands. 'I just don't know, do I?'

'You got no idea what you were doing?'

Josh shook his head. 'None.'

'Rest, that's what you need,' said Marshall. 'Give it a few days. A memory is like a woman. You have to let them come to you.'

'No.' Josh smiled, more to himself than to Marshall. 'I need to chase.'

'Meaning?'

'I'm a hunter. I like to track things down. Women, memories, whatever. That's who I am.'

'You don't know who the hell you are, boy,' answered Marshall.

'But I do know that much about myself,' said Josh quickly. 'Like you said, I'm a soldier. We don't wait for things to come to us.'

Marshall laughed. 'The clever ones do.'

Josh stood up, using the crutch for support. It still hurt, but he needed to push himself: he knew that until he started exercising his muscles again his strength was never going to return. 'Maybe I'm not a good one,' he said, looking back towards

63

Marshall. Josh stretched his arms to relieve the pain in his shoulders. 'Take me back to where you found me.'

'What for?'

'It might trigger something,' said Josh. 'If I could see the place, then maybe I'll get a sense of what happened. Maybe I can find some evidence about who attacked me.'

He sat down again. The pain in his leg was growing worse, making it hard for him to stand for any length of time. 'Now,' he said. 'I want to go back now.'

Marshall shook his head. 'Too hot,' he answered. 'Maybe we'll take you in the morning. When it's cooler. And when Kate says you're strong enough.'

Josh caught the words on the lips, just as he was about to speak. An instinct was burning within him: to tell the older man that he wanted to be taken to the place where they'd found him, and he wanted to be taken there now. No, he reminded himself. Until I have my strength back, I have to depend on these people. I'm an invalid. *I can do nothing for myself.*

'Tomorrow, then,' said Josh stiffly.

Marshall grinned. 'At dawn, before the bull snakes are awake.'

Josh looked out across the scrub. A truck was moving along the road, doing about forty miles an hour. Apart from that the landscape was as bleak and empty as it always was. 'What are you doing out here?' he asked.

'Keeping myself to myself,' said Marshall. 'Soldiering does that to a man sometimes. You might find that out one day for yourself.'

'Not too quiet?'

64

'Not for me, no. I like quiet.'

'What do you do?' asked Josh, looking across at the older man. 'It doesn't look as if there are any jobs out here.'

Marshall took another sip of his beer. 'Veterans from the war,' he replied. 'I run a website that helps keep vets in touch with one another. Gives them help and advice on their benefit payments, medical treatment, the rest of it. There are still a lot of men out there who are in pretty bad shape, both mentally and physically, and for many of them it gets worse as they get older. A lot of them live out in remote places like this because they don't like the noise and the sweat of the cities. So the site helps them stay in touch. Lets them talk. They pay a small subscription, so it doesn't make a lot of money, but it makes a bit. We get by.'

'And Kate?' said Josh, nodding back towards the main building. 'She's a young woman, full of life. What's she doing out here?'

Marshall paused, and Josh could sense the older man growing tense: his hand was tightening its grip on his beer bottle, and his brow was starting to furrow. 'That's her business,' he said.

'Okay,' said Josh, backing away. 'I was just curious.'

'Listen,' continued Marshall. 'I don't mind you being here. You're a soldier, and I like soldiers. But just make sure you keep your hands off my daughter. That way you and I are going to get along just fine.'

*   *   *

The pizza felt sticky and heavy in Josh's hand. It

65

had a thick layer of cheese on top, plus some wedges of ham and pineapple. I can't remember whether I like pizza or not, Josh said to himself. *But I certainly don't like it with sodding pineapple on it.*

He took another bite, flicking one of the pineapple chunks onto the ground, then chewing the slice quickly. Get it inside you, he told himself. Every bite you take will get you a bite closer to being stronger again. *And strength is what you need.*

'I had a memory,' said Josh.

Kate looked surprised. She turned to face him, a smile flashing across her lips. 'Just now?'

'Earlier,' answered Josh. 'As I was waking up this afternoon.'

It was a little after nine at night, and the final rays of sunlight had just dipped below the horizon. The fierce redness of the sunset against the reddish-browns of the desert landscape had held Josh's attention for more than an hour: he had been happy just to sit and watch the gradual fading of the light, and the smears of colour it left behind. By the time Kate had come out of the kitchen with a giant pizza and a pitcher of iced tea he had been feeling better than at any time since he'd been shot. The pain from his wounds was ebbing, and the headache was tuning down to just a mild, irregular drumbeat.

Now a moon was starting to rise in the sky, arcing across the distant mountain and bathing the flat land in a silver light. Ahead of him, Josh could see a huge inch-and-a-half-long bug crawling across the scrub, its eyes glinting through the darkness. The creature had a thick black skin, and was moving at speed across the ground.

66

Is that dangerous? wondered Josh as he watched the spider's progress. That's the real risk from losing your memory: a lifetime's experience of knowing how to look after yourself is lost in a split second.

'Morning is the time when you're most likely to find some memories stirring within you,' said Kate, looking up towards Josh. 'Whenever you feel yourself waking up, try and keep your mind empty and relaxed. Eventually some memories will sneak back in there.'

'There was a shot,' said Josh, looking towards Kate. 'A gunshot.'

'Aimed at you?' she asked. 'Was it someone shooting at you?'

Josh shook his head. 'No, I don't think so,' he answered. 'I hear a shot. And then I see a boy running. Across some kind of dark landscape. Then that's it. The memory goes.'

'It's a start,' said Kate. 'It's locked up in there somewhere. We just have to find a key that opens the box.'

Josh took a further bite of his pizza, flicking another piece of pineapple on the ground and watching the spider crawl towards the discarded fruit. 'The key's pretty well locked up right now.'

'Try some of the stuff you were watching on TV,' said Kate. 'Maybe that will trigger something.'

'Hasn't yet,' said Josh, taking a sip of the iced tea.

'Iraq,' said Kate. 'What does that mean to you personally? Have you been there?'

Josh paused. Something. He could feel it in his brain, a slight flickering of recognition. But nothing more came. 'No,' he replied. 'Nothing.'

'Okay,' said Kate. 'Let's try something else.' She

hesitated. 'What's my name?'

Josh looked at her and grinned. 'Kate.'

'My father's name?'

'Marshall.'

'What did I give you for breakfast yesterday?'

'Cereal.'

Kate nodded. 'And how was the weather?'

'Hot,' answered Josh. 'Bloody hot.'

Kate poured herself a glass of iced tea. She was wearing a pale blue linen skirt and a white blouse, the most dressy clothes Josh had seen her in. He noticed the smooth outline of her legs beneath the fabric. Her skin was tanned a rich, light brown from constant exposure to the sun. The bright locks of red hair against the tanned skin gave her an exotic appearance that was all the more captivating for being so unusual. Most redheads had pale skins, reflected Josh. She was an unusual woman. In a thousand different ways, no doubt.

'There are two different types of memory loss,' said Kate. 'Anterograde, which means the patient can't learn anything new. And retrograde, which means they can't remember anything that happened before a certain point. They can remember general stuff, but nothing personal. We've just tested you on the past couple of days and you're doing fine. You remember everything that happened since you came here. So what you are suffering from is retrograde memory loss. That tells us there isn't any brain damage. Rest. You'll get it back.'

'And if I don't?'

Kate shrugged. 'You'll just have to learn again. Everything. From scratch, like a kid.'

Josh glanced towards Kate. For the first time

since he had woken up here two days ago he could feel himself starting to relax. The itching in his neck was subsiding, and his leg was almost strong enough to stand on without him having to use a crutch. He could move without his whole body rebelling in pain.

Everything's going to be okay, he said to himself. I don't know how or when. But I can sense it. *I'm going to pull through this.*

'What are *you* doing out here?'

He sipped on his iced tea and looked at Kate, at the same time gesturing towards the desolate landscape.

'Don't you like it?' she asked.

He could detect the hint of defiance in her voice. 'It's a wilderness,' he replied.

'I like it. It's natural. Unspoilt. The way the world should be.'

Josh looked out onto the scrubland. Some of the pizza was still sitting at his side, but he had eaten as much as he could manage this evening. 'I don't mean that,' he said. 'You're a doctor, but you don't practise. You're an attractive young woman, but you live out here, a hundred miles from the nearest decent-sized town. I'm sorry, I don't get it.'

He looked at Kate. 'What are you hiding from?'

Kate stood up briskly. Her manner had grown cold and distant: her shoulders were hunched up into her neck, and her gaze flicked past Josh as if she were searching for something in the distance. 'You need some rest,' she said. 'That's an order from your doctor.'

*　　　*　　　*

69

Josh woke up with a start. His head was spinning and his breathing was ragged. He was about to speak, but he could feel Kate's hand covering his lips.

'Quiet,' she whispered fiercely in his ear. 'There are men approaching the house. Police.'

Josh struggled to wrap the sheet around his naked body. He could feel the tension flooding through him. Glancing outside, he could see that it was night: the yard was in shadow, with only some moonlight throwing a few pale beams across the pathway.

'What shall I do?'

'Hide, quick,' said Kate. 'There's a place under the floorboards.'

Josh got to his feet, using his crutch to walk across the yard to the kitchen. He could see two police cars turning the corner, driving along the narrow strip of road that led up to the house. 'Quick,' said Kate at his side.

Marshall was waiting in the kitchen. He was holding up a layer of lino, pointing to a patch of exposed floor. 'Down there,' he snapped, pushing aside two planks to reveal a trapdoor. 'There's a space just big enough to hold a man.'

Josh looked into the darkness. He could see almost nothing. Next to him, Marshall switched on a flashlight. The beam illuminated a set of six steps that led down to a curved space. Josh started to step downwards, leaving his crutch behind. His leg still throbbed painfully as his weight rested upon it. Using his hands, he levered himself into position.

The rectangular trench measured ten feet by ten. It was five feet deep. The space had been cut into the earth below the foundations of the bungalow, with strips of wood used to prop up its sides. Josh lay down on his back. 'I'm going to switch the flashlight off now,' said Marshall. 'I'll get you out when they've gone.'

The flashlight flicked off, and suddenly Josh was plunged into blackness. He could see nothing, only hear footsteps moving above him. The air down in the trench was hot—at least forty degrees—and stale. Josh could feel the sweat starting to form on his skin. He could sense the cracked earth all around him, and a few feet away he could smell the pipe that led down from the bathroom towards the septic tank.

Why do they have a one-man hiding place beneath their house? thought Josh. *Who the hell are these people?*

He heard a knock on the door. One set of footsteps, then another. Two men. Josh was certain they were men. The steps were heavy and deliberate, walking slowly through the house as if they were searching for something.

Voices. They were too muffled for him to make out at first. He strained his ears, struggling to catch the words being spoken just a few yards above him.

'An Englishman,' he heard a voice saying. 'We're looking for a man with a British accent. He's in the area somewhere.'

Josh could hear Kate speaking, but he couldn't catch what she was saying. A whisper was all that filtered down, the words indistinct.

'He might be dangerous,' he heard the man saying. 'Only might be, mind. We just want to bring him in for questioning.'

They think I did it. They think I shot somebody. And—who knows?—maybe I did, thought Josh to

71

himself. *What kind of man am I? What might I be capable of?*

Another pause. Kate was speaking again but still Josh couldn't catch the words.

'You haven't seen anything suspicious in the area?' asked the man. 'We think he might be pretty badly hurt too, so he couldn't have gone far.'

Josh could hear Kate now. 'We haven't seen anybody,' she said. 'And, as you know, it's pretty isolated up here. If there was anyone, we'd've seen them.'

'Mind if we look around?'

Now Josh could hear Marshall walking across the floor. 'Feel free,' the older man said.

Josh lay completely still. He could hear the footsteps tramping across the floor above him. And he could hear the sounds of cupboards being opened and beds being moved.

Suddenly he felt something moving across his skin. The thing's touch felt dry and coarse, with the texture of an old belt. A snake. Josh could feel his flesh starting to creep. Goose bumps were rising on every inch of his skin, and a shiver of cold fear started to run down his spine. His hand was trembling, and he had to focus his mind to try and steady it.

I'm learning new things about myself all the time. I have a fear of snakes.

Stay still, he told himself. Stay perfectly still and you'll be okay.

The snake moved further across his torso. Josh caught a glimpse of its eyes, glinting back at him. His own eyes had become more accustomed to the darkness and he could make out that the reptile had wide bands of red and black skin interspersed with narrow ones of white and yellow. Its head was completely black, with a snubbed snout, and its long tongue flicked lazily across Josh's chest to lick some of the sweat from his body. Was its bite venomous?

Hold steady, man, thought Josh, tracking the snake's movements. Just keep your nerve.

He could hear footsteps moving towards the door. 'Nothing in the other building?' he heard the policeman say.

'Just a guest room,' Marshall replied.

More movement. Then Kate said something that Josh couldn't catch. The snake started to move up along Josh's body towards his neck. Its tail was flicking against his buttocks.

'Sure?' Josh heard the policeman say suspiciously.

'Sure,' said Marshall. 'Go take a look.'

Another pause. Josh felt a desperate need to scratch the bandage on his neck. The snake was pushing up against the wound.

Another inch, thought Josh, and I'll have to move.

'You can contact us in Fernwood,' he heard the man say. 'You see or hear anything strange, then you let us know. And don't attempt to approach this guy. He might be dangerous.'

Josh took a deep breath. The snake was pushing its head against his bandage, nuzzling it open with the hard bone of its snout. It can smell the blood in there, he realised. And it wants a taste.

Above him he could hear the sound of a starter motor turning, then of an engine running. The police car was starting to pull out onto the roadway. Slowly he counted to five, making sure

73

that the car was safely away from the house before risking betraying himself with any sudden movements.

Now I know I'm a wanted man, Josh reflected sourly. And Kate and Marshall are protecting me. *I should be grateful, but why are they doing it?*

With a swift, violent movement, Josh flicked his hand upwards. He grabbed the snake by the throat, squeezing as hard as he could on the thin tube of flesh, skin and bone until the breath emptied out of its body, its tail flapping against Josh's legs, lashing at the skin.

He cast the corpse to one side.

Already, Marshall was beaming his flashlight down into the trench. 'You okay?' he shouted.

FIVE

Friday, June 5th. Dawn.
The Chevy Avalanche pick-up truck bounced along the pitted surface of the road. Josh wound down the window, letting the morning air rush over his face. Traces of red were splattered across the sky. His mind was fresh from another five hours of sleep after the police had left and the caffeine from the coffee he had drunk for breakfast was still flowing through his veins.

'Much further?' he said, looking across at Marshall.

The older man was gripping the wheel of the pick-up truck. 'About two miles,' he said, his voice tired. 'I'll tell you when we're there.'

The drive had taken just under an hour, and they

74

had left the house at six. The route had taken them through a rough, mountainous landscape, the surface of the ground pitted with boulders and dried-out trenches. The first town, Fernwood, was just over a mile away, but that was a just a gas station with a diner and general store attached, and a collection of a dozen houses. Since then, they had passed through two more towns, both of them just as small. A pair of ranches had been signposted off the road. Otherwise, nothing. Cococino County was as empty of people as Josh's mind was of memories.

Cowboy country, thought Josh as he gazed out of the window.

The truck started to slow down. The Ford Ranger had been left back at their house— Marshall was still fixing some of the damage it had taken in the fight at the start of the week. As they turned the corner, Marshall jabbed his foot on the brakes, and the tyres made a screeching sound as they gripped the surface of the road.

'Here,' said Marshall.

Kate was sitting between Josh and her father. She looked at Josh, scrutinising his expression as he looked out over the valley. To the right, behind them, there was a high ridge of red-rock hills. The road twisted along their side. To the left, the land was flat, rolling out several miles into the distance, its smooth, sandy surface punctuated only by cacti and the occasional boulder.

Nothing, thought Josh, a pang of disappointment stabbing at his chest. *It is as if I never saw the place before in my life.*

Marshall pushed open the driver's door and hopped down onto the ground. Kate offered Josh her hand to help him down, but he shook his head. The crutch would do just fine. The pain in his leg was still there, but he was getting used to hobbling, and he knew that the more he exercised it the better.

He was wearing an old pair of Gap jeans that Marshall had lent him: they were a size too big, and he'd had to put an extra notch in the belt to pull them tight enough around his waist. On top, he wore a blue denim shirt that he'd found in a cupboard. Doesn't matter what I look like, he told himself. In this gear, I'll just blend into the landscape. *Another cowboy without much money to spend on his wardrobe.*

'Somewhere around here,' said Kate, stepping away from the side of the road. 'This is where I found you.'

Josh followed a yard behind her until she stopped beside a ridge. He paused, smelling the air: the dust, the rock and the heat combined to create a hazy, earthy odour that reminded him of somewhere. A camp, maybe. On a hillside. With men, and noise. And screaming.

Josh tried to get a grip on the memory, but it had already slipped from his grasp. Lost, he thought. *Down into the pit where the rest of my memories are.*

He stepped forward. Kate was pointing to a ditch that measured thirty feet across and ten feet deep. 'Here,' she said. 'I found you right here.'

Josh knelt down on the ground. He closed his eyes, hoping that the darkness would stir something inside his mind. Empty. He looked down, running his fingers into the dust. A few yards to the right, there was a patch of rusty brown. Even after five days' exposure to the baking sun, it was clear what had made that stain. Blood. Human blood.

My blood, thought Josh.

'Remember anything?' asked Kate.

Josh shook his head. 'Blank,' he replied.

He stood up, looking out across the horizon. Two hundred, maybe three hundred yards distant, he could see a cordoned-off strip of the road, with a taped barrier. A car was drawing up to it, moving at no more than ten miles an hour. As it stopped, a man in uniform and wearing sunglasses climbed out.

'Police,' said Josh. 'I'm going to see what they know.'

Kate grabbed his arm, tugging back at the sleeve of his shirt. Her strength surprised Josh, and he could feel himself losing his grip on the crutch. 'No,' she snapped. 'The police are looking for you.'

Josh brushed her hand away. 'I just need to find out what happened here.'

'It's too risky,' said Kate.

'I'll be the judge of what risks I run.'

Marshall glanced at both of them, as if he was assessing the respective strengths of two boxers in the ring. 'I'll come with you,' he said. 'Kate, you follow us in the car.'

Josh started to hobble down the road. He was becoming more practised with his crutch, swinging forward with long, confident strides. Every third step he was putting some weight on the wounded leg, tolerating the pain that rippled through him every time it touched the ground. He knew that if you were fit, your muscles would rebuild themselves more quickly.

A couple more days and I might be able to walk

77

normally again. So long as I keep the nerves and muscles exercised.

Marshall was walking at Josh's side, his arms folded across his chest. 'You let me do the talking, boy,' he whispered. 'They hear your accent, they're going to be suspicious right away.'

The policeman was standing by himself. About three hundred pounds, with a belly that was bursting out of his khaki Sheriff's Department shirt, the man was leaning against the hood of his Ford Taurus Estate. There was a big polystyrene cup of coffee on the bonnet of the machine, and next to it a box of six doughnuts. Three of them were already eaten. Obviously a man who liked his breakfast.

'What happened here?' said Marshall, nodding gently towards the policeman.

Josh glanced up at the cop and smiled.

'Kid got shot, back on Monday,' said the policeman. 'Didn't you see it on TV?'

Marshall laughed. 'Been out of the county a few days. Who was he?'

The policeman reached behind him for a doughnut, keeping his gaze fixed on Marshall all the time. 'Kid named Ben Lippard,' he replied, starting to chew on his food. 'You know him?'

Marshall shook his head slowly from side to side. 'No. Was he mixed up in something? Drugs?'

The policeman looked across to Josh, his stare locking onto his crutch and the thick white bandage wrapped around his neck. He finished his doughnut, then wiped some saliva away from his chin with the back of his hand. 'What do I look like? A fucking newspaper? You want to find out what happened, you go buy one.'

Marshall backed away a step, raising his hand. 'Hey, steady, pal,' he said. 'I just wanted to find out. That's all.'

The policeman took a step forward from the car. 'Who's your friend?' he asked angrily, jabbing his thumb towards Josh. 'How'd he get so badly hurt?'

'Mountain climbing,' said Marshall quickly. 'We were up at the Grand Canyon for a few days. Had a bit of a fall.'

'I lost something near here,' Josh interrupted. 'A wallet. Some ID. You find anything like that?'

As soon as he spoke, Josh noticed Marshall shooting him a deadly glance: Doesn't matter, Josh decided. I'll take some risks with the police if I have to. Maybe I shot this boy, and maybe I didn't. *If I don't start asking questions, I'll never find out.*

'Are you the man?' asked the policeman.

'What man?' said Josh.

The policeman took another step forward. Now Josh could smell the jam and sugar of the doughnut on his breath. 'What man?' repeated Josh, a ragged edge of anger creeping into his tone.

'There was a third man, guy who got injured on the murder scene,' said the policeman. 'He left some traces of blood in the sand. We got his DNA, so we know who he is.' He looked more closely at Josh. 'I'm wondering if it might be you.' He paused. 'That accent. Is that Australian, or British, or what?'

Josh was about to speak again but Marshall stepped swiftly in front of him. 'He's a veteran. First Iraq war. He . . .' Marshall paused. 'He has some problems.'

The policeman looked past Marshall, still staring at Josh. 'I'm taking you down to the sheriff's office.

79

We need to check out who you are.'

Josh started backing away.

'No need to run,' said the policeman, his tone rising. 'I'm not saying we'll keep you. Just check you out, ask you a few questions, then send you on your way.'

Marshall's fist landed hard in the policeman's stomach. Josh was surprised by the power of the blow that the older man struck, followed through with all the force of his shoulder. The kind of blow that a professional boxer would deliver, thought Josh. *That man knows how to fight.*

The policeman doubled up in pain. He was too fat for his job, and his belly was full of sugar and air. The punch winded him, knocking him sideways and loosening his balance. His right hand slipped down to the leather holster flapping at his belt and his fingers grasped the weapon. He started to pull it free but Marshall had already swung his leg up towards the man's crotch. His boot landed hard in the man's groin, and a scream rose from the cop's lips as the pain shot up through his body.

His hand was still on his gun, a Sig-Sauer P226, a neat, compact black metal handgun that was used by the US Navy Seals and FBI as well as by hundreds of local sheriffs' departments.

Josh stepped forward, swung his crutch in the air, then smashed it hard into the policeman's hand. It struck his knuckles with the force of a metal cane and the gun fell to the ground.

Marshall bent down swiftly, grabbed the gun and jabbed it up against the policeman's head. The man was sweating with fear: a thin film of liquid was streaming down his red, blotched face. He looked wildly towards Marshall, then at Josh. 'Don't hurt me,' he whimpered. 'I got a wife, kids. Please don't hurt me.'

Josh picked up his crutch from the ground, using it to steady himself, then leaned towards the man.

'Whose blood was found at this crime scene?' he said, his tone harsh and determined. 'What's his name?'

'I don't know.'

Marshall rammed the gun harder against the side of the cop's head. 'Tell us,' he said slowly. 'Tell us now, or your brains are cactus fertilizer.'

The man's nose was starting to bleed. 'I don't know, I tell you—I don't know. The name is classified. I'm just guarding the crime scene.'

'Maybe you want me to make it simpler for you to understand,' growled Marshall. 'Tell us before I count to three, or you're a fucking dead man.'

'No, no,' pleaded the policeman.

'One,' said Marshall.

The cop was starting to shake with fear. 'No, please.'

'Two,' said Marshall, his tone even harsher.

'I don't know anything.'

Marshall cocked the P226. 'Three,' he said. He pronounced the word with an air of finality.

'I don't know,' said the policeman again.

Marshall's finger was taking first pressure on the trigger. He glanced towards Josh.

'Christ, no,' said Josh. 'He doesn't know anything.'

'Then we finish him,' said Marshall.

'That's murder,' said Josh angrily. 'Bloody leave him. He doesn't know anything.'

'No, we finish him now,' snarled Marshall.

His face was red, and his stare was locked onto

81

Josh who could see the violence building up inside the older man. The gun was squeezed tight in Marshall's hand, as if he was on the brink of shooting.

Josh leaned down, gripped Marshall's hand tight, and pulled the gun away. 'Leave it,' he snapped. 'We kill a cop, we're in real trouble.'

*   *   *

Kate had put a hamburger down on the table, followed by a bottle of beer. Josh took the food, picked out the fried onions from it and started eating.

'Why are you helping me?' he said, looking up at the woman.

After getting back to the house, Kate had given Josh another injection that had put him back to sleep for eight hours. She insisted that he needed the sleep, and Josh hadn't felt like resisting. He knew from what they had learned out in the scrubland that morning that a boy had been killed at the same time as he had been shot, and the police were searching the area for a man with an English accent.

And now he also knew that Marshall could be violent. Maybe Kate as well.

Maybe I killed the boy? *Maybe they did?*

'Why shouldn't I help you?' said Kate, her tone cool. 'I'm a helpful person.'

She was wearing black jeans that clung tight to her curves, and a white T-shirt with a black diamond printed on its back. When Josh had woken up later that afternoon she had dressed the wounds on his neck and his leg, clearing away the old bandages and replacing them with new ones. Without her and Marshall he'd probably be dead by now. Or languishing in an Arizona jail.

Josh took another bite of the hamburger, then looked back up at Kate. 'You could have just pulled me out of the ditch, patched me up, then sent me on my way—that would've been helpful. Nobody goes to this amount of trouble unless they have an angle.'

'I'm a doctor, remember?' said Kate, a flash of anger in her eyes. 'I'm *meant* to look after sick people.' She sat down opposite him, reaching across the tiny Formica table and taking a bite of the hamburger for herself. Anger makes her hungry, Josh noted. She devours her food the same way she devours arguments: with a ravenous appetite.

'No,' he replied, shaking his head. 'A doctor would just take me to a hospital, patching me up on the way if they had to.' He paused, letting the silence hang between them. 'A regular doctor, that is.' His gaze flicked towards her. For a moment, Josh wondered if he'd gone too far. I hardly know this woman, he reminded himself. I have no idea where the boundaries are.

Then her face sagged, her spirit deflating like a tyre that has just been punctured. She sniffed, and wiped away a small tear that had started to form in the corner of her left eye.

'It's painful for me to talk about,' said Kate.

'What's painful?'

'The reason.'

'What reason?'

'The reason I'm here,' she said. 'The reason I'm helping you.'

Josh pushed away the hamburger, leaning forward on the table. He reached forward, brushing the edge of her palm with the tips of his fingers. Briefly, she looked as if she were about to pull her hand away, but then she let it stay in place. 'Look at me, Kate,' he said. 'I'm all shot to pieces. I don't even know who I am. I'm no threat to anyone. You can talk to me.' He paused. 'Hell, I probably won't even remember anything you say to me.'

Kate laughed, throwing back her red hair as she did so, although Josh noticed that there was not much happiness in her expression. She looked down at the floor. 'I was married,' she said. 'To a man called Danny.'

'Who was he?'

'A soldier, like you.'

Josh nodded, but remained silent.

'A Navy Seal. We grew up together, down in New Mexico. Small town. High school sweethearts, the whole thing. He joined the Navy straight after graduation, while I went off to medical school. But we always stayed together, no matter how far apart we were. Nobody else ever mattered.'

'Where is he now?'

'He's dead.'

Again, Josh reached out for her hand to comfort her, but this time she took it away.

'He was killed in Afghanistan. Just over two years ago. He was stationed at a place called Khost, along the Afghanistan-Pakistan border. He was part of a special-forces unit. Men sent out alone into the small villages, working under cover, looking for al-Qaeda leaders.'

'One of them killed him?'

'I don't know who killed him. He was shot in a

84

struggle, that's all I know. Three times through the chest. Nobody knows who did it. He was left for dead beside some road somewhere. He was there for thirty-six hours in a ditch, without anything to eat or drink or any kind of treatment. A woman from one of the local villages took him in, and started nursing him. She gave him food and water, and tried to put some bandages on his wounds.' She paused, wiping away another tear. 'But it was already too late for Danny. A hospital might have been able to help him, but this woman had no antibiotics, not even any proper disinfectants. He died after three days and the US Army picked his body up a week later when word finally got back to them about where he was.'

'But she helped him, didn't she?' said Josh. 'That's what this is all about.'

Kate looked up at him, her gaze locking with his. 'She saw a soldier in a ditch, and she did what she could to help him, even though he might be the enemy.'

'As I might be.'

Kate looked away again. 'I don't think so,' she replied. 'But that's what I'm doing out here. Taking some time to myself to get over losing Danny. He was the only man who ever meant anything to me, and now he's gone.'

She stood up, walking towards the sink to pour herself a glass of water. 'And that's why I had to help you. Who knows? Maybe there's a wife out there somewhere, worrying about where you are and what's happened to you. I'll do what I can because I know how she'll feel if you die.'

85

SIX

Saturday, June 6th. Morning.
Josh put the crutch to one side and started walking.
He pressed his wounded foot against the dusty
ground, testing the nerves to see how much pain he
could bear. The leg stung, as though it was being
bitten, and the pain rippled up through it into his
groin. Josh gritted his teeth and hobbled towards
the kitchen.

*I've got to lose the crutch. It draws too much
attention to a man.*

The sun had already climbed high in the sky and
the air was getting hot. Josh hadn't checked what
time it was, but he guessed that it was between ten
and eleven. Another twelve hours' sleep, he
figured: Kate had given him his regular cocktail of
sleeping juice and painkillers the night before.
Another half-day closer to getting my strength back.

He had tried to hold on to his thoughts as he
woke up, but there had been nothing there this
morning: the only thing he remembered was Kate
sobbing about her lost husband just before he went
to bed, and his attempts to comfort her.

But what use is it? he asked himself. *How can you
comfort a woman who has lost her husband?*

Josh pushed open the kitchen door. Kate was
already at the table, the remains of some cereal in
front of her. She looked up at Josh and smiled.
'You feeling better?' she asked.

Josh nodded. 'Some,' he replied.

'The crutch,' said Kate. 'Where is it?'

'Back in the room,' answered Josh. 'I wanted to

86

walk without it.'

Kate stood up, looking down at the leg. 'How does it feel?'

'Hurts a bit,' said Josh. 'When I put pressure on it.'

'Don't push it too far. You'll end up with a permanent limp if you don't let it heal properly.'

Josh poured some coffee from the pot next to the sink. He stirred in just a dash of milk and took a sip of the resultant strong liquid. The headache had subsided this morning for the first time in the past week. Now his head felt surprisingly clear, settled and relaxed.

I can think again.

He glanced towards the television playing in the corner and punched up the volume. The weather girl was just wrapping up her forecast. A forty-degree high, and no hint of rain. Not even a cloud. Why do they bother with a forecast? wondered Josh. It's a desert. *Of course it's bloody hot.*

'Returning to our main story of the week, the Ben Lippard murder in Coconino County,' said the newsreader.

A picture had come up on the screen. A boy. About sixteen, and a thrash-metal fan, Josh guessed, judging by the long black hair that fell down past his shoulders. His face was long, and thin, but with eyes that were sparkling with curiosity and boyish life.

So young, thought Josh, looking at the face staring back at him.

'And there is still no sign of his friend Luke Marsden who went missing on the same day,' continued the newsreader.

Another picture flashed onto the screen. Another

boy, also about sixteen. He had a rounder face than the Lippard kid with sandy hair cut away from his face. He was wearing a pale blue shirt with a couple of buttons open at the neck, revealing a strong chest.

'Nobody has heard from Luke Marsden since the day of Ben Lippard's murder last Monday,' continued the newsreader. 'The sheriff's office say they are urgently looking for Luke, but have so far failed to make contact with him.'

Josh looked at the picture again. The boy's face had the innocence that nearly all teenagers have, but there was an edge to the half-smile that was playing on his lips. A smart kid, thought Josh. A kid who knows more than he lets on.

'The sheriff's office has told this station that if anyone sees Luke they should contact them immediately,' continued the newsreader.

Something was happening in Josh's mind. An image had started to play out in front of him. He could see a flat landscape, with rocks in the distance. He could see the sun burning down from the sky. He could see scrub, and a cloud of dust. He squeezed his eyes tight shut, blocking out all the light, and concentrated his mind, closing out the sound of the television. A boy. He could see a boy.

A gunshot.

Another boy was falling.

Ben.

Then a voice. Josh redoubled his concentration, trying to relax his mind so that nothing would soften or blur the moving picture that was playing out in his mind. One of the boys, Luke, was shouting something. He was looking towards Josh and his lips were forming words but although Josh

88

could see he could not hear.

Try, he told himself.

What did he say to you?

'And now, with the latest sports round-up,' said the newsreader, 'here's Dan Smotten.'

Josh cursed and opened his eyes, noticing that Kate was looking at him. The picture had gone, blown right out of his mind. He took a breath, concentrating, struggling to bring it back.

Nothing.

'A memory?' asked Kate, her tone hopeful.

Josh nodded.

Kate stood up from her chair, walked across the room and gripped Josh's arm. He could feel her nails digging into his skin. 'What?' she said quickly. 'What was the memory?'

Josh nodded towards the TV screen. 'Him,' he replied slowly. 'I was there. I saw Ben murdered. And I saw Luke. He was running away from me and he was shouting at the same time.'

Kate's nails dug harder into the skin of Josh's forearm. 'What?' she insisted. 'What did he say?'

Josh shook his head from side to side. 'I don't know. The memory is blurred. I can see, but I can't hear. I can feel him looking at me, and see his lips move, but I don't know what it is he is saying.'

'Try, Josh, try.'

Josh broke free of Kate's grip. He took another hit of the coffee, letting the caffeine flood into his veins, hoping that the energy would put him back in touch with the memory. Nothing. His mind was still a blank.

'I can't see anything else,' he replied. 'It's gone.'

'It's a start,' she said. 'Once your memory starts recovering, it should all start coming back to you.'

'So long as you stay safe,' said Marshall as he stepped into the room.

'I know something about that murder,' said Josh. 'I don't know what it is exactly, but I know *something*. I was there.'

'Maybe it *was* you,' said Marshall. 'The Sheriff's office certainly seems pretty damned keen to talk to you.'

The question had been rattling through his mind for the past few days. Am I a murderer? he kept asking himself. *Could I shoot a boy in cold blood?*

'Do the letters S-A-S mean anything to you?' asked Marshall.

Josh paused. His mind was jumping all over the place, making associations, but he couldn't pin anything down. The headache was coming back: the chisel was starting to tap away insistently at the inside of his skull again. 'No, nothing,' he answered blankly.

'The Regiment,' said Marshall. 'Hereford.'

Josh shook his head. 'Nothing. Why?'

Marshall took a step closer. There was still a bruise on his arm from the fight with the policeman yesterday, and his eyes had the rough appearance of a man who had slept badly. 'Couple of days back, when we were shooting together,' he said, 'you chose a Sig-Sauer P228 like it came natural to you. Like you already knew that gun. So I checked around with some of the veterans who use my website. I wanted to know which British regiments might have trained with that handgun. One guy had the answer.' He paused, looking towards the light beaming in through the window. 'The SAS. British special forces. They used to use Browning High Powers but then they moved on to Sig-Sauers, both

90

the P226 and the P228 models.'

Josh let the words settle in his mind, rubbing his hand against the thick stubble that was growing fast on his face. He repeated the three letters a couple of times to himself. He closed his eyes and tried to relax his mind, intoning the letters silently in his head. No, nothing. No triggers, no flashes of recognition, no pictures. *I don't even know what the sodding letters stand for.*

'Mean anything to you, boy?'

Josh shook his head. 'I already had one memory today. I think that's my lot.' He attempted a smile but could tell it was not likely to be reciprocated.

'You're SAS,' persisted Marshall. 'The guns you know. The way you handle yourself when you shoot. I'm sure of it.' He took another step towards Josh, so close that he could smell the shaving foam that had just been washed off the older man's cheeks. In Marshall's eyes, Josh could suddenly see a flash of the same anger and violence that he had seen yesterday: in that second Josh was certain that Marshall was a killer.

Maybe it was *you* that shot the boy? thought Josh. *Maybe that's why your daughter happened to be in the area.*

'What I want to know is this,' continued Marshall. 'What the hell is a British special forces man doing in the backwaters of Arizona tracking a pair of runaway teenagers?'

Josh could feel his own anger starting to build. The chisel was getting worse, slamming into the side of his skull, and his neck wound was playing up, sending tiny jabs of pain running down from his neck into his spine. 'I don't bloody know, do I?' shouted Josh. 'I've lost my fucking memory.'

91

'What are you, boy?' snapped Marshall. 'What the hell are you?'

Kate stood up. 'Easy, Dad—he's not well.'

Josh held his hand against his brow. 'I can't handle this any more,' he said. 'I'm going into that police station tonight to find out who I am, and what the hell I've done.'

'You're not going, man!' shouted Marshall.

Josh stood up straight. 'Nobody gives me orders,' he snapped. He brushed past Marshall, heading towards the door.

'You're going to walk the whole way,' shouted Marshall. 'It's ten miles.'

*   *   *

Josh and Kate had been watching crap TV for hours. Marshall had gone to bed. Josh looked at Kate. 'I need a smoke,' he said. 'You got any cigarettes?'

Kate shook her head. 'I'm a doctor, remember?'

Josh stood up. 'I'm bloody gagging for one now. Maybe I could borrow the car and drive into town to get some. There should be a gas station open, even at this time of night.'

Kate turned to look at him. 'You've been okay without them until now.'

'Well, now I need one.'

'Good time to give up,' said Kate. 'If you made it through three days, you're over the worst. Take some advice. Quit.'

Josh grinned. He reached down into his pocket. The car keys he'd picked up from the table earlier were right there. Doesn't matter what she says, he told himself. I need to get into town.

92

'I'm going,' he said.

Turning around, Josh walked swiftly from the kitchen and out into the back yard. The night was quiet and still. He walked across to where the Avalanche pick-up truck was parked, pressed the key button, and watched the doors unlock. He sat himself down in the driver's seat, glancing around for the ignition, and checking out where the other controls were. He fired up the engine. Suddenly, the door burst open. Kate was staring at him, her eyes burning with anger. 'Where the hell are you going?'

'I told you, I need a smoke.'

'Then I'm coming with you.'

Kate sat down in the Avalanche's passenger seat, slamming the door behind her. Josh pulled the car out onto the road, heading in the direction of the small town. 'Just on your way in,' said Kate coldly, 'there's a Texaco gas station. You'll get some cigarettes there. Since you seem to need them so badly.'

Christ, thought Josh. With this woman on my case, I really *will* need to start smoking.

They both remained silent for the twenty minutes that it took to drive into town. When he saw the Texaco sign, Josh pulled up. 'I'll be just two minutes,' he said.

'Don't be any longer,' said Kate. 'And you can't smoke in the car. Marshall doesn't like it.'

Josh walked towards the counter. He had no intention of buying any cigarettes. So far as he knew he didn't smoke, and he certainly didn't plan to start now. It was just an excuse to get away from Kate. He stopped at the counter, picked up two packets of gum, and looked up at the boy behind

93

the desk. 'Where's the gents'?' he said as he handed over a dollar bill.

The boy nodded towards a back door. Josh walked up to it and went through. There was one door that led to the toilets, and another that led outside. He stepped quickly through it. The gas station backed onto some scrubland, leading down to the town. Despite the aching in his leg, Josh started running into the darkness.

By the time Kate realised he'd slipped out of sight, it would be too late.

The rocks provided some cover. Josh hobbled between the boulders, leaning against one, then another to support himself as he moved forward. Keep going, he told himself.

High above him, the moon was casting a silvery light down on the plain. The town of Boisdale had a population of ten or fifteen thousand people judged Josh, thinking back to the map he had studied at Kate's house. It had a Wal-Mart, a Motel 6, and a carpet factory that was the main local employer. If you want quiet, Boisdale was the place to find it, reckoned Josh as he looked down towards the neat row of suburban dwellings that led down towards the centre of the town.

Nobody comes here? *So why the hell did I?*

The Sheriff's office was on the edge of town, on Roosevelt Avenue. It was a big, square concrete block, set fifty yards back from the road. About a hundred metres long and thirty deep, its front was protected by a wall. At the back was a fifty-square-metre courtyard. Josh raised a pair of binoculars he had brought with him to his eyes and peered down into the yard: he could see a shooting range, a pound for keeping the dogs, and a row of motorcycles.

If I can keep out of the way of the dogs, that's how I'm going in.

He edged forward. The boulders were littered along a patch of scrubland that led up to the start of the town. From here it was thirty yards to the sheriff's office. He had equipped himself with a grappling rope taken from Marshall's garage, plus the Sig-Sauer P228. It's just a small-town sheriff's office, he told himself. It's already two in the morning. At most there's going to be one fat old night guard on duty, and he's probably fallen asleep in front of the TV. I shouldn't have any trouble breaking in here.

Somewhere in there they may have my blood sample. If they've tested the DNA, they will know who I am. *In a few minutes I'll know as well.*

Josh moved down next to the back wall, walking as quickly as he could on his wounded leg, and as he did so he could feel the adrenalin starting to surge through his veins. Then he paused. A snake was crawling across the ground. Josh remained perfectly still, letting the animal pass, but he realised that he was sweating with fear. He looked up at the wall. It was seven feet high, made from concrete breeze-blocks. About fifteen, maybe twenty years old, he judged. Old enough for the mortar between the blocks to be crumbling. He dug his nails into the space between the blocks. There was some give there. Enough for a man to get a grip.

Whoever I am, this comes naturally to me.

Josh cast aside the rope and started to scale the wall. He used the strength in his shoulders, trying to avoid using his wounded leg as anything more

95

than a dead weight. He stuck his fingers into the mortar, pulled, then rested his legs, balanced himself, and started again. In three swift movements, his fingers were gripping the top of the wall. He hauled himself upwards, lying flat on its one-foot-wide top, looking down into the courtyard below. A seven-foot drop. So long as I don't land on the wounded leg, or on my neck, I'll be fine.

But suddenly Josh could hear the sounds of a siren wailing: his eardrums were starting to rattle as the screeching noise seeped into his brain.

His gaze darted forward. A searchlight had flicked on at the back of the courtyard, bathing the building in a harsh, brilliant light. Josh could feel it dazzling his eyes. A shot rang out. Then another. Josh tried to look into the courtyard, but the light was too harsh.

Run, man, he told himself. *Run like every dog from hell was on your trail.*

Using his arms, Josh started to lower himself down from the wall. He pressed his feet and knees together, the same position he'd adopt for a parachute drop. His feet deflected the blow, then he rolled to the left to lessen the impact.

He turned to look back in the direction he'd come from, back up through the boulders, two, maybe three hundred yards, to where Kate had parked the Avalanche.

If she's still there, maybe I can make it.

Another volley of fire rang out from inside the station. Josh could see dust flicking down from the wall where the bullets were raking the concrete, sending flakes of it puffing into the air.

Christ, he thought to himself. They're not looking to make an arrest. *They're shooting to kill.*

96

'Not the road,' snapped Josh. 'And switch off the lights.'

'Oh, right,' said Kate. 'And how the hell am I meant to drive?'

Josh leaned across, flicking the light switch off with his hand. The lights died and the Avalanche was suddenly surrounded by darkness. He grabbed the steering wheel and yanked it hard to the right, pulling the truck off the tarmac and into the scrubland. From scouting the area earlier that day, Josh knew that the land stretching away from Boisdale was flat: there were a dozen miles until you hit a range of mountains that rose up sharply from the wilderness. It was pitted with craters and boulders. You would drive through it only with extreme caution.

Not at night, and not without lights on, thought Josh. *Unless it was your only chance of survival.*

The Avalanche started to bounce across the scrubland, the suspension rolling with each blow to the undercarriage. Pain shot through Josh as each thump lashed into him with the force of a leather whip. Kate was gripping the steering wheel, hanging onto it as if it were a rope from which she was dangling from a precipice.

He looked across at her. 'Out on the road, the chopper can pick us off. We might as well be waving a big flag saying "Shoot me". But a single truck in the darkness, in scrubland, with no lights on. That has a chance.'

'Yeah, but they'll find a wrecked truck in the morning,' said Kate. 'With a couple of corpses in it.'

'That's one possibility,' said Josh roughly. 'But we stay on the road, we're corpses for sure. They're not looking to take us in for questioning. They want us dead.'

The Avalanche swerved sideways as its front left tyre crashed over a boulder, then sank into a small crater. The truck shook as if it was about to break up, then found its grip again and jerked forwards.

Josh looked behind him. The light of the moon was starting to dim as a cloud drifted across it, and suddenly the plain was plunged into total darkness. Josh could hear the chopper: the noise of its blades cutting through the air filled the sky. Behind them the chopper's searchlight was sending out a narrow beam of light, flashing onto the ground, seeking its target. Looking forwards, he could only see a wall of blackness, into which they were driving at an ungodly speed.

Prayer time.

'You're doing great,' said Josh, glancing across at Kate. 'Just keep the wheel straight, and try to ride with all the knocks. We'll be okay.'

They drove for what seemed like an hour but which, when Josh checked his watch later, turned out to be just twenty minutes. The chopper's lights could only illuminate a narrow stretch of land at a time: by keeping an eye on that they could tell they were moving further and further away from it. Josh reckoned that they were about a mile away. They both remained silent, Kate clutching onto the steering wheel, Josh listening to the sky, monitoring the sound of the chopper.

'Here,' said Josh eventually. 'Stop here.'

In twenty minutes they had covered several miles of open scrubland. The sight and sounds of the chopper were no more. They had seen and heard nothing for at least five minutes. If the police had no fix on which direction they had been driving in, then they could be anywhere within a thirty mile radius of the road. They had vanished. For now.

They'll come looking for us in the morning, thought Josh. *We'll be okay until then.*

He stepped down out of the Avalanche. The temperature had dropped from the scorching heat of the day to a mild ten degrees centigrade at night, and there was a slight breeze, making it feel still cooler. The moon was still shaded by a cloud. It was impossible to see more than a few yards ahead, and he wasn't going to risk switching on the vehicle's headlamps. Darkness I can handle, he told himself. *So long as no one is shooting at me.*

'What the fuck happened back there?' asked Kate angrily. 'You fucking tricked me. You were trying to break into the police station to find your file, weren't you? You must be fucking nuts.'

She was standing in front of him. Sweat soaked her blouse: through the damp material Josh could see the outline of her breasts. 'I triggered an alarm when I went over the wall,' he said. 'That place was wired up like the Pentagon. It's not just some sheriff's office in Hicksville. The place must be crawling with Feds.' He paused. 'What do they have in Boisdale to protect it with that kind of firepower?'

'Nothing,' said Kate. 'It's just a factory town. Fifteen thousand people. Used to be twenty-five thousand, but times haven't been so good in the carpet business.'

Josh took a swig of water from the bottle on the passenger seat of the Avalanche. 'Something,' he said firmly. 'There's something there, and I'm betting it's to do with those boys.'

101

'They're just teenagers,' said Kate. 'At least that's what it said in the news. Hoodlums.'

Josh passed the water bottle across to Kate. 'Bollocks,' he said. 'Unless I've lost my mind as well as my memory, there's something going on in this town. And I reckon those two boys were at the centre of it.'

'What?' said Kate. 'What do you think it is?'

Josh shook his head. 'I don't know.'

'Think,' Kate ordered him.

'First we rest,' said Josh.

He looked around the area where the Avalanche had come to a halt. There was a ridge in the ground, leading down to what looked in the murky light like the dried-out remains of a river bed. Across from that were some large boulders where Josh reckoned they might find some shelter in the grooves in the rock carved out by water. 'Over there,' he said. 'It's just after two in the morning now. Sun rises about six. We sleep for two hours, then start walking. Once the sun is up, they're going to be able to follow the tracks of that truck into the scrub. We don't want to be anywhere near it when they find it.'

Josh looked at Kate. 'You should go home. It's too dangerous for you out here.'

'I'm staying,' she said.

SEVEN

Sunday, June 7th. Morning.
In the distance, Josh could see the police cordon blocking off the main road. Two patrol cars were slewed across the highway, stopping and checking everyone entering the town. Me, thought Josh. It's me they are looking for.

A dangerous time to start scouting around. But I don't have any other choice.

'Where do we start?' asked Kate.

'Let's pick up the trail at the motel,' said Josh. 'Place like this, any strangers in town are going to be passing through the motel.'

Josh looked down from the hill. They were a mile outside the town, to the east, on one of the hillsides that rose up towards the canyons in the far distance. Josh had woken at four a.m., using the alarm on his wristwatch, surprised to find Kate curled into his chest and sleeping soundly. The rocks were a reddish sandstone, not a hard granite: you could sleep on them in moderate comfort. His wounds ached, but no worse than usual. He woke Kate with a gentle shake, then started walking. The chopper would find the Avalanche within a couple of hours once the sun had risen. They had to be at least four or five miles away by then: that meant two hours of solid walking.

Josh's first decision had been to hide the Avalanche. As soon as dawn broke, there would be police helicopters out, scouring the scrubland. Leave it in the open and the truck would lead them straight back to Kate. They had to hide it

103

somewhere that would be invisible from the air; it could take weeks to track it on foot.

He'd scoured the area in the dark. There was a dried-out creek, but he rejected that because it didn't provide enough cover. Then he found a small stand of trees, but that wasn't going to work either, he decided. The Avalanche was a big truck, and a helicopter was going to spot it underneath any tree if it was flying low enough. Eventually he found a group of tall boulders arranged in a haphazard circle, which formed a natural shelter. He drove the Avalanche inside. It was a tight squeeze, and he tore a big gash in the side panel of the machine as he tried to ram it into the limited space.

'I'll pay you for the damage,' he joked to Kate. 'If the insurance doesn't cover it.'

After hiding the Avalanche, they started the long walk to town. Josh stepped carefully across the rough ground, telling Kate, a couple of yards ahead of him, to do the same. It was hard walking in the darkness, weaving a path through the boulders, brambles, and cactus. Josh dragged a stick behind him to brush away any traces of the trail. That was slow work. Even so, they made good progress, following an arc that Josh had calculated would take them back towards the town.

After two miles they had found a creek, with some water in a pool surrounded by thick evergreens. There was nobody around and Josh stripped down to his boxer shorts, washing himself in the cool water. Kate slipped into the pool in her pale blue cotton bra and pants, then dried herself with her T-shirt before slipping it back on. In the half-light Josh could see that her body was slim and lithe as he watched her splash the water through her hair and face: her figure was toned and tanned, the physique of an athlete rather than a model, but supple and sexy all the same.

She might be a doctor, thought Josh, but she isn't a city girl. *She knows how to survive in the wild.*

'How do you want to get there?' asked Kate, pointing to the town.

'On foot,' replied Josh with a rough grin. 'But if you see a cab, hail it.'

Kate smiled back and started walking. A track led down the hillside away from the patrol cars, then the first section of paved road led up to a truck depot, closed this morning, with just a pair of chrome monsters sitting on its forecourt. Ahead, a mile distant, Josh could see the Motel 6 sign rising thirty feet into the air. They kept walking, pacing their way slowly through the first of the suburban streets that led to the centre of town. It was still only eight in the morning, and although the sun was starting to rise through the sky the temperature was still only around fifteen degrees, and a gentle breeze was blowing.

Kate suggested that they should stop at the diner, on the corner of Coral Street and Roosevelt Avenue, and grab some coffee. 'I'll wait outside,' said Josh. 'You go in and get them.'

When Kate returned, she handed him an extra-large cup of foamy, milky coffee, and two honey waffles, wrapped in white tissue paper. Josh hunched down against the fence of the parking lot and started eating. The waffles tasted thick and doughy, and Josh didn't care for the taste. Still, he told himself, it doesn't matter: I need all the calories I can get.

'Did you see the man in the blue sweatshirt?' said Josh, glancing towards the window of the diner.

Kate nodded.

'What do you make of him?'

Kate shrugged. 'Bald guy reading the sports section of the newspaper,' she replied. 'I didn't make anything of him.'

'He's a Fed.'

Kate took a long sip of her coffee, looking thoughtful. 'An FBI agent? Is that what you mean?'

Josh nodded. 'There's something about the way he's sitting, just minding his own business. It looks artificial, practised—like he learned it on a training course.' He turned towards Kate. 'He's surveillance.'

'For you?'

Josh shook his head. 'I don't know. But I bet this town is crawling with agents—it has to be if they've got a helicopter stationed here. They're looking for somebody.'

And if it's not me, then who the hell is it?

Josh slung the rest of his coffee down his throat, finished off the waffles and started walking. The limp from his wounded leg was starting to heal: he could just about conceal the fact that he'd taken a bullet in the past few days. He hadn't shaved since he was wounded and the hair on his face had started to grow into a thick black beard. A trim, and it would look like he had worn it for years. That, plus civilian clothes, should make him different enough from any pictures of him that might be on file.

Just so long as I don't draw any attention to myself.

They know who I am, thought Josh as he walked on steadily. But do they know what I look like?

106

It was half a mile to the Motel 6, a distance covered in ten minutes at a steady pace. The building was at the end of the long commercial strip: a couple of car dealerships, a hairdresser, a hardware store, and then the motel. As he glanced up at it, Josh wondered if he had been there before. There was no flash of recognition but if he'd been staying in the town he must have visited the motel.

And even if I don't recognise *it*, somebody might recognise *me*.

Josh nodded towards the entrance. 'We go in together.'

'They might think we want a room.' She smiled. 'For an hour or so.'

Josh stepped inside. The clerk was watching some baseball on the TV. A boy of nineteen or twenty, Josh judged, he had floppy back hair, and two prominent spots on his left cheek. 'You looking for a room?' he said, looking up at Josh.

Josh scanned the boy's face for some sign that he recognised him, but there was not a flicker. The reception was flat-pack standard, the same yellow and black furniture found in every Motel 6 lobby in the country. It looked out onto the main road, and behind the desk was a set of photos of the main local tourist attractions: the Grand Canyon, Death Valley, Phoenix, then Las Vegas. Those were all a hundred miles away or more, Josh noted. The only guests that this Motel had were travelling salesmen.

'We're looking for some information,' said Josh.

The boy glanced first at Josh, then at Kate. His name was Darren, Josh noted from the name tag pinned to his regulation yellow shirt. There was a look of suspicion in his eyes, but also a spark of curiosity. Life was slow on the desk of this Motel 6, Josh figured. Darren was desperate for anything that might liven the morning up.

'What kind of information?' he said.

'Information about guests, Darren,' continued Josh.

Darren turned down the sound on the television.

'We're freelance journalists,' continued Josh. 'We're researching a programme for the BBC. We're interested in the Lippard story. We're just wondering if there are any other reporters in town covering the case who we might be able to hook up with?'

He talked slowly, keeping his tone relaxed. Only liars talk quickly, Josh reminded himself.

Darren's expression was that of a man who knew that he probably shouldn't help but couldn't fight the temptation. 'The BBC?' he said. 'What's your name?'

Josh hesitated. 'Ben,' he said. 'Ben Webster, and this is Kate. We're researchers.'

'Yeah, there *have* been some reporters checking in,' said Darren.

'Who?' said Josh.

Darren looked down at his desk book. 'A TV crew from Phoenix were here for a couple of nights. News Five. They parked their van right there in the lot. But they left this morning.'

'Who else?'

Darren looked down at his book again. 'That was it. I guess the Lippard killing isn't such a big deal outside this town. There's a woman from the local paper who's been writing stories for the *Phoenix Republic* and the *Las Vegas Sun*. She has an office just a few blocks down this strip. She might be able to help you out.'

'What's her name?' asked Kate.

'Elaine,' replied Darren. 'Elaine Johnston. Paper comes out Monday, so she might even be in the office this morning.'

'Can I look at the registration book?' asked Josh.

If I stayed here, I must have given a name, he reasoned to himself. If I see it, then maybe I'll recognise it.

Darren looked uneasy. 'Company rules,' he said. 'I'm not allowed.'

'Just a quick look,' said Josh, attempting a smile.

'No way, man,' snapped Darren.

Josh reached down for the roll of dollar bills in his pocket. He took them out. 'Maybe I could buy you a drink.'

'Like I said, company policy,' said Darren quickly.

Kate glanced up at him. 'We'd be really grateful,' she said.

'This is the only job I got,' said Darren angrily. 'If you don't drop it, I'm calling the cops.'

'Okay, okay,' said Josh quickly. He took Kate by the arm. 'Come on, we're going.'

Outside, the sun was higher in the sky and there was more traffic on the road. Josh hesitated as he left the Motel 6, glancing back towards the two-storey row of rooms stretching back a hundred yards from the lobby. I have been here before, he realised.

I might even have stayed at this motel before I was shot.

'Some more coffee,' Josh said to Kate. He was thirsty again: the same dry, burning thirst in his throat that he'd had ever since he'd been shot.

'Then we go see if this Elaine woman works on Sunday mornings.'

*   *   *

Another man sitting alone and sipping a coffee. This guy had a baseball cap pulled down tight onto his forehead. Josh looked at him once, through the window of the restaurant, then averted his gaze. More surveillance, he judged. He couldn't be sure how he knew. Maybe I've had that training myself, he mused. Maybe that's why I can recognise them.

Kate came out of the restaurant with two cups of coffee and two turkey-breast sandwiches, and walked across to where Josh was waiting. Ten yards away, a couple were getting their kids out of their car, and a group of bikers had just pulled up in the parking lot of the diner. There were six of them: big men, with long hair, muscles that bulged out of their T-shirts, and fat guts that hung out of their jeans. Half past ten. Boisdale was starting to wake up.

'Let's go,' said Kate. 'We can eat while we walk. If we're going to be sure of catching this reporter we need to get to her office now.'

Josh started to walk down the street, taking bites from his sandwich as he did so.

'Josh,' cried a woman's voice from the parking lot.

He ignored her and carried on walking. Who the hell is Josh? he wondered.

'Josh,' she shouted again.

Is that me she's calling?

Quiet, woman, he thought. Too much commotion and you're going to alert that spotter sitting at the back of the diner.

'Hell, Josh, aren't you even going to say hello to me?'

Suddenly the voice's owner was tugging at the sleeve of his shirt. Up ahead, Josh could see Kate spinning around to see what was happening.

Josh looked down. The woman was maybe twenty, twenty-one. She had long blonde hair tied up behind her head, and a thick chubby face. She could have been a size twelve, borderline fourteen. She was wearing tight blue jeans, and a yellow Madonna T-shirt that exposed a roll of tanned flesh around her midriff. A pair of studs pierced her belly button. Around her neck there was a gold cross, and a pair of silver earrings dangled from her lobes.

'What did you call me?'

Suddenly frightened, the woman backed away, letting go of Josh's sleeve. It was his turn to grab hold of her arm.

'What did you call me?' said Josh, his voice angrier this time.

'Josh.' She hesitated, her expression hurt and confused. 'Josh, I . . . I . . .'

'Josh—you called me Josh?'

The woman pulled her arm away. 'Let go of me, you asshole.'

She turned, walking quickly across the tarmac of the parking lot. Josh started to hurry after her. 'Stop,' he snapped.

To his left, he could see one of the bikers stepping away from the Harley Touring bikes— some of them bastardised, with different handlebars stuck onto the original frames. The man was wearing leather trousers, a white linen shirt, and a thick pair of studded leather gloves.

'This guy bothering you, lady?' he asked the woman.

'Get him away from me,' she said.

A tear was already running down the side of her face.

'I just need to—' But then Josh saw that the biker was stepping towards him and further back two more bikers were climbing down from their Harleys, watching closely.

'The lady doesn't want to talk,' said the first one. 'Take a hike, bud.'

Josh knew that he was in no shape for a fight: certainly not for a brawl with three two-hundred-and-fifty-pound bikers.

Now Kate was behind him and was tugging at his sleeve. 'Leave it,' she snapped.

'Yeah, leave it, man,' said the biker, leering in the direction of Kate. 'You already got a girlfriend.'

'We're going,' said Kate, taking Josh's arm and steering him towards the road. A truck went by, belching a thick cloud of dirty exhaust fumes into the air. Josh choked. Behind him, he could see the young woman going into the diner, talking to the biker who had come to her rescue. Sir Galahad, thought Josh to himself. *In her dreams.*

'What are you doing, you idiot?' snapped Kate. 'You get into a fight, the police are going to come and arrest you.'

'That woman,' said Josh. 'She knew my name.'

'Your name?'

'Josh. She called me Josh.'

Kate smiled, her expression brightening.

'Josh,' repeated Kate, rolling the sound on her tongue. 'I like it. Kind of suits you. I would have had you down as a Sam or an Ed. But Josh will do just fine.'

'How did she know who I was?' said Josh.

'Don't you have any memories?' asked Kate hopefully.

Josh shook his head. 'I must have spent time here,' he said. 'Maybe before I was shot?'

But why? he asked himself. *What was I doing here*?

Josh looked back towards the diner. The spotter, the man he had seen earlier, had finished his coffee and folded away his newspaper. He was staring straight at them.

Josh tugged Kate by the arm. 'Quick,' he said. 'I think he's moving in on us.'

Kate glanced towards the restaurant window.

'Don't look,' hissed Josh.

He started walking along the street. From the corner of his eye he could see the spotter walking out of the restaurant, then glancing up and down the street. Josh tried to assess him. My best guess is that he doesn't know who I am. I'm just someone who's acting suspiciously around town, and he wants to find out more.

'The newspaper office,' said Josh.

From the directions that Darren had given them, the office should only be a couple of hundred yards up this street.

'You sure?' Kate asked nervously.

'No,' snapped Josh. 'But it's the best option we have. And don't walk too fast or that guy's going to call down half the FBI on our trail.'

*   *   *

113

Elaine Johnston cast a professional eye over Kate and Josh as they sat in the chairs opposite her. *Advertisers or stories*, thought Josh. *We have to fall into one category or the other. Otherwise, she's not interested.*

'What do you want to know about?' she asked.

'The Lippard murder,' answered Josh.

The office of the *Boisdale Ledger* occupied two rooms, on the third floor of a modern concrete office building that also housed an accounting firm, a travel agency and a couple of farm-machinery distributors. Johnston's desk was a mass of paper. Five empty coffee cups perched on top of a few old files, and there were two packets of nicotine patches, both opened. Today she was the only person home.

'Everyone wants to know about that,' she said.

Johnston was a woman in her fifties, wearing grey slacks and a black sweater. He hair was greying, cut short, but her face was fresh and inquisitive. She was, Josh noted, possibly the only person in Arizona without any kind of a tan.

'We're researching a TV documentary for the BBC,' continued Josh. 'Looking at small-town murder cases. My name is Ben Webster, and this is my assistant Kate. We were hoping that you might be able to tell us a bit more about the case.' He paused. 'Perhaps you could be on the programme.'

'On the BBC?' Johnston laughed. 'Like the Queen, maybe.'

'Maybe,' said Josh, with a smile. 'And there would be a fee, of course.'

'What do you want to know?'

Kate leaned forwards. 'Just whatever *you* know. Take it from the beginning.'

114

Johnston shot Kate a look that suggested she didn't like her much, then glanced back at Josh. She played with her pencil as if it was a cigarette. 'Ben and Luke were just a couple of computer nerds,' she said. 'We got lots of them around here. Nothing different about these two. They were fifteen, at the local high school They were friends with each other, but not with many other kids. The girls weren't interested. Too many spots and not enough money. Not a combination to get the cheerleaders hot.' Johnston laughed. 'Not even here in Boisdale.'

'What kind of families?' asked Josh.

Johnston shrugged. 'They weren't millionaires, that's for sure. Ben's father was a car mechanic. Ben lived with both parents, about six miles out of town. Nothing grand, but a nice home, with an acre of land and a small pool.'

'And Luke? How about Luke?'

'He lived with his mom, Emily, 'bout ten miles from town, off the Havertree Road. Ask around, people will tell you about Emily. She used to be the town drunk. Always falling out of bars at two in the morning. Town slut as well, from what people say. Nobody knows who Luke's daddy is. Maybe Emily doesn't even know herself. If she does, she never told anyone.'

Josh looked across the room to the water cooler. 'Mind if I get a drink?' he asked.

Johnston nodded. Josh stepped across the room, filled a paper cup and gulped down the cold water. His throat still felt bone dry. He held the bandage tight against his neck: some air had seeped into the wound, irritating the raw skin underneath.

'What happened to you?' asked Johnston.

115

'Fell off my bike,' said Josh. 'Emily? She still drinking?'

Johnston shook her head. 'No. Cleaned up her act about five, six years ago. Got religion, although I think that only lasted a couple of years. Anyway, it helped her straighten her head out. She lives outside of town, in what we locals call the empty country, in an old mining house. Just her and Luke. She's devoted to him.'

'The boys into anything?'

'As I said, computers,' said Johnston. 'They were both obsessed with their computers, the way young boys are these days. They both got into trouble at school for hacking into the school computer and changing everyone's grades. We wrote a story about it in the paper. I don't think they meant any harm. They were nice enough boys in their own way. It's a real shame about Ben.'

'They do any drugs?' asked Kate.

Johnston nodded. Her pencil was dangling from the side of her mouth now. 'Some, I reckon. Just some dope.' She laughed, and the pencil dropped to the floor. 'It's not the most exciting town in the world. Quite a few of the grown-ups do a bit of weed from time to time as well. It helps to pass the time, I believe. Emily grows some out on her land. That and some part-time waitressing are her only income.'

'How about crime?' asked Josh. 'Were the boys mixed up in anything like that?'

'Apart from hacking and dope?' replied Johnston. 'No, not as far as I know. They were okay boys. I spoke to the sheriff, Jim Kelly, yesterday. You spoken with him yet?'

Josh shook his head.

'Well, you'll need to.' She looked at Josh, giving him a smile that he found impossible to read. 'I could introduce you if you like.'

'Thanks,' answered Josh neutrally. 'Go on.'

Johnston sat back in her chair. The window was open, and the mid-morning sunlight was starting to stream into the untidy room. 'Right now, they don't have any significant leads. The best theory they have is that the boys were bored at school and decided to take off for a couple of days. Maybe they ran short of money, and tried to rip off one of the local dealers. That's a good enough reason to get shot. They reckon Luke will turn up in a few days, scared out of his wits. He'll tell them what happened, and then this case will be closed.'

Josh stood up, already glancing towards the door. 'Thanks,' he said. 'That was helpful.'

'I haven't told you anything that you couldn't have figured out for yourself by reading tomorrow's paper.'

Josh smiled. 'Still good to hear it in person,' he said. 'From someone who knows.'

'You going to make that programme?'

'We'll have to see.'

'Because I'd be happy to take part.'

Something about the smile with which Johnston delivered the offer told Josh that she didn't expect it to ever be taken up. 'We'll be in touch,' he said.

Then he took Kate's arm and started guiding her towards the door.

'So who are you really?' said Johnston.

'Like I said, researchers,' said Josh. 'For British TV.'

Johnston was following them towards the door. 'I'm a reporter,' she said. 'I have instincts, and I've

117

learned to rely on them. I know when people are shilling me.' She reached across her desk, taking a card from a box perched next to her computer. 'You're involved,' she said, handing Josh the card. 'I don't know how. But when you feel like saying, call me. I'm sure it's going to make a good story.'

EIGHT

Sunday, June 7th. Evening/night.
Josh scanned the street as he stepped out of the newspaper office. There was no sign of the spotter. Whether he was still looking for them or whether he had called in reinforcements or just moved on, Josh had no way of knowing.

The bikes had disappeared too. The street was empty. 'I think it's okay,' he said to Kate, moving swiftly out onto the pavement.

She followed him out of the building. Josh started walking, keeping alert. Anyone sitting in a car, or just hanging around on a corner, would trigger his suspicion. So far, he could see nothing. *Maybe we're in the clear.*

'I don't think those kids were dopeheads,' said Josh.

'That seems to be the local theory,' said Kate.

Josh shook his head. 'Doesn't make any sense to me. There's something bigger than that happening in this town. A couple of runaway teenagers don't cause this much excitement.'

'Look,' said Kate.

She was nodding towards a car across the road.

Josh looked up. Two men were sitting in the front

seat of a car parked twenty yards down from the restaurant. One of them was drinking from a plastic bottle of water, the other was unwrapping a stick of gum. Josh recognised both of them. The two spotters he'd seen earlier.

And if I recognise them, maybe they will recognise me.

'Stay cool,' he said. 'Just keep walking like nothing is happening.'

Josh picked up his pace. The leg was hurting, and it was tough to move at more than a fast walking pace.

Kate was steering him along. A hundred yards, then two hundred, then three hundred. Josh glanced back once. The two men were still sitting in their car. Neither of them had moved. It's okay, he decided. They aren't looking for us specifically. But they are looking for someone.

'We need to get out of town,' said Kate.

'Where?' said Josh.

'Marshall knows people,' said Kate. 'Out in the wilderness. They'll know where to hide us.'

They kept on walking. Up ahead, Josh could see the bright yellow sign of the Motel 6. He glanced towards Kate, but she seemed lost in her own thoughts. Up beyond the motel was a set of dusty hills rising high into the distance. We're walking right into them, he realised. Good hiding country.

Josh tried to concentrate. A new memory was constantly fading in and out like a badly tuned radio signal. But there was no mistaking it. The girl he had seen earlier, the one who had spoken to him outside the restaurant. Her name was Madge. A big Madonna fan: her iPod had every Madonna track ever recorded stored on it, and was constantly plugged into her ear. She was naked. And she was lying in bed in the motel. With me.

Christ, I'm not surprised she was angry. *I slept with her and now I don't even remember her name.*

Josh stopped and turned to face Kate. 'I have to go back to the motel,' he said.

They were almost a mile out of town now, on a dirt track that led away from the main road up into the hills. 'What?' snapped Kate.

'That girl in the parking lot,' said Josh. 'She works at the motel. The evening shift. She . . .' He paused. 'I've met her before.'

Kate laughed angrily. 'Met her?'

'Right.'

'You mean you fucked her.'

Josh nodded. 'She knows who I am,' he said. 'I need to go and speak to her.'

He could feel Kate gripping his wrist, holding tight onto it. 'No,' she said firmly.

'She knows who I am,' repeated Josh. 'I have to speak to her.'

He could feel Kate's hand squeezing his wrist tighter as she struggled to control her temper. 'Okay,' she said, releasing him. 'If you have to.'

'I have to,' Josh said again.

'I'm going to find Marshall's friends,' said Kate. 'They'll be out looking for us. Keep going along this track for two miles. When you see an abandoned mine, take the track heading due north for one mile. You'll see a rock formation to the right. We'll be there for the night.'

Josh turned around, and started walking back into town.

*   *   *

120

Josh paused outside the motel, scanning the building. The town was crawling with policemen and agents, he reminded himself. There could easily be one here.

As he stepped into the lobby of the Motel 6, Madge's expression changed from a pout to a scowl. She was by herself, dressed in the regulation yellow tunic of the chain: underneath the nylon of the shirt, Josh could make out the blue fabric of her bra. He noticed the plump swelling of her breasts inside it. 'What do you want?' she said.

Josh stepped forward, leaning against the edge of the counter.

'This motel is full,' she said, her face reddening with anger.

'Madge, I'm really sorry.'

'We're full,' she repeated.

Josh held his position. 'You don't understand, Madge,' he continued. 'I was hurt. I've been shot twice, and it's affected my memory. I didn't know my own name, who I was or where I came from. I just didn't realise who you were this morning.' He hesitated, making sure that she could detect the lump in his throat. 'Or how much you meant to me.'

Madge's expression softened. She pushed away the hair that had fallen in front of her face. 'What happened?' she said.

'I don't know,' Josh replied. 'Monday, I was involved in some kind of accident. Or worse.'

Suddenly, Madge threw her arms around him and kissed his cheeks with her wet lips. 'I was lying,' she whispered in his ear. 'We've got lots of room. And I'm closing the desk five minutes early.'

121

Twenty minutes later, they were lying in bed together, their bodies naked, stretched out on the crumpled white sheets.

Josh hugged Madge close to him. Their bodies were hot and sticky, her arms still cradling his chest. She reached up and kissed him on the lips, resting her hands against the bandage wrapped around his neck.

'I was so angry when I thought you'd forgotten who I was,' she said. 'I wanted to kill you.'

Josh smiled, removing her hand from the bandage. 'If you want to kill me, you'll have to join the queue.'

Madge turned on to her side, her cheek against the pillow. Room 19 was a compact, pre-designed box, with a double bed, a pair of side lights, and a picture of the Californian coast on the wall. There was a TV, a shower room, and not much else. Grabbing a room whenever she wanted to sleep with a guy was one of the perks of Madge's job, decided Josh.

'They came to question me,' she said.

Josh suddenly jerked out of the post-coital slumber into which he had drifted. 'Who?'

'Federal agents, Josh,' she said. 'They showed me their cards and everything. They said I should talk to them. They said that you were a witness to the shooting of Ben Lippard.'

Her worried stare met Josh's. 'Is that true?'

'I think so,' answered Josh. 'I can't say for certain because I can't remember anything.'

Madge pulled up the white cotton sheet so that it covered her breasts. 'I told them I didn't know anything. I just said Josh is a fine man. He wouldn't hurt anyone.'

122

I hope that's true, thought Josh to himself. *Right now I wouldn't be so certain.*

'They accepted that?'

'They looked pretty pissed off. But eventually they went away.'

'How long was I here for?'

'You?'

Josh nodded. 'How long was I at the motel?'

'Nine days,' said Madge. 'I noticed you as soon as you checked in. You had a nice smile.'

'And what was I doing?'

'You don't know what you were doing?'

Josh shook his head. 'I told you, I don't remember anything.'

'Scouting tourist sites,' said Madge, sounding bored by the question. 'You said you worked for a tour company in England. You were planning routes, finding hotels, checking places to eat.'

I lied to her, thought Josh. *Whatever the hell I was doing here, that sure wasn't it.*

Josh squeezed her tight, caressing her shoulders. 'And who else was staying at the hotel at the same time as me?'

Madge looked thoughtful. 'Usual people,' she replied. 'Salesmen. A couple of stray tourists. People who were moving house. Husbands who'd been thrown out by their wives. I don't pay much attention to the guests at the Motel 6.' She snuggled up close to Josh. 'I certainly don't do *this* with them.'

'Anyone unusual?'

Madge's nose tilted disdainfully. 'One guy.'

'Who?'

'An Italian,' said Madge. 'Carrying an Italian passport when he checked in. I noticed it because

I've never seen one of those before, and we don't get many foreigners in Boisdale. Heck, we don't even get that many people who aren't from Arizona. First, an Englishman, then this Italian. I couldn't help but notice.'

'You said there was something suspicious about him?'

Madge nodded. 'Just the way he acted. I didn't like it.'

'In what way?'

'I don't know.'

Josh looked at her intently. 'Describe him to me.'

'I can show you a picture.'

Josh picked himself up from the bed, and started walking towards the shower. He had to be careful when he washed not to disturb the bandage on his neck. He dried himself off, put the towel on the rack, and slipped on his jeans and shirt.

'Show me the picture, Madge, and I'll love you for ever,' he said. He could tell that she was enjoying the drama and mystery of all this.

She followed him outside. It was after eleven at night, but the air was still hot and the breeze had dropped, making the night sticky and sweaty. Josh could see one car pulling up down in the parking lot but the middle-aged man getting out looked harmless enough: the town might be crawling with spotters but he wasn't one of them. Madge took the metal staircase, then used her staff key to let herself into the lobby: the reception was closed at this time of night.

'Here,' she said, reaching into a grey metal filing cabinet in the small office behind the desk. 'We keep the guest records in here. We photocopy the passports of foreigners, and keep the details on file

124

for three months.'

'Can I see mine?' said Josh.

She took the file and placed it in front of him. For a second, Josh could feel his blood surging through his veins. *I'm about to find out who I am.*

Josh looked down at the photocopy of his passport. Josh Bellamy, born in Sunderland.

That's not it, I'm not a Geordie. I was travelling under a false name, and a false passport. My name might not even be Josh.

Why would I be travelling under a false name?

Madge started rifling through the drawer, then pulled out a single sheet of white photostatted paper. On it was imprinted the image of a man. Josh looked down. Like all passport photos, it was small, with a white backdrop, and the person was wearing their most sombre expression.

The man in this photocopy had dark, smooth skin, just the way Madge had described him. His hair was black, brushed away from his face, and his dark eyes were set far apart from each other. The jaw looked as though it had been chiselled from stone, but the nose was crooked, as if it had been broken. It was a distinguished face, Josh decided: the mask of a man who knew both what he wanted, and how to hide it.

I've seen him before, thought Josh. *I don't know where or how, but I know this man.*

And I feel certain that I'll see him again.

'How long was he here?'

'Just the Sunday and Monday nights,' said Madge.

He arrives just before I get shot, thought Josh. *And he leaves straight afterwards.*

125

It was a four-mile walk back from the motel, taking three quarters of an hour: a mile to get out of town, two miles along the track, then, as the light faded, another mile up into the hills where Kate had told him they would be camping out for the night. Along the way, Josh had been thinking through all the things he had learned from Madge. A hundred different possibilities were running through his head: he needed time to sort them out and start making sense of what had happened to him.

What do I know? he asked himself. My name was Josh—maybe. I was staying in Boisdale. I lied about what I was doing, and I may have travelled under a false name. A man I recognise from somewhere came to stay at the hotel. Then I got shot.

The more he thought about it, the less sense it made.

His legs were aching from the effort of walking so many miles in one day. The wounds needed rest but that wasn't possible, not yet. There was still too much to be done.

He took the dirt track, letting the moonlight light up the path for him, until he hit the abandoned mine. Then he took the turning that Kate had described to him. Another mile dragged wearily by. As he drew closer, he wasn't sure how much longer he could keep going. He must have travelled at least twenty miles on foot in the last twenty-four hours: a punishing walk, even for a man who hadn't recently taken some lead.

Eventually, he saw the boulder formation. Sniffing the air, he could smell a fire, although he couldn't yet see it. Whoever was hiding there was clearly experienced enough to know how to build a fire, yet at the same time shield its light from the main track. Josh stepped forwards, pushing into the collection of boulders, letting his nose lead him.

Then, in front of him, he made out two men who blended into the landscape the same way a boulder blends into a rockfall. Their skin was tanned, leathery and lined. Both of them had grey hair and grey beards, although they looked no more than forty. A fire was burning in front of a cave, sending tiny plumes of smoke climbing upwards into the clear night sky: on top of the flames, its body pierced by a crooked stick, was some kind of small animal. A bird of some sort, figured Josh, as he smelled the charred flesh. Christ, maybe even a snake. *These guys look like they'll eat anything.*

'You okay?' Kate asked, a trace of anxiety in her voice as she emerged from the shadows.

Josh nodded. 'Who are they?'

One of the two men looked up at Josh, then stabbed the tiny creature. The fat from its body spluttered, falling into the fire, sending a sheet of sparks flying upwards.

Kate took Josh by the arm. 'This is Danny O'Brien,' she said, 'and this is Richie Morant.' She looked up at Josh. 'Marshall sent them out to look for us when we disappeared,' she said. 'They're here to help.'

'What the hell is this place?' said Josh, looking around the tiny, rough camp.

'It's a survivalist base,' said Kate. 'Many people believe that the UN is going to invade the United States one day. They've got all the kit here that they need to organise the local resistance. Food, fuel, explosives, some ammunition. The works.'

Great, thought Josh. Nutters.

He looked up. O'Brien was the shorter of the pair. His eyes were a pale grey, and you could see the Irish ancestry in him still: his head was broad and square, like a concrete block, and his shoulders were massive, but his manner was relaxed and genial. Morant, a bigger man, had a thick scar running down his left cheek, and the build of a brickie: he too had huge shoulders and biceps, a beefy torso tapering to a thin waist, then a pair of legs like tree trunks. Both men looked strong and healthy, and there was something wild about their appearance. Their hair was thick with grease. And they carried with them the dry, dusty smell of the desert.

'Is it you?' said O'Brien.

'Is it me, what?' asked Josh, looking towards him.

'Who's set the Feds crawling all over the place,' O'Brien said.

'You can't move for the motherfuckers,' said Morant. 'Nice quiet bit of the desert we had out here. Now it's crawling with agents. United Nations. Foreigners.'

Christ, thought Josh. *Where the hell did Kate find these two?*

'I'm hiding from them myself,' said Josh.

O'Brien nodded, and a smile suddenly flashed across his face. 'Marshall says you're okay, a soldier.'

'I think so,' said Josh. 'He told you about me?'

'Said you might need some help,' said Morant.

He reached out for the animal roasting on the home-made spit, and took it from the fire. It was long and thin, but it had legs: that ruled out a

128

snake. Its flesh was singed from the flames, but the smell was good: a succulent, fatty odour somewhere between chicken and pork. Josh was famished.

'Want some?' said Morant, offering him a chunk of meat. 'It's crane.'

Josh nodded. He took a bite from the greasy lump of flesh now sitting in his hands. It was stringy, with the texture of rabbit.

'I need help,' he said. 'Marshall was right about that.'

'What kind of help?' asked O'Brien.

Josh was sitting next to the fire now. The temperature had dropped, making the warmth a welcome respite from the chilled air. In the light of the fire, he could see the faces of both men more clearly. There was a determination in both of them: an inner core of strength. But also a lightness of spirit.

Josh tapped the side of his head. 'I lost my memory when I got shot,' he said. 'Over in the Sheriff's office, they know who I am. I want to get in there and see my files.'

'Fucking government,' said O'Brien. 'Got no right keeping files on any man.'

'When the fucking UN takes over the country,' said Morant, 'they're going to take down anyone who tries to oppose them. This damned country's going to be finished.'

'Assholes,' said O'Brien. A thick wedge of cooked meat was dangling from his teeth. 'They got no fucking files on us, that's for sure. So far as the law is concerned, we don't exist. And we're keeping it that way.'

'You'll help me?'

'You're a fucking foreigner,' spat O'Brien. 'We only deal with Americans.'

'We don't trust you,' said Morant.

'We only trust our own kind,' added O'Brien.

'Even if I'm against the Feds?' said Josh.

There was a silence while both men paused for thought.

'Marshall told you—' began Kate.

'Marshall's pretty pissed with you for disappearing in the middle of the night,' said O'Brien.

NINE

Monday, June 8th. Night.

Madge gave Josh a long, lingering kiss on the lips. He took her in his arms, holding her tight to his chest.

'My shift doesn't end for another two hours,' she said. 'But I needed to see you.'

'Why?' asked Josh.

Madge looked around the drab foyer of the Motel 6. Her uniform was looking tighter today, as if it had shrunk in the wash or she had put on a couple of extra pounds. 'Because some men were snooping around the hotel last night.'

*   *   *

Josh and Kate had stayed the night in the mountains, hiding out with O'Brien and Morant. They had spent an uneasy night at the survivalist base. Josh wasn't at all sure how much he trusted the other men and he didn't think that they trusted him either.

In the morning, he'd said that he'd go back into town to draw up a plan of attack on the sheriff's office while O'Brien and Morant would put together some kit.

O'Brien had a red Mustang that he assured them was clean and couldn't be traced by the police. He'd let Kate drive it to drop Josh on the outskirts of town.

Then, as Josh was walking past the motel, Madge had run out to speak to him.

'What kind of men?' asked Josh.

'Bikers,' replied Madge, steering him back into the motel. 'Here, I'll show you.'

*   *   *

The back office of the Motel 6 was painted battleship grey, and had just one desk, two telephones and a computer screen. On one side of the desk there was a bank of four CCTV screens, each one just twelve inches square, displaying different views of the hotel: they monitored the car park, the foyer, and both of the two corridors along which the rooms were arranged. Only one flaw, Josh realised. There was nobody watching. The cameras would record a crime, but there would be no one there to stop it.

'This happened last night,' said Madge. She sat down at the desk, spooling back the tape until she reached the section she wanted. 23.19 was the time recorded on the screen in tiny white lettering. 'Look,' she said, her finger jabbing against the screen. 'Here.'

Josh leaned forwards, resting his hands on the table and peering into the screen. He could see three men pulling up their bikes in the parking lot, then walking around to the back of the hotel. They clambered up the fire escape, methodically looking through the back windows built into the rooms. Each man weighed at least two hundred and fifty pounds and had a long beard, but they were surprisingly agile, moving swiftly and silently around the building. They looked different from the bikers who had stood up for Madge in the restaurant parking lot: meaner, and fiercer, moving with an almost military precision. Next, the man who appeared to be the leader of the group walked up to the lobby, breaking its flimsy lock with his bare hands. Once inside, he started rummaging through the registration book, then spent ten minutes sitting in front of the hotel's computer in the reception. At one point he looked up, and the CCTV camera froze, capturing a perfect image of his face. Even obscured by the crash helmet still strapped securely to his head, it was easy to make out his main features. He had the thick, strapping skull of a pirate, with deep, dark eyes, bored like pits into the front of his face. His hair was long, wrapped up behind his head in a ponytail, while his beard was a foot long, jet black, and neatly combed. His skin, from what little Josh could see of it between the helmet and the beard, looked as if he had been suffering from acute acne for at least four decades. The moon has a smoother surface than your cheeks, pal, Josh decided.

I've seen him before, thought Josh. *I don't know where but I've seen that animal somewhere before.*

'What do you think they were looking for?' asked

132

Madge.

'Me,' answered Josh. 'And they'll be back.'

On the motel computer, he printed out two still frames from the CCTV footage, sliding the pictures into the inside of his shirt. 'Motel 6 aren't going to miss one shot, are they?'

Madge shook her head.

Josh planted a resounding kiss on her lips. 'I love you,' he said.

*　　　*　　　*

O'Brien and Morant were already cooking on the fire. The flames were licking around the body of another small animal, and the smell of singed fat and charcoal was already filling the air. 'More crane?' said Josh, looking down.

'Not crane,' said O'Brien. 'No crane around this evening. At least none that we could catch.'

'We don't mind fighting the law, but we do so on a full stomach,' said Morant.

Both men laughed.

Kate was sitting just behind them, her hair tied up behind her neck. She looked across at Josh and smiled. It was just after eight in the evening, and it was already dark.

Josh took the leg of meat that O'Brien had just offered him and sank his teeth into the hot flesh. A dribble of fat ran down the side of his chin, and he brushed it away with a handkerchief. It tasted more like wild boar than anything else, but had a sharper, tangier flavour. Don't ask, he reminded himself. *If you ask what it is, you'll lose your appetite.*

'You guys ready?' he asked, looking across at the two men.

O'Brien and Morant nodded in turn. 'For fighting the cops, there's no time like the present.'

'Let's go through the plan once more,' said Josh. 'We go into town. But first we knock out the FBI agent so that we can use his pass to get us into the Sheriff's office. Once we're inside we look up all the details they have on me, then get the hell out of there.'

O'Brien nodded. 'The bit I like is at the start,' he said. 'Where we knock out the fucking Fed.'

The plan was that Kate would drop them off on the outskirts of town, then drive back to Marshall's to wait for them.

O'Brien made it his business to monitor the movements of every law-enforcement official in the region and prided himself on keeping tabs on all their routines. A Federal agent stopped at the Texaco station two miles outside Boisdale every night not long after midnight, pulling up for coffee and a doughnut. When they'd disposed of the agent they'd proceed into town, using his car.

Now the three men walked in silence: the track was too rough to use a car or a bike. Josh was using a stick to relieve some of the pressure on his leg, but he could move with freedom. I'm not going to let it slow me down, he kept telling himself every time he felt a bolt of pain shooting up his spine.

He sensed excitement in O'Brien and Morant as they reached the gas station. They were just waiting, he realised, for the right moment to teach the Feds a lesson about who controlled this land.

'He'll be here in a moment,' said O'Brien, as they circled round the patch of scrubland at the back of the Texaco station. 'He usually stops between 12.30 and 1.00.'

'And he usually takes a leak,' said Morant. 'Weak bladder, I guess. We'll take him there.' He chuckled to himself. 'Always wanted to smash up a Fed bastard with his trousers down.'

Josh stayed silent. Now he could see a Ford Taurus pulling up at the station, the driver climbing out and starting to fill his tank. The man was around thirty-five, with sandy brown hair, and a dull, undistinguished face, already starting to run to fat around the cheeks. He was wearing grey slacks and a beige short-sleeved shirt.

'Motherfucker,' muttered Morant under his breath. 'Thinks he can come down from Washington and start snooping around our town.'

The man put the gas pump's nozzle back into its holder, then walked towards the gents'. Josh was sitting behind two huge plastic rubbish bins, filled to overflowing with the debris from the station: half-filled cups of coffee, and the remains of the micro-waved burgers sold inside. The smell was mixing with the fumes of gas and diesel and the odours drifting across from the toilet to make Josh feel queasy. Get this over with, he told himself. *I can't stand the stink much longer.*

The door slammed shut on the toilet.

The three men moved out onto the forecourt and stepped into the gents'. It was painted grey, with white tiles running halfway up the wall and Texaco logos above the sinks. The man was standing with his back to them, pissing into the urinal. Josh took a quick glance at him, making a rough mental calculation of his size, weight and strength, then worked out the force of the blow that would be needed to take him down. The man glanced back, nodded, then looked back at the urinal. Josh curled

135

his fist into a ball and drew his arm back, coiling the pressure in his shoulder muscles. Then he released his punch.

The blow landed on the side of the man's neck. The muscles there were loose and relaxed: the man had had no warning of the attack and so had done nothing to prepare himself. The breath was forced out of his windpipe, making him choke. At his side, O'Brien had prepared another blow, delivering his punch straight to the gut. Next, Morant's boot smashed upwards, colliding with the agent's groin, sending a vicious bolt of pain searing up through his body at the same moment that all the oxygen emptied out of his lungs.

Still gripping his penis, some urine still trickling from it, the man crumpled to the floor.

Josh reached down, grabbing the man's throat and squeezing the air out of him. He could see the agent's eyes closing as shortage of oxygen to his brain made him lose consciousness.

But suddenly his eyes were open, staring straight up at Josh, and his hand was clutching at Josh's leg, tearing away at the bandage underneath his jeans, jamming the cotton into the raw wound. Josh bit his tongue to stifle a scream as the pain ripped through him. 'Fucker,' he gasped. He drove his fist hard into the side of the man's face. The agent slumped backward and his hand fell away as his head slammed against the floor.

A slow trickle of blood had started to seep down the side of Josh's leg.

'Not much fight in the fucker, is there?' snarled Morant. 'Let's cut his balls off, and hang them on the door. A warning to the others.'

Christ, thought Josh. I know the enemy of my

enemy is my friend, and all that. *But these guys are bloody nutters.*

Josh took a tissue from his pocket and stuffed it inside the man's mouth. Next he took a roll of duct tape and started to bind up the man's mouth and hands. 'We'll stuff him in the can,' he said. 'This time of night, it should be a couple of hours at least before anyone finds him. That gives us enough time.'

Gratuitously, O'Brien smashed his fist into the man's gut again, making his unconscious body jerk. 'Why aren't we killing him?'

'Because if you kill a Fed, you'll get the whole bloody FBI coming down to the town, that's why,' snapped Josh. The pain in his leg was terrible, his head was starting to ache again and his temper was about to fly out of the room.

'Bring 'em on,' muttered Morant. 'Bring 'em on.'

'Fucking liberal,' said O'Brien, glancing towards Josh.

'Christ, let's just get out of here,' said Josh angrily. He grabbed the agent by the shoulders, heaving his body up. 'Hold his legs,' he snapped at O'Brien. He watched while O'Brien took the man by the legs, then they bundled him towards the toilet cubicle. 'Let's go,' said Josh.

O'Brien and Morant followed him out. Josh paused on the step, checking that no one had seen them. It was 12.45 a.m. now, and the forecourt was empty. The clerk sitting at the desk was the only person there, and he was watching the TV next to his desk. There were CCTV cameras, but they were trained on the cash desk. Nothing was recording people coming in and out of the toilet.

'You get in the car,' hissed Josh. 'I'll pay the bill.'

137

He had taken the jacket off the agent and put it on himself.

'We're not paying for the fucking Fed's gas,' snarled Morant. 'We should have just killed him.'

'Right,' said Josh. 'And you think we can drive out of the gas station without paying the bill and nobody will notice? Get in the car.'

Christ, thought Josh. *It's a miracle these morons have stayed out of jail this long.*

He walked swiftly towards the cash desk, checking that O'Brien and Morant had made it to the car. I'm taking a risk, he told himself, but a manageable one. Chances were the kid on the cash desk hadn't bothered to look at the man as he stepped out of the car and headed to the loos after filling up. And I'm wearing the guy's jacket. So long as the petrol is paid for he'll be happy enough.

They drove in silence from the gas station to the Sheriff's office. All three of them were recovering their breath after the fight. And they were focusing on the battle that lay ahead.

A battery of spotlights was shining down from the front of the Sheriff's office. Josh pulled the Taurus up on the street outside, switching off its lights.

He could feel the nerves in his stomach starting to get jumpy. Of course this was risky, but he had to find out who he was. Morant had assured him that the police station was lightly manned at night: one patrol car and one duty officer. Even so, this town was crawling with agents. It was impossible to know for sure how many people might be in there.

And he was worried that the officer Marshall had beaten up might be there. If so, he would certainly recognise Josh.

I'm taking my life in my hands.

Josh took the wallet from the Fed's jacket he was wearing and looked down at the ID. The name on the badge was Arnie Canestra, FBI Agent Number 2234B. There was a picture, but it was tiny. The memory of the heavy security around the building that he had encountered the other night was still fresh in his mind: they were going to have to make this act convincing if they hoped to get away with it. *Let's just hope that O'Brien and Morant don't get any smart ideas.*

'You stay in the car,' Josh said, looking at Morant. 'Keep the engine switched off, or it will attract attention. But keep it ready to move. We might need to get out of here in a hurry.'

An Italian-American, thought Josh as he stepped towards the entrance to the Sheriff's office. Agent Canestra. *Maybe I should talk like Al Pacino.*

'Walk quickly,' whispered Josh to O'Brien as he stepped through the doorway. 'A man walks quickly through any building, people assume he's doing something important. They are going to be nervous about stopping him.'

The corridor was painted pale cream. There was a duty desk, empty at this time of night. The corridor was lined with pictures of men on the wanted list: rough-looking characters, Josh noted, with pinched, violent faces, full of malevolence and anger. *I wouldn't be surprised to see either O'Brien or Morant up there along with the rest of the losers and psychopaths.*

'This way,' he said softly. Josh walked briskly towards the back office. He could feel his pulse racing. Last time he'd been here, he'd been chased away by a helicopter. So far as he could see, the place looked a lot quieter this evening. Or maybe it just appeared that way.

The corridor led into a large open-plan room. A lingering smell of sugar and coffee filled the air. About twenty desks were arranged opposite each other, all made from the same cheap wood, each with a regulation grey bin at the side. One cop who looked like a local guy was sitting alone at a desk close to the entrance. Another pair were checking their revolvers before heading out on a night patrol. It looked like there were only three of them.

In my jeans and T-shirt I don't look much like an FBI agent, thought Josh. *But in the middle of the night, I'll pass.*

'Agent Canestra,' he said, showing his badge, his tone clipped and purposeful as he nodded towards the one cop sitting at a desk. The man, nearing fifty and with a balding head, was looking down at a pile of papers, ticking boxes one by one.

'Need to check the computers,' continued Josh. 'That okay?'

The man glanced up, grunted something that Josh didn't catch, then went back to his work. Us Feds aren't very popular around here, Josh figured. *Treading on their turf, and nobody likes that.* He noticed the other two cops clock him as they left to go out on patrol.

He chose a desk in the far right hand corner of the office. So far, so good, he told himself with quiet satisfaction. There's a chance I might get away with this.

O'Brien followed him as he sat down, bringing up the opening page on the computer. His eyes started scanning down the rows of files. It took a few minutes to start navigating his way around the system. There were files on local laws, state laws, and federal laws. Procedural files and training files. Budgets and duty rosters. All of it operated from the same central database. Josh couldn't be certain, but it made sense that the local police would keep files on every murder case in the county. And the most likely place to keep those files would be on the computer.

'Open files,' said an icon on the screen.

Josh clicked on it. A list of names scrolled up onto the screen. Josh started scrolling through them alphabetically until he found what he was looking for. Lippard. 'Open,' he commanded the computer with a click of the mouse.

Josh started reading. The main report told him little that he didn't already know. Ben had been shot between eleven and twelve on the morning of Monday, June the first. Four bullets had been found in his body, fired from a Smith & Wesson Mountain Lite revolver. No trace had been made on the gun, nor had the weapon been found. There were no witnesses to the shooting, and the police had so far identified no leads and had no suspects.

Just like I thought. They are groping around in the dark.

Tiny jabs of pain were starting to hammer the inside of Josh's leg. He glanced down and saw that blood was dripping from the side of his thigh. It had seeped into the cloth of his jeans and was trickling down onto the tiled surface of the floor. A tiny trail of red droplets was leading from the doorway to this desk. He glanced anxiously at the cop in the corner.

He was standing up. He can't miss it, the bastard, thought Josh. Even the drowsiest cop has to see a trail of blood leading through his own office.

I haven't got much time.

He scrolled further through the files, his fingers moving swiftly across the keyboard. Against the back of his neck, he could feel O'Brien breathing heavily. 'Quick,' O'Brien muttered. 'All these cops are making me uncomfortable.'

Three words flashed up: 'The Third Man.' Josh clicked on the file, bringing the Word document up onto the screen. He glanced anxiously towards the door. No sign of the cop.

Josh started reading. 'Crime Scene Report, 6/1/05: Report File No: 34521DF. Reporting officer: Dick McNamara. Traces of blood were also found at the scene of the crime, just a few yards away from Lippard's body. Initially that was assumed to be Lippard's blood, but a test showed that it belonged to another person. The blood sample was sent to the National Crime Laboratories in Washington for DNA analysis. The NCL replied three days later. They had identified the person, and were awaiting security clearance before releasing the name and details of the person to the Boisdale sheriff's office.'

The third man? thought Josh, sitting back in his chair and staring intently at the screen. Security clearance? *Christ, what the hell am I doing in this country?*

'What did you say your name was again?' said a voice behind him.

Josh spun around.

The cop was looking straight down at him.

His face was puffy and tired, but the message in his eyes was clear enough. He had decided that Josh was not who he said he was. Now he was weighing up what to do about it.

'Agent Canestra,' snapped Josh. 'This is my colleague Dave Freemantle. We're busy, if you don't mind.'

'You don't look like Feds,' said the cop, delivering his words slowly. 'You've got a weird accent. And there's a trail of blood leading from the doorway to your desk.'

I've got two choices, figured Josh, his mind tabbing quickly through the available options. I can bluff my way out of this. Or run.

He's probably already called in reinforcements. Maybe that's why he disappeared for so long. That patrol car has probably turned round and is on its way back now. He just wants to keep me talking until they show up. There's nothing to gain by trying to talk my way out. *Run, man, while you still have the chance.*

'Like I said, we're busy,' snapped Josh, his tone rising.

'Then what about the blood?' asked the cop.

Josh's elbow snapped backwards, crashing into the side of the cop's jaw. Josh could feel his bone striking against the other man's, the point of his elbow joint digging deep into the soft flesh of the policeman's cheek. At the same moment, O'Brien drove his fist into the man's neck.

The cop reeled, then regained his balance. There was more strength in him than Josh had expected: he was a big man and his rolls of flesh turned out to contain as much muscle as fat. His hand slammed down on the desk, steadying himself, then his knee jerked upwards, smashing into Josh's chest. He could feel his ribcage vibrating with the impact, a bolt of pain shooting out into his body. Josh stepped backwards, steadying himself, then swung his leg forward, driving it hard into the cop's side. Then O'Brien gripped his neck between his forearms, jerking it backwards, and Josh could see the man's face turn red.

Josh heard a snapping sound. *Christ, is that his neck breaking?*

'Punch him out,' hissed O'Brien. 'Punch him out.'

Josh drew back his fist. He could see a look of fear flash across the cop's face. He was wriggling like a fish on a hook, but O'Brien's lock on his neck was strong.

I'll make it quick, pal, thought Josh. *You're better off with me punching you out than you'd be with either of these other head cases.*

Josh punched first with his right hand, then with his left, delivering a swift uppercut straight below the cop's jaw. A trickle of blood started to seep from the man's mouth and nose, and his eyes closed.

'He's out,' snapped O'Brien.

'Then let's get the hell out of here,' said Josh.

He started moving swiftly towards the street door. It was ten yards away, and some blood was flowing more freely now from the opened wound on his leg, spattering the floor with more red droplets. *They've got my DNA already, even if they don't know who I am. They will know that the third man has been here. And they'll turn over every last grain of sand in the desert to find me.*

The sound of a siren ripped through the quiet of the night sky. Josh lunged towards the doorway, looking out along the road. He could see Morant waiting in the Taurus. The car swung out into the road to meet him. But up on the main street, maybe three hundred yards away, Josh could now

144

make out the patrol car accelerating towards them, its siren wailing and its warning strobe sending arcs of blue light spinning out into the night sky.

'They're bloody onto us,' Josh shouted, throwing himself into the passenger seat of the Taurus. Behind him, O'Brien was slamming his own door shut.

'Just bloody drive,' yelled Josh.

Morant was gripping the steering wheel of the Taurus hard. His foot slammed down on the accelerator as the car sped out onto the road leading out of town. Josh glanced behind him. The patrol car was already ramped up to full speed. It was travelling at a hundred, maybe a hundred and ten an hour, gaining on them with every second.

'Faster,' he muttered under his breath.

I've assaulted their office, and punched out one of their own men. *They're not going to be in a mood to take any prisoners.*

'I'm going blindfold,' Morant warned. He switched off the headlamps, plunging the road ahead into darkness. The patrol car was throwing off some light, but that was still two hundred yards behind them. This far from the town there were no more street lamps. Josh could see nothing ahead, not even the curve of the road.

He gripped the side of the seat. This was going to be a rough ride.

Looking across at the speedometer, he could see the Taurus gaining pace. It was hitting a hundred and twenty an hour, and Josh could hear the engine straining as it struggled to gets the revs it needed for that kind of speed. Another glance back. The patrol car was still gaining. A hundred yards behind, figured Josh. A hundred and fifty if we're lucky.

'The fuckers, they're fast,' shouted Morant, a gleeful wild edge to his voice.

'Cross-country,' shouted O'Brien from the back seat.

Josh couldn't be sure whether it was a question or a command.

'Hell, yes,' shouted Morant, struggling to make himself heard above the roar of the car's engine.

The Taurus swerved viciously to the right, its suspension shuddering as the tyres collided with the rough surface of the scrubland. This is just a suburban cruiser, realised Josh. Not an SUV or a 4x4, and it wasn't designed for driving off-road. *Every crevice, curve and rock is going to hit me straight in the spine.*

'The river,' shouted O'Brien from the back seat. 'Head for the river.'

.Josh searched the ground ahead. He was peering through the windscreen, trying to figure out where they were going, but it was impossible to make out anything apart from a few murky shapes. They could be boulders, they could be plants. It was impossible to tell. The car was skidding across the dusty ground like a stone skimming across the surface of a lake, hardly touching its surface.

The river? What the hell do they mean, the river?

He checked the mirror. The patrol car had been thrown as they turned off the road. It had taken the driver a few seconds to react. But now powerful headlamps were beaming out across the open countryside, picking up the trail of the Taurus.

He might be four, five hundred yards behind us, realised Josh. *But he's still got us in his sights.*

'Left, left,' shouted O'Brien.

Josh could feel himself being pressed against the door as the car swerved viciously to the left. Something collided with the car's side with a terrifying thump, crashing into the metal. He could hear screeching and tearing as the Taurus's frame started to buckle. 'Harder left,' shouted O'Brien.

Josh drew a breath. At his side, Morant flashed him a smile. 'Hold on to your seat, boy,' he snapped.

'Why?'

Morant laughed. 'Trust me, you don't want to know.'

Josh gripped the black cloth seat of the car. He wondered whether he should put his safety belt on but decided against it. Whatever the health-and-safety monkeys said, seat belts killed as many people as they saved because they stopped you getting out of the car quickly.

And I may well want to get out of this one in a real hurry.

Josh looked ahead. All he could see was darkness. What Morant was driving by, he couldn't tell. Instinct, or an encyclopaedic knowledge of the terrain. Either way it was working. *So far.*

Suddenly he could hear nothing. The sound of the tyres rubbing protestingly against the surface of the rough ground disappeared. Christ, Josh said disbelievingly to himself. *We're flying.*

The idiot's driven off the edge of a cliff.

Prayer time.

Next, there was a deafening crash as the car hit the ground. Every bolt in the Taurus shook loose, a huge cloud of steam rose up from the engine, and the lights started flashing on and off. Water was gushing all around them, spitting up against the

147

windscreen and seeping through the door until the carpet at Josh's feet was a sodden mess.

This is what he meant by the river.

The engine coughed, then roared. Josh could see Morant stabbing at the brakes, but to little effect. Broken, Josh realised. The steering was erratic, and the suspension had broken in at least two places, making every turn and twist a strain on the car. *One thing's certain. This machine's not passing its MOT.*

'Swing right,' shouted O'Brien.

Morant was twisting on the wheel but the power steering was gone, and Josh could see that the wheels were submerged in two feet of fast-running water. The car was sliding as much as it was being driven. Morant tugged harder on the wheel, and the car started drifting right, skimming across stones and pebbles, then picking up speed as it started to drive along a narrow tributary that—in the direction they were going—led away from the river.

Josh looked behind him. He could see nothing, only darkness.

No sign of the patrol car. *Maybe we lost them.*

The brakes still weren't working, so Morant killed the engine and let the car drift slowly to a halt. 'Shit, that was fun,' he said, climbing out of the car.

Josh stood up, slamming the door behind him. About six inches of water were running beneath his feet. He bent down, scooped up a handful and started to drink. The liquid slowly calmed his nerves, and he paused to examine his injuries. Blood was still dripping from his leg, and the cloth of his jeans was stained red on that side. There was some bruising to his calf and his chest where he'd been rammed against the door of the car and hit by the policeman. Otherwise I'm okay, he told himself. *Not much worse than usual.*

'There's a dried-out creek, right to the left of here,' said O'Brien, pointing to a turn in the stream about a hundred yards ahead of where they were standing. 'Just follow that. It will take you back to Ferndale. From there you can make your way back to Marshall's house.'

'Where are *you* going?' asked Josh.

'Into the wilderness,' said O'Brien. 'We have bases all over this county. They'll never find us because they don't know the ground anything like as well as we do.'

'Well, thanks for the help.'

Morant laughed roughly. 'Hell, we don't need any encouragement to go up against the Feds. I'm just pissed we didn't finish off that guy in the gas station.'

It takes all sorts, decided Josh as he started walking. Even out here.

It was just past two in the morning. It was dark but from the sliver of moon in the sky he could just make out the dried-up bed of the stream that O'Brien had told him about. I can follow that trail, he told himself. It could be twenty miles back to Marshall's house, a four- or five-hour walk depending on how his leg held out against the pain.

There aren't any choices but to walk my way out of trouble, Josh reminded himself through gritted teeth. *I don't want to be around here when the sun rises.*

*　　*　　*

149

Dawn was not far away now, Josh realised. He couldn't see any signs of light breaking over the horizon yet, nor could he see any streaks of orange piercing through the dark sky. But he could smell it. There is a freshness to the air just before the sun rises, he thought. You can sense it in the dew hanging in the air, and in the stillness of the air just before the birds wake for the day.

He had checked his trail a dozen times since he'd been walking, and felt certain that the Sheriff's car that had been chasing them last night had been lost.

They will still be out there looking for me. But for now they've lost the scent.

Josh began to recognise the outline of the land. The house was just a mile away. The creek had led Josh back to Ferndale, just as O'Brien had said it would.

Josh paused. He scanned the empty landscape, looking for any signs of patrol cars, helicopters or any other kind of surveillance. There was nothing. Only a light breeze was blowing across the empty plain.

The sheriff's office don't know about Kate and Marshall, he realised. *They don't know that they are helping me.*

The house looked dead as Josh approached it. No lights, no sounds. He leaned on the frame of the door leading out from the kitchen. The flimsy lock gave way surprisingly quickly. Josh stood alone in the kitchen. He was out of breath and his tongue was parched dry from the walk. Beads of sweat were rolling down his back. He leaned over the sink, splashing his face with water. It felt good against his skin. He reached out for a slice of bread from the packet lying open on the side.

Bread and water, Josh reminded himself. *The basics of keeping yourself alive.*

The light flashed on. Kate was standing in the doorway. A towel was wrapped tightly around her body, tied into a knot just above her breasts. It stopped just an inch below her hips. 'What the hell happened to you?'

'National security,' said Josh. 'I got as far as finding my file. The Feds know who I am, but they haven't told the local cops yet.' He looked hard at Kate. 'Who the hell am I?'

'I don't know, Josh.'

She walked closer towards him, her eyes flashing towards the dark crimson patch on his jeans. 'You're hurt.'

Josh nodded. 'Bit of a scrap.'

A look of anxiety crossed her face. 'You've been shot?'

'No,' said Josh. 'The old wound started bleeding.' He looked down into her eyes. 'It gave us away in the police station, leaking out all over the floor.'

'Come here,' said Kate. 'I'll clean it up for you.'

She led him towards her bedroom. Josh hadn't been to the back of the house before. The room was small, no more than ten feet by fifteen, with a single bed at one side of it. It was painted pale yellow: the only room in the house that looked as if it had seen a paintbrush at any time in the past decade.

This can't be the place where she lives all the time, thought Josh as he glanced around.

It's not a woman's room. There are no cushions delicately arranged. No attempt to match the

151

sheets with the curtains. No cuddly toys or framed photographs. Just a bed, and a dressing table, and a suitcase that has only been half opened.

'Take off your jeans,' said Kate.

'Yes, doctor,' said Josh, flashing a grin at her.

He unbuckled his belt and looked towards the bed. With a look, she ordered him to lie down. Josh lay back against the white sheet: he could smell Kate's perfume on the pillow where she had been sleeping just a few minutes before. The mattress was hard and springy, and Josh could feel the bruises and cuts along his body suddenly start to ache and quiver with pain. His feet were blistered and tired from the long walk, and the sweat was clinging to every inch of his skin.

Give me a can of Special Brew and I'll fit right in underneath any set of arches in London.

The flannel felt wet and cool against the side of his leg. Josh glanced up. Kate had already unpeeled the torn bandage, exposing the wound. The flesh was twisted and charred, the hole that the bullet had made in its surface still clearly visible. The blood had dribbled down his leg, drying into the hairs to make a thin, crimson crust. Kate poured some disinfectant onto her cloth, rubbing it into the skin. As she did so, the nerve endings rebelled in pain, jabs of agony rolling up through his body. Then the pain subsided throughout him, to be replaced by a tingling sensation as if a mild current of electricity had just passed through him.

'That hurts, doesn't it?' said Kate.

Josh wasn't sure if she was worried or amused. 'I can handle it,' he answered.

She was leaning across him, applying more

152

disinfectant to his leg. He could feel her red hair brushing across his chest, tickling him. With only the towel covering her body, her legs were naked and he could feel her skin brushing against his.

He looked up, their gazes making contact.

He paused, allowing his gaze to linger on her for a fraction longer, then reached up with his hand to run his fingers through her hair. It was soft, and immaculately combed. He could hear the small murmur of pleasure escape from her mouth as his hands started to caress her scalp.

His head jerked upwards and he kissed her on the lips.

For a fraction of a second, it was as if nothing had happened. Kate's lips were motionless next to his, and her breathing was calm. Then, like a car with the accelerator jammed down hard, she started to react. Her tongue flicked out to meet his, and her arms slid down across his chest. Her body was smothering him now, her hips grinding into his groin. Josh reached up, untying the simple knot that held her towel in place, releasing her breasts. He held them between his hands, flicking at her nipples with the tip of his tongue, then running his hands down her arched back.

'I think there's something in the medical guidelines about fucking the patients,' she said, a giggle playing in her voice.

'What does it say?'

Her tongue ran down the side of his chest. 'Only if they're cute.'

Josh rolled Kate over on her back. The sex that followed was tender, yet satisfying. She responded to each touch and caress, guiding him towards the zones of her body that would deliver the fastest

153

pleasure: Josh was surprised by how quickly their bodies locked together, as if they had been preparing for this for weeks.

Afterwards, she lay on his chest. Josh could feel her heart thumping against his skin. 'You don't live here, do you?' he said. 'Not all the time.'

'For now, I'm here,' said Kate.

Her voice was tired, uninterested.

'This is not for you, Kate,' said Josh. 'It's a wilderness out here. Your husband's dead, you have to move on.'

She smiled at him. 'Maybe that's what I've just done.'

'Then move out.'

Kate closed his lips with the fingers of her right hand. 'You're not well,' she said. 'You need to sleep.'

At the side of the bed, Josh could see Kate holding a syringe between her fingers. Dawn was breaking through the window: a shaft of orange light was streaming into the room. The needle glistened. 'I don't need it,' said Josh. 'I'll be fine.'

Before he could even finish the sentence, the needle had pierced the skin of his arm and the pale liquid inside the syringe had already shot into his bloodstream. Josh could feel himself starting to grow drowsier.

'I'm your doctor,' said Kate softly. 'If I say you need it, then you need it.'

Josh struggled to keep his eyes open, but sleep was catching up on him fast, forcing him down. As his eyes shut, he could see something. A desert. A rock. A boy shouting, then another one speaking. At him.

Luke. And Ben.

He struggled to hold on to the image. But sleep had already overwhelmed him.

TEN

Tuesday, June 9th. Morning.
Even though his eyes were still closed, Josh could feel the first rays of dawn pressing against them. He squeezed his eyelids shut, maintaining the darkness for a few more moments. An image was playing through his head. A man in some kind of uniform, shouting something. A concrete room. He closed his eyes tighter, trying to empty his mind of every other sensation, pouring all his energy into focusing on the memory. The man was tearing a picture from a wall, shouting at Josh as he did so. But the words were impossible to make out, nor could Josh even be certain that it was him that was being shouted at.

What the hell does that mean?

A noise.

Josh woke up with a start. He looked around anxiously. The room was unfamiliar. It was only when he smelled Kate's perfume on the crumpled sheets that he remembered where he was and what had happened. That scent? *What was its name?*

Josh yawned, stretched, and pulled himself up. The morning air was cool and fresh. At his side, Kate was still asleep: her red hair had fallen across her face. From the slow movement of her lips, he could tell that it would be a while before she woke. He dipped his head and brushed his lips against her forehead, planting a small kiss on her cool skin.

155

If it weren't for you, I'd be dead, he reminded himself.

Walking through to the kitchen, he started boiling some water. There was no sign of Marshall in the house.

Kate had dressed his neck wound last night, using some pure alcohol that Marshall had stored in the house: whether it was for drinking or medical emergencies, Josh couldn't be sure. Probably both. It stung like hell as she rubbed it into the thick scab running across the side of his neck. But by the time she covered it again with a smaller bandage it felt better: the skin didn't itch so much, and he could move his neck without pain running down into his spine.

The leg is strong enough to walk on, if not run. And the neck is starting to heal, Josh thought.

But still no more than the occasional flicker of a memory.

Josh took another sip of his coffee, watching the sun rise over the horizon: the reddish landscape of the rocks and the earth blended into the dawn's rays to turn the world orange. Like I've landed on another planet, thought Josh.

I wonder what kind of family I have? A wife? Children, maybe. I must have a mum and dad, everyone's got one of those. A home town. Places that I recognise, and people that I know. But am I ever going to see them again? *And if I do, will I even know them?*

No mind games, Josh told himself. Pull yourself together, man. *There's work to be done.*

Josh poured an extra cup of coffee, and walked across to the bedroom. Kate had rolled over, her hand resting across her face, and he could see her breasts gently rising and falling as she breathed. He put his hand on her shoulder, giving it a shake.

'Coffee in bed,' he said with a bright smile. 'And there's beans for breakfast.'

Kate rose gently, sitting forward. Her eyes were still sleepy. 'What's the plan? she asked.

Josh hesitated. He'd been turning the same question over in his mind. 'Luke's mother,' he said. 'That's the only lead we've got.'

*   *   *

Music was blasting from the house, the volume turned way up high. Josh leaned forwards in the car, trying to get a closer look. One car in the driveway. No lights on. The chances were that Emily Marsden was alone.

'Shall we go inside?' asked Kate.

Josh nodded, climbing out of the red Ford Mustang. It was getting close to lunchtime, and the sun was already scorching. The building was just one storey, made from rough stone and with a roof that was a mixture of tin and slate. At the back was a yard, a hundred feet long and fifty feet wide. One section of the wall had broken down, and some shrubs were growing between the stones. If you couldn't hear the music, thought Josh to himself, you might think the place was a deserted ruin.

The volume of the music increased as they walked together down the pebbled path that led towards the main drive.

'Dogs begin to bark and hounds begin to howl/Watch out, strange cat people/Little red rooster's on the prowl,' went the song.

Josh paused. I know that song, he thought.

Suddenly he could see a picture in his mind. A house. Somewhere in England, he felt sure of that. A woman, with dark hair and a shapely figure. A girl. Aged two, maybe three, a dummy in her mouth.

'If you see my little red rooster/Please drive him home/Ain't had no peace in the farmyard/Since my little red rooster's been gone,' continued the song, the growing voice delivering the words over a solid drum and guitar backbeat.

The woman was saying something to Josh. The girl was crying. She was looking for her dummy. Josh was trying to comfort her.

A silence. The song had ended, and the next track on the album hadn't started yet. As the music faded, so did the memory, disappearing back into the recesses of Josh's mind.

That girl, wondered Josh. Was she mine?

'The singer?' asked Josh. 'You recognise it?

Kate laughed. 'You really *have* lost your memory, haven't you?'

'Who is it?' asked Josh angrily.

'The Rolling Stones,' said Kate. ' "Little Red Rooster." From the *Rolling Stones Now* album, which came out in 1965, I think. Before either of us was born, anyway.'

Josh nodded. I'll buy it if I can find a copy, he decided. It's sparking memories. Maybe I used to be a Stones fan? There are worse things. Elton John sounded familiar, but not in a good way.

He rang the doorbell, waited for a moment to see if there was a reply, then rang again. The next track—'Surprise, Surprise'—had already started up, the strumming guitars blasting out of the speakers so loud, that the mortar between the bricks seemed to be shaking. Josh rang again then knocked. Nothing. No good, he told himself. You can't hear yourself thinking above this music. *You certainly can't hear the doorbell.*

The door swung open as Josh pushed against it. The hallway was high and dark, with a sofa along one side and two bikes propped up against a wall. Kate followed as Josh stepped inside. Two rooms led off the hallway, and there was a staircase at the back of the building. The music was coming from behind the door on the left-hand side. He pushed it open and stepped forwards.

A woman was standing in the centre of the room. Approaching fifty, she had streaked blonde hair, a thin, wiry frame, and a face that had once been pretty but which had succumbed to the ravages of time and exhaustion. Too much drinking had left thick creases embedded in the skin of her face. Light was streaming down from the two high windows, filling the room which was furnished with two old sofas, both with oriental drapes thrown across them. There was a huge tapestry on one wall, and a mural on another. At the back of the room there was an expensive-looking NAD hi-fi system, the only bit of kit in the room that looked as if it had cost more than a few dollars in a junk store.

The woman turned slowly around, her hips still swaying to the music. Josh saw that she was holding a shotgun, pointed straight at his chest. 'Get the fuck out of my goddam house,' she said.

Josh raised his hands in the air. He sensed that he'd looked down plenty of gun barrels in his life.

You developed an instinct for who was going to pull the trigger and who wasn't. This woman

159

wasn't. *There's a certain look in their eye that people get just before they are about to shoot you, and she didn't have it.*

'You must be Emily,' he said, trying to make his tone as relaxed and friendly as possible.

She stayed silent.

Did she hear me? wondered Josh. He walked slowly towards the back of the room, keeping his hands in the air. Then he flicked down the volume dial on the NAD until the music was just a murmur. Suddenly he could hear himself think again.

'You must be Emily,' he repeated.

Emily laughed. 'In this country, you can shoot a man for turning down your music.'

'Shoot him twice if it's the Stones?' said Josh with a grin. He walked slowly towards her until the gun barrel was only inches from his chest. 'My name's Josh. This is Kate.'

The gun held steady. 'What do you want?'

'Some dope,' said Josh. 'Heard from some friends of ours that this was the best place to get some.'

Emily Marsden lowered the gun, tossing it back on the sofa. Josh flinched. She didn't appear to have any idea how easy it was to fire a shotgun accidentally. 'What kind of accent is that? English?'

'English.'

'Long way to come for some weed.'

'I heard that you grow the best.'

Emily smiled. 'Ain't that the truth. You and your honey take the weight off your feet and I'll go get you some.'

As she left the room, Josh sat down on one of the sofas. Now he noticed that there was a smell of bourbon, dope and perfume in the air: a pleasant

160

enough mixture of scents, but one that made you feel drowsy. He looked towards Kate, noting the suspicion in her eyes. 'Let me do the talking,' he said. 'Just pretend to be my girlfriend.'

Emily walked back into the room, carrying a pouch with a few leaves in it. She took out a pack of tobacco and some Rizla papers, and started rolling a joint. Her fingers worked quickly, Josh noted. She didn't even need to look down. 'Here,' she said, handing across a thick spliff after she'd lit it. 'Try before you buy, that's my policy.'

Josh took a hit of the smoke, letting it fill his lungs. He had a vague memory that it worked pretty well as a painkiller as well as whatever else it was supposed to do. *I could use some of that.*

'Good stuff,' he said.

Emily smiled. 'It's good country for growing any kind of hot-weather plant up here. Just so long as you water it enough. Never rains around here. Hasn't rained for five years now.'

Josh took another drag on the joint, then passed it across to Kate. *Not too much, he warned himself. You don't want to lose your concentration.*

'Here, you try it, honey,' he said.

He looked back at Emily. 'Put whatever fifty dollars will buy me into a bag.'

On the next sofa, he could see Kate sitting back, taking three long hits on the joint in a row before passing it back to Emily. The room was suddenly filled with smoke. 'I heard about your boy Luke,' said Josh, still looking at Emily. 'I'm sorry.'

She started rubbing an eye, and Josh could suddenly see how bloodshot it was. She held the joint between her left index finger and her thumb but her hand was starting to tremble and the tip of

161

the ash tumbled onto the floor. She looked first at Kate, then at Josh. 'It's been nine days now since I heard from him, nine whole days,' she said, her voice fragile and shaky. 'Luke's not like that. He was wild sometimes, the way young boys are. Difficult. But hell, we're close, real close. He'd never go that long without contacting me. He'd know how much I was worrying about him.' She paused, sucking at the joint like it was an oxygen tank and she'd just emerged from being held underwater. 'Not unless something happened to him.'

'We might be able to help,' said Josh.

A look of fear suddenly passed across Emily's face. 'You're not the Feds, are you?' she said, her voice quivering with anxiety. 'I don't grow a lot of dope, you know. Just a bit for myself. And to give to my friends.'

'We're not police,' said Kate.

'Then who the hell are you?'

Josh could see that she was eyeing the shotgun again. 'I saw something,' he said.

There was a silence. Josh could see Emily taking another drag on the joint, her lips trembling. 'You saw Luke?' she said. 'Tell me you saw Luke. Tell me he's okay.'

'I don't know what I saw, not exactly,' said Josh. 'I can't even tell you who I am. But I saw *something*.'

'What the hell are you talking about?' said Emily angrily. 'Either you saw something or you didn't.'

Kate leaned forward in her chair. 'Josh has lost his memory, but he was there when Ben got shot. He got shot at the same time, that's why he's injured.'

'I saw Ben, and I think I saw Luke running away.

162

I don't know what I was doing there, but I think I was involved in some way.'

Emily waved her spliff in the air, spilling more ash onto the carpet. 'Christ, you've been smoking even more of this stuff than I have.'

Kate reached out, trying to hold on to her hand, but Emily snatched it away suspiciously. 'Luke's in some kind of danger, that's obvious,' Kate said. 'The police are going to lose interest in a couple of days. Teenage boy runs away, there's nothing to interest them there. We're the only people who are going to help you.'

'How do I know you didn't kill him?' said Emily. 'How do I know you didn't kill Ben as well?' She paused. 'You both look pretty fucking weird to me.'

Maybe she's right, thought Josh. Christ, I don't even know myself. *Maybe I did kill Ben.*

'Listen, I'll tell you what I know, then you can make up your own mind whether to help us or not,' said Josh. 'I'm British. Some kind of soldier or agent, I think. I figure I was on a mission, and that led me to track Ben and Luke. Then Ben got shot, and so did I. Luke escaped, I'm sure of it. I saw him running.'

'An agent,' said Emily, laughing bitterly. 'Like James damned Bond or something?' She waved her spliff at him. 'I'm not growing this any more.'

'No, think, Emily,' said Josh, his tone turning even more serious. 'Your son's life could be at stake here.'

'I know that—and I'm supposed to waste my time listening to some dope-head who walks into my house and starts talking this kind of shit?'

'You got a better explanation, let's hear it,' said Josh. 'Listen, Ben and Luke disappeared nine days

163

ago. Seven days ago Ben got shot. They'd already gone two days by the time that happened and they were ninety miles away. What do you think happened?'

Now a tear was rolling down Emily's face. 'You said you were there?'

Josh nodded.

'Bullshit.'

Josh closed his eyes, and rolled his head back. 'Limp Bizkit,' he said. 'Does Luke like that band?'

'Thrash-metal crap.'

'His T-shirt,' said Josh. 'He was wearing a Limp Bizkit '02 tour T-shirt. And I reckon it was an extra-large because it was way too big for him.'

'You saw that on TV,' said Emily.

'It hasn't been on TV,' said Kate. 'They've been showing an old high-school picture of Luke.'

'What was he wearing the day he left?' asked Josh.

'The T-shirt,' said Emily. 'The Limp Bizkit T-shirt. Christ, you really *were* there.' She looked hard at Josh. 'Is he okay? Tell me he's okay.'

'He ran, I know that much,' said Josh. 'I can't tell you where he is now, or whether he's still alive, because I just don't know.' He looked hard at Emily. 'But I don't think Luke was just some teenager who went on the run for a few days with his mate because he was a bit bored. I think he was mixed up with something. And I think I was mixed up in it as well.'

'The trouble is, we don't know what the hell it was,' said Kate.

'That's why we'd like you to help us,' said Josh. 'We need to know what Luke was involved with.'

Emily remained silent.

164

'What was it?' persisted Josh. 'What was Luke involved with?'

Emily still remained silent, her stare fixed on the floor.

'We're the only people who are going to help you, Emily,' interrupted Kate. 'The *only* people.'

Emily walked across to the window, looking out as if she was searching for something in the empty, scorched landscape that lay around the house. The sunlight streamed though her hair, making it look almost white. Her lips started to move, but no sound emerged.

'Luke might still be in danger,' said Josh.

Emily nodded. She turned around so that the sun was now behind her. Josh noticed how pale she looked, as if all the blood had suddenly been emptied from her veins. 'Hacking,' she said. 'Luke was into hacking.'

She walked back across the room. 'He and Ben, they used to go up to his room and play around on their computers for hours and hours. I didn't know much about what they were doing. Myself, I can't even turn the damned things on. But they got into trouble for it at school, after they changed everyone's grades on the school computer. I told them to stop.' She shrugged. 'But how are you to stop a boy playing around on his computer? And anyway, it seems pretty harmless. Better than running wild, shooting guns and riding bikes. That's what all the other boys around here do.'

'So you think the hacking might have been what got him into trouble?'

Emily sat down on the sofa. She folded her arms on her lap. For the first time since Kate and Josh had come into the room, she seemed to be unwinding: it was as if she had decided to trust them, and that was relaxing her.

'About three months ago, Luke started talking about how we wouldn't have to live in this old shack any more,' she started. 'It's always been tough for us financially. I do some waitressing and I grow some dope. Neither of those professions pays very well, as you probably know. We get by, that's the best you can say. Luke started telling me that soon we wouldn't have to worry about money any more, that everything was going to be okay. We could buy a big car, a house in California, maybe another one down in Jamaica. He was getting into reggae.'

Emily reached across the sofa and rolled herself a cigarette, one with just tobacco in it this time. A thin stream of smoke blew out of her nostrils. 'I just humoured him. Yes, yes, Luke, I used to say. I'm looking forward to it. Buy me an SUV as well. One of those big Mercedes ones, or maybe a Lexus. Something fancy. Then he used to get cross, and start telling me that he really *was* going to make a lot of money, that he was doing something on his computer that was going to make him a fortune.'

Emily jabbed the cigarette in the air, her tone turning darker. 'Then he disappeared. And I can't help thinking that maybe he was doing something on his computer. Something that got him into trouble.'

'Have you told the police about this?' asked Josh.

Emily shook her head. 'I don't want to get him into even worse trouble. I mean, if he was doing something on his computer, it probably wasn't legal. But they knew he was into hacking because of what happened at school. And they took his

166

computer away for examination.'

'And you have no idea what he might be doing?' asked Josh.

'Like I said, I didn't take much notice of it at the time. Just boy's talk. Bravado. It was only after he disappeared that I started to think there might be something to it.'

'He never mentioned any websites he was visiting, nothing like that?'

Emily stubbed out her cigarette. Her expression was thoughtful, as if she was weighing different options. 'No,' she said finally. 'But he had *two* computers. The police took his desktop, the one up in his room. But Luke had a laptop, the one he used to take around to Ben's house. That's the one he mainly worked on, I think. The desktop was just for playing games and stuff.'

'And the police didn't take that one?'

'I didn't tell them about it.'

There was a silence. Some cigarette smoke was drifting through the air. Josh knew what question he wanted to ask next, but decided to pause before pressing it. Better to wait, he told himself. She knows the question. *She just doesn't know the answer yet.*

'You said you were a soldier?' she asked. 'That you might have been looking for Luke?'

Josh nodded. 'I'm not going to kid around—I don't know who I am. But I think I was involved with Luke. I think he's out there somewhere. And I'm going to try and find him.'

'You want his laptop?' said Emily. 'You think that might help?'

'If there's something on it, we'll find it,' said Josh.

'Follow me,' said Emily.

167

She stood up and walked out of the room. Josh followed closely behind, with Kate beside him. He could feel his heart thumping inside his chest. This was the first real breakthrough: if they could find out what Luke had been hacking into, they would have unlocked a door.

Slowly, the jigsaw of who I am is about to be reassembled.

The midday sun was frying the scrubland outside the house. At least forty, Josh judged as he stepped out of the building. Emily's house was on an open stretch of plain, at least twenty miles from any hills, in a dip in the land: the heat gathered up each last atom of moisture, sweating it out of every grain of dust.

Boiling hot scrub. *After the Gobi Desert this must be the cheapest real estate in the world.*

The barn was just a shack, with some farm equipment that looked as if it dated from the 1930s rusting inside. A trailer was slung onto the back of a tractor, with a tarpaulin sheet stretched across it. Emily pulled it aside, taking out a sleek black Dell Inspiron. 'Here,' she said. 'This is what he used.'

Josh took the laptop under his arm. 'We'll bring it back,' he said.

'I don't care if you bring it back or not,' Emily snapped. 'Bring *Luke* back—that's what I want.'

'I'll try,' said Josh.

Emily turned around and started to walk back towards the house.

'One other question,' said Josh. 'Who's Luke's dad?'

Emily looked startled. 'His dad?'

Josh nodded. Sometimes you asked a question without being quite sure why, or what the answer

168

might be. When you are stuck in the middle of a mystery, you have to examine every angle. Otherwise, you'll never find the way out. 'If something has happened to Luke, maybe his father was involved somewhere along the line,' said Josh. 'Who was he?'

Emily looked at him contemptuously. 'It doesn't matter,' she snapped. 'That's private.'

Josh turned around. No point pressing, he realised. He was clearly stepping into dangerous territory. 'Well, if you ever think it might be relevant, get in touch.'

'Just bring him back,' said Emily. 'I just want him back with me, that's all.'

ELEVEN

Tuesday, June 9th. Midday.
The coffee was steaming in a pot in the centre of the table. Josh took a long drink of the thick black liquid, refilling the cup as soon as he had drained it. The coffee washed down his throat, gradually sweeping away the tiredness that the dope he'd smoked at Emily's house had left in his system. He glanced out at the sweeping, empty scrubland. The sun was beating down, scorching the life out of everything beneath it, but a stronger wind was blowing today, sending vicious swirls of dust spinning up through the boulders, and clumps of weeds rolling along the ground.

'We are the pilgrims, master/We shall go always a little further.'

Josh spun around. Marshall was standing in the

169

doorway, a bottle of beer in his hand.

'Recognise it?' he asked, stepping forward into the room.

Josh shook his head. 'No,' he replied.

That wasn't quite true, he told himself. As he'd heard the words recited *something* had stirred within his mind. A shadowy memory of a long, concrete room. A barracks. Some men standing around. Another man shouting. A rainstorm.

They were just fleeting, disjointed images. You couldn't piece them together. *They didn't make any sense.*

'What is it?' Josh asked.

'The SAS,' answered Marshall. 'The Regiment's poem. You sure it didn't stir anything?'

'Maybe something,' said Josh.

'Then that's who you are,' said Marshall. 'British special forces—I was right.' He walked up to the front door, opened it and stepped outside. 'Heard you had quite an adventure with my two friends.'

Josh nodded.

'You know how to handle yourself.'

'I'm still alive.'

'You can't stay here,' said Marshall. 'There's going to be deputies crawling all over the county by the end of the day.'

'Don't worry, daddy, we're going,' Kate interrupted.

Marshall looked at Kate and nodded. She looked different this afternoon, Josh noted. Calmer, more relaxed. Her skin was shining, and although she was trying to disguise it, there was the hint of a smile in her eyes. Josh wasn't sure what was behind it, but he hoped that Marshall wouldn't notice.

'Where?' said Marshall.

170

Kate placed a laptop down on the kitchen table. 'To find out what's on this. It belonged to Luke, that boy.'

'You got anyone who can help us with this?' asked Josh, the question directed at Marshall.

The older man nodded, raking a finger through his grey hair. 'I know the guy you need. Lives up in Utah. About two hundred miles north of here. Goes by the name of Kessler.' He paused, as if searching around for something in his memory. 'Sam Kessler.'

'You think he will help us?' Kate asked.

'If I tell him he has to he will,' snapped Marshall.

'Then I'll pack a bag,' said Kate. 'We're leaving.'

Josh dug deep into the pocket at the back of his jeans. The previous pair was still stained with his blood, but he had borrowed another pair of Marshall's: at this rate, Josh noted, the older guy wasn't going to have much left in his wardrobe. He pulled out two pictures. They were creased and smudged, but still recognisable. They were stills from the video clips that Madge had given him yesterday, showing the leader of the group of men who had broken into the Motel 6. Josh felt sure that the men had been looking for him.

'This guy,' said Josh, his finger jabbing down at the table as he pointed at the man. 'Any chance that you or one of your friends might know who he is?'

Marshall picked up the photograph, scrutinising the man portrayed there. 'Ugly-looking mother.'

'It would be better if I could find him before he finds me,' said Josh.

'And what makes you think that I might know him?' There was a dangerous look on Marshall's

171

face, Josh realised. His stare was boring into him like a drill. For a moment, he wondered whether Marshall had heard him slipping into Kate's bedroom last night.

'I didn't say that—I only asked if you might know who he was—but you seem pretty well connected around here,' Josh replied.

A smile broke out on Marshall's face, as if Josh was the funniest guy he'd ever met. 'You catch on quick.' He picked up the pictures, folded them, and tucked them into the breast pocket of his denim shirt. 'I'll see what I can do,' he said. 'Call me. I'll let you know if I discover anything.'

*   *   *

The road twisted down to the ranch house through a steep valley. It was no more than a dirt track, pitted with holes, and the suspension of the Mustang clattered as it bounced down the hill. 'Think he'll be pleased to see us?' said Josh.

'No,' replied Kate, with a curt shake of her head.

Josh looked out from the car. On one side the hills rose up towards the sky, but on the other side a flat plain stretched out for several miles. A river trickled along near the horizon: at this stage of the summer, it had dried to just a few inches of water. He could just make out some trees growing in a thicket about a mile away. A pack of semi-wild horses were watering themselves by the river. Otherwise, it was just grassland and scrub. There was not another building anywhere in sight.

This is about as remote as you can get within a civilised country. A good place to hide.

The house was just one storey, made from wood.

A porch ran along its entire front. To the right there was a giant set of solar panels and to the left a fifteen-foot satellite dish pointed up to the sky. Electricity and TV, noted Josh. All a man needs to survive.

He hopped out of the car and walked towards the door. It was just after five in the evening, and the heat of the day was starting to ebb. From Ferndale, it had taken them four hours straight to drive here, heading due north up through Arizona, crossing over the state line into Utah, and turning due east, crossing another fifty miles until they hit Kanab, the closest town to the ranch house.

'Are you Sam Kessler?' said Josh to the man who opened the door.

The man nodded. To Josh, he looked at least fifty, with a face that bore the scars of a difficult life. His hair was black but had thick streaks of grey running through it. He wore it long, tumbling down over his neck, and he had a thick moustache that almost hid his mouth. His eyes were round, set close to his nose, and his jaw was thick with folds of fat.

'You're Marshall's friend?' said Kessler.

Josh nodded.

'Then you better come in.'

Marshall had only given Josh the sketchiest outline of Kessler, and of how he'd come to know him. He'd been in Vietnam, but had then made a career for himself in computers, working for the big companies in Silicon Valley across in California, until a decade ago he'd moved out to this decaying horse ranch in Utah. He lived by himself—his wife hadn't thought much of the wilderness and had moved back to California after a couple of years—

and supported himself by freelancing as a computer-security consultant. If local companies wanted someone to make their systems secure, Kessler was the man they turned to. 'If anyone can find anything on that computer, Kessler can,' Marshall had said to them just before they'd left.

'I'm grateful for your time,' said Josh, stepping into the hallway.

Inside, the hall had stone flooring and wooden walls. It was decorated with riding ornaments: saddles, stirrups, horseshoes and whips. Kessler led them through into the kitchen. There was no offer of coffee or even a glass of water: Josh decided that asking would be a mistake.

'Where's the kit?' said Kessler.

Kate took the laptop from its bag, putting it down on the table. Kessler glanced down, then raised an eyebrow. 'What's the problem?'

'It's empty,' said Josh. 'All the files have been erased.'

Kessler sat down at the table. He flipped open the laptop, switched it on and looked at the screen. 'Maybe there's nothing there,' he said. 'Maybe somebody just bought it.'

Josh sat down at the other side of the table. 'No, there was definitely something there,' he said firmly. 'I think they deleted the files.'

'Who did it belong to?'

Kessler's stare shot up to meet Josh's as he posed the question.

'That doesn't matter,' said Kate quickly.

'It matters to me,' said Kessler. 'In my experience, computers are kind of personal. People don't like other people fishing around in their kit, the same way they don't like them breaking into

174

their houses—or screwing their wives.'

Josh glanced at Kate then back towards Kessler. 'That doesn't matter,' he snapped. 'The guy this machine belonged to won't mind you looking at it. We're trying to help him.' Josh paused. 'Trust me.'

'Trust you?' Kessler laughed. 'I've only just met you—how the hell am I going to trust you?'

Josh reached out for the laptop, snapping its cover shut. 'If you don't want to help us, that's fine. We're sorry to have wasted your time.' He started to lift himself from the seat.

'I'll tell Marshall that you weren't able to do anything for us.'

Kessler raised his hand. 'I'll look at it,' he said wearily. 'Give me a couple of days. I'll tell you if I can find anything.'

Josh placed the laptop back down on the table. 'Two days is too long,' he said. 'I need it done now. We can wait here while you take a look at it.'

'I work on my own terms or not at all,' said Kessler. 'I'll get to you as fast as I can. But this isn't Hackers-While-U-Wait. Take it or leave it.'

'I'll take it,' said Josh. 'Thanks.'

Kessler took back the laptop and put it on the side of the table. 'I'm going to give you a cellphone,' he said. 'It's a secure line. All traces of who it belonged to have been erased, and I'm the only person who has the number. Any message transmitted through it can't be traced. I'll call you on that when I'm ready.'

Josh nodded. Kessler was clearly a man who had plenty of clients who liked to keep their business very secret. 'Just make it as fast as possible,' he said. 'We'll be waiting to hear from you.'

Josh handed over two twenty-dollar bills to the clerk at the gas station, and waited for his change. He glanced out towards Kate who was sitting waiting for him in the Mustang. The sun was setting but the air was still hot and dry, and Josh added a couple of bottles of cold Coke and some biscuits to his purchases.

We're getting closer, he told himself. I can smell it. I may not know who I am yet but I know about endgames. *And this one is starting to come together.*

'You got a phone?' he asked the clerk.

'Out back, by the toilets,' said the clerk, handing across the change.

Josh started walking to the back of the gas station. An image was flashing through his mind. O'Brien, Morant and himself attacking an FBI agent as he stood at a urinal. Step carefully, he told himself. You don't want to get coshed while you're making a call of nature.

He fed fifty cents into the phone's coin box, checking the surrounding area as he did so. So far as he could see, it was empty. They had taken a back road through Utah back into Arizona, keeping clear of the Interstate in case there were any police checks at the state or county boundaries. The road was empty. Even at the gas stations there were only a few customers.

Marshall picked up the phone after a couple of rings. 'Kate with you?' he said as soon as Josh said hello.

'Yup, she's fine,' said Josh.

'Kessler helping you?'

'Reluctantly,' said Josh. 'What do you have on

him?'

'Doesn't matter,' said Marshall. 'He helped, didn't he? That's all that counts.'

True enough, Josh reckoned. 'Any leads on the man in the picture?'

Josh felt certain that if Marshall could identify the man in the picture that he'd given him, then that would be another lead.

Something in the drawn-out silence that followed his question suggested to Josh that he was going to be told something, but not everything. With Marshall, he never felt he was getting more than half the story.

'I reckon it's a guy called Jim Flatner,' said Marshall eventually.

'Who's he?'

Another pause, while Marshall seemed to weigh up how much to say. 'He's a biker.'

'I figured that from his clothes,' said Josh. 'Either that or he's some old queen who likes to dress up in leather.'

Marshall chuckled. 'He hangs out in the empty country, about twenty miles east of Scottsdale. There's about thirty of them living out in the mountains. Mostly men, but there are a few girls there as well. A few kids, too. It's kind of an alternative community.'

'What do they do?'

'Anything that pays,' said Marshall. 'Some drug dealing. Fencing stolen goods. That kind of thing. They try not to bother the local community, and the locals stay out of their way.'

'They were looking for me,' said Josh. 'I'm sure of it.'

'I think you can be twice as sure now.'

Josh gripped the phone tighter in his hands. He looked out across the forecourt of the station. Kate had climbed out of the car, and was walking up and down impatiently. A truck had pulled up, filling up its tank with diesel. 'Why?'

'Your friend Madge,' said Marshall. 'She's dead.'

Josh paused. An image of the girl lying in his arms was playing out in his mind: the way she was just a few days ago, when she was full of passion and life. 'What the hell happened?'

'There was a story on the local news,' said Marshall. 'Said she killed herself. Threw herself off a bridge in Boisdale.'

'That's a lie.'

Marshall chuckled again. 'Probably the oldest lie the police ever heard.'

'I was with her just couple of days ago,' continued Josh, glancing at Kate. 'She wasn't the kind of girl who kills herself. She had no reason to, and even if she had she wouldn't do it. She just wasn't the type.' Josh paused. 'Somebody killed her. And if they killed her, they'll want to kill me as well.'

Josh started walking back towards the car. Why the hell would anyone want to kill Madge? he wondered to himself. Christ, it must have been because she was in touch with me. I told her that if she found out anything more, then she should get in touch with me at Marshall's house.

He could feel his stomach churning with guilt. Just that tiny sliver of information cost the girl her life.

Could those bikers be working for the Feds? No, that doesn't make any sense. Then who? Who the hell are they and what do they want? What can I possibly have known that was worth all this?

Josh made a decision. He didn't want to just hang around and wait for Kessler to come up with something. Find those bikers—and find out who they are working for, he told himself.

* * *

A fire was burning down in the camp. Josh held the binoculars to his eyes, scanning the tiny community. From his vantage point high up in the hills, he could count about fifteen homes. They were made from wood, canvas and corrugated iron: rough, shanty-town shelters that could be taken down as quickly as they had been thrown up.

He turned towards Kate. 'You reckon he's down there somewhere?'

She nodded. 'This is his territory,' she said. 'It's only a few square miles of desert, but Marshall says Flatner rules it like some medieval warlord.'

After hearing of Madge's death, they had driven straight into the mountains where Marshall said the bikers had their camp, stopping only once at a gas station to grab a pair of microwaved burgers. Josh sensed that there was little time for delay. The conspiracy was closing in on them fast. If they'd found Madge, soon they would find both him and Kate. And it might be sooner than they knew.

Take the fight to the enemy. I don't know where the hell I remember that from, but it was good advice.

They'd parked the Mustang three miles away, and had covered the rest of the distance on foot. It was too dangerous to approach the camp in a car. There was only one dirt track leading up through the mountains, and Josh had to assume that it was watched. The bikers could have posted lookouts.

179

Or they could have rigged it up with electronic sensors. It didn't matter which. Either way, Josh had to assume that it was under surveillance. They would certainly detect a car.

The trek had been a long and hard one. The first mile was fine, but after that the country had started to rise sharply upwards, and Josh had found the ground heavy going. They had stopped on the way to pick up some supplies from a gas station: four litres of water, some tinned beans, bacon and biscuits, and some matches, plus a couple of cheap plastic rucksacks to sling their kit over their backs. The weight of the gear was making the going tougher. Josh could tell that his leg was still far from healed: there was nothing he could do about the damage inflicted on his muscles, however. Recuperation will have to wait, he told himself. Right now, the best I can hope for is to stay alive.

Josh folded away his binoculars and put them back in his pocket. He'd seen a fire at the centre of the camp, and he could see some men sitting around, smoking joints and drinking beer. But at this distance, and in this darkness, it was impossible to get a clear line on any of their faces. 'We won't see anything tonight,' he said. 'Too late and too dark.'

'And what are you hoping to find exactly, Josh?' said Kate.

He turned to face her. Not for the first time in the few days that they had spent together, he found himself wondering what was driving her on. At times she was considerate, at others angry, sometimes helpful, and sometimes just difficult. Maybe I've forgotten what women are like, he wondered to himself. *Maybe I never knew.*

'The key,' he said. 'My memory is there somewhere, I know it. I get glimpses. All I need is something to unlock it all.'

'And you think that it might be here?'

Josh shook his head. 'I won't know it until I find it,' he replied.

Kate had started unfurling the cloth that they had picked up along with the rest of their supplies. It looked like a picnic rug, with a plastic sheet on one side. The mountainside was rising above them, with the valley and the camp stretched out down below. They were about halfway up on a steep incline, with a set of boulders shielding their position from anyone looking up from the camp. Josh broke out some biscuits and a bottle of water, and went to lie next to Kate on the rug.

'I'm frightened, Josh.'

He put his arm around her, grateful for the warmth of her skin next to his. The exhaustion of the day had seeped into every bruised limb: the wound on his leg was weeping with pain and his brain was spinning as he tried to make sense of everything that had happened in the past few days.

The same question played itself, over and over, like a tape stuck in a loop. *What can I have done that this many people want me dead?*

Kate was running her lips down the side of his neck. He pulled her tighter against him, aware of her breath on his skin. He started to roll her over onto her back, but she pushed him away playfully, pinning his arms down and slowly unbuttoning his shirt with her teeth. He reached out, glancing towards the stars, then at the magnificent mane of red hair streaming above him. Taking each button of her blouse in turn, he undressed her with the

181

same care and attention with which he would field-strip a treasured gun. As he did so, he listened to her whimpers and moans of pleasure as they disturbed the silence of the desert night.

Josh closed his eyes. Suddenly, he was startled to find another image playing in front of his eyes. Another woman was making love to him. A brunette. With long dark hair and deep brown eyes, she had skin that was smooth, supple and tanned to perfection. There was a metal stud in her belly button. And her face was sculpted as if from marble, with delicate eyes, a straight nose, high, narrow cheekbones, and a wicked, mischievous mouth.

Who is she? Josh wondered. A girlfriend. *A wife?*

'You okay, baby?' Kate whispered in his ear, as she rode him towards her own climax.

Josh shuddered, then nodded. Memory can be a dark and dangerous place, he thought. There is so little I know about myself.

Kate rolled away from him, her passion exhausted, and for a few minutes they lay still and silent, their bodies bathed by the starlight shining down on the mountains. Kate reached down for her shirt, pulling it back up over her breasts. Then she squeezed herself tight against Josh, as if looking for shelter from the cold of the night.

'You don't have to be with me,' said Josh. 'This is my fight. I can handle it on my own.'

Kate swung her head from side to side, her lips reaching up to peck at Josh's mouth. 'Now that I've found you, I'm not letting you out of my sight.'

TWELVE

Wednesday, June 10th. Dawn.
Josh struggled to shake the sleep from his eyes. He could tell that it was set to be another baking-hot day, but the night had been cold and there was still a chill in the air. His bones felt stiff from the rough ground on which Kate and he had slept, and the wound in his leg was teasing his nerves: a vicious tingling sensation was running down the main artery, shooting into his knee. It feels like a cheese grater rubbing against my skin, he reflected. *From the inside.*

'Any memories, Josh?' said Kate.

She opened a bottle of Coke and passed a plastic cup across to Josh, and he took it between his hands, letting the cola drink's caffeine sink slowly into his veins. A coffee would have been good, but it was too dangerous to light a fire up here: the smoke would reveal their position. Down below, the camp was starting to stir to life. He could see some men walking through the rows of tin and canvas shacks: big, bearlike creatures, with beards, and tattoos on their bulging forearms. A few yards from the shacks, a group of children were playing on some old tyres attached by ropes between a pair of up ended cars to make a simple swing. In the centre, he could see some women starting a fire. At least they're probably women, thought Josh. *They had longer hair, bleached blonde, and not so many tattoos.*

'Nothing,' he replied. 'It's going to be a long hard slog to get them back.'

He sat down on a boulder, using the binoculars to continue his search. 'There,' said Josh. 'That's him.'

He passed the binoculars across to Kate. Whilst she peered down at the camp, he tracked the man walking across the rough scrubland. It was Flatner, Josh felt certain of it. He was flipping open a mobile phone, and pacing around while he talked.

'Yeah, definitely,' said Kate.

'What the hell are they all doing down there?' asked Josh.

She shrugged. 'Bikers—who knows what the hell they do?' she answered. 'Most of them aren't as weird as they look. Lots of them have jobs and families and houses and stuff. They come up here for a few days, mess around with their Hondas and Yamahas, do some drugs, and trade some stolen goods.'

'Bloody funny place to do it.'

'Look to your left.'

Josh glanced to the left of the camp. He could just about see some long rows of cacti, their ground-hugging green compact bulbs broken up by strings of light purple flowers. There were different kinds of cacti growing all over the wilderness, but these looked fresher. They were arranged in straight lines. Someone was cultivating them.

'Peyote,' continued Kate. 'It grows wild along this valley. It's one of the oldest and most effective psychedelic drugs known. The desert tribes of the South-West used it. So did the Aztecs. And now the bikers as well. You get good prices for that stuff in California.'

Josh looked across at Kate. 'Do you think there might be a good electronics shop anywhere nearby?'

Now that he'd seen that they were carrying mobiles, he knew what he needed: an interceptor that would allow him to eavesdrop on their calls.

'There's a mall outside Scottsdale,' she replied. 'They've probably got one there. Why?'

'Flatner's conversations. I want to listen to them,' replied Josh. 'I want to know who he is and what he's doing.'

*   *   *

The journey was a long and arduous one. From Kate and Josh's base in the mountains, it was a three-mile walk back down to the car. At least no one had nicked the Mustang, thought Josh as he put the keys into the ignition. Next, there was a twenty-mile drive to The Village, a mall just outside Scottsdale. Josh had been wary on the road, keeping a close eye out for police patrols, and now he watched the security guards closely as they stepped inside. As soon as they arrived, he picked up some cheap plain-glass spectacles from a drugstore: they would change the shape of his face and make him harder to recognise. Then he found a public toilet and gave himself a wash. Next he made for a barber's shop to get the beard that he had been growing trimmed and his hair cut, telling the girl to give it a left parting—so that it would help him look different to any picture of him that might exist. A man who stinks of the desert, and who looks like he hasn't washed or shaved in a week stands out, he figured. Just the smell would be enough to mark you out.

'I don't know about cleanliness being next to

185

godliness, but I do know that it helps you stay in the shadows,' he pointed out to Kate as he directed her towards the hairdresser to get her own hair shampooed and blow-dried.

The electronics shop was a huge barn, filled with sockets, connections, wires and plugs. When Josh explained that he wanted an LAN receiver, the clerk sitting at the information desk had looked puzzled. 'Check your stocklist,' Josh told him sharply. Sure enough, they had a Yellowjacket in the storeroom. Eight hundred dollars, explained the clerk. Josh whistled, then started counting out the cash. The three thousand dollars in cash that he'd had on him when he was shot had already been whittled down to just a thousand bucks.

I'd better find out who I am soon, he thought to himself. *And I hope I have some sodding money in my account.*

'How does that work?' asked Kate. They were back up the mountains.

The three-mile trek from where they had concealed the Mustang had put the dust and grime back into her freshly done hair, but she still looked magnificent, thought Josh. Her eyes were burning with curiosity, and the spirit of adventure was warming her blood, bringing a glow to her cheeks.

Josh held the Yellowjacket Wireless Receiver in his hand. The device measured eighteen inches long, by ten across, and weighed just one pound. It was encased in a frame of thick black plastic, with a tiny liquid-crystal screen displaying the radio frequencies as you scrolled through them.

I know how to use this, thought Josh to himself, looking down at the receiver. I don't know where or when, but somebody taught me how to spy on

186

people. 'A cellphone transmits over a local area network to its closest base station,' he said. 'Most phones and networks are digital these days, so that makes them pretty hard to hack into unless you have access to the encryption software run by the phone company. That's enough security for the average user, although if you are really worried about it you can scramble your own calls. These guys aren't doing that.'

'So what does *this* thing do?'

'This device is a high-powered radio receiver,' said Josh, 'with a built-in digital decoder. The encryption doesn't kick in until the call reaches the base station and gets processed by the computers of the phone company. But if you can intercept the call between the cellphone and its base station, you can tune into it as if you were tuning into your local radio station. All we have to do is sit back and listen.'

Josh hunkered down behind a boulder. The Yellowjacket was lying in the sand next to him, along with a bottle of water. It was three in the afternoon now, and the sun was still hanging high above him in the sky. Even at altitude the heat was punishing. Beads of sweat were running down his back, soaking his shirt, and the air was so dry and overheated that it was scorching the back of his throat. A snake was winding its way through the boulders: a nasty-looking yellow and black creature. Josh watched it slither its way across the boulders. He held a sharp rock in his hand, ready to smash the reptile to death if it came any closer.

A man could fry to death out here. If the snakes didn't poison him first.

Using his thumb, Josh was scanning through the

187

frequencies on the Yellowjacket. Most mobile systems transmitted at between 2,300 and 2,600 megahertz, a narrow range of radio bands. Which one any particular phone was using depended on the network operator, and the amount of voice traffic that they were carrying.

The receiver locked on to a signal. Josh plugged in the earphone and started listening.

'I need an FA135,' said a voice.

'We haven't got any.'

'Where can I get some?'

'No idea, man. Try the Honda dealer in Phoenix.'

Brake pads, realised Josh. One of the bikers down in the camp was looking for some new brake pads for his Honda. He swivelled the dial, locking out that call and looking for another one.

'I can deliver you the stuff Tuesday, man. That okay?'

Josh listened intently. What stuff?

'I can handle three. Think you can get that many?'

'No way, man. Three Mercedes by this week, no way. There aren't that many Mercs to steal in the whole of fucking Arizona. I can get you a couple of Mercs, maybe a Beamer and a Ford. A nice pick-up, a Ranger, whatever.'

'Forget it. I'll take a Merc and a Beamer if you can get them, but no Fords. We can't even sell the new ones, so forget the hot mothers.'

Josh leaned back against the boulder. He took a bottle of water, putting it to his lips, letting the liquid pour down his throat, taking a couple of degrees off his body heat. Got to be careful with the water, he thought. The bikers are doing a lot of business up here in the hills. They talk a lot. *It could be a long wait.*

*   *   *

Josh pushed the earphone into his anticle, pressing the tiny lump of black plastic tight against his flesh, making sure that he caught every word. Dusk had started to fall across the valley, and there was a fire burning down in the centre of the camp. Even high up in the hills, Josh could smell the charred flesh of the animal roasting on the spit: the odours of the juices of the cooked meat were making him hungry as he nibbled his way to the bottom of the day's second packet of biscuits.

Then he sat bolt upright. The rest of the bikers, he reckoned, were just dope-heads and small-time crooks. If there was anything important happening down there, it was going to be channelled through Flatner. He was their leader.

And suddenly there was a new voice on the line. 'I want him dead Flatner,' said the voice. 'Do you understand me? Dead, as of today. And that Luke boy as well.'

'Do you hear me?' repeated the voice, its tone rising into a nasal, bullying whine. 'Dead.'

He wants who dead? Josh asked himself.

Me?

Josh fiddled with the scanner on the Yellowjacket, making sure that it stayed locked on to the call.

'We've got men roaming the area,' answered Flatner. 'We're going to nail him.'

'And the boy?' said the man.

'We're still hunting.'

'Redouble your efforts,' said the voice. 'Spend

whatever money you have to. Hire whoever you have to. The expense doesn't matter.' He paused on the line. As Josh looked down on the valley, he could see Flatner standing just outside the camp, his huge shoulders hunched upwards and his brow furrowed. 'I need both of them.'

'Understood, sir,' said Flatner. 'We're already measuring up the coffins,' he chuckled as he snapped the phone shut.

It's not often that a man gets to listen to his own death sentence, reflected Josh as he pulled the plug from his ear.

Looking down at the Yellowjacket, he started punching the dials on the device. He was working purely from instinct—he had no memory of when or where he might have received the training to do this—but he knew that it was possible to access the incoming call number. The numbers were digitally encoded, but the device slowly unpicked the code until the incoming call data was clearly described in soft green lettering on the instrument's LCD screen.

Josh looked down at the eleven digits displayed in front of him. 08732 611544.

That's the number of the man who wants to kill me. All I need to know now is his name.

He looked up at Kate. She was stretched out on the rug, dozing gently. He had been sitting there for hours waiting for the one call that would give him the breakthrough he needed.

Inside Kate's rucksack a cellphone rang.

Josh jumped, worried that even the quiet ring tone might give away their position.

'Yes?' he said.

'That Josh?'

190

Josh recognised the voice: the same gruff, unhelpful tone that he had listened to yesterday. Kessler. 'You found something?'

A pause. Even over a mobile line, Josh could see the man's face, the skin around his beard twitching as he calculated how much information he wanted to reveal. 'You bet.'

'What is it?' said Josh. 'What's on the computer?'

Another pause. *Can't you just get to the point, man?*

'We can't speak on the phone.'

'I thought you said this was a secure line.'

Kessler laughed drily. 'I'm not telling you on any kind of phone.'

'I'll come to your house, then,' said Josh. 'Tonight.'

'No way,' said Kessler quickly. 'I don't want you coming anywhere near my house.'

Christ, what's he found?

'Where, then?'

'About a mile west of Kanab, just after you cross into Utah from Arizona on Interstate 89, there's a mall called The Waterfall. In there, you'll see a Taco Bell. It's open twenty-four-hours. When can you get there?'

Josh thought for a moment, running the calculations in his head. An hour to walk back to where the car was hidden, then at least a two or three hours' drive. 'Three hours, maybe four,' he replied.

'Then I'll see you there at midnight,' said Kessler. 'Don't go inside. I'll meet you in the parking lot. Look for a yellow VW Beetle.'

'Fine, we'll be there.'

'And listen—I'm doing this as a favour for

191

Marshall,' continued Kessler. 'I'll talk to you for half an hour. After that I never want to see you again.'

THIRTEEN

Wednesday, June 10th. Midnight.
There were only two other cars in the parking lot as Josh steered the Mustang through the entrance to the Taco Bell. A pick-up truck and a new Audi. Josh killed the Mustang's engine, and leaned back in his seat. No sign of a yellow Beetle. He'd made sure they'd arrived a few minutes early so he could check that the parking lot was safe before they went in. He'd seen two cars at Kessler's ranch: a Ford and a Land Rover. *No sign of a Beetle. Maybe he's fixed himself up with a different car just for this trip. To make sure that no one can trace him.*

He's scared. *And he doesn't look like a man who scares easily.*

'Can you see him?' Josh said, glancing across to Kate.

She shook her head. 'We've still got ten minutes,' she replied. 'A computer nerd. I've got a feeling he's going to be punctual.'

'Want something to eat?'

'Hell, why not? When you drive two hundred miles to a Taco Bell you might as well treat yourself. Make it a half-pound burrito combo, with some cheesy fiesta potatoes on the side.'

She looks thin enough, thought Josh as he walked towards the counter inside the restaurant. *Not like most of the customers at Taco Bell.*

It was now ten to midnight, he noted, checking the clock on the wall. They had walked quickly down the mountainside, back to the curve of the road where they had hidden the Mustang behind a heap of boulders. The drive had been a fast one. There was little traffic at this time of night. And Josh's adrenalin was pumping furiously, pushing him forwards. *If we can crack what was on that computer, maybe I'll know what I was out here looking for.*

Returning to the car, he handed Kate her burrito and took a bite from his own Double Decker Taco. The combination of beef, flour, cheese and lettuce tasted good. Fast food is what you need on the run, he reflected. *Constant hits of sugary, over-flavoured food to keep your energy levels up.*

Just then, the Beetle drove into the parking lot. Josh and Kate climbed out of the Mustang.

Kessler stepped from his car and walked the few yards across the parking lot to where Josh and Kate were standing. His eyes swivelled from side to side, checking the space for surveillance. One man was sitting inside the restaurant, eating a Tostada and listening to some music on his iPod. Otherwise the place was empty. As Kessler reassured himself that no one could see him his manner slowly unwound.

'Cheesy potato?' asked Josh, offering him one of the out-sized chips.

'I'm not hungry,' snapped Kessler.

'Golden potatoes topped with warm nacho-cheese sauce,' continued Josh, reading from the side of the carton. 'They're delicious.'

'Let's make this quick,' said Kessler.

'Suits me,' answered Josh, putting down his food on the car. 'What did you find?'

Kessler put a black leather computer case down on the bonnet, unzipped it, and took out the Dell Inspiron. The machine lay silent and inert, a harmless-looking lump of plastic, wire, and silicon. 'Take it,' said Kessler, a rasp in his voice. 'I never want to see it again.'

Josh put his hand down on the computer. 'I will,' he said softly. 'But first I want to know what's on it.'

Kessler wiped his brow. Even though there was a cool breeze blowing through the night air, a few beads of sweat had formed on his forehead. 'The hard drive had been wiped,' he said. 'Done it pretty well, too. Whoever owned this machine clearly knew a bit about computers. They knew how to get right inside the operating system and carefully erase all traces of what programs it had been running, and what websites it had visited.'

'But it wasn't all wiped clean?' Josh asked.

'Just about. But Windows is a hell of a program. There are layers and layers of code in there, with different bits plugged into the thing as they update it every year. I reckon even Bill Gates doesn't really understand it any more.' Kessler paused to smile at his own joke. 'Eventually I found a few traces. Took me all day but there were bits of code wrapped inside other bits of code. Once you unpeeled those you had a few keys. And I didn't like what I found.'

Josh reached down to pick up his taco. 'What?' he said quickly.

'Ever heard of a company called Porter-Bell?' said Kessler, his eyes flicking upwards nervously.

'Vaguely,' interrupted Kate. 'Software, right? Run by a billionaire called Edward Porter.'

194

Kessler nodded. 'A vicious company,' he said. 'Among the hackers and phreakers and the rest of the alternative software community, they are nick-named Hanging-Bell. That's because if you touch one of their patents, or stray onto any of the bits of commercial territory they control, they come after you like a posse on speed. They make Microsoft look like a bunch of Boy Scouts. Nobody messes with them. Not if they've got any sense.'

'What do they make?' asked Josh.

'Industrial software,' said Kessler. 'The really big pieces of kit that are used to control complex urban systems. The chances are that if you stop at a red light, or ride the subway to work, then you'll be relying on some Porter-Bell software. They are global, and in that space they are the best there is.'

As he listened to the explanation, Josh could sense himself growing more and more uneasy. 'Let me guess,' he said. 'Luke was hacking into it.'

'Big time,' said Kessler, his gaze sweeping across the sparse parking lot. 'What I found on his computer was a shadow. That's traces of a different operating system that has a different basic programming language to Windows. It's a proprietary system, one that belongs to just one company. I looked it up. It was designed by Porter-Bell. The kid must have been good, because that company has more security than the Pentagon. But I reckon there's only one explanation for what I found in that Dell. He'd been into their systems and stolen some of their codes.'

Josh whistled. He already had a sense of what he was about to hear, but asked the question anyway. 'What kinds of codes?'

'Security codes, of course,' replied Kessler. 'In

195

particular, the codes for power-grid systems. You know about those?'

Josh shook his head. *Maybe I don't want to know, either.*

'Porter-Bell installs and operates power-grid software, the kit that gets the juice from the power station to the kettle in your kitchen,' said Kessler. 'It's like the holy grail of hackers. Get access to that software, and you could switch the power on and off at will. Gradually, Porter-Bell has been installing new software around the world, with upgraded systems that were meant to make the software invulnerable to attack.'

'Where were the upgrades?' said Kate. 'Where did they start?'

'Three different cities,' said Kessler. 'London, Paris and New York.'

'Christ,' said Josh. 'You think Luke was responsible for the Three Cities attack earlier this year?'

Kessler nodded. 'And that's why I don't want anything more to do with you.' He finally took a cheesy potato. 'I'm talking to you now, and after that I hope that I never have to see you again.' A slow smile crossed his lips. 'Heck, maybe *nobody* will.'

With his right hand, Kessler pushed the computer further across the bonnet of the car: he touched it only with the tips of his fingers, as if it might be contaminated. 'Here's what I think happened,' he continued. 'I think this kid managed to hack into the codes, and then turned off the lights in those three cities to see if the program he had written worked. Maybe he's a great hacker, or maybe he's just some punk who happened to get lucky. That

196

happens from time to time—you get some bright kid who gets a few breaks and cracks into the Pentagon computers. But however he did it, your kid didn't know what he was messing with.'

'Meaning what?' says Kate.

'Meaning, crack open that code, and Porter-Bell wants to kill you, the Government wants to arrest you, and every nut, psychopath and terrorist is going to try and steal it off you.'

A malevolent smile was playing on Kessler's face and Josh was sure that he could detect just a hint of jealously in his voice. 'Think about it. The ability to turn off the power anywhere in the world at will. Everyone wants it, and you've got it. There ain't no safe place in the world for you to hide.'

Kessler turned around, walking back in the direction of the parked Beetle. 'Next time my lights go off, I'll be thinking of you.'

Josh watched as the car pulled out of the parking lot, disappearing along the slip road that led back out to the highway. He took the last bite out of his taco, and threw the remains of the food in the bin.

'Come on,' he said to Kate. 'Let's get out of here.'

'To where?' Kate asked. 'Where the hell are we going?'

'To find Luke,' replied Josh. 'Before they do.'

FOURTEEN

Thursday, June 11th. Dawn.
Kate lay at Josh's side, her eyes still closed, her red hair draped across her face. Josh stood up, and

197

walked gingerly towards the Mustang. Reaching for a bottle of water, he threw some down his throat, drinking a quarter of a litre in one gulp. Slowly, he could feel himself starting to wake up.

The ground beneath them was dusty and harsh. Josh could feel a wind blowing across his face: grating, violent gusts of air, filled with grit, that seemed to smash into his skin.

As he looked around, he briefly wondered where he was. Behind him he could see a gently sloping hill dotted with pine trees. Below him he could see the narrow road twisting into the distance. Further away he could see a river meandering its way towards the horizon.

Neither of them had had enough energy to drive far last night. After Kessler left, they took the Mustang out into the back roads along the state border. It was too dangerous to risk checking into a motel, and neither Josh nor Kate knew enough about this countryside to find adequate shelter for the night. So after driving through the darkness for twenty minutes, Josh turned off the road, ploughing along a dirt track that twisted its way through some fields. They might as well stay there, he had decided. They weren't going to find anywhere better.

As they lay down together, pulling the one blanket they had in their kitbags over their heads, Kate suddenly grabbed hold of Josh, pulling his body close against her: her fingers clawed him as if she were clinging onto him in fear that he might escape from her.

Josh had fallen immediately into a deep sleep, blocking out all his senses. As he drifted off, an image suddenly drifted through his mind. The brunette. The one he had seen a few days ago. Her lips were moving. She was shouting. But he couldn't hear anything she was saying.

Now Josh paced around to try and warm himself up. They had learned so much in the last twenty-four hours. Flatner was looking for Josh, as well as for Luke. Someone was paying him to do it. And he wanted Josh dead. It was a fair conclusion that whoever that was, he'd also had something to do with Josh's shooting.

Then again, Luke had been hacking into the software systems of Porter-Bell. His mother had told them that he'd been talking about how he was going to make a lot of money sometime soon. That wasn't hard to figure out. He and Ben had cracked some lucrative code, and had thought that they could make some money out of it.

Edward Porter, Josh had concluded as they completed the long drive. That's the link. *We need to know a lot more about him.*

He walked across to Kate. 'Wake up,' he said gently, passing her a bottle of water.

Her eyes opened, drowsy at first, then fiercely alert. She snapped out of her sleep, looking around her. 'Where the hell are we?' she said, glancing up at Josh.

'Nowhere.'

Kate took the water, drinking a few mouthfuls, then using the rest of the bottle's contents to wash her face and hands. Some of the dust and grime from the field was sticking to her shirt and jeans, and some earth had lodged itself in her hair.

'What's the plan?' said Kate. 'Where do you want to start?'

'Your house,' said Josh.

There was a pause. 'You think he's there?'

Josh shook his head. 'No,' he answered. 'But Marshall has a fine collection of guns. I'm going to see if I can borrow some. For the next stage of this battle, I think we need to be armed.' He chuckled harshly. 'To the teeth.'

'It's two hundred miles back there,' said Kate.

'Then we'd better get started.'

* * *

Josh walked carefully towards the house. His eyes were scanning first left, then right, and his ears were tuned for the slightest noise: a whisper of wind, the wings of a bird, or the movement of a snake through the sand, any of them would have alerted him instantly. But there was nothing. The place was as still as a graveyard.

If anyone is there waiting, then I'm done for, thought Josh. It's at least two hundred yards to the house. *They will see me long before I can see them.*

He picked up his pace. There was no cover, and no way of approaching the building without being seen. Checking that Kate was still behind him, he started to run towards the front door.

'I don't like it,' said Kate suddenly. 'Something's wrong.'

The hinge of the door was hanging loose. Josh stood next to the entrance to the house, holding on to a fragment of wood that had once been part of the door.

'My God,' said Kate. 'What the hell happened?'

It was only as they approached the porch that they could see the extent of the damage that had been done to the house. They stepped inside

200

together, noticing at once that the television was still on. The door had been smashed in. An axe, Josh guessed, given the way in which the wood had splintered and split. The hall had been left untouched, but both the bedrooms had been turned upside down, every drawer flung open, the contents tossed onto the floor. The mattresses had been ripped open with knives—the stuffing was bulging out of them. Across the floor the scattered debris was lying in a heap.

And Josh noticed something else as well. *There was no sign of Marshall.*

Josh moved through to the kitchen. Every cupboard door had been ripped from its hinges, the food tipped out, and every box and jar thrown open. Flies had started to invade the house, settling thickly on the food spread out everywhere: a couple flew away as Josh stepped into the room, but the rest just carried on eating. Looking down, Josh could see that the intruders had discovered the hiding place beneath the floor: the boards had been ripped apart and the staircase smashed up.

'Where the hell is my dad?' said Kate, her voice ragged.

Josh took a moment to survey the damage. Professionals, he concluded. They knew how to search a building quickly and efficiently, and they didn't care how much damage they did. 'They were looking for me,' said Josh.

Kate shook her head from side to side. Her expression was concentrated, intense. 'No,' she said. 'They were looking for something smaller than a man, something that might be hidden here. They've ripped open mattresses. They've opened up all the food jars. A man can't hide in one of

201

those.'

'Then it's the computer,' said Josh. 'Luke's computer—that's what they want.'

'Or a disk,' said Kate.

'Christ, I hope they haven't attacked Luke's mother,' said Josh.

Josh walked quickly through to the room where he had slept. The bed had been knifed to shreds. Next, he strode to the back of the house, to the small room where Marshall kept his guns. Nothing. The rack was still there: a thick, solid slab of finely polished wood, with a dozen oblong slots in it. But the weapons were all gone.

'The guns,' shouted Josh to Kate. 'All taken. And there's still no sign of Marshall.'

Josh walked back to the kitchen. Kate was standing by herself, next to the sink. The glasses were all broken, but she'd found a plastic beaker and was taking a sip of water. Josh could see her eyes flickering toward the TV. Whoever had ransacked this place must have left it on. Probably checking the TV actually worked, figured Josh. Not just an empty box with something hidden inside it. *Like I thought, professionals.*

The newsreader was the kind of highlighted blonde who dominated every news channel in America. 'In a terrifying reprise of the Three Cities Attack earlier this year, the power was dramatically switched off in four different cities for precisely one hour this morning,' she was saying.

Josh put his arm around Kate's shoulder, watching the news intently. He could feel the tension rippling through her as he held her body next to his.

'At precisely nine o'clock this morning the power

got switched off in Orlando, Seattle, in the historic holiday town of Jamestown in New York State, and in Harrison in Tennessee. In each incident, the power shutdown caused widespread panic and confusion. Road systems stopped working, factories, office buildings and schools had to be closed and hospitals had to shut their doors since even their emergency back-up generators couldn't cope with the demand for electricity. Although the power has now been restored in each city, reports are coming in of several injuries in both Seattle and Orlando, mainly caused by traffic accidents as the street lights went down. Air traffic control was suspended in the cities, and all flights in and out have had to be diverted. There are also reports of widespread looting in Orlando as local police failed to stop panic spreading through the streets.

'So what caused this latest blackout? There is plenty of speculation about a terrorist assault, just as there was with the Three Cities Attack earlier this year. Some people are saying that it could have been a blow against Microsoft because Seattle was one of the cities where the power was shut down and that is where the software giant is based. Other people are saying it could be an attack on the Kennedy Space Centre, based near Orlando, although no rocket launches were scheduled for this morning.

'A spokesman for the White House said that they were at this stage ruling out the possibility of a terrorist attack, and that a full investigation was now under way into how the power failed in four cities across the United States at precisely the same moment. The White House is due to make a fuller statement later today. After this break, we go over live to our correspondent in Orlando to find out how local people are coping with the aftermath of the blackout.'

Josh looked towards Kate. 'Luke,' he said simply. 'He's still out there.'

'Or his software,' said Kate. 'Maybe somebody else has got hold of it by now.'

'You think they took Marshall?'

'Maybe they killed him?'

Josh shook his head. 'You see any sign of a struggle?' he replied. 'Blood on the floor? Gunshot holes in the wall? No. I reckon if they had taken Marshall there would have been a fight. He left before they got here.'

She's brave, thought Josh. Her father has disappeared, and yet she appears confident that he's okay. *Maybe she just has a lot of faith in the old guy.*

'But they've linked the two of us,' said Josh. 'I reckon they got Marshall's name from Madge before they killed her. That's why they came out here. Whoever did this, they now know that you and Marshall have been helping me.'

Kate walked to the back of the hallway. A computer was plugged into the wall, and although the cable linking the screen to the keyboard and the power box had been ripped apart it looked to have been undamaged. Kate spent a few seconds checking the machine, then fired it up. 'That number you took, the man who called Flatner telling him to find you,' she said. 'Have you still got it?'

'We haven't got enough time,' snapped Josh. 'How the hell do we know when they'll be back?'

'We have to know for certain,' said Kate.

204

'Without that, we have nothing.'

Josh sat down next to her. There was a stillness to the house. The sun was beating down outside, its rays spilling across the broken and scattered furniture. There was not even a hint of a breeze and the insects that populated the yard had fallen quiet. Josh read out the number that he had already committed to memory. '08732 611544.'

I may not remember much, but I can remember that.

Josh watched as Kate fired up the Internet connection. She was searching through a succession of different websites, then sent out some e-mail from her Hotmail address. Her expression was one of total concentration: her stage was fixed on the screen and her fingers were moving swiftly across the keyboard. In her left hand, she was playing with a pencil, toying with it in her mouth as if it was a cigarette. *She looks just the way she was when I first opened my eyes.*

Standing up from the desk, Josh started to walk back through the shattered house. Sometimes it was best to give people a few moments to themselves, he decided. He started sorting through some of the rubbish, trying to figure out what kinds of weapons had been used. Some sharp knives, he figured. An axe. Maybe a hammer and a wrench. *The bastards brought a whole branch of B&Q with them.*

The yard was empty. Josh stood outside, shielding his eyes from the burning sun. He looked out across the dusty plain, his eyes scanning the horizon for any kind of movement. Nothing. The landscape looked lifeless. Whoever had come here, they had left no trace of themselves.

I won't be sorry to see the back of this godforsaken country.

He took a sip of water, trying to clear the headache that was scratching against the inside of his skull. What the hell am I doing? he wondered to himself. Why don't I just hand myself in to the police?

'Found it,' shouted Kate from the back of the corridor.

Josh walked swiftly back to where she was sitting. She was leaning into the computer. He looked down. On the screen, he could see an e-mail, but it seemed to have been sent from an anonymous account. The words were printed in small bold lettering. 'The number 08732 611544 is a private cellphone number operated by Verizon Wireless. The account is registered in the name of a Mr Edward Porter.'

'So it's him,' breathed Josh. 'That's the fucker who sent Flatner to kill me.'

Kate nodded, her expression impassive.

'It's starting to make sense,' said Josh. 'Luke and Ben hacked into their software. So they want to kill him. That figures. Unless the software is invulnerable to attack, no city anywhere is going to want to install it to manage their power system. Those two boys could end up costing that company billions of dollars.'

Josh turned away, looking towards the kitchen. 'But why do they want to kill me?' he said. 'I don't get it. I *just* don't get it.'

'Maybe they don't want to kill you, Josh.'

He looked at Kate, puzzled.

'Maybe they want to find you,' she continued.

'What for?' snapped Josh. 'What the hell for?'

'Maybe you know something, Josh—don't you see?' said Kate.

Josh turned to face her. Her voice sounded raw and ragged. 'But what?' he said coldly. '*What* do I know?'

'Think, Josh,' she said, her voice sounding choked. 'Can't you remember *anything*? Anything at all?'

Josh slammed his fist down on the sideboard, the wood, already splintered and broken, shaking under the force of the blow. Some dust fell to the floor. 'I can't bloody remember, I tell you,' he shouted. 'This is useless. I need a hospital, I need the police.'

'No, Josh, no,' said Kate.

Her voice sounded suddenly scared, desperately anxious. She rushed to him, putting her arms around his body and hugging him to her chest. 'It's going to be okay, baby.'

Josh shook his head. 'I need help.'

'*I'm* here to help you,' she said.

'You go to the police, a hospital, Porter will know about it, then kill you,' said Kate. 'Hell, if they think you had anything to do with shutting down the power system, they might not even bother to question you first. We need to fix this together. We need to find Luke.'

Josh took a sip of his water. A single sentence was drumming through his mind. She's right. *She's right*.

'I need to know more about Porter,' said Josh. 'You have to know what sort of man your enemy is.'

Josh sat down at the computer. In the next twenty minutes, he started to compile a brief biography of Edward Porter, culled from the archives of a dozen

207

different business magazines. Porter had been born in California in 1950, and had graduated from Berkeley in physics and computing. He'd spent two years in the 5th Marine Regiment, fighting in Vietnam, but had left the armed forces after being wounded in the leg. Next, he'd spent five years working first for IBM, then for Cray Supercomputers. He'd founded Porter-Bell in 1977 with a partner, Sam Bell, but Bell had left the company in 1980. It had grown rapidly in the 1980s, first with a series of military contracts, then expanding into building city and industrial systems. As factories and power systems became automated during that decade, Porter-Bell developed and built the software that controlled them. It made a fortune.

In 1992, the company listed on the NASDAQ technology exchange, making Porter an instant billionaire. He was now estimated to be worth at least ten billion dollars, and Porter-Bell dominated its sector of the market. Twice divorced, with a string of mistresses, Porter had a reputation as a mean, combative entrepreneur, who ran his company with ruthless discipline and crushed the competition with relentless ferocity. Scouring the web, Josh found that there were countless articles testifying to the ferocity with which rivals who tried to muscle in on Porter-Bell's territory were flattened. For the last two years, the US Justice Department had been trying to prosecute the company for a series of anti-trust violations, but its lawyers had fought the actions all the way.

'We have to find Morant and O'Brien,' said Josh. 'Maybe they will know where Marshall is. And if they don't, they'll be able to get us guns and

208

ammunition, and maybe even reinforcements.'

'We don't need weapons, Josh.'

'What the hell *do* we need, then?'

'We need your memory back. That's the only way we can get to Luke before Porter and Flatner get to them. That's what this is all about. We have to get to Luke before they do.'

'But where is he?'

Kate stood closer to him. 'You know where he is, Josh,' she said softly. 'You just need to remember, that's all.'

*   *   *

The road twisted ahead of them. Kate was driving the Mustang, steering it along the road that led away from the house and out into the mountains. A truck passed, then a car, but there was no sign of any patrol cars, nor of any of Flatner's bikers.

The road is safe, thought Josh. *For now.*

'How far?' he asked.

'A couple of miles,' said Kate.

She was driving them to one of their mountain hideouts. This one was thirty miles to the east of Boisdale, in a dusty mountain range that had once been home to a couple of tin mines but had long since been abandoned by everything except a few snakes and the occasional flock of wild cranes. Kate knew that Morant and O'Brien moved from camp to camp and she had a good hunch that this was where they would find them. For five hundred dollars, they could equip Kate and Josh with a pair of mules and enough food to last them for a month: they could collect water from creeks and wells out in the scrub. Morant would give them a map of the water sources that the survivalists used and the caves they slept in at night. They knew this terrain better than anyone else alive. *It won't be comfortable, thought Josh when Kate explained it to him, but we'll survive.*

The plan, thought Josh, running it afresh through his mind, was to get out into open country. His sense was that if Luke was hiding, it would be out there somewhere. He didn't have the resources or the knowledge to travel far, not without being detected. And if anyone can find him, we can. *Then, maybe, he can tell me what happened.*

Dusk was just starting to fall. The sun was dipping down towards the horizon and the light was fading. Shadows from the mountains far to the east were lying across the road, spiked and threatening, like snakes lying in wait for their victims. Josh kept his eyes focused on the road, aware that if their enemies knew Kate was helping him, then they could trace this easily enough.

The next few miles will be the most dangerous. Until we get out into the empty country.

A hitch-hiker was thumbing a lift on the side of the road: a boy of eighteen or nineteen, noticed Josh, with a rucksack at his side. For a brief moment, Josh wondered if it might be Luke. 'Keep going,' he muttered to Kate.

Josh checked the rear-view mirror, expecting to see the boy shaking his fist or giving them the finger: cars were rare enough on this empty stretch of road for a hitch-hiker to be angry with anyone who didn't stop.

But he wasn't doing anything, Josh noticed. He looked hard into the mirror, straining to make out the shape disappearing into the distance. Then he twisted round to get a better look. The boy had turned around, walking a couple of yards off the road. His shoulders were hunched, and he was holding something in his hand. Christ, thought Josh. A mobile. He's making a call.

'Slow down,' he barked.

'What?'

'Slow the bloody car,' repeated Josh.

Kate turned to look at him, fear flashing through her eyes.

'He's a spotter—that bloody kid's a spotter,' said Josh.

Kate slipped down the gears on the Mustang, putting it into second, letting the car crawl along the road at a nervous twenty miles an hour. Behind them the boy was moving swiftly across the scrubland, his phone still in his hand. He didn't look back. It was impossible to tell whether he knew they'd seen him.

Josh scanned the area, his stare swivelling across the flat empty desert to the west and the mountain range rising up to the east. He tried to block out the noise of the car, straining to detect any other sounds. We'll hear it soon enough, he said to himself grimly. The sound of attack.

'You going after him?' asked Kate.

Josh shook his head. 'No point,' he snapped. 'He's already told them we're on the road.'

'Any turnings?'

Josh scanned the road. The tarmac stretched out onto the horizon, as straight as a ruler, with no sign of any crossroads. 'Nothing,' he said bitterly.

'Want to go cross-country?'

Josh looked both right and left. The mountains half a mile distant on the right would provide some

211

cover. Maybe they could even find somewhere to
hide there. But there was no way they could drive
through them. They would have to take their
chances on foot. On the left, the scrub was
stretching into the far distance, its flat surface
punctuated only by cacti and jagged, dangerous-
looking boulders. There was nowhere to hide out
there, realised Josh. They would be picked up
within a few minutes.

'No,' he said briskly. 'Too risky.'

Now he could hear the rumble of motors,
growling out across the flat scrubland like the first
warning of a distant storm. They were somewhere
to his right, about a mile distant, sneaking through
the mountains. I know that sound, he told himself.
The oily roar of an engine revving into life. A
motorbike. *Maybe a whole bloody army of them.*

'All right, I reckon it's Plan B,' said Josh.

Kate looked at him, and even though he could
see the tension rippling through her, there was a
hint of amusement in her eyes. 'Okay,' she said
softly. 'What's Plan B?'

'Run like a rat on roller skates—and start
praying.'

Kate's foot jammed down on the accelerator.
The Mustang roared, its engine howling as it
started to pick up power and speed. Josh cursed
himself for not taking the wheel for this stretch of
the journey, but it was too late now.

He checked behind. Three motorbikes were
powering down the side of the mountain, driving in
a tight V-formation. They were eight or nine
hundred yards away but doing at least eighty or
ninety miles an hour, and closing fast. A furious
cloud of dust was being kicked up into the air as

their back wheels bit into the caked mud of the desert. They spun out onto the tarmac, hurtling towards the Mustang at well over a hundred miles a hour now.

'Faster, faster,' snapped Josh.

He could see the sweat trickling down Kate's face as she hammered the accelerator. The Mustang's two-litre engine was roaring as she struggled to extract some more power from the machine. By now they had climbed past a hundred, and were touching a hundred and ten miles an hour. The tyres were screeching against the hot tarmac. There's not much acceleration left in this tin can, realised Josh. And the bikers are still gaining on us.

He looked in front. About half a mile ahead, more bikes, four this time, were shrieking out from behind a boulder, their engines already revved up to maximum speed. Two were in front, with two more flanking them as outriders. Definitely Flatner's men, decided Josh. As they sped towards the Mustang, he could see the men riding them: burly, leather-clad creatures, with tattoos on their arms and helmets slung down low across their faces. Except for the leader: he was wearing a Nazi helmet, with a pair of cattle horns drilled into the sides. Not much use if you had a crash, decided Josh. *But good for scaring people.*

'Which way?' shouted Kate, her eyes swivelling desperately towards Josh.

The bikes five hundred yards ahead were bearing down on them, and the bikes behind were gaining speed. Trapped, thought Josh.

I outwitted these fuckers right after I was shot, he decided. *Maybe I can do it again.*

'Keep going,' he barked. 'Drive straight into

213

them, then swerve at the last minute and try to get past them.'

Kate's hands were vibrating on the wheel. Josh's stare was locked on the road ahead, tracking the four bikes flanking the road as they sped towards each other.

Four hundred yards, he calculated. Three hundred . . .

'Turn,' he shouted.

Kate hauled the wheel hard over. Too much pressure, Josh realised the instant she had made her move. The Mustang skidded, its wheels losing contact with the ground. It had gone into a backspin as the momentum from the rear wheels overwhelmed the vehicle, turning it through ninety degrees within a fraction of a second.

'Hold the wheel, hold the wheel,' shouted Josh.

Reaching down, he grabbed the handbrake, yanking it up to try and control the spin. The brake discs howled as they clamped against the wheels and Josh released his grip. No good, he told himself. *We'll have to take our chances in the scrub.*

A cloud of dust rose up from the side of the road as the Mustang slewed off it. He'd counted seven bikes in total, closing in fast, but now he could see nothing except for the swirling dirt all around them. The smell of burnt rubber filled the air. 'Go forward,' he shouted. 'Just go forward.'

A shot. Josh recognised the sound instantly: the thud of a cartridge fired from a sawn-off shotgun.

The back window of the Mustang crashed inwards, splinters of glass flying into their backs like a hailstorm. Josh felt two shards pricking his skin: one on his neck, the other in his back, and a hot trickle of blood ran down the edge of his spine.

Another shot, then another. Josh heard a ripping sound. A tyre. The Mustang skidded again as first one tyre blew out, then another. The power in the engine was starting to fade as the lead pellets from the shotguns ripped through the car's bodywork, smashing into the suspension, brakes and engine.

Josh looked up. Kate was still clinging to the wheel, frantically trying to bring the machine under control. The dust clouds were still obscuring their vision. Josh could just make out some boulders. A ditch that might be a dried-out creek. Then the mountains behind.

And now, looming through the dust clouds like shadows in the night, the outlines of two bikers.

Death on wheels.

Another shot. This time the bonnet flipped open, the sheet of metal catching in the wind and shooting straight upwards. The engine snarled, then stalled. To his right, Josh could smell petrol leaking onto the ground. 'Get out, get out,' he shouted. 'They're going to kill us if we stay in here.'

The Mustang was slowing fast, down to fifteen or twenty miles an hour, losing power, its steering gone. It was skidding across the surface of the ground, out of control. Josh flipped the door open. He could see moving scrub, the ground pitted with gravel and rock. Just roll out, he told himself. And pray you don't crack open your skull on one of those stones.

'Just jump,' he shouted to Kate. 'It's your only chance. Just jump and run like hell.'

'I'm not leaving you,' she shouted, straining to make her voice heard over the sound of the engine and the gunfire.

'We'll rendezvous with O'Brien and Morant,'

shouted Josh.

Josh tightened his shoulder muscles. The trick to hitting the ground at speed was to wrap yourself into a ball so that the force of the impact was deflected throughout your body. You used your arms to protect your face and your head: that was where the worst injuries would be sustained. Go, man, go, he told himself. *This is your only shot at saving yourself.*

He kicked back from the car with his legs, tumbling out onto the ground. At his side, he could see Kate doing the same as the Mustang ploughed onwards under its own momentum, heading straight for the jagged edges of a massive boulder formation.

The ground impacted against his ribcage first. Josh could feel his bones rattling. None broken, he hoped, although it was impossible to tell through the pain of the fall. He rolled one yard, two, then three. The ground felt rough and harsh, grating into his skin. His jeans snagged on something. A rip opened up, then something cut into his skin. He could feel his wound throbbing, the worst it had been for days. Slamming his hands down, he gripped into the dirt, breaking a nail as he dug his fingers into the ground, bringing himself to a halt.

Josh looked up. Kate was already on her feet, running. He could not see where she was heading.

Next, he looked ahead. The Mustang was moving straight for the boulders. As it struck, a horrific noise erupted: the sound of metal being shredded by rock. The vehicle shuddered, then a storm of sparks flew up where the metal was scraping along the boulders. Josh closed his eyes, already aware of what was going to happen next. He heard the air

216

being sucked forwards, then felt the first waves of the explosion brush against the skin of his face. The heat was scorching: a wave of hot air, blowing round him with gale-force strength. The fireball rose straight up into the sky, scattering parts of the car in every direction and sending a huge, oily cloud of thick black smoke boiling up. The sun was briefly blocked out, and the air smelled of petrol, scorched metal and fried dust.

Slowly, the force of the explosion subsided. As the clouds of black smoke cleared, Josh could see two bikes driving straight towards him. The riders were each holding one end of a rope in their hands, sweeping it across the scrubland like a fishing net. Josh stood to his feet, swallowing the pain, and then he started to run. One of his shoes had come loose and was catching on his foot, threatening to trip him. No time to stop, he told himself, willing himself forwards. *Another second, and they've got me.*

In the next moment, he felt the rope smash into the centre of his back. It started dragging him down, pushing him hard onto the ground. Josh tried desperately to pick himself up, but it was too late. The two bikes had screeched to a halt, kicking up a wall of dust, and the rope was pinning him to the dirt, cutting into the skin of his arms, and digging deep welts into his back. The pain jabbed through him.

I'm done for. *Dead in a miserable desert, where only the wolves and the vultures will pick over my bones.*

The bikers came to a halt, stepping quickly towards him, both men holding an end of the rope tightly in their fists. The leader stood over Josh,

217

peering into his eyes. The horns on the Nazi helmet were glistening in the sunlight. 'Make it easy for yourself,' he muttered, spitting a mouthful of stale breath into Josh's face. 'Try to sleep.'

Josh could feel a fist smashing into the side of his neck—once, then twice. His eyes began to cloud over, a dazzling mist drifting across his line of vision. He could feel the pain rippling through him. It started in his neck, then ran down his spine, settling in his gut.

Another fist, this time on the other side of his neck. The blow glanced upwards, the fist colliding with his ear. Josh could feel consciousness starting to abandon him. His mind was shutting down. Before his eyes, he could see a picture. The brunette, the woman he had seen twice now. The little girl with blonde hair, three or maybe four, opening a present, then holding out a Barbie doll. She was saying something. Her lips were moving. *But what? If only I could hear as well as see her.*

Josh willed himself to stay awake, to hold on to the image. It faded, clouding before his eyes. He went under, blackness overwhelming him. Then, briefly, he was awake again. Someone was lifting him up, one man taking his legs, another his shoulders. The bikers. *Where the hell are they taking me?*

As his body swayed from side to side, consciousness started to fade and Josh could feel himself going under again. Another image flashed in front of his eyes. This time it was Luke. Running. Then the boy was turning around, shouting something. What was it? 'Touch,' realised Josh. He was shouting 'Touch,' plus some other words that were indistinct. Touch, thought Josh, the word rattling through his mind. What the hell did he want me to touch?

The image faded as quickly as it had arisen, and suddenly Josh could see nothing. He opened his eyes, but the vision had gone. He could see only the darkness. Is this what it's like when you die? he wondered. *If I've been captured, that might be the best I can hope for.*

FIFTEEN

Thursday, June 11th. Noon.
Where's the cyanide pill? thought Josh.
Where's the sodding cyanide pill?

He closed his eyes, then opened them again, hoping against hope that maybe it was just a dream. As he pulled his eyelids slowly open, it took him a few minutes to adjust to the darkness of his surroundings. He was lying on a rough dirt floor, his hands bound tightly behind his back and his feet strapped together. A stake had been driven into the ground and the ropes wrapped around his legs had been tied to it, making it impossible for him to wriggle forward more than a yard. The room measured ten feet square, and looked to have been dug out of some kind of dried mud: a hole, driven straight down into the ground. Looking up, he could see that it was covered by some thick sheets of metal. Not a glimmer of light was breaking through. Josh could hardly even see his own body in the darkness.

It was impossible to tell what time of day it was. His watch had been taken from his wrist.

219

It could by any time of day, any day of the week.

What happened yesterday? Josh asked himself. What the hell happened?

A sudden jolt of cold fear ran down his spine. *Christ, not more memory loss.*

But slowly, in his mind, he started to reassemble the events of the last twenty hours. He had been with Kate, he remembered that. They had been driving, on their way to meet O'Brien and Morant. They had been attacked. The bikers had been there in force: at least seven of them, maybe more in reserve. It had been impossible to run, and they'd had no weapons with which to fight. The last thing he remembered was Kate running for her life across the open scrubland, while the bikers punched him unconscious.

I don't even know if she is alive or dead. I don't even know if I'm going to live much longer.

Josh tried to stretch his limbs. Assess the state of the damage you've taken, he decided. His neck hurt badly. The bandage on his gunshot wound had been pulled off, and the punches he'd taken to the side of his head had broken the skin open again. It had been bleeding, he could tell, and some dirt might have got in there, but the flow of blood had staunched itself while he'd been unconscious, and some fresh scabs had started to form. The nerves in his leg wound were throbbing with agony, as if his leg was being drilled open. And his ribs were aching from the fall from the car and the beating he'd taken from the bikers: none of them seemed to be broken, but the muscles were strained and they ached every time he moved.

So far they haven't roughed me up much at all. Just brought me back and tossed me in this hole.

Concentrate, he told himself. Don't give in to despair. *So long as you are alive you can pull through this.*

His bladder was aching. Josh was desperate for a piss, but it was impossible to stand or even squat. 'Hey,' he shouted, looking up. 'Who's there?'

His voice was hoarse, and rasping. Something was hurting the back of his throat as he tried to speak but he couldn't identify what: so many different types of pain were already assaulting him that it was hard to tell them apart.

'Who's bloody there?' he shouted again, louder this time.

A chink of light opened in the space above him. Josh's stare shot up to track the movement. A ray of fierce sunshine burst through, sending a narrow shaft of light down into Josh's face. He tracked the movement of the covering as it slid open. A rope ladder dropped down into the hole, then Josh could see a man starting to climb down into the pit. His boots came into view first, then his black jeans, then his leather jacket, his black beard and his thick ponytail. Josh recognised him at once. Flatner.

'How you doing today, pretty boy?' Flatner said, looking down.

Josh struggled to sit up, but the tight leash made it impossible: the best he could manage was to raise his face a few feet from the ground.

'I need a piss,' said Josh.

'And so do I,' said Flatner.

With deliberate slowness, Flatner unzipped his flies and pulled out his penis. Holding it in his hands, he sprayed Josh with his urine. The liquid felt warm as it splashed against the cloth of Josh's

221

jeans and T-shirt. The smell made Josh cough in disgust. His own bladder could contain itself no longer: his own urine started running down the side of his leg, forming a noxious puddle on the ground.

'Talk to me, man, talk to me,' said Flatner roughly. 'You'll save yourself a lot of pain.'

'Fuck off,' Josh spat.

Josh rested his head back on the ground. The air inside the hole was already thirty or thirty-five degrees, and the sunlight now beaming in was making it even hotter. I'm going to take a beating, he told himself. *I just have to try and survive it as best I can.*

'You can make this easy for yourself, or you can make it hard,' said Flatner.

Josh looked up, making eye contact with Flatner for the first time. His expression was as hard as rock: solid and unyielding. 'What do you want?' he asked.

'The kid, Josh,' said Flatner. 'I want to know where the kid is.'

'Which kid?'

Flatner knelt down, leaning close into Josh's face, so close that Josh could smell his sour breath. 'A word of advice, man,' he said. 'Don't try to be funny and don't try to be clever. You know which fucking kid.'

'Luke?'

Flatner nodded just once.

'I don't know.'

The punch was delivered to his ribcage. Flatner's fist collided with the side of Josh's chest, sending a dull pain though his body. That was just a friendly warning, Josh warned himself. *The man can deliver a far more violent blow than that.*

'I'll ask you again,' said Flatner. 'Where's the fucking kid?'

'I don't know,' Josh repeated.

The punch was harder this time, delivered to the same point on his ribcage. The wind emptied out of his gut, and he could feel his skin turning numb. 'I don't know,' he said again.

He could see Flatner starting to draw his fist back, readying the next blow. 'No, listen,' said Josh, a ragged edge creeping into his voice. 'I really don't know.'

Flat's fist was poised to crash down against Josh's ribcage. 'Don't know?'

'I lost my memory,' said Josh.

Flatner smiled, revealing a huge set of jagged teeth. His eyes looked down at Josh, dark and morose. 'Don't try to get smart with me, pretty boy.'

'It's true,' snapped Josh. 'I was shot in the neck, and the leg. My memory's gone to pieces. Even if I did know where the hell Luke was once, I sure as hell don't know any more.'

From his back pocket, Flatner pulled out a page torn from a newspaper. 'Recognise this?'

Josh shook his head.

'It's the *New York* fucking *Times*, man. Paper of record, right?'

Josh remained silent.

'And it has a report here about what it calls The Four Cities Attack. Couple of days ago the power gets turned off in four different cities around the United States. Just like The Three Cities Attack a couple of months ago. Want me to read you what it says?'

Flatner paused for breath, not looking to Josh for

a response.

'It says this: "The timing of the attacks has been described as simultaneous, but according to power-industry experts the blackouts started in different cities at slightly different local times. In Jamestown, the power went down at 9.01.00; in Orlando at 9.01.15; in Seattle at 9.01.30; and in Harrison at 9.01.45. Each blackout started at precisely fifteen seconds after the last one. But according to power-industry sources that may have just been the result of differences in local systems, and in the length of time it takes for the systems to shut themselves down."' Flatner put the paper down on the ground at his side. 'What do you think that means?'

'No bloody idea,' said Josh. 'Like it says, differences in local power systems.'

'You think so? Then maybe you're as fucking dumb as you look. Four cities. Jamestown, Orlando, Seattle and Harrison. That mean anything to you?'

Josh shook his head.

'You're a dumb son of a bitch. J-O-S-H. It spells fucking Josh. The kid shut down the power in those four cities deliberately, and he spaced out the attacks because he knew you were so fucking stupid you might have trouble figuring it out for yourself. J-O-S-H. Spells Josh.'

Flatner raised his fist as if he was about to launch another punch. Instinctively, Josh could feel himself flinching. 'Now are you still going to tell me you don't know where he is?'

The letters were spinning through Josh's mind. J-O-S-H, he repeated to himself. Luke is sending me a message, he has to be. *But what the hell is he*

224

trying to say?

'I don't know,' mumbled Josh.

The punch landed on his ribcage again, sending vibrations of pain rippling up into his chest. Josh clamped his teeth together, trying not to scream out in pain. The side of his chest was numb, and even though he couldn't see it he could sense the flesh and muscle swelling under the impact of the blows.

'Now tell me where the fuck he is,' roared Flatner.

'I don't know.'

'Tell me, you son of a bitch.'

'I don't know.'

Flatner's arm was raised high, ready to strike again. 'Tell me.'

'I don't bloody know.'

'Tell me!'

'I don't know.'

Flatner struck once, then again, both times hitting Josh in the same section of his ribcage. Josh screamed with pain. Each blow was worse than the last one: the flesh was softened, already wounded, and every nerve was set alight each time Flatner thumped him.

'I don't even know who I bloody am,' screamed Josh.

Flatner reached for his shoulder, yanking Josh forwards so that he was lying with his face at Flatner's feet. 'Your name is Josh Harding,' he said. 'You are a British soldier, working undercover in the United States. You were sent here just after the juice got turned off in London. Your mission was to find out what happened and to stop it happening again.'

225

Flatner drew himself up, standing above Josh, his thick muscles bulging as he crossed his forearms. 'But you know what, pretty boy? Right now, you don't belong to the British fucking army. You don't belong to that bitch you've been going around with. You don't even belong to yourself. And unless you start thinking about how to get your mouth working again, you're just going to be fertiliser for a fucking cactus.'

He turned around, starting to climb the rope ladder up out of the hole. Josh watched as he slowly slid the metal covers back into place. Just as he was finishing, Flatner stuck his head down, blocking out what remained of the light. 'I want you to lie here in the dirt, and I want you to think of the worst thing that can possibly happen to a man,' he growled. 'And I want you to know that it's going to happen to you soon if you don't tell me where the fucking kid is.'

Josh lay silently. He turned onto his side, trying to take the pressure off his bruised ribs. Harding, he thought to himself. Flatner said that my name is Josh Harding. Josh racked his brains, trying to see if the surname could summon up any more memories.

If I can't think of anything to tell him, I'm going to take a terrible beating.

And now, in the darkness, Josh could at last feel a memory stirring within him. He was sitting in a concrete room. A man was standing in front of a group of soldiers, lecturing them, his expression serious. Josh couldn't remember the names of any of the men who sat there alongside him, but he could hear the words as clearly as if they were playing on a radio right next to him. The man in

226

front was telling them how any member of the special forces had to expect to be captured at least once in his career. And if he was taken prisoner, he had to expect to be tortured. 'We don't do the nice Geneva Convention wars,' he was saying. 'We go into the places where we aren't meant to be and we do the rough stuff. We get captured, we expect to get slapped around a little. Goes with the territory. You want to dish it out, you have to learn how to take it as well. That's what I'm here for. To teach you how to take it.'

The man went on to outline a few simple techniques for surviving torture. Josh struggled to keep the memory intact, trying to make sure that he remembered each word exactly as it was spoken. *This could mean the difference between life and death.*

You have to be physically fit, the man was telling them. That goes without saying. But you have to be mentally fit as well. You have to know how to stay on level terms with your tormentor.

There were five lessons that had been drilled into them. You have to have a 'mental home base': a mental safe house, into which you could retreat to protect yourself against the inevitable fits of depression and despair. You need a 'Focus Word', either a prayer or a poem that you can latch on to, to help get you through the day. You need to use visualisation to help you cope with the pain, turning the pain into an object such as a football that you can kick away. You have to use all your imagination and powers of imagery to try and construct fantasy worlds into which you can escape. And you have to create a 'magic box': a place outside yourself into which you can pour all your fears, anxieties, and pain.

At the time, me and the rest of the blokes thought it was just a load of psycho-bollocks. Now I'm not so sure. Now I might need it.

'You have to want to survive,' their lecturer had concluded, writing the words up on a blackboard. 'You have to know what you are living for and why. That's the only way you can make it through the pain.'

Josh repeated the words to himself, running his own private tape loop in his mind.

You have to want to survive

You have to want to survive.

But how can you want to survive, how can you know what you are living for, when you don't even know who you are?

SIXTEEN

Thursday, June 11th. Night.

The cover slid open, letting a chink of moonlight shine down into the hole. Josh turned onto his side, ignoring the pain still jabbing upwards from his ribs. He could see the ladder being tossed into the pit, and he could see a pair of thick leather boots starting their descent towards him.

'It's night-time, Josh,' said Flatner, laughing. 'Your nightmare is just starting.'

Josh kept silent. He had no clear idea what time it was. He knew that torture victims were supposed to try to keep track of the hours and the days as a way of keeping themselves sane, but it had proved impossible: with neither light nor sounds, there had been nothing to mark the passage of the hours. *It could be Thursday, Friday, any day.*

'Feeling good?' Flatner asked.

Josh glanced up. Another pair of boots was clambering down the ladder. Within a few short seconds, another of the bikers was standing at Flatner's side. Josh looked at the man's face, but in the murky light it was hard to make out any distinguishing features. His hair was matted and black, and his beard grew down more than a foot. He wore shades pulled down over his eyes, and his head was wrapped in a Confederate bandanna. Otherwise, he looked the same as all the other bikers Josh had seen walking through the camp.

Another monster. They have their own species developing here, thought Josh. *The missing link between the great apes and the morons.*

'Not in the mood to talk, pretty boy?' said Flatner. 'Then we'll just have to juice you up a little bit.'

Anticipation was the worst part of the process, Josh realised. For the last few hours, he had been lying in the dark imagining the different types of torture that might be inflicted upon him. The bones in his fingers could be broken one by one. His skin could be burnt. A limb could be amputated every day until he agreed to speak. There could be sexual abuse, or a hundred different forms of mental torture: they might use white noise, water drips, drugs. It was hard to believe there was any cruelty that they would regard as too extreme.

The same question repeated itself in his head again and again. *How much pain do I have to suffer before they believe that I don't know where Luke is?*

229

'Strap him, Mark,' snapped Flatner.

The second biker moved across to where Josh was lying and knelt down. Close up, Josh could get a better view of him. Mark was thin, with the build of an athlete, and looked no more than twenty-five, Josh judged. In his eyes, he had the cold professional glare of a man who took pride in his work. He's done this before, sensed Josh. And he enjoys it.

If the Waffen-SS was still recruiting, he'd be first in the queue.

Mark was holding what looked like a thick leather belt in his hand. It was ten inches wide, with thick Velcro straps to help secure it to the body, and with a grey battery case clipped to its back. Mark opened up the belt, threading it around Josh's waist. Using his hands, he tugged at the Velcro, squeezing it into position.

'Too tight for you?' Mark asked, leering down at Josh. 'Well, hell. I don't give a fuck. A few minutes' time, that's going to be the least of your worries.'

'What is it?' snapped Josh.

'A stun belt,' said Flatner. 'The cops use them on prisoners. Put one of these babies around them, then if they complain about anything you just press a button from up to a hundred yards away and the belt delivers an electric shock. 50,000 volts frying up your body from all sides. Well, that's usually the maximum dose used by the law enforcement boys, but you know what, I think they're just a bunch of pussies looking after another bunch of pussies. So I tweaked this one. Took it up to 100,000 volts. Makes things a bit more interesting. At the same time it's giving you a shock, it makes a noise like one of those car alarms. A hundred and ten decibels.' Flatner laughed. 'Your guts are going to be frying and your ears bleeding,' he chuckled. 'And you know what the best thing is? You won't even know when it's coming because you won't be able to see me press the button. That doubles the shock.'

Magic box, Josh told himself. Take yourself away to the magic box. *That's the only way you'll get through this.*

'Get the blanket, Mark,' Flatner ordered.

Josh watched as Mark unfurled a blanket that was already dripping with water.

Electricity, realised Josh. They're going to electrocute me. And they're going to put me on a wet blanket while they are doing it so that the shock is administered evenly throughout my body. Hold yourself together, man. *This is going to be rough.*

'Move your ugly butt, man,' said Mark. 'I need to get this underneath you.'

'Fuck off,' spat Josh.

Mark's boot slammed into Josh's shoulder, the leather top colliding hard with the collarbone, sending a harsh pulse of pain surging out across his upper body. Instinctively, he rolled away at the impact. As he did so, Mark laid the wet blanket on the ground.

'You're a dumb fuck,' shouted Flatner. 'You're going to have to learn to cooperate.'

The blanket was spread out on the ground now, and two cables had already been chucked down the hole. Mark had attached the end of one to the underside of the blanket, putting the other cable to the top side. Josh lay on the ground next to the blanket, unable to move any further away. 'Lie on

231

it,' said Mark softly.

Josh remained silent.

'I said lie on it,' repeated Mark.

Josh tightened his muscles, preparing himself for the inevitable blow. Soak up as much pain as you can, he reminded himself. Never cooperate until you have to. *Only total strength, total conviction, and total self-belief are going to get you through this.*

The boot landed in the centre of his back this time. His spine shuddered under the force of the kick. And although he resisted, it was impossible to stop himself rolling forwards onto the blanket. Immediately, Mark strapped a rope across him, using what looked like a tent peg to stake it into the ground. Trapped, realised Josh. The juice is going to start flowing any minute.

'Give it five,' shouted Flatner, looking up towards the edge of the hole.

Josh braced himself. The first jolts of electricity started jabbing at his feet, followed by an assault on his shoulders. Within seconds his whole body was being tossed around. The senses had shut down along his spine, and it was the nerves at the end of his body that were taking the worst beating: each of his toes and fingers felt as if it were being set alight in turn.

Somewhere he could smell burning. *My shirt? My skin? I can't tell.*

A scream rose up, starting in Josh's gut, tearing through his lungs, and exploding from his lips. It's okay to show pain, he told himself. It's okay to show fear. *This is about survival, not about proving yourself.*

'Cut it,' shouted Flatner.

A last surge of power tore through Josh's body,

then faded away. He lay limp and breathless. The dampness of the blanket was seeping up into his skin, making his body itch all over. Small puffs of steam were rising up from the fabric, mixing with the already fetid air of the hole. Josh could feel some vomit rising in the back of his throat, but he struggled to keep it back.

'That was just a taster, pretty boy,' said Flatner. 'Just like a minor accident. The kind of thing that might happen when you change a light bulb.' He leaned down, the end of his beard brushing against Josh's skin. 'Now talk to me.'

You can beg, bargain, and plead, thought Josh. *But unless you can give them what they want, they aren't going to let you go.*

'I don't know anything.'

Josh was surprised by how weak his voice was already sounding: it was as if all the character and grit had already been shaken out of it. His throat was parched dry, and he could feel his body starting to dehydrate—one of the most common side effects of electric shocks.

'I didn't want to hear that, Josh,' said Flatner. 'I didn't want to hear that.'

A pause. Josh tried to count the silence. Six, maybe seven seconds. *A brief respite to prepare yourself for the next assault.*

'Frying time,' shouted Flatner.

Josh could feel his body convulsing violently as the wave of electricity rushed through him. It was impossible to say any more where the pain started and stopped: it was as if every nerve in his body was being attacked simultaneously. 'No,' he shouted. 'Please, no.'

Voice the pain, he told himself. You have to voice

233

the pain. *Let it all flow straight out of you.*

'Cut it,' shouted Flatner.

The power dropped again, leaving Josh limp and lifeless. He felt as if all the blood was draining out of him. 'Now, pretty boy, let's have it,' said Flatner. 'Where's the kid?'

'Listen, you have to believe me,' said Josh, his voice raw. 'I don't know. I might have been in contact with him, but I don't know anything anymore. Take me through it step by step, I'll tell you everything that I know. I just don't know *where* he is.'

'Don't play for fucking time, pretty boy. I'm not that stupid.'

'I'm not playing for bloody time. I just don't *know.*'

Josh's hands were shaking like a pair of leaves being tossed around in a gale. Not fear, he noted. Part of the involuntary muscle movements you could expect after a long series of electric shocks.

This is going to get a lot worse, he thought grimly.

'Fry him,' shouted Flatner.

Another surge. Josh felt as if he'd been hit from the inside, as the pain exploded throughout his body. He closed his eyes, trying to think about the last time he'd been lying alone with Kate, imagining her hands running across his skin and her lips soothing away the pain. Anything, he told himself. *Anything to take your mind to a better place.*

'You ready to squeal yet, pretty boy?' said Flatner. 'Or you want me to soften you up a bit more? Get that tongue nice and loose.'

'I don't know, I tell you.'

Flatner turned around and started to climb the

rope ladder. His massive body stretched it down, and he rose slowly as he slung one arm over the other. 'You're not a weak man, Josh Harding, I'll give you that. You're a tough stupid fuck. But you'll break, hear me? You'll fucking break. Because no man can survive the hell you're about to go through.'

The cover of the hole slid shut. Josh was plunged into darkness again. His body felt wet from the moisture on the electrocution blanket and from the sweat that had poured off him.

Stay still, he ordered himself. Let your body relax. Try to unwind, get some sleep. *Only by resting can you hope to pull through.*

Josh closed his eyes. All the time, he was worrying about the damage that was being done to his body. Even if he lived, it was impossible to tell whether he would ever recover properly: the electric shocks would leave burn marks on his skin, but those would heal. It was the long-term damage to his nervous system that worried him.

Then his mind was drifting. He thought about Madge, then Kate, but found that did nothing for him. Madge was dead, probably killed by Flatner, and Kate could well be dead as well.

Who the hell am I? What kind of life will I have out there if I get through this?

A jab of pain. Instinctively, Josh's body jerked upwards. His bones felt brittle and strained. The pain subsided, and he fell back onto the wet blanket. Tears of misery and stress were starting to roll down his face. A vicious noise was rattling through the hole, making Josh's ears bleed with pain. The stun belt, he realised. They're going to keep me here in the dark, delivering occasional

235

random bolts of pain and noise from the belt.

He started to remember some of the other things he been warned about during his torture survival classes. The human mind is rarely so ingenious as when it is devising new forms of cruelty. The torturer's training manual ran to a hundred volumes. But the most effective techniques were all psychological, not physical. Sleep deprivation, sexual abuse, random beatings, all were parts of the armoury. A trained soldier could be expected to withstand a heavy load of physical pain. Yet mental anguish killed even the bravest of spirits eventually.

There was no better form of mental torture than surprise. Sometimes a man would be blindfolded and then pushed downstairs, so that he couldn't see himself falling. Other times the torturer would strap his victim to a chair before assaulting him from behind. The stun belt was just a refinement of some age-old techniques.

While I've got this belt on, I can't sleep, can't relax, can't lower my guard even for an instant.

*   *   *

Josh rolled over on the blanket, looking at the shaft of light shining downwards as the covers were taken off the hole. He could see a rope ladder being chucked down and a pair of heavy black boots starting their ominous descent.

Another day in hell.

'Breakfast time, pretty boy,' shouted Flatner.

Josh could feel himself coughing. Whether he had slept at all during the night he couldn't say. There might have been a few minutes when a kind of nervous exhaustion had overtaken him. But rest?

No. That wouldn't be the word for it.

Because the stun belt had been triggered at least a dozen times during the last twelve hours. Short sharp attacks that left Josh feeling like he'd just taken a hundred thunderous blows to different parts of his body. There wasn't a vein left within him that didn't feel as if it was swollen and puffy. His eyes were bloodshot and streaming with pale liquid. Hunger was hollowing out his stomach. And the growing stench of urine within the hole was making his stomach heave.

'How you feeling today, pretty boy?' Flatner asked. 'Feel like talking?'

'I need some food,' said Josh.

'You need some food?' Flatner laughed, the roar echoing up the narrow sides of the hole. 'Shit, man. Should have called for room service.'

'I need food, and water,' repeated Josh. 'I'll bloody die if I don't get something soon.'

His throat burnt as he spoke. His tonsils seemed to be engorged, and his tongue had swollen. Every word was delivered through the pain.

'Well, shit, man, you're tugging at my heartstrings.'

'You're a fucking idiot,' snapped Josh. 'I'm no bloody good to you dead, am I?'

'You're no fucking good to me *silent*, pretty boy,' said Flatner. 'If you're not saying anything, you might as well be a corpse for all I care. Least I wouldn't have to listen to your fucking whining all day.'

'Listen,' said Josh. 'I'm telling you, I can't remember anything. I need treatment. I need help. Give me that, get my memory back, and I swear I'll help you.'

Flatner chuckled. 'You're a twisty little fuck, Harding,' he said. 'I'm not so dumb I'm falling for a line like that.'

'I'm telling you I need help. When I know where Luke is I'll tell you. What do I care about some stupid kid?'

'You'll tell me?'

'Of course,' said Josh. 'Just give me some food and water. Some rest. Get my memories back, and I'll tell you everything you need to know.'

A punch landed hard in Josh's stomach. The skin was already so numb that he hardly felt it. But he coughed violently, some bile rising up in his parched throat and landing on the back of his tongue.

'You need some more fucking pain, that's what you need, pretty boy. I'm going to fry you to within an inch of your life. Then you'll talk to me.'

Change tack, Josh told himself. Keep pushing every button you can until you find something that works. 'I know who you work for.'

Flatner paused. 'I work for myself, pretty boy. That understood?'

'You work for Edward Porter, the boss of Porter-Bell. He's the guy who's paying you to torture me.'

'So?' replied Flatner, his tone amused. 'There's always somebody paying for everything.'

'There are several people who know about that. Anything happens to me, it's going to be traced back to Porter, then to you.'

Flatner laughed, then landed a heavy slap across the side of Josh's cheek. He could feel his jaw ache under the impact. 'Nobody's going to give a fuck about what happens to you, pretty boy. For one, you don't exist. And for two, by the time I'm

238

finished with you even the vultures won't recognise you as a human being.'

Josh rolled back. He tried to think of some words, tried to summon up some memories, anything at all that he might be able to cling on to to get him through the next dozen or so hours. Most dying men cried for their mothers. He'd heard them on the battlefield, weeping for them as the bullets tore the life out of them. *I don't even know who my mother is—or was. Whether she is alive or dead.*

I'm living for two things only. Finding out who is responsible for all that has happened to me in the last few weeks—and then ripping their stupid brains out of their miserable heads.

*   *   *

Josh tried to bury his face into the hardened mud, desperate to find some way to keep the noise out of his ears. The decibels were screaming around him, making it impossible to think. Every few seconds, the belt sent a new shot of electricity up through his body. He jerked, then shook, as shock surged along his spine, shooting off along the main arteries within his body until they felt as if they were about to explode.

Then it stopped. Josh slumped forwards, catching his breath. The atmosphere within the hole was fetid and stale. Not a breath of air was circulating, and he'd been here for at least two nights now, filling the cramped space with the stench of his own urine and sweat.

Fear, realised Josh. *That's the main thing you can smell in here.*

239

Flatner had been down here twice more, taking a malicious pleasure in attaching the electrodes to the blanket. Each time, Josh had been subjected to a half-hour or more of brutal physical and mental pain: huge doses of electricity were mixed with beatings and abuse. Every round of abuse had been matched by another round of furious denials from Josh.

He doesn't believe me. I'll be dead before he realises the truth.

Josh started poking his fingers into the dried mud. It was impossible to say when the hole had been dug. Given that it hadn't rained for at least five years in this patch of desert, it could have been there at least that long. His fingernails scratched into the hardened earth. Maybe something has been left down here, Josh mused. A tool that I might be able to use as a weapon. Maybe a scrap of some old plant that I can eat. Or just a trace of moisture that I can rub against my parched lips.

A fingernail broke but Josh ignored the pain. Compared with what he'd just been through, it was nothing. He burrowed further, getting down one inch, then two. Nothing. It was useless, he realised, rolling over onto the blanket. The ropes tagging him down chafed against his skin.

The stun belt will start up again in a minute, just when I least expect it, he told himself grimly. Flatner will be back down, with more threats, more shots of electricity, more beatings. There's nothing left for me. Just the darkness and the pain.

I'm broken. That bastard just doesn't realise it yet.

Somewhere up above him, Josh could hear a scratching sound. One of the covers was moving. His heart sank within him. What was left of his

240

spirit deserted him. Flatner, he guessed and another round of beatings.

A rope this time, without a ladder, Josh noticed as his stare turned upwards. A figure was sliding downwards. Thin and dark. Not Flatner, realised Josh. Not Mark either. Maybe they're tired. *Maybe they're sending in the B team to rough me up a bit.*

The man landed softly, alighting on the ground with the silent agility of a cat. His gaze focused on Josh with a mixture of pity and curiosity. Now Josh could see him clearly. He was dressed in black jeans, a black T-shirt, and around the lower half of his face he had wrapped a black cloth. Whether it was to hide his face or to protect himself, Josh couldn't tell. Only his eyes were visible: brown, and gleaming out of the darkness.

Not a biker, thought Josh. *Whoever the hell he is, he isn't a biker.*

'Who are you?' said Josh hoarsely.

The man remained silent. He moved across to where Josh was lying. In his left hand, Josh could see the curved outline of a steel blade, its handle crafted in wood and ivory. The blade flashed forwards. Instinctively, Josh flinched, trying to prepare himself for the knife penetrating his flesh. Not butchery, he said inwardly. He'd heard of torturers cutting men open. *Please, God, not that.*

The rope sprang loose. Josh held his breath as the man cut one rope, then another. The blade on the knife was as sharp as a razor, slicing through the bindings with ease. One by one, Josh could feel his limbs released from their captivity. 'Who are you?' he repeated, his voice louder this time.

'Stay completely quiet,' said the man, his voice barely a breath above a whisper. 'I'm here to help

241

you.'

For a brief moment, Josh wondered if he might be dreaming. An hallucination, maybe. He knew that happened to torture victims sometimes. The pain and the despair overwhelmed their minds and the victims slipped into trancelike states where they genuinely believed that they were being rescued. Josh closed his eyes, struggling to concentrate. He could feel the ropes snapping loose, and the man's hands on his chest rolling him across the dirt floor.

It's not a trance, he told himself. *It's bloody real.*

His eyes snapped open. The ropes were all cut now. Slowly Josh sat up. His body felt limp, weaker than it had ever felt before. The muscles were slow to respond to his commands, and Josh immediately started to wonder if he'd suffered some long-term nerve damage from the massive quantities of electricity that had surged through his body in the last two days.

'Can you stand?' whispered the man.

Josh struggled to his feet. His knees felt soft and flabby, as if the bone had been taken out of them, and his feet were having trouble keeping a grip on the ground. The man slung an arm around his shoulder, hauling him upwards. Josh clung on to him, as if he was hanging on to a lifebelt in a stormy sea. Slowly, they inched their way across the hole's floor to where the rope was dangling.

Who the hell are you? wondered Josh. *What are you doing here?*

'Think you can climb?'

I can hardly bloody stand up, pal, thought Josh. *But I could climb the sodding Eiffel Tower if it meant escaping from this hell.*

'I don't know,' he said. 'I'll try.'

242

'I'll stand behind you, and help push you up.'

Josh gripped the rope. He reckoned he'd scaled a million different ropes in his life, and this one was only twelve feet long, lying against a dried-mud wall with plenty of grip in it. It shouldn't be any harder than climbing a staircase. *Unless your body had been shot to pieces by two days of torture.*

He clamped his right hand around the rope, followed by his left. His grip was limp and feeble. Summoning up all his powers of concentration, he squeezed hard on the rope and started to drag himself upwards. His shoulders were buckling under the strain, and his bones felt as if they'd been stretched on a rack. You can do this, he told himself silently. One burst of effort and then you'll be free.

Josh could feel the man beneath him using his back to help support Josh's weight. He gripped harder on the rope, hauling himself upwards foot by foot. He could see the lip of the hole, just two feet away. Kicking down, he rested his feet on the other man's back, using his support to help lever himself another few inches upwards.

Maybe Kate sent him, thought Josh. Maybe he's one of Marshall's survivalist friends.

His fingers grabbed up towards the edge. Below him, the other man was now climbing up the rope himself, still using the strength in his back to help propel Josh upwards. For a thin man, he had the toughness of a person twice his size. Josh's nails dug into the hardened mud at the surface. Above him, he could see the night sky. He levered himself up another few inches, bringing his eyes level with the ground. One more heave, he told himself. *And I'll be free.*

243

Josh had no idea what might be waiting for him once he got out of the hole. He didn't even know where he had been imprisoned: he assumed it was in the biker's camp, but he had no way of telling for sure. If there was anyone guarding the site, he had to assume that he'd be shot on sight.

I'll take my chances. *Right now, a bullet is a fate I'd gladly settle for.*

His gaze swivelled first right, then left. A grunt escaped from his lips as, with one last effort from his tortured muscles, he dragged himself over the edge. The hole had been dug about fifty yards from the main camp. He could see the tents and the shacks, and the parked rows of gleaming, chrome-laden motorbikes, but little sign of life. Judging by the position of the moon, it was three or four in the morning: the dead of night. About ten yards from the hole a man was lying face down in the dust. A knife was sticking out of his back. And a trickle of blood was seeping down into the ground.

The night guard, reckoned Josh. At his side lay the controller used to trigger the stun belt.

'Go,' whispered the man below him. 'We haven't got much time.'

That accent, thought Josh. Not quite English, and not quite American either. I can't place it.

Josh scrambled onto the surface. Within an instant, the man was lying at his side. 'There,' he said. 'There's a horse behind that boulder. Think you can make it?'

Josh nodded. *I'd run right across a bed of razor blades in my bare feet to get out of this place.*

His feet kicked back against the ground. The strength is always there when you need it, he reflected as he started running the two hundred

244

metres towards the boulder. Sometimes it's buried so deep that you don't even know it is there. But if you can dig it out, you can survive.

Josh didn't look back as he ran. He just sped forwards, ignoring the pain in his legs. The breath came hard and heavy in his lungs but he kept going. The other man was running at his side. A little over fifty yards, he told himself. *Then you'll have escaped.*

The horse was an elegant grey stallion, the side of its neck dotted with brown freckles. Josh didn't know much about horses, but he could tell at a glance that this one was built for speed. A leather rein tethered the animal to the stump of a tree, and the horse was idly chewing some of the weeds sprouting through the rocky ground.

On this terrain, there could be no better getaway vehicle.

'Get on its back,' said the man. 'This isn't going to be comfortable, but it *is* going to be quick.'

The man got up on the horse first, pulling himself up in one swift, well-practised movement. I've seen him, thought Josh. Somewhere. There was no saddle, just a cloth slung over its back. Nor were there any stirrups, just a leather bridle and rein.

The man grabbed Josh's hand, yanking him upwards. Again, Josh was impressed by the power he packed into his slight frame. Josh landed on the horse's back and sat astride the animal, clinging on to his rescuer's shoulders.

'Hold on tight,' whispered the man. Then he delivered a swift kick to the stallion's side and suddenly they were in motion. Josh gripped hard, adjusting to the rhythm of the gallop. He could feel the adrenalin surging through him as he looked

245

backwards and saw the biker's camp receding into the background.

I'll be back, he vowed. *And when I return my hands will drip with your blood.*

The stallion sped over the open countryside. Josh had little idea where he was going. He clung on tight, grateful to be breathing free air again. His body had taken a terrible beating. Hunger and thirst were eating away at him, but he sensed that if he could just get clear of this place then he might survive. Right now, that's all that counts, he thought. Survival.

The horse was sure-footed and the man was an expert enough rider to steer it through the rough terrain. They were heading north, Josh noted, up towards the heartlands of Arizona. He glanced back a couple of times, but the getaway had been clean enough. If the bikers had found their murdered guard by now, then they hadn't sent out a search party yet. Even if they did, it should be too late by now. The stallion was putting good distance between them and the camp, and taking them across terrain that couldn't be covered on a bike.

My rescuer can ride fast, noted Josh. Without stirrups.

Something sparked in Josh's mind. Without stirrups?

The animal whinnied beneath them, then halted as the man tugged on its reins. 'Here,' he said, pointing down towards a dark pool of water between some rocks. 'He needs to drink. So do you.'

The horse had already stuck his muzzle into the pool, and was taking huge draughts of the water. Josh climbed down uneasily, careful not to hit the ground too hard. He walked unsteadily towards the pool. His legs were shaking beneath him. Keeping to a straight line required all his concentration. Slowly, he knelt down. The thirst was burning within him, but he knew that after two days without water he had to be careful. Too much, too quickly would be damaging. *Just a few sips.*

The man was standing at his side. 'Drink, drink,' he said. 'It'll do you good.'

Josh dipped his hand into the water. It felt cool and refreshing. He lifted his hand and let the water trickle across his face. Next, he used his fingers to rub some of the liquid into his lips. The skin was cracked and parched, and stung at the touch of the fluid. Gradually he started to lick some of the water out of his hands, letting just a few drops at a time into his mouth.

He felt dizzy and disorientated. I haven't slept for two days, he reminded himself.

The horse was finishing its drink, raising its head from the pool and chewing on a clump of weeds. No stirrups, thought Josh again. *Why does that keep bothering me?*

Josh looked again at the man. He was holding on to the reins of the horse, the leather held tight in his grip. The black bandanna was still strapped tight around the lower half of his face, masking him from view.

Josh took another sip of water, letting the cool liquid settle inside him. He could feel it affecting his ragged, electrocuted nerve endings, making his body tingle. Arabia, he thought to himself. That's where men learn to ride horses without stirrups. Arabia. Josh looked down into the pool. In a shaft of moonlight, he caught a glimpse of his own reflection. He scarcely recognised the man looking back at him. There was several more days' growth of beard and his hair was matted with sweat and streaks of blood. His skin was pallid, and there were scratches all down the side of his cheek. But it was the eyes that shocked Josh the most. They had a hunted, scared look.

Suddenly, Josh could see the face of his rescuer reflected next to his own in the pool. I've seen you before, he repeated to himself. The man who'd been staying in the Motel 6, the one who had said he was an Italian, the one who Madge gave me a picture of.

You're not an Italian. You're al-Qaeda.

Josh turned around, looking up into the man's face. He tried to smile, but his lips were still too cracked. 'Thank you for rescuing me.'

The man raised his hand. 'You won't be thanking me soon,' he replied.

The hand slammed into the side of Josh's face. He could feel himself growing dizzy. His body wobbled and in the next instant he crashed face down into the cold water.

SEVENTEEN

Saturday, June 13th. Afternoon.
The light hit Josh's face. He struggled to open his eyes, adjusting his vision to the sunshine streaming in through the open window. Blinking hard, he looked around. A white room. A white bed. With white sheets. And a white towelling bath robe wrapped around him.

248

Where the hell am I now? A hospital, maybe.

He sat bolt upright, feeling his body ache as he stretched himself forwards. It took him a moment to collect his thoughts. My name is Josh Harding, he told himself. I am a British soldier. *And, right now, I'm in some serious shit.*

His memories came flooding back, filling his mind with a hundred different bits of information at the same time. He had been captured by the bikers. He'd been rescued. But his rescuer was, he felt certain, an al-Qaeda agent.

I haven't been rescued at all. *I've just swapped one prison for another.*

Josh paused, taking a moment to asses the damage that had been inflicted upon him in the last two days. There were plenty of cuts and bruises where he had been punched by Flatner, but probably no permanent damage there. It was the electricity that had taken the heaviest toll. Any damage that might have done would be internal. It might be days before his nervous system was working properly. Maybe never.

But it doesn't look like a prison, decided Josh, glancing round the room. It was clean. It was light. There was a glass of water by the bed. A television sat on a simple wooden stand in one corner. Nothing was holding him down. No chains. No handcuffs. No bars. *But it still doesn't mean you're a free man. The worst jails don't look like jails.*

'Are you feeling better this afternoon?'

Josh looked up. It was the man who had rescued him last night. He was dressed in cream chinos and a dark blue polo shirt. There were touches of grey in his hair. His face, without the bandanna to mask it, had a harder edge to it. It was tough and craggy, and the cheeks bore the marks of old wounds. It was the face of a man who had spent much of his life in combat.

I've seen you before, Josh realised. *And not just in the picture that Madge showed me.*

'I don't know,' said Josh. 'It'll take a few days to learn how badly I'm hurt.'

A woman stepped into the room. She was dressed all in white: white tunic, white tights, white gloves, white shoes. And she wore a white linen veil across her face. Her dark brown eyes and black hair were the only part of her body that Josh could see. In one hand, she was carrying a bowl of water, in the other some cotton wool and a bottle of disinfectant.

'We need to dress those wounds,' said the man.

The woman remained silent. She leaned over the side of the belt, removing the sheet. Apart from a new pair of boxer shorts, Josh was naked. The woman dabbed the cotton wool into the water, then pressed the bottle of disinfectant to it. Starting with the neck, she started washing the wounds, bruises and scratches on Josh's body. His skin stung as she did so, but her touch was delicate and gentle.

'What am I doing here?' asked Josh.

The man raised a finger to his lips. 'Quiet,' he said. 'You need to recover your strength.'

'I need to know where I am.'

'No, quiet,' said the man. He smiled, flicking on the television. 'Here, watch some television. Try to relax. Get your strength back.'

Josh lay back on the bed. There was nothing obvious to keep him in place. The man didn't appear to be armed. He couldn't hear any guards outside. Still, he knew that there was no way he could just get up and walk out of here. Sometimes you didn't need to see your jailers. *The strongest chains were the invisible ones.*

There was a weather forecast on the television. It was tuned to CNN. Another bright sunny day for Arizona, Josh noticed. *At least they haven't taken me out of the country.*

'Our top story this hour,' started the newsreader as soon as the weather forecast had finished. 'Another terrifying Cities Attack. We'll be back with all the details after this break.'

Josh stared at the television. His chest was stinging where the woman was dabbing disinfectant into the raw flesh of a wound. Maybe one of the places Flatner had kicked him.

A dog-food advert faded away, then the news started up again. Three o'clock, Josh noted. He'd been asleep for a long time. 'Our top story this hour: another terrifying series of blackouts, this time in the United Kingdom,' started the newsreader. 'At precisely nine this morning, local time, the power was switched off in four British cities. Liverpool, Harrogate, Peterborough and Exeter. In each city, the power went off at just after nine in the morning, and the blackout lasted for precisely one hour. In scenes that have become distressingly familiar across the world, there was widespread chaos in each city as the power shut down. Schools and hospitals were closed, traffic ground to a halt, and factories and offices emptied for the day. In Liverpool there was an outbreak of looting as a shopping mall came under attack from an angry mob. Now, almost ten hours later, police are still struggling to bring the city under control.'

251

Luke, thought Josh instantly. *He's still out there. He's still operating.*

'There is now heightened speculation that the blackouts that started several months ago with the Three Cities Attack are the work of a terrorist network, suspected to be al-Qaeda,' continued the newsreader. 'Power industry experts are saying it is impossible that the simultaneous shutdowns of so many networks in so many different cities could be a coincidence. The fact that Britain, America's closest ally in the War on Terror, has been targeted has only fuelled speculation that the blackouts are part of the terrorist campaign waged against the West.

'Prime Minister Tony Blair issued a statement this afternoon, saying that the nation would not flinch in the face of these attacks, and saying the outrage justified his decision to support the US in the invasion of Iraq. However, Liberal Democrat leader Charles Kennedy said he believed that Britain should now withdraw its troops from Iraq. We'll be back with more reactions to today's events right after this break.'

The television suddenly went dead. The man put down the remote at the foot of Josh's bed and turned to him, a half-smile playing on his lips. 'So you see, Josh Harding, there is much for us to speak of.'

The woman had finished with Josh for the time being, dressing the last of his wounds and applying a final plaster to a cut in his skin. She bowed, staying silent, then withdrew from the room. Josh shut his eyes. Something was happening. An image was sliding behind his closed eyelids, hazy at first, like an out-of-focus picture, but gradually

252

sharpening. *A memory.*

Josh struggled to concentrate as the picture hovered in front of him. A concrete room. He was standing in front of someone. Josh was dressed in white robes, and was dirty and unshaven. The other man was older, dressed in a uniform. He was shouting at him. Josh was shouting back. Bugger it, thought Josh. I can't hear anything. What the hell were we arguing about?

He kept his eyes closed. He could see himself shouting at the man, then standing up. He was moving across to the wall. A picture was in his hands. He was tearing the picture, throwing the torn strips of paper onto the floor.

But even though the picture was shredded by his own hands, Josh could see the face clearly enough. The same face that was standing right next to him now. Khalid Azim. *One of the most wanted al-Qaeda terrorists in the world.*

'I know who you are,' said Josh, his stare meeting Azim's.

'I am your rescuer,' said Azim.

'Your name is Khalid Azim.'

Azim nodded. 'I'm glad to see that your memory is coming back to you,' he said. 'It should make the next few hours so much easier.' He paused. 'For both of us.'

'I've tried to kill you once,' snapped Josh. 'Next time, I will bloody succeed.'

Azim laughed. 'You don't have much in the way of small talk, do you?' he said. 'Still, never mind. For what we have to discuss, only a few words will be needed.'

He walked slowly the length of the small room to stand right next to Josh. 'I have been tracking you

253

for some weeks, following you from place to place. Even after you were shot, I stuck to you, watching you from afar. It was only after those idiots on bikes took you captive that I realised I had to intervene. They were going to kill you, either on purpose or just through sheer bloody carelessness. And that I couldn't allow. Why? Because I knew that if I followed you, you would eventually lead me to what you know I want.' Azim paused, rubbing his left hand reflectively over his jowls. 'Luke. I want to know where Luke is.'

Turning around, he gestured towards the television set. 'They are talking as if these attacks on power stations around the world were organised by al-Qaeda. If only they were, I keep saying to myself. If only they were.' He paused. 'Think of the power that would put into our hands, Josh. Anywhere in the world, at will, with the flick of a few switches, we could plunge whole nations into darkness. Chaos, confusions, riots and anarchy— they would all be ours, at the mere touch of a few buttons. And so they will soon be, Josh. So they will soon be.'

Azim clapped his hands together. The woman walked back into the room. She was carrying a tray on which were a jug of orange juice, a bowl of mixed fruits and a plate of sandwiches. Carefully, she placed it down at the side of the bed. Josh eyed the food hungrily. It was two days since he had eaten anything, but he kept his hands still.

How the hell do I know they are not about to drug me?

'Luke has the software, doesn't he, Josh?' continued Azim. 'And we want it. As soon as we have it, these blackouts really will be the work of

254

al-Qaeda, just as they are describing it on the news.'

'I don't know where he is,' snapped Josh. 'Even if I did, I wouldn't tell you.'

Azim took an apple from the fruit bowl, rolling it between his hands like a cricket ball. 'I don't think you've been paying attention, Josh. Maybe you've taken too many blows to the head. It might have made it hard for you to concentrate. We saw the first attack. Jamestown, Orlando, Seattle, and Harrison. It spells Josh. Now we see there is another attack. What did they say on the news? Liverpool, Peterborough, Exeter, and Harrogate. But I bet when we get all the details tomorrow, we'll find that there was a delay in the sequence of the blackouts. I imagine it went Harrogate, Exeter, Liverpool and then Peterborough.'

Azim took a bite from the apple, a sly smile playing on his face. 'J-O-S-H H-E-L-P,' he said, spelling out each letter carefully. 'I think he's trying to tell you something. Don't you?'

'I don't know what he's bloody trying to do,' said Josh, the anger rising within him. 'And anyway, it doesn't bloody matter. You can kill me if you want to. You'll get nothing from me.'

Azim laughed. 'That SAS bravado—I like it,' he said. 'The bulldog spirit. It is one of the things we can all admire about the British. But let me tell you this. You'll break. They all break. Within a day or two you'll be begging me to kill you. And at some stage I'll put you out of your misery. But only when you've told me where the boy is.'

'Then you might as well kill me now,' spat Josh. 'Get it over with, and save us all a lot of trouble.'

Azim passed across another apple. 'Eat

something.'

'Fuck off.'

Azim placed the apple down on the white cotton sheet. 'Eat something,' he repeated. 'We need to build you up again, get your strength back. Why? Because a strong man will feel the pain more acutely than a weak one. And I want you to feel the pain, Josh. I want you to feel every second of it.'

Before leaving, Azim put a gun to Josh's head, holding it tightly against his temple while the nurse snapped a handcuff onto the side of the bed, securing Josh's left hand. Another cuff chained his left foot to the bed's frame, and the bed itself was fixed to the floor. It didn't matter how violently Josh shook himself, he couldn't make it move an inch. Next the woman returned with a syringe, jabbing the needle hard into his thigh, injecting the pale-coloured liquid straight into his bloodstream. Whether it was a truth serum, a poison, or just a tranquiliser Josh didn't know but within minutes he'd fallen into a deep sleep.

*   *   *

When Josh awoke he had no idea how long he had slept. A few hours or a whole day, it was impossible to tell. He was alone in the room, with just a single pale light shining down from the centre of the ceiling. The TV was switched off. The door was closed, and Josh couldn't hear a single sound from the corridor outside.

I don't even know what kind of building I'm in.

He reached across to the side of the table, taking an apple with his right hand. His left was still chained to the bed. Azim was right, realised Josh as he took a big bite of the fruit. If my strength returns, I will feel the pain more acutely. *But I'll also be able to withstand it for longer.*

The food tasted good. It was two, maybe three days since he had eaten. His stomach was empty and, as with the water, he knew that he had to pace himself. Too much food, eaten too quickly, would only make him feel sick. His body wouldn't be able to take it.

Stomach ache, he thought with a rueful smile to himself. *Somehow, I've got a feeling that's going to be the least of my worries.*

The door opened. Azim walked slowly into the room, his gaze running over Josh. They must know I'm awake, he realised. He scanned the room, looking for cameras, but could see nothing. That doesn't mean anything. Azim knows I'm awake. He's watching me somehow.

'You slept well, I hope,' said Azim.

Josh remained silent. In the few minutes that he had been alone, the lessons on torture and how to survive it had been swirling through his mind. This was going to be different from the beatings he'd taken from Flatner and his thugs. Now he knew that he'd need to withstand the greatest subtleties of mental torture.

'We gave you an injection,' said Azim. 'It should have helped to clear your mind.'

The jab, thought Josh. They've put something into me to try and bring my memory back. They want me to remember everything—so they can squeeze the information out of me.

And the worst of it was this: it was working.

Since he'd been awake, Josh's mind had been working with new clarity. He knew that his name

257

was Josh Harding. He knew that he was a serving soldier in the Regiment. He couldn't say for certain, but he thought he was about thirty. He knew he'd been in the Army for twelve years, and in the special forces for five. And he knew that he'd seen Azim before—and tried to kill him.

I am a long way from a full recovery. But it's starting. My memories are coming back. And that's going to make this a hundred times worse. Flatner couldn't break me because there was nothing to break. Now I'm going to have to use will-power to make sure that I don't tell them anything.

I have to learn how to take my secrets to my grave.

Azim reached out for a pear from the fruit bowl. He took a knife and started peeling it, offering the fruit in cubes to Josh. 'The Prophet teaches us when to be merciful and when to be cruel,' he said. 'First we take care of you, then we bleed you for the information that we need. That is our way.'

Josh took a slice of the pear. He could feel the fear eating away at his gut: nothing had happened yet, but he could be certain that it would. 'I know nothing,' he said. 'You saw the beating I took from those bikers. If I didn't tell them anything, I certainly won't tell *you* anything.' He looked up towards Azim, his expression hardening. 'I'm a British soldier. I know when I'm done for, and I'm enough of a man not to complain about it. So if your fucking Prophet is so merciful, just kill me now and get it over with.'

'Brave words, Josh,' said Azim. 'And soon we'll set about our gruesome business. Then we'll see if the strength of your spirit matches the strength of your language. But first, I should make you an offer. You should understand that I am not a cruel

258

man. I take no pleasure in what is about to happen. Talk now. Save yourself the pain that is about to come.'

'Piss off.'

Azim clasped his hands together, as if in prayer. 'The torturer abandons his humanity as much as his victim does. Spare us both the indignity. Talk to me now. Tell me where Luke is.'

'I don't know,' spat Josh. 'And if I *did* know, what's the bloody point of telling you? You'll kill me anyway. You're not going to release me. Not now that I know you're here.'

Azim nodded. 'Of course,' he replied. 'Your demise is inevitable now—we both know that. And let me assure you, in a few hours' time you'll welcome it more eagerly than you ever welcomed a woman into your bed. Death is not so frightening to men such as us. An honourable death—what more could a warrior ask for?'

Azim paused, turning away from the bed and walking to the back of the room. He reached around the half-open door, collecting a small wicker box, then turned back towards Josh. 'But there are many different ways to die. A death with honour on the battlefield. A death in your own bed, with your wife and children around you to say goodbye. None of those are so bad. But this isn't going to be like that. It will be a nasty, squalid, vicious death, filled with fear, despair, defeat and the stench of self-loathing. That's what awaits you, Josh.'

Azim walked closer to the bed, the wicker basket swinging in his hand. Josh watched it closely, trying to see what it contained. It measured ten inches by twenty. Enough room for a whole array of instruments of torture, noted Josh grimly. Knives, manacles, thumbscrews. It could be anything.

'Once more, Josh,' said Azim. 'Just tell me where Luke is.'

'I don't bloody know,' shouted Josh.

He gritted his teeth. Close your eyes, he told himself. *Let your imagination take you away to a better place.*

But his eyes wouldn't shut. Josh watched with mounting dread as Azim opened the small basket. His hand slipped inside, then emerged. Sticking up from his tightly clenched fist was the head of a snake. 'You don't like these, do you, Josh?' said Azim, a soft smile breaking out on his lips.

The reptile had been sleeping. Its neck was held tightly within Azim's fist, and its long thin body drooped down into the basket. Slowly it was starting to wake up. One bright green eye opened, then another. The snake's skin was black, mottled with greens and blues, with ridges running down the side of its thick, leathery skin. Its tongue darted from its mouth, then shot back inside as it closed one eye.

'What the fuck is that?' snapped Josh.

'An Arizona Black Rattlesnake, also known as a *Crotalus cerberus*,' said Azim.

'Keep it away from me!'

Azim smiled. 'Talk to me, Josh. Then I'll get rid of the beast.'

'I told you—I don't bloody know anything.'

Azim put the snake back in the basket and clapped his hands together. The woman re-entered the room. She was still wearing the veil wrapped across her mouth, yet Josh could look straight into her cold brown eyes. He could feel himself

260

recoiling from her presence.

'Handcuff him,' commanded Azim.

Josh's left hand was already manacled to the bed, as was his left foot. The woman approached him, a set of steel handcuffs held before her. She sat down next to Josh. Slowly she reached out for his right hand.

'Leave me alone,' shouted Josh.

Within a second, Azim had whipped a pistol from inside his tunic: an American-made Mauser M2. The snubbed steel nose of the weapon was now nestling against Josh's ear, cool and hard against his skin. 'Do as she says, Josh.'

'Kill me now, you bastard,' shouted Josh, a note of hysteria in his voice. 'Get the bloody thing over with.' The gun was pressing tighter against his skin. He could feel it pressing into the bone of his skull. 'Hold still, man,' whispered Azim. 'Let her cuff you.'

Josh rolled sideways, snatching his hand away from the woman. She pushed herself on top of him, straddling him with a thick and powerful pair of thighs. He could feel her weight, hot and sticky against his body, making it impossible for him to move any further. The gun was still pressing against his head and Azim's finger was twitching on its trigger. The woman spat in his face. A warm ball of saliva landed hard against his cheek. As Josh brushed it aside, she grabbed his right hand, snapping one cuff into place. Her movement was swift and practised. In a fraction of a second she had placed the other cuff round the bedpost and snapped it shut. Josh was trapped. Both hands were secured and so was one foot.

I can't move, he told himself grimly. *I can't*

escape.

'Infidel pig,' sneered the woman. She spat again, this time landing a ball of saliva just next to Josh's eye. Her breath smelled of onions and sugar, and so did her spit. But with both hands cuffed, it was impossible for Josh to wipe it away.

Now the woman climbed away from his chest, straightening out her white skirt as she stood back on the floor. Azim picked up the wicker case, lifting out the snake again. The reptile opened an eye, looking around the room lazily. Gripping it by the head, Azim put it down at the foot of the bed.

'Want to tell me where Luke is?'

'Piss off.'

Azim pulled a dead mouse from his pocket. He held the small corpse up by its tail, then placed it down on Josh's chest. Dead for a day or two, reckoned Josh from the look of the animal. It was already starting to smell like the sewers it had probably come from. He could see the snake focusing its beady green eyes on it.

'He's hungry,' said Azim. 'And when he starts eating, he doesn't stop.'

Azim looked down at Josh, his expression sympathetic. 'Talk to me.'

'Fuck off.'

Azim leaned across him. In his right hand he was holding a black wooden cane with which he tapped the snake on its back. Suddenly, its eyes, filled with anger, fixed on Josh.

Azim turned around and walked towards the door. 'When you're ready, call for me. I'll be listening.'

Josh could hear the door shutting. His stare was riveted on the snake. The reptile's head had reared up, and it was sniffing the air. Slowly it started to advance. Its head moved across Josh's leg, then the rest of its three-foot-long body started sliding over him.

He could feel himself starting to tremble. Get a bloody grip, man, he ordered himself. *You show any fear, this animal's going to bite you for sure.*

The snake was moving closer. It stopped at Josh's groin, sniffing the skin for several minutes, its tongue flashing in and out of its mouth. Then it moved on upwards. Its skin felt like a rubber tyre: thick and fleshy, yet also tepid. Its eyes looked up towards Josh. At first it seemed to be afraid, but then it grew in confidence as it noticed that Josh wasn't making any move to protect himself.

The snake knows, thought Josh. It knows that I can't move. *It's laughing at me.*

It paused, sniffing the mouse. Its tongue darted across the animal's skin, licking the gradually decomposing flesh. Then its teeth sank into the mouse's body, tearing at it ferociously. Small bits of fur dropped onto Josh's chest, mixing with the saliva drooling from the snake's open mouth.

Josh could feel his hands shaking. The fear was taking control of him. Don't bite me, he muttered to himself, repeating the phrase over and over. Please God, don't bite me.

The beast paused, looking up towards Josh. Then it sniffed the hairs on his chest. Its tongue flicked against them.

Stay still, man. Stay as still as a rock and maybe it won't bite you.

Shall I call Azim? No, Josh told himself, gripping onto the side of the bed. You can't tell Azim *anything.*

263

Just kill me with one bite, thought Josh, looking towards the snake. Get it over with.

The movement was so sudden that its swiftness bewildered Josh. One second the snake was eyeing him idly, as if calmly assessing his strength, then he could see its tongue flicking out and its head dipping downwards, like a seagull swooping on a fish in the sea.

The teeth felt icy cold as they sank into Josh's chest. The snake's sharp fangs easily pierced his skin. He could feel his flesh being punctured. Next he felt the reptile's tongue flash forwards. A stinging sensation burned through him.

The venom.

The snake has bitten me.

Josh could feel blood starting to seep out across his chest. The snake whipped around and started slithering back down his body.

Already Josh was starting to feel dizzy. His vision was clouding. He could feel his limbs beginning to stiffen as his skin turned numb. His body felt chilled, as if the air-conditioning had been turned on.

Blackness. Josh tried to open his eyes, but the eyelids refused to move. An image was floating through his mind. The brunette. And, next to her, the little girl. Paula, realised Josh. The brunette's name was Paula. And the little girl was called Emily. He could hear her laughter as he played with her, and the sound of her breathing gently in his arms as he cradled her to sleep.

My daughter. *I have a daughter.*

Who I might never see again.

The venom had him in its grip now. Josh couldn't open his eyes, nor could he move. His breathing was slow. A terrible pounding was beating against the side of his head.

Stay awake, Josh ordered himself.

But he could feel his consciousness departing. As the darkness overwhelmed him Josh wondered if he was dying.

EIGHTEEN

Sunday, June 14th. Morning.
Josh's head was splitting as he gradually emerged from a deep sleep. He opened one eye first, adjusting it to the bright light shining over him. Then the other. I should be dead, he thought. That sodding snake's poison should have killed me. But then bloody Azim would never get any info out of me, about Luke or anything else. He and that bitch nurse or whatever she is must have shot me full of anti-venom serum as soon as I'd passed out.

He could see Azim peering down at him, a smile playing on his lips. 'Good morning, Josh,' he said, his tone ingratiating and insincere. 'Welcome to another day in hell.'

Josh rattled his handcuffs. The metal frame of the bed creaked and groaned as he shook it angrily but all he was doing was hurting himself, he realised. The two sets of cuffs holding his arms in place were still locked tight, as was the single set securing his left foot. The metal rings around his wrists and ankle cut into his skin as he struggled to pull himself free.

'Stop fighting, Josh,' said Azim. 'And talk to me.'

Josh stayed silent. He was still trying to collect his

thoughts, to remember where he was, who he was, and what he had to do.

My name is Josh Harding. I'm a British soldier. *And I'm about to die for my country.*

'The Americans are amateurs when it comes to torture,' said Azim. 'Flatner and his idiots, they knew nothing. Just like those idiots in Abu Ghraib back in Iraq. Brute force, that's all they understand.'

He was toying with a thin glass tube, turning it over and over in his hands. 'But torture is a subtle art, as subtle in its own way as the arts of love. Your victim is like a woman. You must coax him to give up his secrets, just as you would coax a woman into giving up her innocence.'

'And what if your victim doesn't know anything?'

'But he will, Josh, he will,' said Azim. 'You see, a man's memory is a delicate thing. The Arab world has its own traditions of medicine. The greatest doctors of medieval times were all Arab. Much of their wisdom might have been lost, but there are still lessons that have been passed down through the ages. And one of them is about memory.'

Christ, thought Josh. *This guy's trying to bore me to death.*

Azim held up the glass tube between his fingers. Inside Josh could see a pale red liquid. 'A memory can be restored through care, treatment and rest,' Azim continued. 'But it can also be restored through pain and suffering. The careful application of pain can sharpen and sensitise the nerves until the mind yields up its secrets. Trust me, when you want to die enough, then your memory will come back.'

'What the hell is that?' said Josh, nodding

towards the tube.

'Blood, Josh. Your blood.'

Josh could feel his stomach muscles tightening.

'We took a pint while you slept,' continued Azim. 'And we're going to keep taking pints from you. Our blood is our strength. You're a soldier, you know the truth of that. Without our blood, we are nothing, we are weak. And that's how I want you, Josh. Weak.'

Azim flung the tube down. Josh could hear the glass cracking and splintering. He could see the liquid spill out, spreading a thick crimson stain across the floor. My own blood, he thought in appalled fascination.

'Talk to me,' barked Azim.

'Piss off.'

'Talk to me,' shouted Azim again, his voice louder this time.

Josh struggled to stay silent. A rage was burning within him. His head was spinning, and his vision weak. With mental fingertips, he was clinging desperately to the memories that he'd recovered last night. Paula. My wife, or maybe ex-wife. And Emily. My daughter. Suddenly he could see her smile and hear her laugh as vividly as if she was cuddling up to him in his arms. That's something to survive for—and something worth dying for, too, he thought.

'You're a fool, Josh. You're going to tell me, and then you're going to die. Make it easy for yourself.'

'Piss off,' yelled Josh again, summoning as much strength as possible into his voice.

Josh tried to lash out with his hand, trying desperately to strike Azim, but the chain binding him to the bed cut into his skin. He could see Azim

267

pulling a white handkerchief from his jacket pocket. He slowly unfolded it, revealing three white pills. 'Here,' he said, leaning down in front of Josh. 'Take them.'

'What the hell are they?'

'Two aspirin, and one warfarin,' said Azim.

Josh hesitated. Aspirin was a painkiller, and warfarin was a drug given to heart patients and anyone else who needed their blood thinning. Christ, realised Josh, aspirin thins the blood as well, that's why it too is recommended to heart patients. If you get a cut after taking those three pills it will be impossible for the body to form a clot to stop the bleeding. The blood is going to pour out of you like a tap.

'Fuck off,' spat Josh. 'If you want me to bleed to death, then just cut me open, you bastard.'

He glanced up. The woman had walked into the room and was standing at the foot of the bed, with a syringe in her hand. She stood close to the bed, looking down at Josh.

'Take the pills, Josh,' said Azim. 'It will hurt less than the injection, and the end result will be the same. Any anticoagulant can be taken as a pill or a jab, as I'm sure you know.'

'Just get her away from me,' shouted Josh.

'Talk to me, then,' snapped Azim.

Josh stayed silent.

'Jab him,' Azim said, glancing towards the woman.

The needle stabbed into the flesh of his thigh. Josh tried to struggle, but against the cuffs on his hands and leg it was useless. The woman stirred the syringe around, searching for a vein, then squeezed hard. The liquid disappeared. Josh yelped as the

268

needle was pulled roughly out of his body.

'I'll give you another chance,' said Azim coldly. 'Tell me where Luke is.'

'Do your worst, you bastard.'

Azim drew a knife from his pocket. Nothing fancy. Just a plain steel kitchen knife, four inches long, the sort of thing for chopping onions. Doesn't matter, thought Josh grimly. It'll do the job.

'Spare us both the misery, Josh,' said Azim.

Josh bit his tongue, preparing himself for the pain that he now accepted was inevitable. Azim leaned over the side of Josh's body, examining him the way a butcher might examine a steak that he was about to carve. He held the knife steady in his hand, then jabbed it into the top of Josh's shoulder. Josh cried out in pain as blood started to seep from the wound. He could feel himself getting drowsier as the drugs took effect. Blood was gushing from the wound, turning the sheets bright crimson.

Josh closed his eyes. The strength was draining out of him, as if he was about to die.

*   *   *

The sound of the television roused Josh from his slumber. He opened his eyes, blinking hard at the screen. The news. A blonde woman was mouthing the words, but Josh was struggling to concentrate.

More blood, he realised. They took more blood out of me while I was sleeping. The strength is literally draining out of me.

'Another terrifying Three Cities Attack,' said the newsreader on the TV screen.

Josh tried to calm his mind as he focused on what

269

she was saying. A harsh neon light was filling the room, and the television was turned up loud. His throat was parched, and his limbs felt numb and lifeless. Hunger was gnawing away at his gut.

'In a pattern that is now terrifyingly familiar, there were blackouts today in Little Rock, Arkansas, in Birmingham, Alabama, and in Jersey City. In each city, the power was switched off at nine a.m. local time precisely, and remained switched off for one hour. Local law-enforcement authorities reported widespread panic, confusion and chaos as traffic systems, airports, schools and hospitals were all shut down. But after this fourth attack—the third in just a few days—the emergency services already have in place a well rehearsed plan for dealing with them. Within minutes of the attack, National Guard personnel were patrolling the streets, preventing the outbreaks of looting and rioting seen in earlier incidents. Still, two people in Birmingham died when a truck rammed into a hairdressing salon after failing to spot an emergency traffic signal. And one person died in Little Rock when the power was turned off during heart surgery and the hospital's back-up generators failed to switch on in time.'

Josh squinted at the screen, trying to shake off the pounding headache beating at the inside of his forehead and the terrible waves of fear that were assaulting his nervous system. Another attack, he told himself. Luke's still out there. But where the hell is he? *And why the hell does he keep doing this?*

'After yet another attack, more and more people are becoming convinced this must be the work of terrorists, possibly al-Qaeda,' continued the newsreader. 'A spokesman for the Pentagon said earlier today that, despite earlier denials, the

270

possibility that terrorists may have worked out a way to hijack power systems is now being taken seriously. We are going to go over live now to our correspondent at the Pentagon, Ken Flagstaff. Ken, what's the latest you're hearing?'

Azim flicked off the television. He stood over the bed, looking down at Josh, his expression a mixture of pity and contempt. 'We don't need to listen to some prattling reporter outside the Pentagon, do we, Josh? We know who's responsible for these blackouts. All we need to know now is where to find him.'

Josh looked first at the blank TV screen, then up at Azim. He could feel himself starting to become afraid, and the emotion disgusted him. He had felt many different emotions in his life: despair, anger, confusion, rage—they were all part of what a soldier expected to experience on the field of battle.

But abject, cowardly fear? I hoped I could always resist that.

'So where is he, Josh? Where is he?'

Josh shook his head. 'I've told you that I don't know.'

Azim clapped his hands together. The woman walked into the room. She was still dressed all in white, and she still had a veil wrapped around her mouth, as if she refused to breathe the air of a room that Josh had slept in. Her brown eyes turned icily towards where he was lying, and Josh sensed that she was enjoying herself: there was a hint of amusement in her expression as she advanced towards him at a snail's pace.

She had a wicker basket in her hands. Through the silence, Josh could hear the sound of something

271

rustling.

Please God, not another snake.

'First we get J-O-S-H. Then we get H-E-L-P.' Azim paused. 'And now we get L-B-J. What does that mean, Josh?'

He shrugged. 'Lyndon B. Johnson. An American President during the Vietnam War.'

Azim shook his head. 'I don't think so. Unless it's some kind of clue. I think it's a message. He asks you for help, then he tells you where to find him. I think the letters L, B and J mean something. Either in that order, or in some other sequence. But that's the signal. So where is he, Josh?'

'I don't know, I've told you that.'

The woman stepped closer. Josh thought that he could smell the snake inside her basket.

'Tell me, Josh,' said Azim, his voice growing louder. 'Tell me, and I'll let you die like a man.'

'I don't know,' shouted Josh. 'I've bloody told you that.'

Azim clapped his hands together. Silently, the woman unfastened the basket. The head of a snake slipped out. Its pale green-eyed stare darted hungrily around the room. About three feet long, with banded black, red, and ivory skin, the muscles in its neck were straining as it looked across at Josh. From its manic writhing Josh could tell that the animal was starving. Probably not been fed for a couple of days, he realised with mounting dread. *The bastard is going to bite everything in sight.*

Azim tapped Josh's chest with his cane. 'We're going to keep doing this until you tell me,' he said flatly.

'I'd tell you if I knew,' Josh yelled. 'Just keep it bloody off me.'

272

'The pain will stir your memories, Josh. When you genuinely want to die, then you'll tell me.'

'Just keep the snake off me, please. Please.'

Josh could hear his own whimpering and hated himself. He was willing himself to be strong, but the strength was ebbing out of him. Another day, another two days, maybe three at most. *I'm starting to break. I can feel it.*

'Just one bullet, Josh, and this can all be over,' said Azim. 'Just tell me what I want to know.'

Josh remained silent, clenching his fists. Another place, he told himself angrily. *Take yourself to another place.*

'Let it out,' said Azim angrily, turning on his heels and walking out of the room.

The woman placed the open basket at the foot of the bed. The snake slithered out, its long thin body sliding up across the sheets and rubbing against Josh's body. It moved roughly across him.

Josh screamed, a curling howl that seemed to fill the tiny room.

The snake paused and looked at Josh, first in surprise, then with curiosity. It flicked its tail angrily against the skin of Josh's thigh. Then it started sniffing his chest.

I know, thought Josh, suddenly terrified by the knowledge sweeping over him. I know what L, B and J means. *And I know where I can find Luke.*

*   *   *

Josh rolled over onto his side. There was a terrible pain in his chest where the snake had bitten him. Looking down, he could see the marks where its fangs had dug deep into his skin, and he could see

273

where his own blood had dripped onto the white sheets.

He tried to see if the snake was lying somewhere in the room, satiated and sleeping. But he could see no sign of it.

He had been lying awake for an hour now. The ceiling's fluorescent lights were shining down on him. He no longer had any idea what time it was. Nor what day it was. The fruit had been taken away, and so had the water. His body felt weak and exhausted. Josh had no idea what it was like to die, but he wouldn't have been surprised if it felt something very much like this.

He could remember the snake sinking its teeth into his chest. He could remember losing consciousness as the waves of fear, pain and disgust had washed through him. And he could remember something else as well: a set of memories that had come flooding back into his mind just before he'd gone under. Josh couldn't be sure if it was the blood loss or the snakes' venom that was making him remember.

But he ordered himself to hold on to them. *Those memories may be the thread on which your life is hanging.*

Josh struggled to concentrate, slowly reassembling the elements of the story. The initials meant something. L, B, and J were a code, a set of letters that he and Luke had agreed with each other. He couldn't recall the precise time or place, but he could see the picture as clearly as if it were playing on the TV in front of him. He and Luke were sitting in the mountains somewhere. There were rocks and boulders behind them, and scrubland stretching below them. A small campfire

274

was burning next to them, providing the only illumination apart from the stars and the moon in the sky. Luke had a laptop open on his knees. The machine was plugged into a car battery placed next to them in the dust. They were discussing something, although not all the words were clear to Josh. He could see Luke's lips moving, but he couldn't hear all the words. Word by word, Josh started to piece together what had been agreed between them. If they were separated in the next twenty-four hours, then Luke would contact Josh by switching off the power in three different cities. The first letters of those cities would be a code: use the code and it would give you the GPS coordinates of where the other person had hidden themself. L, B, and J, were the letters. All Josh would need was a GPS machine that could be picked up for a few dollars in any electronics store and that would tell him where Luke was.

I know, he realised. *I know where Luke is.*

Josh, help. L, B and J.

But what possible help can I be to him now?

The best I can hope for is to die quickly without revealing where he is.

Josh lay silently in the bed. The handcuffs were still holding his hands and one foot in place, and he had stopped trying to move. The next few hours and days were going to be the hardest of his life, he told himself. As long as his memory had been shot to pieces, it had been possible to take the torture. That's why commanders send out their men with only the minimum of information. That's why terrorists organise themselves in cells, with no contact between different groups even in the same town. You can't reveal any secrets you don't know,

275

no matter what they do to you.

But now I know. And at some point they're going to squeeze the information out of me. The willpower of even the strongest man will snap eventually. *It's just a matter of finding his breaking point.*

Josh steeled himself. At some point Azim would be back. So would the woman. They would have snakes with them. Maybe something worse. My best hope is to provoke them, he told himself grimly. I need to rile them. I need to get their blood up so high they make a mistake.

I need to push them over the edge. So that they kill me.

Josh could feel the silence all around him. He didn't want to die, he knew that. Enough memories had come back to him in the past few days for him to know that there was a life back home waiting for him. There was Paula. He thought they had split up, but she was still the most beautiful woman he'd ever seen. Maybe they'd all get back together some day. There was Kate too. He still had no way of knowing whether she'd escaped Flatner and his thugs. If she was okay, if he escaped, maybe there would be something between them. And most of all there was Emily. A little girl with the looks of an angel. Emily. My daughter. Whatever happens, I must act in a way that would at least make her proud of my memory.

I don't mind dying if I have to. So long as it's dignified.

The door slid open. There was a creak where the hinge needed oiling, and Josh had learned to fear the sound. He glanced upwards. The woman was slipping silently into the room. In the past day, Josh

276

had also started to recognise her scent: a mixture of onions, cheap perfume and disinfectants. His stomach was already churning as he took in the vile smell. He could see a long syringe in her hands, its metal tip sparkling under the neon light. *My blood,* realised Josh. *They're coming to drain more blood from me.*

He lay perfectly still. Azim had a cold intelligence that Josh could only respect. The woman was more hot-blooded. Her eyes were full of anger and contempt. The rage within her was always going to make her vulnerable. If she was provoked, she might lash out.

Of the two of them, she's more likely to make a mistake. She's the one who might kill me.

She was leaning over him now, looking at his skin. Josh kept his eyes closed, tracking her movements by the stale smell of her breath. *She thinks I'm asleep,* he told himself. He felt the needle jab his shoulder. The metal tip was thick, and he could feel his nerves stinging as it pierced the skin and started probing its way towards the vein. *Now,* he told himself. *Strike.*

Using all the strength he had left, Josh bucked upwards with a sharp jerking motion. 'Get the fuck off me, you bitch,' he roared.

The woman looked petrified, as if Josh had just risen from the grave. The hypodermic fell out of her hand and onto the floor. For a moment she froze, unable to move. Josh was heaving himself up, ignoring the pain of the handcuffs cutting into his wrists. 'Untie me, you bloody bitch,' he shouted. 'Untie me before I bloody kill you.'

The woman slapped him hard on his cheek.

'Kanith, kanith,' shouted Josh.

I may not have learned much Arabic in my time as a soldier. *But I know the word for 'Fucker'.*

He could feel her solid palm hitting his skin, and the flesh underneath started to swell. 'Get back to your bloody camel, bitch,' shouted Josh.

He spat up into her face, putting a gob of saliva directly into her eye.

She hit him again and again, the fury rising within her. The blows rained down on Josh's body and he could feel his strength ebbing away under the punishment. The veil had fallen away from the woman's mouth, and he could see her full face for the first time: an ugly, sour set of features—a pinched, thin mouth and a heavy, brutal jaw.

This is it, thought Josh. I'm going to die. But at least I'll take my secret with me . . .

Azim ran into the room. He yanked the woman hard by the shoulders. 'Stop it, Nadia, in the name of all that is sacred, stop it,' he yelled. 'You'll kill the man. You'll kill him.'

The woman resisted Azim, still trying to strike Josh with her fists. She hit his face again, then his ribs. The pain raged through Josh's body. I haven't eaten, I haven't drunk, I've been tortured for four days, I've got no strength, no endurance left. Lose consciousness now, and I'll never wake up.

'Stop it *now*,' roared Azim, throwing both his arms around the woman in an effort to control her.

'He insulted me,' she spat. 'He dies.'

Azim slapped her hard across the face. A trickle of blood started to seep from her nose. 'Calm,' said Azim. 'Calm down.'

Her breathing started to slow, and her fists dropped to her side. A tear was running down the side of her face.

278

Josh lay still on his back. Every inch of his body was screaming out in pain. The bruises and swellings on the front of his chest were turning purple, and he could still see the punctures where the snakes had bitten him. Still alive, he told himself grimly. I can't even get myself killed.

And I can't do another round with the snakes.

Azim turned to him and smiled. 'Clever, Josh, clever,' he said. 'You want us to kill you. And we will, don't worry. A nice clean bullet to the head. Right after you tell us where Luke is.'

Another day, another two days, that's how long I have to hold out. Luke has sent me a message, but if I don't respond in two or three days he must realise that something has gone wrong. He must realise it's time for him to move on. He won't keep waiting for me.

Take the punishment for another forty-eight hours. Then tell them. *And let it all end with a simple bullet to the head.*

'Get the snake,' snapped Azim.

The woman stooped to collect her veil from the floor. She rearranged it over her face, then stalked from the room.

'The snakes aren't bloody working,' said Josh. 'Haven't you got anything else?'

Azim rubbed his hands together. 'Torture is not a pick 'n' mix buffet,' he said. 'That is the trouble with the infidels. They have no attention-span any more. If they don't get instant results they lose interest. That is not the way a real torturer works. He picks his point of weakness and he scratches away at it until the stress and the pain become unbearable.'

He leaned down close to Josh's face. 'You see,

279

I've heard the screams, Josh. I've heard the moans and the howls as the reptiles sink their teeth into your flesh. And I know that snakes are *your* weakness.'

The woman had walked back into the room, the wicker basket in her hand.

'Please, no,' said Josh, the anxiety already building inside him. 'I've told you, I don't know anything.'

The woman unfastened the basket's lid and the snake inside shot out: this time it was one with yellow eyes and a skin that was jet black. Josh could feel himself recoiling: every muscle and nerve in his body screamed with pain, begging him to snap, to reveal where Luke was.

Josh closed his eyes, but despair was starting to overwhelm him.

'Luke, Luke . . .' he started.

Azim turned to look at him, his stare burning with curiosity.

'Yes, Josh? What about Luke?'

'Luke, Luke . . .'

The words had taken Josh himself by surprise, tumbling out of his mouth as if he could no longer control his own tongue. The snake was edging along the side of the bed, its eyes darting from side to side. A dead mouse was already dangling from Azim's hand, ready to be placed on Josh's chest.

'What about Luke? Where is he?'

'L, B and J,' stuttered Josh. 'It means . . . you need . . . I . . .'

No, he screamed silently to himself. No, hold on, man. If al-Qaeda gets hold of that software they'll wreak havoc on the whole world.

You mustn't break for at least another forty-eight

hours.

Just take the punishment. You're a bloody soldier.

'What does it mean?' shouted Azim.

'Fuck off,' spat Josh. He felt relief flooding through him as he regained control of his tongue. 'Fuck off,' he spat again.

'The snakes will chew you to ribbons, Josh,' shouted Azim. 'Just tell me.'

Josh pressed his lips together.

Azim turned around and strode from the room. 'You're breaking, Josh,' he said coldly as he left. 'I can smell it. You're breaking. And in a few minutes you'll be mine.'

The snake was slithering up the side of Josh's leg, its tongue darting out of its mouth. Josh could feel sweat pouring off his body as he steeled himself for the reptilian attack that was inevitable.

Somewhere in the distance, Josh heard an explosion. And gunfire.

NINETEEN

Sunday, June 14th. Evening.

The explosion had come from fifty, maybe a hundred yards away, Josh judged.

The snake was advancing up towards his neck, its dry skin scratching against his chest. Josh could ignore it because he was listening out for more explosions, more gunfire. He could hear feet running along the corridor.

A rescue. Please God, let it be a rescue.

Then Azim burst into the room, the woman at his side. 'Unchain him,' he shouted. 'Get him to the

281

car. I'll fight them off.'

The woman leaned over Josh, unlocking the two pairs of handcuffs. With a sweeping movement of her hand, she struck the snake on the side of its head, knocking the startled reptile to the floor. She had a .45 Colt automatic in her grip. Then Josh was dragged to his feet. The gun was pressed against his head, and he had only a pair of boxer shorts for protection.

'One wrong move, and I'll shoot you,' she hissed.

Josh could feel the adrenalin surging through his veins. A few minutes ago he'd been ready to die. Now there was the possibility of survival.

Stay calm, he told himself. Think clearly. *You've got a chance.*

Azim had left the room again. From somewhere in the distance, Josh could hear another burst of gunfire. A machine gun, he reckoned, from the sound. He got unsteadily to his feet. It had been two days since he'd been allowed to walk, and his body had taken a terrible beating. His balance was unsteady, and he needed the woman's hands on him to help him hold himself up.

'Move,' she shouted, pointing to the door. 'Move.'

Josh edged his way to the corridor.

'Faster,' she shouted. 'Move, *kwanii*, move.'

Josh picked up on the Arabic expression. *She's calling me a faggot.*

Another man was standing in the corridor. A guard, guessed Josh. He pointed a Colt pistol like the woman's at Josh, and nodded him towards the doorway. Suddenly Josh was starting to get some bearings. The building was a cheaply built bungalow. One central corridor ran through it and

Josh's room had been at the end. He could see a living area and kitchen at the front, and through a doorway lay a dark patch of lawn fronting the road.

The gunshots seemed to be coming from the front of the building, but amid the noise of shooting it was impossible for Josh to get a precise fix on their location.

Josh could see another guard running with Azim to the front of the bungalow. Both guards were young Arab men, stocky, dressed in jeans and black T-shirts with bulging muscles and trim black beards.

'This way, this way,' hissed the first guard, urging Josh on along the corridor towards the back.

I'll make my move any moment now, Josh decided. *If I die trying, then that's what I wanted all along.*

Josh reckoned he'd already figured out Azim's plan. The terrorist wanted to hold off his opponents for a few minutes to buy himself enough time to hustle Josh into a van and get him out of the area. To another safe house.

They passed a window and Josh glanced out. In the gloom of the evening he thought he could make out at least three men crouched behind boulders in the scrubland outside. They were at least thirty yards away. Their faces were obscured but he could see the muzzles of their rifles. At the end of the corridor, Azim and his guard were stationed behind the metal door frame, using it to protect themselves, their own weapons ready.

Azim began to lay down a deadly barrage of fire that would make it impossible for the attackers to advance.

A stand-off, thought Josh.

283

'Faster, faster,' shouted the woman, her voice breathless.

Both the guard and the woman had pistols rammed hard into Josh's flesh. A terrible thought struck him, slowing him down. Maybe I'm not being rescued? Maybe it's just Flatner and his thugs come to take me back?

Maybe I'm better off making a run for it and letting them shoot me now.

The woman shoved him through the back door. Immediately, Josh could feel the blast of warm air hitting him in the face. His vision was blurred. He paused, taking two deep breaths.

The back of the building gave onto a square compound, marked by a boundary of rocks but no fence. The tarmac driveway circled the building and ended up there, in a parking space ten yards from the back door.

A white van was sitting on the tarmac. The woman pointed to it. 'There,' she hissed. 'Get in.'

Josh started to move. The woman was gripping his arm, and ahead of them the guard had already unlocked the van's door and was gesturing to Josh to get inside. A thin mattress was laid out on the floor, and chains, ropes and manacles were attached to the inside of the van. Great, thought Josh. *A bloody travelling torture chamber.*

'Get in now, man,' hissed the guard, in an accent that was part American, part Saudi Arabian.

No, decided Josh. I'm not bloody getting in there, pal. *You can shoot me if you want to, but I'm not bloody going.*

He swung his elbow sharply upwards, smashing it into the woman's jaw. It was a move he'd first learned as a defender for the school football team,

284

and he'd found it as effective as anything he'd ever learned. The woman spun around, shocked by the sudden pain shooting through her face, her gun loose in her hand.

A deafening roar rolled out across the yard which was instantly filled with the smoke of the explosion. A stun grenade, reckoned Josh. Or some kind of home-made mortar shell. He closed his eyes and mouth to protect himself. He could feel the heat of something burning, and he started to run to get away from the blaze.

'Stop or I shoot,' shouted the guard, his voice ragged and tense.

Feel free, pal. My funeral can't start soon enough.

Josh kept running, his eyes still tight shut, stumbling forwards. He wanted to get round to the front of the house where the attackers were.

He heard a shot, then another one.

Somewhere nearby he could hear a bullet slamming into the ground.

'Quick, this way, man,' snapped a voice. 'Fucking run, man.'

Josh recognised the coarse croak. O'Brien.

Josh swivelled to the left. He heard another shot. The guard was shooting blind.

Josh pushed forwards, picking up speed. He was holding back the pain as best he could.

Death or freedom, pal, he yelled inwardly as he willed himself forward. *Either is better than going back to that hell.*

'Here, over here,' shouted O'Brien, somewhere off to Josh's left.

Another explosion. Someone was laying down a heavy barrage of stun grenades and smoke bombs. Rescue tactics, Josh realised. Put down enough fire

285

and confusion to get your man out without killing him in the process. *These guys know what they are doing.*

The air was thick with sulphurous smoke. Josh swerved further to the left, avoiding the explosions, letting himself be guided by the lethal heat behind him and the noise ahead.

'Jump, man, jump,' shouted O'Brien. 'Over the ridge.'

Josh glanced up. The ridge to the right of the compound that surrounded the bungalow was just ten yards away. The ground rose up steadily until it reached its full height. He would just have to take a run and jump at it. There was no other way.

Ten yards, then five. Despite the waves of pain crashing through him, Josh did his best to pick up all the speed he could. Then he jumped, pushing back with his legs to gain as much height as he could. For a brief instant he was flying through the air. Then he landed hard on the ground. It took another second to find his balance again. He opened his eyes. O'Brien was kneeling in a ditch in the classic firing position, an XM8 assault rifle—a weapon issued only to American troops and still in extremely restricted circulation even among criminals—tucked against his shoulder. With a distinctive brown plastic casing and a black metal barrel, the weapon was capable of laying down a ferocious 750 rounds of deadly fire a minute.

A hand reached up, dragging Josh down behind the bank of earth that O'Brien was using for cover. 'You okay, man?' shouted O'Brien, starting to stand up.

A shot rang out. A splatter of blood hit Josh on the chest, smearing his bruised skin. For a second he thought that he'd been hit. He was waiting for the pain to kick in. Then he saw O'Brien drop to his knees. Blood was pouring from a head wound and there was a pitiful whimpering sound coming from his lips. Dying, realised Josh. Only seconds left. No point in even putting him out of his misery.

Josh's eyes swivelled desperately around. Where the hell did that shot come from? he wondered. He was positioned behind a ridge of earth overlooking the bungalow. The van the guard had been trying to put him in was already engulfed in flames, filling the area with thick, ugly clouds of black smoke, and the guard was lying bleeding on the ground. There was no sign of the woman.

From the noise of the gunfire, Josh reckoned that there were three, maybe four men attacking the house. About as many defending it.

Josh reached down and grabbed the XM8. The barrel of the weapon was wet and slippery with O'Brien's blood. Another shot whistled over the ridge. It glanced against the casing of the gun, knocking it from his grip. Josh stumbled backwards, his balance thrown by the force of the impact. He noticed that the noise of the gun battle and the grenades had stopped. For a moment there was silence. Then . . .

'Hold it right there, Josh.'

Josh recognised the voice immediately: it was cold and precise. Azim.

You can take me if you want to, Josh told himself, but not alive.

The XM8 was lying in the dirt. Josh glanced up. He could see Azim standing ten yards away, walking slowly towards him. The terrorist was holding a Swiss-made Sig-Sauer P220 handgun, the

287

American version with a stainless-steel casing, a weapon noted for its reliability and accuracy. It was pointed straight at Josh's head. And Azim didn't look like a man who would miss a shot like that. Not at ten yards.

I'm not going back, Josh told himself. *I'll take a soldier's death if it's offered to me.*

He reached down quickly for the XM8, planning to grab it in one movement and then turn it on Azim. The chances of survival were poor, but Josh no longer cared. His heart was thumping furiously as he began the move, but his mind was suddenly calm. You make a decision, he told himself. And once it's made, that's it.

Another shot. The XM8 jumped off the ground and into the air, striking Josh's hand. By the time it landed again, the trigger mechanism had been bent out of shape by the impact of the Sig's bullet. 'Hold it, Josh,' Azim shouted again. 'Stay still, and put your hands in the air.'

Josh pulled himself upright. The XM8 was useless now, he realised bitterly. He looked up at Azim. There was a smile on the man's lips. 'Morant is dead. O'Brien is dead. There is no one to help you,' he said coldly. 'Now, do as I told you and put your hands in the air.'

Josh remained perfectly still. Whether he was the only man left standing it was impossible to say. He couldn't hear or see anyone. Right now it was just him against Azim. One against one.

You're not taking me, Josh repeated to himself, the phrase hammering inside his head. You're not taking me alive.

Azim was walking slowly towards him, taking tiny cautious steps. The Sig was aimed straight at Josh's head. My only hope is to rush him, Josh thought. Throw my body against him, and hope that his reaction times are too slow for him to shoot me first. My chances of survival? *Above zero—but only just.*

'Give me the bullet now,' snarled Josh. 'Just bloody give it to me now.'

Azim wiped a bead of sweat away from his brow with the back of his left hand, while using the right to keep the Sig aimed straight at Josh. 'A nice, clean soldier's death here on a battlefield of your own choosing? We've already had this discussion, Josh. It's not going to happen.' There was a mocking, lilting tone to his voice as he spoke: the sound of a man charmed by his own rhetoric.

'Just give me the fucking bullet,' shouted Josh.

'Your friends have tried to rescue you and they've failed. You're mine now, and you'll break. I know it, you know it.'

The throbbing inside Josh's head was getting worse. L, B, J, he repeated to himself. That was the code from Luke. *I know where he is.*

'Give me the bullet,' he shouted.

'Start moving sideways, very slowly, Josh,' Azim ordered. 'Do exactly as I say.'

'Hold your ground, Josh.'

Josh spun around. Marshall was standing ten yards behind him, holding an American-made M1 Garand sniper rifle. Its long narrow barrel was pointed straight at Azim. Josh judged that Marshall must have crept round the back of the ridge. Josh looked up at him. In the older man's eyes he could see the calm, implacable expression of an old soldier. *A man who would be happy to kill you if he needed to.*

289

'Hold your ground,' Marshall repeated, his voice firm and clear.

Josh stood steady, every muscle in his body tense but rock solid. He could see Azim's finger twitching on the trigger of his Sig. The gun was still trained on Josh, but his stare was fixed on Marshall.

'Back away,' Azim hissed. 'Or I'll kill him.'

'You need him alive,' snapped Marshall. 'Wounded, crippled, mutilated, whatever. But his brain needs to be alive. You need what's inside it.'

'I need nothing from you,' hissed Azim. 'Back away now, old man. He means nothing to you. Don't throw away your own life.'

Marshall kept the rifle trained on the terrorist. One bullet, thought Josh. He knew that the older man was, at best, only an average shot. *If that aim isn't true, we're all corpses. Or worse.*

The Garand fired. Azim rocked backwards. The bullet had hit him in the shoulder.

'Run, Josh, run,' shouted a voice.

A woman. Kate.

She was standing next to the Mustang, twenty yards away. A single thought ran through Josh's mind. *Escape.*

Azim was stymied by Marshall's gun. Josh started running, surprised at his own speed and agility. His feet pounded against the ground.

Behind him, Josh could hear a shot, then another. He raced towards the car. 'Drive, drive, drive,' he shouted, his lungs burning as he yelled the word.

As he reached Kate he could see her expression changing. A look of horror flashed into her eyes. Her shoulders sagged, and her face creased up. Josh looked behind him. Marshall had fallen to the ground.

The bullet hole in the centre of his forehead was clearly visible.

Dead.

'Into the car,' shouted Josh.

Kate remained motionless, frozen like a statue.

'Into the car,' shouted Josh again, louder this time.

Using the back of his hand, he slapped her across the cheek. She stays like this, he told himself, we all die. 'You can't help him now,' he shouted. 'Drive the bloody car.'

She opened the door of the Mustang. Josh threw himself into the passenger seat, instinctively diving for cover. At his side, Kate had turned on the ignition. The engine roared to life, revving furiously as she jammed her foot on the accelerator and turned the car hard along the dusty track.

'Drive like hell,' he shouted.

The car spun away on a surge of power. Josh looked briefly behind him. Azim was struggling to his feet. With his left hand, he was clutching his shoulder, trying to staunch the flow of blood that was weeping from the bullet wound. With his right hand, he was holding the Sig-Sauer P220. And pointing it straight at the Mustang.

TWENTY

Monday, June 15th. Afternoon.

It was the smell that brought Josh back to consciousness. He lay with his eyes closed, inhaling the aroma of fresh coffee that was wafting across to where he lay. I don't want to open my eyes, he told himself. I just want to lie here. *Smelling freedom.*

'You need to drink something,' said Kate. 'It will make you feel better.'

Josh opened his eyes. Kate was kneeling beside him, her red hair tied back behind her head. She looked tired and drawn, her face smudged with tears, but after the trauma of the last few days it was a relief for Josh just to see a friendly face.

He looked up, noticing the shimmering brightness of the sky above him. As he glanced around, he could see the high boulders and deep crevices of the mountain range.

'Where are we?'

'In the mountains,' answered Kate. 'We're safe— we're in another of the survivalist camps.'

Josh took the coffee that she'd made him. They were sitting behind a rock formation on a patch of ground with a small cave at one side. Kate had dressed him in some blue chinos and a black sweatshirt: anonymous, easy-wearing gear, just right for a man on the run.

Looking down, Josh could see the plain stretching out below them. There was one road, maybe three or four miles distant, and a dirt track, along which Kate had driven the Mustang. The car was parked about twenty yards away: there were some scratches and dents, but it still looked to be intact.

Safe, thought Josh, savouring the word. *Safe.*

He took a first sip of coffee. There were bandages around his chest, and the wounds on his neck and legs had been freshly treated. His body was clean, and his beard had been trimmed. He could feel swellings in his chest where he had been

292

bitten by the snakes, and there was a numbness in his shoulder where his flesh had been cut open by Azim. The extent of the damage would take a few days to become clear. He couldn't quite be sure how long he had been sleeping. At least twenty hours.

'I'm sorry about Marshall,' he said.

Kate's expression remained stoical. 'So am I,' she replied.

Josh fell silent. It was a terrible thing to lose a father. Once the fog of amnesia had started to clear, the memories had come flooding back to him. Now he had a clear recollection of comrades who had fallen during his time in the Regiment. He knew that he had broken the news to wives who had lost husbands, and to parents who had lost sons. And he knew that there were no words of consolation, no explanations, and no justifications that would ever make even the tiniest dent in the grief they faced.

There was nothing you could say to dim the intensity of the pain. Nothing.

'You okay?'

Kate looked away. 'It was his choice,' she said softly. 'He knew the risks he was running.'

'You shouldn't have done it,' said Josh. 'I'm not worth it. You should have left me in the ditch. This isn't your fight.'

'When I start something I finish it—I told you that.'

Josh shook his head. 'No,' he said softly. 'Trust me, sometimes you have to know which battles to fight, and which to skip.'

'Well, this one I fight.'

'Why?' snapped Josh. 'I'm just some guy you

293

found in a ditch. I know your husband died, but you have to stop torturing yourself about that. You have to move on.'

'Move on? They've killed my father,' said Kate. 'Now it's my fight too.' She was cradling her own cup of coffee in her hand. How long she'd been awake, Josh couldn't say. He knew that she'd escaped with him last night, but how long the drive up here had been he couldn't say: he'd lost consciousness soon after they'd made their getaway in the Mustang. She must have driven them up here, then treated his wounds and given him something to help him sleep. She was a brave woman, he reflected: she had lost weight in the past few days, emphasising her elegant chiselled features, but there was iron in her heart.

'That software is important. If it falls into the wrong hands then it would be incredibly dangerous,' said Kate. Her eyes flashed. 'Marshall cared about that. I care about that. So we'll do what we have to do to stop that happening.'

Something's not right, thought Josh. *Something still doesn't make sense.*

'We need help,' he said. 'We can't fight this on our own any more.'

'What kind of help?'

Kate's tone was nervous, as if she was frightened of something.

'My memory,' said Josh. 'It's back. Not all of it. Lots of things are still fuzzy. But enough.'

Kate leaned across, taking his hand. 'You know where Luke is?'

Josh nodded. He took another gulp of the coffee, his eyes scanning the empty horizon. In his other hand he held a thick biscuit from the camp supplies

294

and started chewing on it. The food was doing him good, he reflected: he was still weak, and his nerves were still in a poor state, but he was still alive, and so long as he ate and rested there was no reason why he shouldn't recover.

Rest, he thought grimly, and maybe one day I'll feel fit and healthy again.

'There was a code,' Josh said.

'I saw it, the third attack in a few days,' Kate said. 'J, B, L, or B, J, L, or something.'

Josh smiled. 'I know what it means. Luke told me, shortly before I got shot. He's waiting for me. I just have to go and find him. The code tells me where he is.'

Kate reached out to touch Josh's shoulders with her outstretched palm. Her skin felt good against his. The fleeting caress was soft, feminine, caring: the kind of touch that he had thought he would never feel again. 'Where, Josh?' she said softly. 'Where?'

'Like I said, we need help. We can't fight this on our own. It's too big.'

'But Luke is waiting for *you*.'

Josh wondered if he could hear a hint of irritation in her voice. 'My memory is back. I know who I am, and what I have to do,' he said.

Kate took her hand away from his shoulder. 'And that is?'

'My name is Josh Harding. I'm a British soldier, serving in the SAS, but on secondment to anti-terrorist operations. I was sent out here on a mission to find Luke. And I found him.' Josh hesitated. The pieces of the jigsaw were reassembling in his head, but he knew that the picture was still some way from being complete.

295

'Now I know where he is, my duty is clear.' He paused, looking down to the wilderness below. 'I report back for duty.'

'For duty?'

Josh nodded. 'I'm a soldier, like I said. That's what we do.'

Kate shook her head. 'You told me that you've been tortured, Josh,' she said. 'You said that first they electrocuted you to within an inch of your life. Next you had snakes biting you almost to death. You're weak, Josh. Your nerves are shot to pieces. You're not thinking straight.'

Josh could see the intensity in her expression: her stare was focused completely upon him, as if he were a patient on her examining table. 'Trust me, Josh. I'm a doctor. I know about these things.'

'I have to check back in. I know where Luke is, but I can't handle this on my own any more. I've already been captured twice. I can't expect you to help me again. I need to go and get reinforcements, go and get Luke, bring him in, and get this thing over with.'

'You're missing something.'

Josh said nothing.

'Why were you shot, Josh?' Kate persisted. 'Why is Luke just sending messages to you? Why isn't *he* calling for the reinforcements?'

She paused, lowering her gaze to the ground. 'There's something else going on. What happened between you and Luke?'

Josh shook his head. 'I can't remember.'

'Try, Josh, try.'

Josh concentrated. The memories were swimming in and out of his head. Catching them was like trying to catch fish in the river with your bare hands. As soon as you grabbed for them, they were already gone. What was I talking to Luke about, he asked himself?

His head was throbbing with pain and frustration. Nothing was clear. 'I have to check back in with my unit,' he said flatly. 'It's my duty.'

'Just tell me where Luke is,' said Kate. 'We'll go find him together.'

'No,' snapped Josh. 'I have to go back in.'

'You're an idiot.'

'No—I have to get back to the Regiment.'

'That's a dumb choice.'

'I'm a soldier,' said Josh angrily. 'We don't have choices. We just have our duty. Without that, we're nothing.'

*   *   *

Josh held the phone in his hand. From their hiding place, it had been an hour's walk down into the valley and across the plain before he'd found the road. Then it had been another half-mile before he'd found one of the payphones dotted along the highway for stranded motorists. The pain had been intense, stumbling his way through the scrub and boulders. The swelling in his chest from the snakebites was getting worse: two thick purple bruises were spreading out across his chest. And his legs were still weak from the electric shocks.

My body is weak, but my nerves are even weaker, he told himself. Kate is wrong. I have to get back to base. *I can't do this by myself.*

'My name is Josh Harding,' he said, as soon as the call was answered. 'I need to speak to the Administrative Vice-Consul.' He was ringing through to the British consulate in Los Angeles, the British government office nearest to Arizona. Every British embassy and major consulate in the world has an administrative vice-consul: supposedly a person in charge of the running of the office, but in reality the representative of The Firm, Regiment slang for the security services. The vice-consul would know who he was. And he would know what to do. If a Regiment operative was in trouble anywhere in the world, that was who they called.

'He's in a meeting,' said a secretary when Josh was put through.

Josh checked his watch. It was six-fifteen. Dusk was starting to settle over the wilderness. It was quiet. There was the low murmur of a breeze, but nothing else.

It was the quiet space between day and night, reflected Josh. A good time for a man to disappear.

'Tell him it's Josh Harding,' he snapped. 'From Hereford.'

'I'll put you through,' said the secretary. 'Right away.'

'Kenneth Adams here,' said a voice on the line. 'Who's this?'

The accent was pure Oxbridge, noted Josh. It probably belonged to a man in his mid-thirties, who'd drifted between the Foreign Office and The Firm. Maybe sandy-coloured hair, maybe dark. *Either way he'd be a Rupert.*

'Josh Harding.'

There was a pause. Josh could imagine the surprise on the man's face.

'Bugger it, man, where the hell have you been?' said Adams. 'We've been looking for you everywhere.'

I bet you have, thought Josh. *Could have tried a bit bloody harder as well while I was getting my balls fried for Queen and Country.*

'I got held up,' said Josh. 'But I'm coming in.'

'Where are you?'

Josh rolled his eyes up towards the sky. Thick streaks of red were smudged across the horizon as the sunlight ebbed away. The moon was already making its ascent. Bloody nowhere, he thought sourly.

'Arizona,' he replied. 'Keeping a low profile.' He paused, checking his watch. It was getting late, and he needed a few hours' rest before he attempted another journey. 'I've got access to a vehicle. I could be in LA by the morning.'

'Stay right where you are,' said Adams fiercely. 'Give us the coordinates, and we'll pick you up right now.'

'I can come in under my own steam,' said Josh. 'I'll see you in the morning.'

'No,' snapped Adams. 'Just tell us where you are and we'll get our American friends to lend us a Black Hawk for the night. We want you back on dry land.'

'I need to rest,' said Josh. 'It can wait until morning.'

'You're coming in tonight, Harding,' said Adams. 'And that's an order.'

Welcome back to the world of the Ruperts, Josh told himself. *Maybe I was better off without my memory.*

*　　　*　　　*

299

The thunderous roar of the Sikorsky Black Hawk UH 60 shattered the silence of the scrublands. Dust and clumps of twisted grass were swept up, caught in the whirlwind of swirling air beneath the machine's rotor blades.

Josh stepped forward from behind the boulder where he had taken shelter. It was just after ten at night. It had taken him an hour to walk back to their hiding place, then there had been a brief but furious exchange with Kate when he'd told her that a chopper would be picking him up within a couple of hours.

'Come with me,' Josh said again as he heard the first rumble of the chopper echoing out across the mountains.

'No way,' she snapped back.

'I still need help,' said Josh. 'We'll find Luke together.'

'You're a fucking idiot, Josh,' she shouted. 'There's something wrong, I tell you. Something else that you haven't remembered. This is a trap.'

'This is the British Army,' said Josh, 'Don't be ridiculous.'

'It's your neck on the block,' Kate said coldly, turning away and disappearing among the boulders. 'But if you need me, if anything goes wrong, I'll be waiting by that phone booth you used on the road.'

Her words were still echoing in his ears. *If anything goes wrong, I'll be waiting.*

Nothing's going to go wrong, Josh told himself as he stepped forward towards the waiting Black Hawk. A man he assumed was Adams was beckoning him forwards with impatient movements of his arms. He wasn't quite as Josh had expected:

300

he was shorter and stouter, with greying hair, and with a thick layer of fat bulging over the waistband of the trousers of his black suit.

But I'm back with my own tribe, reckoned Josh. Within the hour, I'll be part of the Regiment again.

'Are you Josh Harding?' said Adams.

Josh climbed on board the Black Hawk. The moment his feet left the ground, the machine soared upwards. The roar of the rotor blades through the open doors felt like it was splitting open his eardrums, and the swirling dust clogged his lungs and hurt his eyes.

He could feel his spirits lifting as the huge blades of the chopper lifted it high into the sky. Support. Back-up.

'That's me,' shouted Josh.

'Then get to the back of the bloody chopper,' Adams shouted back.

Josh started to walk to the back of the helicopter. The machine swayed noticeably in flight and he had to hold on to its metal walls to steady himself.

He looked down the length of the chopper. At the back were two military policemen, sitting with their weapons held ready. Like Adams, they were wearing headphones so that they could talk to each other over the roar of the Black Hawk's engine. Their expressions were sombre. Glancing back towards Adams, Josh could see the signature breast pocket bulge of a man carrying a handgun in a shoulder holster.

'Why the policemen?' said Josh, looking at Adams.

'Because you're under bloody arrest.'

Josh blinked. No, he told himself. I must have misheard. It must have been the noise of the Black

Hawk. *He must have said something else.*

'I don't . . . *What?*'

'You're under arrest,' snarled Adams. 'Now sit bloody still.'

'What the fuck for?' shouted Josh.

'Insubordination,' said Adams. 'Disobeying orders. Then desertion. They'll court-martial you. And from what I hear about you, I hope they bring back the sodding firing squad.'

Josh's gaze roamed through the Black Hawk. The pilot was sitting at the controls, taking the machine up above the desert. Both of the MPs were gripping their standard-issue Heckler Koch MP5 sub-machine guns. They'll shoot me if they're told to, and won't even think twice about it, Josh thought.

Adams was still to the back of him, now hunched down on one of the metal seats that lined the interior of the Black Hawk.

'It's not bloody true,' Josh snarled.

'Save your whingeing for the court martial, Harding,' snapped Adams.

'The power failures, the blackouts, the attacks— there's going to be more of them,' said Josh. 'I'm the only man who can stop them.'

'I've told you to shut it.'

'I'm the only man who can stop it,' shouted Josh, his voice raw with anger. 'Can't you bloody understand that?'

Adams looked towards the MPs. One of them looked at Josh, his finger poised on the trigger of his MP5. 'You're under arrest,' he barked. 'You'll have your chance to defend yourself.'

'There's going to be a catastrophe.'

'I don't care,' shouted Adams. 'You're a British

302

soldier. Just follow the bloody orders.'

'The orders are fucking stupid.'

'Doesn't make any difference,' snapped Adams. 'You follow them all the same. You break them, you deserve whatever shit gets thrown at you.'

Josh looked out of the chopper's door. The air was rushing past at three hundred miles an hour. Darkness had already fallen, but the Black Hawk was equipped with electronic guidance. It could probably find its way back to LA without a pilot, never mind without any light.

A river: Gazing down, Josh could just make out its twisting contours. He started racking his brains, trying to dredge up whatever memories he could. A river from Arizona, running west. The Colorado. It had to be. If the pilot was tracking that, at some point they were going to hit the Hoover Dam. A dam meant a lake.

Josh smiled inwardly. A lake. That meant a man could jump from a helicopter and have a chance of surviving.

Maybe only a one in ten chance. *But it was still something.*

I have to escape, he told himself. I *have* to. Not to save myself. But if I don't get to Luke soon, then Azim or one of his thugs will get to him first. Then the whole world will be in trouble.

Josh started to make his calculations. The helicopter door was open. The Black Hawk was designed for close-quarter military contacts, designed to put down fresh troops and pick up casualties in a hurry, which was why it was usually flown with a side door open. They were flying at about two thousand feet, snaking their way across the open countryside. Josh was sitting on one of the

303

bucket seats, across from the doorway, not far from where the MPs were sitting.

Josh stood up and walked towards Adams. He could feel the two MPs tracking him with their stares. 'You're making a bloody mistake,' he said.

'What?' shouted Adams, straining to hear him above the noise of the Black Hawk's engine.

'I said you're making a bloody mistake,' said Josh, not bothering to raise his voice.

'What?'

Adams leaned forward, trying to catch Josh's softly spoken words.

You're mine.

With a sudden swift movement, Josh thumped him in the chest with his left hand. In the same instant, his right hand whipped down and grabbed the gun from beneath Adams's jacket. It was a simple Glock 19, a gun that Josh was familiar with. He gripped it tight, jabbing the barrel against Adams's right ear.

'Hold bloody still,' he shouted at the two MPs. 'Hold bloody still or I shoot.'

Both men froze, staring hard at Josh.

'Hold your fire,' said Adams, speaking into his mouthpiece so that the two MPs could hear him on their headphones.

Glancing from the side of the chopper, Josh could see that they were now flying over Lake Mead. I just have to get to Luke, he repeated to himself. *I just have to get to Luke before Azim does.*

He grabbed Adams by the scalp, yanking hard on his greying hair. With the Glock still pressed against the man's ear, Josh dragged him down to the front of the Black Hawk. The pilot was staring back at him. A man of twenty-four, twenty-five,

Josh couldn't help admiring the way he was holding the Black Hawk on a rock-steady course despite the fracas. 'Take her down,' snapped Josh. 'Take the bloody thing down.'

'You're making it worse for yourself, man,' Adams shouted.

'I'll be the judge of that,' roared Josh, tugging harder on the man's hair.

'Just put the gun down, Harding. I'll make sure you get a fair hearing.'

Josh ignored him, looking back towards the pilot. 'Just bring the fucking thing down,' he growled.

'Don't,' barked Adams.

The pilot held the Black Hawk steady on its progress across the lake.

They're trying to outsmart me, thought Josh. They know I can't bring this bird down while I'm holding a gun on Adams. *I'm buggered.*

Unless . . .

Josh fired once, then twice. The bullets smashed into the Black Hawk's control panel. A shower of sparks flew out of it, spitting up into the pilot's face. Now Josh jammed the pistol back against Adams's head. Already he could feel the chopper starting to sway and swerve through the air as the controls jammed, then died.

Josh glanced at the altimeter.

Now we're going down.

Fast.

Sixteen hundred yards. *At one hundred, I jump.*

Josh could feel the Black Hawk start to plummet. It was as if his legs had collapsed beneath him. His heart was jumping up into his throat. The pilot was wrestling desperately with the controls, trying to regain control of the machine.

'You're a fucking madman, Harding,' shrieked Adams. 'You're going to die.'

'At least we'll all go together,' shouted Josh.

One thousand one hundred yards.

The lake was so close that Josh could almost smell it.

The two MPs tried to stand up, but as the Black Hawk lurched through its descent they were thrown back down again.

'Finish him,' yelled Adams. 'Finish the fucker.'

Five hundred and fifty yards.

One of the guards was holding his MP5 straight in front of him, trying to point it straight at Josh, but the Black Hawk was swaying violently as its descent gathered speed. The nose was starting to turn down as the aircraft hurtled faster towards the black, icy waters of the lake.

Two hundred and ten yards.

A burst of gunfire rattled against the metal walls of the machine. Amid the violent motion, it was impossible for the guard to maintain his aim.

Josh glanced towards the open door.

A hundred and sixty yards.

He let go of Adams and kicked back, compressing all his strength into his calf muscles to give himself maximum lift. His body started to arc through the air towards the open doorway. A churning vortex of air was swirling just outside.

The air hit Josh hard, first in the face, then in the chest, thumping the wind from him and making it almost impossible to breathe. For a second it seemed as if he was hurtling horizontally, flying level with the Black Hawk. He could hear the sound of gunfire behind him. One bullet, then two, then three.

Nothing hit.
Suddenly he could feel himself falling at a terrifying velocity. The Black Hawk was high above him. The swirling wind started to spin him around. His head was dizzy, and it was hard to keep his eyes open against the rush of oncoming air.

He flung his arms and legs wide, maximising the surface area of his body. Slowly he could feel himself starting to get control. His body was stable, his spreadeagled state buffering him from the full impact of the rushing air. Up above, he could see the Black Hawk starting to bank, turning hard as it continued to descend rapidly.

Josh put all his strength into trying to hold himself steady. But there was nothing he could do about the accelerating speed of his fall. And in a few seconds he was going to hit the water.

Below him he could see its icy blackness.

TWENTY-ONE

Monday, June 15th. Night.
In the last seconds of the fall, Josh had arched his body into a smooth diving position, his arms stretched out in front of him and his hands clasped together. His head had been tucked just behind the arms, slightly bowed so that the first impact from the water would come on the crown: the skull there was the thickest lump of bone in the body, designed that way by evolution to protect the brain, and if you had to take a hard blow that was the best place to take it. He had held his legs together behind him, as straight as poles.

The perfect diving position.

It had made no difference. The impact had been a moment of shattering terror. As first his hands, then his head and his shoulders had sliced into the water, he'd felt as if every bone in his body had suddenly been pulverised.

The pain hit him first, rippling up through him in wave after wave. He lost control of his muscles. Then the icy cold of the water numbed his body, freezing the blood in his veins. His breathing stopped, and it felt as if his heart had stopped beating.

For a moment, Josh was convinced that he was dead. It seemed unimaginable that he could survive any more punishment.

Then the motion stopped. A splitting headache was throbbing inside his skull. Josh could feel that he was no longer moving. The water was still swirling around him, and a strong underwater current had started to catch hold of him, dragging him forwards.

He was probably thirty feet below water, he reckoned. Slowly, he started to kick his legs. They responded lazily at first. There was little strength left in his muscles to fight against the current. He tried again, harder this time. Both legs started to move and Josh could feel his body start to move.

It had been impossible to take a proper mouthful while he'd been in free fall. Now he was desperately short of air.

I just hope I've landed close to the shore. Even if I get to the surface in time, I haven't the strength to swim very far.

Josh kicked hard, using his arms to help drag himself back up to the surface. He opened his eyes.

The water was fresh and clean, but it still took a moment to adjust his vision. He looked straight up. He could see something moving. A shallow wave. The surface.

Then his head broke through. Josh opened his mouth, taking great lungfuls of air. The oxygen filled his chest, hitting his bloodstream and instantly clearing his splitting headache.

Alive.

The word sent a jolt of exhilaration through him. He looked quickly around the dark, choppy waters of Lake Mead. About three hundreds yards ahead of him he could see the massive wall of the dam that had created the lake. The current was dragging the water slowly towards it, allowing the Colorado River to continue its journey towards the coast. To the north, reckoned Josh, was Nevada. To the west, California. And safety? he wondered bitterly to himself. *That probably wasn't in any direction at all.*

Now, straight ahead of him, he could see the Black Hawk crash into the water. A huge wave rolled out as the machine was sucked down. It was at least a mile away, but through the dark night air Josh could still hear the shouts as the crew jumped out. And then he could see a dinghy starting to move away from the crash site.

It's a massive lake, he told himself. *They've little chance of finding me.*

Josh started swimming. He reckoned it was a good two hundred, two hundred and fifty yards to the closest shoreline. A pebbled beach and some conifer trees were all he could make out.

The shoreline was a national park, and it must be close to midnight by now. There shouldn't be anyone around. Just the occasional bear.

But I've got to move, Josh told himself, because in a few minutes Adams will have half the American army out here looking for me.

He swam furiously, dipping his head below the surface of the water and surfacing only when he had to for air.

If I can keep my strength, I can do this, Josh told himself. I just have to believe.

After ten minutes he reached the shore, his teeth chattering from the cold. The beach was made up of tiny pebbles. Josh lay still for a moment, recovering his breath. He cupped some water in his hands, drinking as much as he could get inside himself, then crawled forwards. The trees were ten yards away. He curled up behind one of the massive pine trunks. The shoreline was completely empty.

I need a few minutes to rest, he told himself. *Then I make my escape.*

His clothes were sodden. Every inch of his skin felt damp and chilled. He struggled to pick himself up, standing uneasily. Got to get away, he told himself, staggering forwards. Got to get away.

If they find me, they're going to kill me.

*   *   *

Josh walked for two hours through the forest that ran down to the lakeside. He knew there would already be hunting parties out looking for him, but the national park surrounding the lake covered a hundred and fifty square miles. Locating a single man would take a team of hundreds. *For a few hours at least he should be safe.*

He still had money on him. Two hundred dollars in cash, and a pocketful of loose change: the notes were dripping wet but would dry out in time. Eventually he found a small road and, after walking along it for an hour and a half, a payphone placed there for anyone who broke down in their car. He called Kate on the payphone that she'd said she'd be waiting by and told her what had happened. 'Stay right where you are,' she told him. 'Hide in the woods. I can drive down there in a couple of hours.'

After speaking with Kate and giving her his position, Josh retreated fifty yards back from the road, into a thicket of tall pine trees. He pushed some leaves together to form a bed, then lay down, his eyes closing almost instantly. He breathed deeply, drawing in the rich restorative oxygen of the woodlands. For the first time in weeks, his mind was clear. He knew who he was. *And he knew what he had to do.*

He rested for two hours, catching enough sleep to get some strength back into his system: the ability to sleep on demand was one of the first lessons he'd learned in the army. Then he trudged back up to the road, settling behind a group of trees close to the spot where he'd told Kate to meet him. It was past two in the morning, and the narrow strip of tarmac running through the forest was empty. His heart pounded inside his chest in the twenty minutes he had to wait until he saw the Mustang pull around the corner. Kate was the only person he could think of who could help him now. *And if they didn't get to Luke soon, then Azim would find him.*

After the Mustang pulled up to the side of the

road, Josh waited a couple of minutes, making sure it hadn't been followed, then ran out to meet Kate. They drove the car fifty yards into the woods so that it wouldn't be visible from the air, then went back towards Josh's hiding place. The air was damp and cold, and a light breeze was whistling through the trees. But it felt good to have her back at his side.

'How much damage have I taken?' said Josh as Kate started to examine his wounds.

'Too much,' she replied. She bathed the wound in his neck with a swab of disinfectant, then replaced the bandage.

'Normally, I'd recommend at least a week or two of complete relaxation and recuperation,' she said with a gentle smile.

'Doctor's orders?' said Josh.

Kate nodded. 'But you're a bad patient,' she said. 'The kind that doesn't listen to their doctor.'

He reached up to kiss her. Her lips felt warm and soft and moist, and as her tongue stabbed against his skin he could feel some of his wounds starting to heal. When a man feels certain that he is about to die, Josh reflected, there are many things that he thinks about. There are a hundred different regrets that flash through his mind: places he never visited; people he never met; the daughter he wouldn't see again. But foremost among them is the realisation that he'll never hold a woman in his arms again, never feel her yield under his touch, nor hear her whisper in his ear.

Over the last few days, there had been many moments when he'd felt he was about to die. There'd been times when he would have welcomed death as warmly as if it were a long-lost brother.

But now that he'd escaped death's clutches, he was grateful to be alive. Every moment, he resolved, was there to be savoured as if it were a succulent piece of fruit hanging from a tree.

So Josh held Kate tight, drawing strength from the warmth of her body. She lay down next to him, resting on the strip of ground surrounded by the tall pine trees that filled this bank of the lake. For a few minutes, Josh was content just to feel her embrace. It was only after a while that he started to unbutton her blouse, and slowly and gently make love to her.

'You told me something wasn't right,' he said, lying next to her when they had finished.

Her lips caressed his forehead, soothing him more effectively than any tranquilliser could. 'Don't worry, baby. It doesn't matter. We'll go find Luke now.'

The first shafts of daylight were breaking through the trees. 'Christ, it's morning,' said Josh. 'We've wasted time.'

Kate looked behind her. The sun was rising above the horizon. Through the trees they could see the still waters of the lake, the orange light of early morning playing across its surface. 'It would be nice just to enjoy this place for a few days,' she said. 'It's so beautiful.'

Josh hugged her closer to him. 'After we've completed the mission,' he said. 'We'll go somewhere together.'

Kate nodded: 'Here?'

'Maybe. But next time I'm not jumping out of a bloody helicopter.'

There was a silence between them. It was foolish to talk of the future. There was too much to do.

'You know where Luke is?' said Kate.

Josh nodded.

* * *

They drove due north from the lake, tracking the minor roads. When they reached a small town, Josh waited in the car while Kate went into the mall to run her errands. His eyes scanned the horizon carefully. He could see a security guard patrolling the outer perimeter of the car park. He could see a man ambling through the parked cars, checking each one. Just some guy who's looking for his own vehicle? wondered Josh. Or a Fed? Josh ducked, shielding his face so that no one could see him.

You watch everyone like a hawk, Josh told himself. That what it's like to be a hunted man.

Kate slammed the Mustang's door shut. 'Here,' she said, handing across a large Burger King paper bag.

Josh glanced down at the food. A Bacon Double Cheeseburger, a Whopper with cheese, two extra-large portions of fries, and a big carton of Coke. The first meat he'd have eaten in days, he suddenly realised. *I need it.*

He pulled the Mustang out of the parking lot and started heading due north, away from the town. There was a sheriff's office by the side of the road, and as they went past it Josh instinctively felt himself gunning the accelerator. Take it easy, he warned himself. This is a big country, men get lost for years. So long as you stay calm you can buy yourself the day or two you need to find Luke.

His head had been spinning ever since his arrest. That was the last thing he'd expected. For the first few hours he'd been driven just by the adrenalin of his escape, then by finding Kate again. But he still didn't know what he could have done to make the Army turn on him so viciously.

My memory, he reflected grimly. It's still shot full of holes. Something happened between me and Luke. Something that is still unfinished. Something that the Army didn't like.

I just don't know what it is.

I have to find him. I have to find out what happened in those few hours and minutes before I was shot.

He pulled the car into a lay-by at the side of the road. The forests that surrounded the narrow stretch of irrigated land bordering Lake Mead had long since faded from view, and they were now driving through the harsh wilderness that separated the lake from Las Vegas. There were signs on the road offering land for sale at a dollar an acre. But no takers, decided Josh: it was a brutal landscape, untouched by rain for years at a stretch, where even the toughest, hardiest of animals would struggle to survive.

Josh took a bite of the Whopper, gobbling down the food. He needed protein, carbohydrates, and sugar, and he needed them fast.

The main battle still lay ahead. He would need whatever strength he could summon up.

'Did you get all the stuff?' he asked Kate.

She nodded. 'A GPS locator. And a copy of *London Calling* by the Clash.' She hesitated, holding up the slim black machine that could locate any spot in the world from a single set of coordinates, and then a copy of the CD, with its iconic cover of Paul Simenon smashing his bass

315

guitar against the stage of a concert hall. 'The GPS device I understand. It'll tell us where Luke is, so long as we have the right numbers to feed into it.' She held up the CD, glancing at its cover. 'And this. Well, I don't know.'

Josh grinned. '*London Calling*, right?'

'He's in London?'

Josh shook his head. 'Three letters, that was the signal. L, B, and J.'

Kate looked confused. 'Okay, tell me.'

'The first three tracks of *London Calling*. The title track, that's an L.'

Kate flipped the CD over, looking down the track listing. ' "Brand New Cadillac". Followed by "Jimmy Jazz".'

'Right. L, B, and J.'

'So where is Luke?'

Josh reached across for the CD. He ripped off the plastic covering and pulled out the inner sleeve. 'Take the times of those three tracks, then feed the number of seconds into our GPS locator. So if the track lasts three minutes, twenty-eight seconds, put in twenty-eight.' He handed the CD back to Kate. 'Whatever comes out, then that's where Luke is.'

Her fingers worked feverishly. Josh sat patiently, chewing his way through the rest of the Whopper, then attacking the Bacon Double Cheeseburger. He took a handful of the fries and slipped them into his mouth. At his side, Kate was holding the GPS device in one hand and the CD in the other. Her fingers were hitting the tiny plastic keyboard with the force of a carpenter banging a nail into a wall.

'Swansea,' she said, her tone excited. 'He's in Swansea.'

Josh felt a couple of fries lodge themselves in his throat. He started coughing violently. 'What's he doing there? With the bloody Taffies?'

'What?'

Josh looked at her expression. Blank. She's never heard of Swansea, he thought.

'Where is it?' he asked.

'Swansea, Arizona,' said Kate. 'About a hundred miles north-east of here. In the middle of just about nowhere.'

'Then that's where we're going,' said Josh.

Josh slipped the CD in the Mustang's audio system, then fired up the engine and pulled the car out into the road. The first sweeping, howling chords that opened the album boomed up through the Mustang's speakers.

'London calling,' yelped Joe Strummer's rasping, hoarse voice as the song cranked up.

Josh tapped his fingers against the dashboard, allowing the beat of the music to surge through his veins. Instinctively, he started to mouth the familiar words. For an apocalypse, there was no better soundtrack.

TWENTY-TWO

Tuesday, June 16th. Noon.
The road twisted up the side of the mountain, its surface pitted with holes and strewn with dust and boulders. Josh was gripping onto the wheel of the Mustang, letting it roll with the bumps. His body had taken so many knocks in the past two weeks that he could no longer locate the pain precisely:

317

there was just a dull, insistent ache that seemed to be burning up every nerve in his body.

It had taken three hours to drive here, longer than Josh had expected. They had stopped once at a gas station to shower and get some coffee. Then they had stopped at an all-day store to pick up some fresh supplies for the day ahead: water, matches, some tinned food and biscuits, plus as much spare petrol as they could get into a selection of jerrycans and fit onto the back seat of the Mustang.

The route had been a long and hard one, taking Kate and Josh through the empty back roads of western Arizona. They drove up through high mountains, coloured a mixture of reds, bronzes and yellows, and twisted their way through steep valleys filled only with boulders and a few stray cacti barely managing to stay alive in the miserable soil. The heat of the morning was baking, and as Josh looked up at crystal-blue skies uninterrupted by even a whisper of cloud he could feel himself growing wary of the sunshine. They were only a few dozen miles from Death Valley, the hottest place in North America, where the heat still claimed a few careless tourists every year.

Swansea was a mining town, started by the Clara Consolidated Gold and Copper Company in 1909. It had remained inhabited until the mine finally shut down in 1924. At its peak, it had had a population of 750 people and a railway that connected it to the main Arizona transport arteries. As well as the mine, there had been a smelter, a barber's, a hotel and a sheriff. Now nothing remained. Unlike many of the Arizona ghost towns, it wasn't on any of the tourist maps: it

318

was too new for anyone interested in the history of the Old West, and it had been home to none of the famous gunfighters of an earlier era. Year by year, it was turning back into the dust from which it had been built.

Josh's gaze flickered up to the horizon. The ground levelled off at an altitude of around a thousand metres. There were deep gullies and crevices etched into the side of the mountain where the rain had washed off its sides, but as they climbed higher the ground became smoother, its surface covered with fine dust. 'There,' said Josh, spotting the small collection of tumbledown buildings emerging in the distance. 'That's it.'

The road broke out onto a plateau, and suddenly widened. The layout of the town was clearer now. A main street, with a collection of ruined buildings. A flat mountain top. And just beyond that a huge ditch, hundreds of metres long and at least fifty metres deep, sitting like a giant scar on the side of the town: the familiar debris, reflected Josh, of opencast mining.

He pulled the Mustang up at the side of the road. It was difficult to say where the town started or ended. The buildings broke down into splinters of wood and rubble, and whatever fences there might once have been had long since rotted away. Josh paused at the beginning of the street. At its edge was a sign, broken in two. '*Swan—*' it read. '*Popu—*'

'Whoever was the last man out of this place wasn't worrying about turning out the lights,' said Josh.

Kate smiled. 'It's the last man *in* that we need to worry about.'

Shafts of sunlight were shining right through the

319

ruined structures as Josh started to walk down the main street. Twenty husks of buildings lined the eight-foot-wide track, but the walls were tumbling down, and weeds and cacti had started to take root in the mortar, turning it to dust. If you looked carefully, you could just make out what they might once have been—a bank, a hotel, an ironmonger's.

There had never been anything grand about Swansea, Josh decided as his eyes scanned the buildings. It had been built quickly and cheaply. The façades showed no signs of decoration: wood planks and steel girders flung together as fast as possible.

He picked his way carefully through the debris littering the street. This is just what I need, he thought. *A man with no past hides out in a town with no present.*

'Can you see anything?'

Josh noticed he was whispering, as if it was somehow wrong to raise your voice in this place. *As if you might wake the dead.*

Kate shook her head. 'But he's here somewhere,' she whispered back. 'I'm sure of it.'

Josh noticed the smell of the air. The accumulated dirt of decades had covered the place. Every broken wall and shattered slate seemed to be caked in a layer of filth. The wind had blown bricks, beams and plaster mouldings out into the streets where they had lain for years, breaking into fragments, embedding themselves in the surface of the ground. Nothing, he realised. Usually, you could smell a man. He left his scent imprinted on the air. Here there was nothing. Just the smell of decay.

'You sure you got the coordinates right?'

320

Kate nodded. 'Swansea,' she said. 'That's how the coordinates came out. You sure you got the *code* right?'

Josh nodded. 'We talked about it. That memory is quite clear. Luke's a rock kid—he knows all the classic albums off by heart. I think he must have learned them from his mum. We agreed on a whole bunch, and the tracks would be the clues. The Beatles and The Stones, of course. And Van Morrison. Some Dylan.'

'So where the hell is he, then?'

'Water,' said Josh.

'We got some in the car.'

'No,' said Josh. 'I mean, there has to be a water source somewhere. Nobody can build a town unless there's fresh water. Luke's a smart kid. He'll be hiding out by the water.'

Kate looked at him, her eyes sparkling. 'So where is it?'

'Easy,' answered Josh. 'Look for the smelter. You can't run one of those without water.'

He started walking towards the smelter. Swansea's main street ran in a dead straight line with buildings on either side of it. Behind the buildings there were a few relics of what might have been residential houses. Straight ahead of them, Josh could see the mine. Its rusting hauling gear still rose high above the landscape. Next to it lay the disused conveyer belt that had taken the ore and started sorting it before depositing it in the smelter. The mine had been opencast. In this derelict country, no attempt had been made to cover up the damage after the mine had shut down. Huge pits were sunk into the sides of the mountains, and huge piles of rubble where

321

explosives had been used to break up thousands of tons of rock lay in massive, crumbling piles.

A barbed-wire fence had been put up around the plant, but it had long since rusted. Josh pushed open the door and stepped inside. The machinery lay silent all around. He walked quickly towards the door of the smelter. Rust had settled into the hinges of the door, making it stiff. He leaned his shoulder into the door, giving it a hard shove. Once, then twice he heaved his weight against the door. The third time, the hinges cracked and the door swung open.

Josh stepped inside. The smelter still had a smell of charcoal and metal that had lingered through the decades since it had last been used.

'Luke,' shouted Josh. 'Luke.'

His voice echoed against the tin roof.

'Luke,' he shouted again, louder this time. 'Luke?'

The words coiled around the derelict building, bouncing off the walls. Each time it bounced back it lost a fraction of its strength, and Josh could hear the sound gradually dimming, like the fade at the end of a record. Where the hell are you? Josh asked himself. *Why aren't you answering?*

I just hope you haven't left already. You won't survive out there by yourself, not for a minute. *Too many people are looking for you.*

A flashlight came on, its beam trained on Josh. He jumped, instinctively recoiling from the harsh light. Raising his forearm to his eyes to shield them, he turned around. A thin pale figure was stepping out of the shadows.

'Is that you, man? Is that really you?' said the boy.

Josh looked closer. The figure was obscured by the light blazing out from the torch. Josh took a step forward. 'Luke?'

The light switched off. Josh could see clearly now. A thin boy, fifteen or sixteen, with straggly blond hair, thick lips, and a complexion that was pale and waxy. His eyes were sunken and there were dark shadows across his cheeks. His Limp Bizkit T-shirt had a couple of gashes in it. And he smelled strange: an acrid mixture of sweat, fear and dirt.

'Christ, you look terrible.'

Luke shrugged. 'You don't look so great yourself.'

Josh took another step forward. He reached out a hand, placing his palm against Luke's. The boy's hand was cold and sweaty, and his fingers were trembling. Scared, realised Josh. Scared the way an animal is scared. *Or a child.*

He pulled Luke closer, putting his arms around him and hugging him to his chest, the same way he might have greeted a long-lost brother. For a moment they remained silent.

'It's okay, man, it's okay,' said Josh. 'I'm here now. It's going to be okay.'

A tear was starting to trickle down the side of Luke's face. 'Hell, man, I've been so frightened. So fucking frightened, you wouldn't believe it.'

'We're here now,' said Josh. 'It's going to be okay.' He took the torch and started to look around. Luke had been living here alone for two weeks. Some dried leaves had been bundled into a pile to make a bed. A solar panel had been fixed up to provide enough electricity to run a laptop, and a tiny portable satellite dish had been set up to give the computer access to the Internet. Otherwise,

Luke had been entirely by himself here, speaking to no one, frightened out of his skin. No surprise that he's starting to crack, realised Josh. There are many brave grown men who wouldn't be able to take that.

'Let's eat,' said Luke, nervously. 'We need to talk.'

Josh looked around. Luke's ideas, like those of many teenagers, of what he needed to survive while on the run were foolish. He had a dozen two-litre bottles of Coke, several boxes of crisps, and endless packets of biscuits. But little fresh water, no fruit, no bread, and no cereals. Another reason he looks in bad shape, thought Josh. He's just eating sugar and starch.

'Who's she?' said Luke, jabbing a finger towards Kate.

'Kate,' said Josh. 'She's a doctor. She's been helping me the last couple of weeks. I've been really lucky to have her along.'

'Are you okay, Luke?' said Kate. 'I can examine you if you want.'

Luke shook his head. 'I'm okay. Scared. But okay.'

He poured out three servings of Coke into some plastic cups, and took a hefty swig of his own, downing it in one gulp. Josh could see that his hand was still shaking nervously.

'What the fuck happened, man?' Luke said suddenly, looking accusingly towards Josh. 'You were meant to help me.'

'I don't know,' answered Josh.

'Hey, you were meant to get me out of here,' said Luke, sounding angrier. 'That was the deal.'

'I don't know about that, either,' said Josh.

Luke looked startled. Josh noticed how the fear in his eyes, which had started to abate in the last few minutes as he'd grown angry, had suddenly returned. 'You don't know much.'

'I lost my memory,' said Josh. 'After I got shot. What happened immediately before that is a blank.'

'Your memory? Shit!'

'You'll have to tell me everything that happened between us, Luke,' said Josh. 'So let's all sit down. And you start at the beginning.'

TWENTY-THREE

Tuesday, June 16th. Night.

'It started with me and Ben. Just a couple of kids, right? We hang out together at school because we're both into computers. We started out playing games, all the usual stuff. Then we did some programming, and started following some of the hacking websites. Nothing sinister. We were just testing ourselves, I reckon. Seeing what we might be able to do.'

Luke was sitting on the pile of leaves that he had swept together to make a bed for himself during the last two weeks. He had a cup of Coke in one hand, a biscuit in the other. Josh was sitting next to him, his legs crossed. Kate was sitting just behind him, her hands resting on Josh's shoulders. Above them some pale shafts of light were beaming down through the cracks in the ceiling of the smelter.

'We did some stuff like hacking into the computers at school, changing grades. We got into a bit of trouble for that. We were hacking into the phone company so that we could get our calls for free. We hacked into a few other company systems as well. Not to do any harm. We just wanted to have a look around, see what we might be able to do.'

'Like what?' said Josh. 'Why were you doing it?'

Luke looked up, a hint of a smile on his face. 'Why does anybody do anything? Money, right? You met my mom. Do we look rich? I mean, I love my mom, don't get me wrong, man, but she's a wacko. Right?'

Josh smiled. 'She takes her own path through life.'

'I never had a dad, at least not one that I knew. We never had a proper car or a proper house, or any of that stuff. So all the time I'm thinking, what if I could make some real money. A million dollars, two million dollars, something like that. Buy a place by the beach in Jamaica, where mom could just sit around smoking weed all day. Maybe go to London, visit some of the places The Clash used to play. Like that place on the cover of their first album.'

'The Westway?' said Josh. 'Forget it.'

'Well, whatever, man. I just wanted to get out of Hicksville. Me and Ben, both of us, that's what we wanted.' He paused, taking another hit on his Coke. 'You get onto the hacking websites, and go into the chat rooms, and you get all these stories from guys who hacked into corporate websites. You know, you get kids who hack into the Starbucks system and start messing with the prices of latte. Or whatever. And they're, like, the company pays them a million bucks or something just to tell them what the flaw in the system was and how they could fix it. All these stories going around of kids making millions just by sitting in front of their computers.'

'It's men, Luke,' interrupted Kate.

Luke looked up at her. Her red hair was tumbling down her neck, and her eyes were staring right into his. The perfume, noticed Josh. The perfume was drifting across the space between them, sweetening the fetid air of the smelter.

'What?' said Luke, his gaze darting up towards her the way a puppy's eyes flick up to its owner.

'When you're a bit older you'll realise that men talk a lot of rubbish. They sit around in bars, saying they've nailed this girl and that girl, done this deal and that deal. Usually, it's just bullshit.'

Josh laughed. 'Usually? It's *always* bullshit.'

'You think those kids didn't get money off Starbucks and the rest? Is that what you're saying?'

'I think it happens,' answered Kate. 'I just suspect it happens a lot less often than the people in the chat rooms say it does.'

Luke nodded. From his expression, Josh could tell that he was disappointed. Part of being a teenager, he reflected. One by one your illusions get chipped away, like the paint being stripped off a piece of wood. *Get used to it, pal. Life has a lot more disillusion in store for you.*

'Whatever, that's what Ben and I thought. I guess we were naive. We figured we could hack into some corporate system, maybe they'd pay us some money just to go away.'

'Porter-Bell, right,' said Josh. 'That's where you started.'

Luke nodded. 'There's kind of a buzz about it in the chat rooms. Hanging Bell, they call it, because they come down so heavy on hackers and because it's so tough to get into their systems. We figured we'd have a crack. After all, what did we have to lose? Nothing. It's not like we have girls calling us up for dates every night. We just hang out, playing with our computers.'

'The Three Cities Attack,' said Kate. 'That was you?'

Luke remained silent for a moment. A look of fear crossed his face, as if a nasty memory had just broken through. 'We got lucky, I guess. That's the thing about hacking. You just try different things, and see what works. They got firewalls, barriers, everything you can think of around this system. But Luke and I designed this worm. You know what a worm is?'

Josh shook his head.

'It's like a piece of software that tunnels into a system and comes out the other end. You wrap the instructions inside another bit of code, and that's what allows it to get through. The system doesn't recognise what's coming through.'

'Like hiding a gun inside a laptop or something when you're going through Customs?'

Luke grinned. 'Just like that. Usually they don't get through. The firewalls are built to detect worms, along with everything else the hacker can throw at them.'

'But this did?' asked Kate.

'Well, we did a couple of dozen, and they kept getting thrown right back at us. Then we made it. A perfect worm. It sailed right into their system, undetected, and then, once it was inside, the thing unwrapped itself. And for a few minutes we had control of their system.'

'So you did The Three Cities Attack?' Josh asked.

Luke nodded. 'Ben and I planned it together. We figured we needed something pretty spectacular, something that was going to grab their attention. So we figured London, Paris and New York. They all use Porter-Bell software for their power grids, and they all use the latest version, which was all we had access to. So we switched it all off.' He flashed a smile at Kate, and Josh could tell that he was trying to impress her. 'It was a hell of a buzz, I can tell you. All that power, and all that chaos. All caused by Ben and me. We got a hell of a kick when we watched it all on TV.'

'Until people started saying it was terrorists,' said Josh.

'That frightened us a bit. I guess we hadn't really thought very much about what kind of reaction there might be.'

The light was fading from the ceiling. It was past eight, Josh noticed, and the burning heat of the day had already subsided, replaced by the chill that descended on the wilderness at night-time.

'We contacted Porter-Bell,' continued Luke. 'We didn't use our real names or anything. We're not that stupid. We just set up a dummy Internet address, told them we had access to their software, and told them to be in touch if they wanted to do some business.' He paused, as if trying to sort out all the memories lodged in his mind. 'They told us to get lost at first. Said they'd been contacted by hundreds of cranks from all over the world asking them for money. So we gave them a couple more demonstrations. We didn't turn the juice off for a whole hour. Just for a minute or two at a few

329

places. Nothing to make the evening news.' Luke clicked his fingers together. 'But enough to let Porter-Bell know we had the power.'

'Then they wanted to play ball?' asked Josh.

'You bet. Once they knew we weren't just cranks, that we had a way into their system, they were all over us. Wanted to meet up right away. But again, Ben and I weren't that dumb. We knew we had to play it cool. I mean, what we were doing was illegal. And we wanted a lot of money. Five million dollars. Enough to set us both up for the rest of our lives. So we arranged to make a swap on a neutral piece of ground. They'd give us the money. We'd give them the worm.'

Luke looked up towards Josh, his eyes suddenly dark and intense. 'Then you showed up.'

Josh thought it was like watching a film you'd first seen as a kid: the outline of the story was dimly familiar, but you couldn't colour in any of the details. 'What the hell was I doing there?' he said.

Luke shrugged. 'Search me, man.'

'What did I say? I must have told you something.'

'I don't know how the hell you found us,' continued Luke, glancing between Josh and Kate. 'Ben reckoned it might have been because we were using a dummy Internet address we'd set up with one of the British Internet service providers. We didn't want to use an American one because we might have been traced. And we figured British was best, because that way we'd understand the language.'

Josh could feel something stirring within his mind. As Luke explained the sequence of events, more memories were flooding back. Fragments of meetings, orders and journeys were flashing

330

through his brain, lighting up a path that had until now been shrouded in darkness. 'That's how we got you,' he said. 'British Intelligence were onto you as soon as the power got switched off in London. The British are bloody nervous about a terrorist attack on London, and we assumed it was our old pals at al-Qaeda. We were monitoring Internet traffic, and came across your e-mails to Porter-Bell. Then we used our search powers to get the ISP to tell us where you were.' Josh clenched his fists. Suddenly he knew what he had been doing in America. 'I was sent out here to find you.'

Luke grinned. 'You succeeded. And that's when things turned interesting.'

'What did I want?' asked Josh.

'You said that you were an SAS agent, sent over to the US because one of the cities attacked was London. Your task was to track us down and make sure it never happened again. You also had to find out who it was, because the British Government was convinced that al-Qaeda was planning to use our software to launch an attack against them. If there was any possibility of al-Qaeda getting hold of this software, that had to be stopped from happening. So that was your mission. To find us, and to get the software before anyone else did. You told us that every intelligence agency in the world was trying to track us down, and so was every terrorist group. Your intelligence was that al-Qaeda was trying to capture us, because they wanted the software to launch their own attacks. If we went to the meeting with Porter-Bell, you said, we'd be killed almost certainly.'

Josh shrugged. 'Makes sense.'

'Then you offered us a deal. You said that if we

331

could help you track down the al-Qaeda man who was looking for us, you'd arrange for us to be smuggled out of the country, and we could keep whatever money we managed to squeeze out of Porter-Bell. You said that no one was really interested in us. So far as you were concerned, catching the al-Qaeda people on our trail, that was what you wanted to do.'

'Did I mention a name?'

'What name?' asked Luke.

'The name of the al-Qaeda operative who might be tracking us.'

Luke paused for just a fraction of a second. 'Azim. A guy called Khalid Azim.'

Azim, thought Josh. I was trying to capture him all along. And I still am. *Except this time I want him dead*.

'You took that deal?' asked Kate.

'Ben and I figured we were running out of choices. We'd already noticed strange things happening, around town, around our school. There were rumours of Federal agents checking through the state. We suddenly got a sense of what we'd unleashed. Everyone in the world was looking for us. If we were to get out alive, if we were to get our money, then we needed help. And you were the only guy making an offer.'

'So what did I want you to do?'

'This Azim guy, he was your main focus. It was him you wanted.'

More memories. The meetings with Ben and Luke. Josh could recall talking to them slowly, winning them over, earning their trust the hard way: by listening to them, understanding what they wanted, then doing his best to deliver. 'You and

Ben took off for a few days, I remember that,' he said. 'We figured out a safe place in the mountains for you to lay up. Then we fixed the meeting with Porter-Bell. But we left a trail of clues on the Internet as to where and when the meeting would be. Enough clues that we could be certain that Azim would also be there on the day to try and get the software from us.'

There was a breath of excitement in Josh's voice as he recalled the events of those few days. He'd discovered that Azim was in the area, tracking down Luke to steal his software for al-Qaeda, and he'd realised that this was his one chance to catch him: the night he'd escaped his clutches on the Afghanistan border could be buried for ever. 'That's when I'd get him. Then I'd spirit you away. You'd get your money, and I'd catch one of the most wanted terrorists on our list.'

'We camped out the night before the meeting with Porter-Bell in the mountains,' said Luke, taking up the story. 'Sunday, May thirty-first. All three of us were sitting around a campfire, like a bunch of desperadoes. Man, it was fun. We swapped this code, just in case anything happened and the three of us got separated.'

Josh grinned. 'That was when we discovered we both liked The Clash.'

'And all the other 1970s rock greats,' said Luke. 'Proper music, as my mom likes to call it.' He fell silent. 'And then you fucked up, man. When the shit went down, you weren't there for us.'

Josh remained silent.

'What the fuck happened, man?' said Luke, his voice turning ragged. 'Why weren't you there for us? We trusted you, man. We fucking trusted you

333

with our lives.'

TWENTY-FOUR

Tuesday, June 16th. Night.
Josh could see the pent-up anger in the boy's eyes. The story had been with him for days now, a noxious stew of betrayal and anger.

Believe me, thought Josh, if I could turn back the clock, I would.

He remembered that they had been standing at the side of the road. It was an empty stretch of track, deep in the heart of the Arizona wilderness. Josh knew the ground intimately by now. It was the same place where Kate had found him after he'd been shot. The same place he'd been back to with Marshall. The same place where Ben had been murdered.

Josh had scouted it out the day before. The ground next to the road was completely open but there was some cover in the boulders, where he was planning to lay up and provide covering fire when it was needed. He had equipped himself with an MP-5, issued to him by the British consulate in Los Angeles. And he had a stash of stun grenades in case the battle turned rough.

'You remember now, don't you?' said Luke accusingly.

Josh nodded, but remained silent. What had taken place in the next few minutes was now playing vividly across his mind. It was a scene, he suspected, that would remain etched on his soul until he sank into his grave. There are many terrible things that can happen on a battlefield, he reflected bitterly. A hundred different ways to die, and a thousand ways to get wounded. But there is nothing worse than betraying a comrade.

'It went like this,' said Josh. His voice was hushed, as if he were speaking in church. Outside, he could see the stars starting to brighten up the night sky. He could see both Kate and Luke tracking every word. 'Luke and Ben were sitting at the side of the road. You looked innocent, young. A couple of boys exploring the wilderness, maybe hitching a ride. I had the moves all worked out in my mind. The Porter-Bell people were going to come up, give you the money, and take the software. At some point, Azim was going to make his move. When that happened, I'd take him out. If there was any rough stuff from the Porter-Bell guys, I was going to take them out as well. Either way, I'd make sure you and Ben got out okay. If the plan went the way I wanted it to, Porter-Bell would have the software, so there'd be no more blackouts anywhere in the world. And I'd go home with Azim's scalp. A hero. *At least, that's what I thought.*

'Azim was there somewhere. I'd tracked the man for six months through the Afghanistan-Pakistan borderlands. I'd had him in the sights of my rifle once before. I could smell the bastard. I couldn't see him but I could sense him moving through the boulders and rocks like a breeze. He was out there somewhere. And when he showed himself, I was going to take him. The job would be finished. Properly, this time.

'Then, at the appointed time, a group of three bikers pulled up at the side of the road. The leader was a big, burly man, with a ponytail and beard,

335

driving a big Honda bike. He had two other bikers flanking him. I recognise him now as Flatner, although I didn't know that at the time.

'Next there was a car. A Jaguar XJS, black. Not a car you see very often in Arizona. A man climbed out. In his late forties, maybe early fifties. He was dressed in blue jeans and a loose-fitting white linen shirt. He had black aviator shades covering his eyes. I recognised him, of course. Ed Porter.

'I was scanning the horizon. I had the rifle in my hand, and a set of binoculars. I'm a good shot, always have been. Show me a man's head at a range of up to five hundred yards, and I'll hit it ninety-nine times out of a hundred. Nobody knew I was there. Nobody *could* know. When Azim showed his hand, he was going to die.

'I was hooked up via a scrambled mobile phone link to The Firm back in Vauxhall. I had told my commanding officer, a Rupert called Mark Bruton, exactly what I was going to do. He'd approved the plan. He'd told me he didn't believe that Azim was still alive, but if he was they certainly wanted him dead. And so long as I made sure the software was safely back with Porter-Bell so there could be no more blackouts, then they were happy with the plan. All I had to do was execute it.

'Everything was set. I was certain that nothing could go wrong.'

'But it did, man,' said Luke. 'You fucked up.'

Josh nodded. He could feel the guilt passing across him like a dark cloud. 'Here's what happened,' he said softly. 'Luke and Ben were standing at the side of the road. Luke had his laptop in his hand. Porter approached both of you, with Flatner at his side. Porter was holding a black

336

canvas bag in *his* hand. The money. Then everything started to move very quickly. Azim had hidden himself in the sand, just a few yards away. The bugger had literally buried himself, with just a straw sticking above the surface of the ground so that he could breathe. He rose up out of the ground like a zombie from its grave, clutching an AK-47 in his hand. In one swift movement, he strode up towards Ben, and jabbed the gun against his head. "There's dozens of us," he was shouting. "All over the area. Just give us the software, and drop your weapons, and you'll be okay."

'I had him. I had the bugger in my sights. In that moment, I knew that all I had to do was squeeze the trigger and he'd drop down dead. The shot was going to be a clean one, right through his skull. Nobody could survive a hit like that. Nobody.

'Then this voice comes through on my earpiece. It was Bruton.

' "You there, Harding?" he's shouting down my bloody ear. "You there?"

' "Here," I replied.

'My gun was still trained on Azim at this point. I could still drop him. I just had to squeeze the sodding trigger.

' "There's been a change of plan, Harding," says Bruton. "We reckon it's too dangerous to have a couple of teenage headbangers running around with the power to switch off the electricity in London or Paris or New York whenever they're feeling a bit bloody bored. HMG wants them dead."

' "I gave them my word," I snapped back at him.

' "Well, no one gives a bugger about your word," says Bruton. "Slot them. Now."

' "With respect, sir, fuck off." '

' "You're heading for a fucking court martial, Harding," Bruton shouted back at me. "Now, sl—" '

Josh hesitated. He took a sip of Coke and chewed on one of the biscuits. Telling the story, reliving it exactly as it had been played out that day, had left him drained and exhausted. He glanced up at Luke: the boy's expression was turning from surprise to fascination. I'll make it up to you, Josh vowed silently to himself. *If I can . . .*

'I ripped the earpiece out,' continued Josh, his tone growing firmer all the time. 'I didn't want to listen to any more of that bollocks. Bruton was telling me to slot Ben and Luke—it was a direct order. But I wasn't about to do that. No way.

'I looked back down. I'd lost vital seconds arguing with that idiot. It was chaos down there. Flatner and his two henchmen had pulled out their guns. Pistols. I recognised the make, Desert Eagles, the biggest automatic handgun in the world. One of them had grabbed Ben away from Azim. He was waving a gun at him. Two more Arabs had arrived as if from nowhere. Both of them were holding rifles. They were pointing them at you, Luke. They were trying to get the computer away from you but you were standing your ground.

'There wasn't any time to think. I couldn't get a clear shot at Azim. The moment had passed. I picked myself up, gripped the MP-5 tight in one hand, put a stun grenade in the other. And then I started my charge. There was only one thought in my mind. I had to save you and Ben. I'd given you my word, and I was bloody well going to live up to it no matter what the cost. You don't leave a mate

338

in danger. That's the first rule of my Regiment. *And I was ready to live or die by that rule.*

'It was bloody chaos down there. For a few seconds there were bullets flying everywhere. It was bloody murderous. I fired once, then twice. I think I wounded one of Azim's men. Maybe two. I don't really know. There were so many people waving guns around, it was impossible to get a grip on anything. The whole mission was a complete fuck-up.

'I saw you, Luke. And I saw Ben. Flatner was about to fire at you. I just shouted, "Run Luke, run. Run for your fucking life." And then I saw you starting to head out across the open scrubland. You looked back at me, and said, "I'll be in touch, I'll be in touch."

'Then I could see the gun pointed at Ben. I could see Flatner's finger on the trigger, and he was starting to squeeze it. I hurled myself towards him, trying to knock him off balance and ruin his aim. And that was it. That must have been when the bullets hit me. One in the neck and one in the leg.

'Because that's the last thing I remember.'

'I trusted you,' said Luke. 'But I shouldn't have. And Ben died because of that.'

Josh shook his head. 'My Regiment let me down,' he answered. 'Azim is one of our most wanted terrorists. I could have taken him, then rescued you, but they changed the orders on me at the last moment.' He smashed his fists together, trying to deal with the anger that was building up inside him. 'The bastards. They turned on me. And now they want to arrest and court martial me for disobeying an order.'

'So you can't help me?'

'That's not what I meant,' said Josh. 'I said I'd help you and I will.'

'Like, how, man?' said Luke. 'You fucked up big last time.'

The words stung Josh. At school, he'd flunked a couple of his GCSEs. That was one reason why he'd joined the Army, to make something of himself. During his training for the Regiment, he'd failed a couple of courses and had had to retake them. His marriage to Paula, the way he'd remembered it, had failed, and had left Emily without two parents to raise her: talking to Luke had unlocked the floodgates, and all his memories had come back to him now. And earlier this year, he'd failed to take out Azim when he'd had the man in his sights. Every time you failed, it diminished you as a man, until there was nothing left but a walking collection of disappointments, defeats and regrets.

I won't fail this time. I can't.

'In the Regiment, we have a saying and it's a good one,' said Josh. 'We bring our enemies out into the open, then we can take them. That's what we're going to do. We get Flatner and his boys, and Azim and *his* boys, out here. And we take them down. When all our enemies are dead, we've won.'

Luke smiled: some of the youthful vigour had started to return to his eyes. 'Where?'

Josh looked out through the door of the smelter, onto the dusty abandoned street. 'This looks like a good spot. We fight them right here.'

*   *   *

The meat was skewered on a piece of old wood.

340

Kate was bathing the dead crane in its own fat, turning it gently over the campfire, making sure that it was evenly cooked on all sides. The smell was drifting across to where Josh was sitting: a beguiling mixture of poultry and steak that would tempt the most demanding gourmet.

'You ready to do this?' said Josh glancing across at Luke.

He nodded. They were sitting cross-legged on the dusty ground inside the old smelter. Outside, Josh could see that it was a clear night. The stars were beaming down on the mountains, and a half-moon was illuminating Swansea in a pale, silvery light. *Looks better than the Welsh one*, reflected Josh, smiling to himself. *It's quieter, and the food is better, too.*

The laptop computer was open on the ground between them: a Dell Inspiron with a blue cover, similar to the machine that had been analysed by Kessler. The solar panelling was generating enough power to recharge its batteries during the day, and so long as they didn't overuse it, it would be enough for their needs. A portable satellite link was hooking into the Internet, allowing them to send and receive e-mails: usually these services were very expensive, but Luke knew how to hack into the system of one of the operators, allowing him to access the web for free. *If I'd had that kind of kit when I was a teenager, I wouldn't have had to join the Army*, decided Josh ruefully. *I'd be fighting electronic wars. A lot safer than the other kind.*

'I'm ready,' answered Luke.

His fingers started tapping on the keyboard. Josh and Luke had discussed the plan, and had agreed exactly what they were going do. Luke would send through a message to Porter-Bell, using the same dummy e-mail address that he had been using earlier with Ben. He'd tell them that he was still willing to trade his software for five million dollars. All they had to do was agree, and he'd set up a time and place for the meeting.

'They've taken the bait,' said Luke, looking up towards Josh.

Josh was surprised by the speed of the response. It was less than five minutes since Luke had sent his message, and they had already got back to him. He keeps turning the juice off, realised Josh. *It's making them as nervous as a raghead in a Texas bar.*

'What's it say?'

'They agree to our terms, unconditionally,' said Luke. 'Five million. Whenever, wherever we want it.'

Josh looked across at the message.

'What shall I say?'

'Not tomorrow,' said Josh. 'We need a day to prepare. Thursday.'

'What time? Noon?'

'You've been watching too much TCM. Midday will be too hot. Make it dawn. And tell them we'll give them the place tomorrow.'

Luke started tapping on the laptop's keyboard.

'Why dawn?'

Because all the best soldiers die at dawn. With their boots on.

Josh laughed and smiled at Luke. 'Because there's no point wasting a whole day shooting these bastards.'

TWENTY-FIVE

Wednesday, June 17th. Dawn.
The sun was breaking across the horizon, its first bright beams flashing across Josh's skin. He could feel Kate sleeping in his arms. Her red hair was lying across his cheek, and her arm was stretched out over his chest. The warmth of her body felt reassuring next to his skin, and he could measure the beating of her heart as she breathed.

Perhaps we *will* have a shot together when this is over, he reflected. *Maybe, just maybe, I could make a relationship work this time.*

Her perfume was still lingering on her neck, but it was mixed with the sweat of the night so that only fragments of the smell still remained on her skin. *Clandestine* by Guy Laroche, realised Josh. The name had been somewhere inside his head for weeks. A nurse he'd spent the night with once had worn it, and when his wife had smelled it on his clothes she'd promptly chucked him out. *That's one memory I'd have been better off without.*

My memories, he realised. They're all back. My family, my school, my mum and dad, my ex-wife, my daughter. They're all there. All back in the right box.

I know who I am, and what I have to live for. *I know what I'm prepared to die for as well.*

Josh lifted himself from the ground. It was just after seven in the morning. Kate had curled up next to him, both of them resting on a pile of old leaves that had been swept up from the streets. Luke was a dozen yards away, his body covered by what

343

looked like some ragged overalls he had found in one of the abandoned locker rooms. Let them sleep, thought Josh. I need to scout this place by myself.

He stretched, and walked out of the smelter, down into the main street. Swansea felt fresher in the morning: it was as if the ghosts had abandoned the place, and the buildings looked almost as if they could be occupied again one day. A flock of cranes were drifting overhead in close formation, and one of the grey birds had settled onto a slab of crumbling rock. It cast a wary glance at Josh, then decided to ignore him.

A mining town, Josh mused. The place must have been packed with explosives once.

He started rooting through the empty buildings. The hotel still had the remains of a check-in desk, but the staircase had collapsed, and all the furniture had long since been removed. The kitchen still had an old rusting stove in it, but no sign of any fuel. Next, he tried what looked as if it had once been a hardware store. The counter was still there, although the polish of the surface had long since faded. The shelves had collapsed leaving a dusty pile of debris. Josh picked up the first of a series of tin containers. The can crumbled in his hand, the brown metal flaking like a piece of pastry.

A bunch of heavy steel nails dropped to the floor. Josh gathered them up carefully. Put together into a home-made bomb, they might make useful shrapnel. He walked through to what must have been the stockroom. Looking at some piles of tea chests, he started levering them open one by one. Most were empty. Eventually he stumbled across

344

one filled with hunting knives. He took them out one by one. They hadn't been used since they'd been left here eighty or more years ago, and their blades were still as sharp as razors.

Now we're getting somewhere, thought Josh. *Our own armoury.*

For the next hour, Josh kept searching. The sheriff's office, the houses, the blacksmith's—he inspected each building from top to bottom to see what he could scavenge. By the time he had finished, he was covered in a thin film of dust. His hands felt as if they had been dipped in history. But he had gathered a useful haul: several litres of heating oil from one of the old houses; a dozen cases of shotgun shells from the sheriff's office; some glass bottles from the saloon; and a collection of vicious-looking heavy steel hammers from what had once been the blacksmith's.

Enough kit to do a lot of damage. *If you have time to prepare and you know how to use it.*

Walking back towards the smelter, he kicked up the embers of the fire that they had built last night, tossing another broken floorboard onto the flames to rekindle it. Boiling some water, he brewed up some rough-tasting coffee, pouring it into a pair of the plastic cups that he and Kate had stashed in their kitbag.

'Okay, campers,' said Josh offering both Luke and Kate one cup each. 'No time to kip. We've got work to do. I want this place ready to blow up like it's the bloody fourth of July.'

*   *   *

Josh pointed to the entrance to the town. 'Here,'

345

he said to Luke. 'We should plant them right here.'

A road snaked up the side of the mountain: when Swansea had been a working town, it had been a two-lane paved road, but in the years since then it had collapsed into a single dirt track.

'How deep?' asked Luke.

'An inch, no more,' said Josh. 'Cover them with a layer of dirt, and pat it down so it's not too obvious that the ground has been freshly dug.'

For the past hour, they had taken the shotgun shells and carefully opened up their caps. Using some old string, they had bound the shells together in clusters of four. Bury them beneath the surface, and anyone who trod on them was going to get their foot blown off. It was a simple, rough landmine. *But I've seen them used by men I've fought in Bosnia, and I know how lethal they can be.*

They worked for an hour, digging the pits and laying down the charges in neat formations at different spots around the town. *As soon as anyone attacks, we'll draw them onto the landmines.*

'Okay,' said Josh, as he inspected the last of the charges. 'On to the bottles.'

For the next hour, they filled several old glass bottles with nails, then poured heating oil into them and capped out each one with six inches of twisted rag. Josh crept carefully on top of the crumbling hotel, careful not to break any of the rotting beams that were still barely supporting what remained of its roof. Using some cord, he tied the bottles to the roof, spacing them a dozen feet apart.

A combined nail and petrol bomb, he reflected grimly. Anyone near one of these babies when they blow is going to be feeling very sorry for themselves

346

in the morning. *If they ever wake up.*

'Just memorise where they are,' said Josh to Luke as he climbed back down into the dusty street. 'Look at each one a hundred times, and keep on telling yourself where it is until you can remember it backwards.'

*   *   *

'Shall I tell them where?' asked Luke, glancing across at Josh.

Josh had studied Kate's map of the area, and discussed it with her. He didn't want to let anyone at Porter-Bell know they were hiding up in Swansea. It would be too easy for their hired killers to infiltrate the area during the night, take them by surprise, and murder them all while they slept. Instead, they would give them a meeting place an hour's walk across the mountains and tell them to be there at eight a.m. tomorrow. When they arrived, they would find a note redirecting them towards Swansea. That way, they should arrive in the town around nine. *And we'll have dusted off the welcome mat.*

'Give them these GPS coordinates,' said Josh. 'And tell them not to even think about getting here early. Any tricks and the deal's dead. And so are they.'

Luke tapped the message into the keyboard, then pressed *send.*

'You really think Azim is going to get these e-mails?' asked Josh.

Luke nodded. 'I'm just using my regular old e-mail box. Anyone who knows anything can hack into that.'

347

Josh nodded. 'Then he'll know where we are, and he'll come and get us as well. He wants that software more than he wants anything on the planet.' He tried to smile, but it died on his lips. 'Get as much sleep as you can,' he said softly. 'Tomorrow is going to be a hell of a day.'

* * *

Josh cradled the pistol in his hand. It was a Wilder Survivor: a slim hunting handgun with an extended eight-inch barrel and a wood-sided grip. The Wilder was the one gun they had between them. Luke had brought it with him. He'd been carrying it ever since he'd left his house. Must be his mum's, Josh figured, and she'd probably picked it up from one of her old boyfriends.

But one gun is all you need. So long as it has the right finger on its trigger.

He toyed with the pistol, lining it up to his eye and making sure that its aim was true. He had twenty rounds of ammunition, and he didn't want to waste any of them on practice shots. The Wildey was a gun he knew almost nothing about: he'd seen Charles Bronson use one in *Death Wish 3* but that was the only time he'd encountered it. *Still, if it was good enough for Charlie, then it's good enough for me.*

Experience had taught Josh that every gun was like a woman: unique, temperamental, and to be handled with care. They fired a fraction to the left or to the right, they had to be held up or down, and their triggers liked to be squeezed hard or gently. If you didn't know their winsome little ways you didn't stand a chance.

348

I've got a few hours to get to know your character, thought Josh as he examined the Wildey. *And my life may depend on it.*

So for the next twenty minutes, Josh stripped the Wildey down, checking that every part of the gun was working just as it should be.

A quarter-moon was hanging in the sky. Josh was sitting just outside the smelter, on what might once have been a kerb but was now just a broken piece of rock. He glanced along the empty street, and for a moment he could see it as it must once have been, filled with people, horses, noise, dirt and life. To watch it all winding down, he reflected to himself. That must have been hard. To have seen the families quit one by one, and then to be the last person left, alone.

Time to go home, thought Josh. Time to see my girl again. Time to hold her in my arms, take her to McDonald's, pick her up from school, take her to the cinema, build her a swing in the garden. Do all the things that a dad is meant to do. But it's a long and nasty twenty-four hours from here to there.

Even if I survive tomorrow, the bloody system will still want to arrest me. No, Josh told himself firmly. I'll bloody fight them, the only way I know how. So long as I get Azim, they can't court-martial me. They can throw the bloody book at me. They almost certainly will. But the man who brings in the head of one of the most wanted al-Qaeda terrorists in the world—well, they can't throw *him* out of the Regiment. *They might want to, but they haven't got the guts.*

Josh kicked up a piece of dirt from the ground in front of him. He was struggling to control the anger inside him: it was surging through his chest, making his pulse race and his blood boil. Bruton had stopped him from taking down Azim twice already. *He's not going to stop me a third time.*

Josh squeezed the soil between his fists. Tomorrow his blood will be soaking this ground.

'What are you thinking about?' asked Kate.

She was holding a bottle of water in her hand. Sitting down next to him, she slipped an arm around his back and nestled her cheek into the side of his face. Her skin nuzzled against his, and he could feel the passion running beneath the surface.

'I'm thinking that you should get the hell out of here,' he said. His tone was flat and blunt.

Kate drew her face away and looked at him. Anger flashed in her eyes. 'I'm staying right here.'

'No,' said Josh sharply. 'It's too dangerous.'

Kate laughed: a hollow, shallow laugh that seemed to mock Josh. 'Like digging you out of a ditch wasn't too dangerous? Like taking you into my house wasn't too dangerous? Like hiding you from the cops? Like rescuing your butt when you were about to crack under torture?' She paused, the words choking her as her face reddened with anger. 'Like watching my father die as he tried to save you?'

A pang of guilt stabbed at Josh. Marshall took a bullet for me, he realised. But that's soldiering. You put yourself on the line, and you take a bullet for your unit. That was the way it worked. Marshall was an old soldier. *The rules of the trade were familiar to him.*

'That's the point,' he snapped. 'You've done enough for me. I can't let you take any more risks.'

'I can handle myself.'

Josh stood up. 'You've no idea how bloody

dangerous this is going to be. I don't know how many men are coming to get us tomorrow. Five, six, maybe a dozen. How the hell can I tell? I've got one pistol, some home-made landmines, and a teenage boy who's never been closer to combat than a game on his Playstation. My chances? Pretty bloody miserable.'

'Then why are you doing it?'

'I've no choice.'

Kate tossed back her mane of red hair. 'Everyone has a choice.'

'I'm a soldier. We don't have choices. We have orders.'

'Your orders were to shoot Luke and Ben.'

'I have my own orders—those are the ones I follow,' said Josh. 'My orders are that I keep my word to Luke. And that I take out Azim, because he is an evil, dangerous man. And I don't care what the Ruperts say. I do it my way.'

'And my way is to stay right here,' said Kate. 'I don't care about the danger—I want to see it through.'

Josh shrugged. 'I've warned you. It's your decision.' He paused, looking straight into her eyes. 'But stay out of danger. I owe you my life. The least I can do is pay that back by keeping you safe.'

TWENTY-SIX

Thursday, June 18th. Dawn.

Josh took a swig from the water bottle, letting the liquid splash over his face. He glanced up at the sky. It was already a blazing, fierce blue, even

351

though it was still only eight in the morning. He glanced anxiously along the main street of Swansea. Empty, as always. Yet in a few hours it would be as full of life as it had ever been. *And as full of death as well.*

In the past hour, he had walked down the side of the mountain, traversing rough, difficult terrain. Probably no man had walked across it for half a century or more. He surveyed the dirt-track crossroads where Porter-Bell had been told to leave the money if they wanted Luke's software. The place was empty, just as Porter-Bell had promised. The attacks of the past week, used by Luke to communicate with Josh, must have scared the company witless. Perhaps now they just wanted to hand over the money, get the software, and close the whole miserable chapter. After scouting the area to make sure that it was still empty, Josh pinned a note to a stick and stuck it down in the middle of the crossroads. We'll meet you in Swansea, it said. As soon as you can be there.

As he surveyed the empty town again, Josh ran the plan through his head for the hundredth time. It was eight now. In half an hour the Porter-Bell team would find the note. Assuming they had some all-terrain vehicles with them—maybe Jeeps, maybe quad bikes, maybe sports bikes—they would be here half an hour later. We should expect them at nine.

Late last night, he'd told Luke to send a public e-mail confirming the time, then another one, encrypted, just to Porter-Bell, changing the meeting time from eight to eight-thirty. With any luck, Azim should only intercept the first message, telling them to meet at eight. That way he would be

352

here first—at eight-thirty. *His neck delivered straight into my hands.*

Azim gets here in half an hour. We kill him, then the Porter-Bell mob show up. We get the money, give them the software. Job done. Then we get the hell out of here.

Bruton can burn on his own stake, decided Josh. *If they want robots for soldiers, they should bloody well build some. From now on, I make my own decisions on how this war should be fought.*

'You ready?' said Josh, glancing across at Kate.

She was standing in the shadows of the abandoned hotel, ten yards away, ready to let fall some of the petrol bombs on its roof. 'Ready,' she said firmly.

'When I say so, just get up on the roof, and toss the bombs into the street,' he said. 'Don't worry about aiming, that's not the point. They'll make a big enough explosion to take out anyone who gets in the way. Got that?'

'Got it.'

'You ready?' called Josh, glancing towards Luke. The boy was standing in the doorway of the old sheriff's office, fifteen yards away.

'Hell, man, can't wait,' said Luke.

Josh could hear the bravado in the boy's voice, but he could also see the fear in his eyes. Don't do anything stupid, Josh said silently to himself. Don't be too tough. Combat is bloody frightening, and you have to know when to hide as well as when to fight.

'Stay alert,' he snapped. 'We're not expecting anyone for at least another twenty minutes. But they may come at any time. The worst thing you can do in any battle is get taken by surprise.'

The stage is set, let the battle rage down, Josh told himself. *And if it consumes us all in its fire, then so be it.*

He fingered the trigger of the Wildey Survivor. If I could change anything, I'd have more guns, he mused. Some assault rifles, a machine gun, some grenades. Maybe a battalion or two as back-up. In the meantime, I'll have to make do with this pistol.

Soldiers don't choose their weapons or their battlefield. *If they did, there wouldn't be so many military cemeteries in the world.*

A noise. Josh's head spun around. The sound of a distant rumbling, as if thunder was rolling through the sky. He glanced up. The sky was clear. Holding the gun in his hand, he slipped behind the doorway of the hardware store. Some dust drifted down onto his head.

Another noise. Louder this time. A motorbike.

Eight-twenty. *There shouldn't be anyone here yet.*

Josh listened harder. The rumbling of the machines was maybe a mile away but getting closer all the time. It was a low roar, echoing out across the barren countryside. A minute away, maybe. Perhaps only thirty seconds.

Azim, decided Josh. It must be him. *And this time we meet on equal terms.*

The noise of the bikes was getting louder. Josh could almost smell the fumes of their exhausts. He could sense the wheels churning up the dusty ground, and the swirling plumes of black smoke trailing behind them.

Josh slipped out of the doorway and started to move down the main street. He kept close to the wall in case there were any snipers taking up position anywhere in the mountains.

354

He was planning to charge the attackers once they were in among the landmines. Kate and Luke would stay back, away from the danger. Maybe we can finish this without involving them at all, he decided. With luck.

'Take cover,' barked Josh towards Kate in the hotel. 'You see anyone you don't like, bomb the fuckers.' Then he glanced at Luke, still waiting in the doorway of the sheriff's office. 'Keep your head down.'

'I'm coming with you,' shouted Luke.

'No, you're bloody not,' snapped Josh.

Luke stepped forward. 'I'm coming,' he insisted.

'Stay where you bloody are,' yelled Josh. 'And that's a fucking order.'

He walked further forward, taking care to keep out of sight, each movement a careful step into the unknown. He could feel the sweat breaking out on his fist as he gripped the Wildey tight. He could also feel his ribcage vibrating as his heart thumped hard against his chest. As he reached the end of the street, he leaned hard against the last fissured stone wall and looked carefully out across into the wilderness that tumbled away from the edge of town.

I'll draw them into the minefield. And let the explosives send them back to whatever hell they crawled out of.

The three bikes arrived on the horizon. The machines were Honda XR650s: big, powerful off-road bikes, with raised handlebars, mud flaps, and huge spiked tyres, designed for cutting through mud and dust. A man weighing at least two-hundred and fifty pounds was sitting on each one. They were clad in leather from head to foot, and had shades pulled down over their eyes and helmets over their heads.

It was strange. They looked like Flatner's men, but whether they were his or Azim's, decided Josh, it didn't matter. Either way the choice was a simple one. *I kill them or they kill me.*

Fifty yards in front of him, he could hear the bikes halt, a man shouting, then the roar of throttles as the three bikes leaped into action again. The first bike was speeding out across the sand, the other two following closely in its wake. Great clouds of dust swirled around the accelerating machines. As he watched the lead biker, Josh could see him drawing a pistol, holding the gun in his right hand and the handlebars of his Honda in his left.

The minefield that Josh and Luke had prepared was twenty feet in front of them.

A shot. The bullet bounced off the stone wall, ricocheting harmlessly away. Josh knew that he'd been seen and kept his head down. The bikes must by now be tracking through the start of the minefield, gliding across it like stones skimming across the surface of a lake.

Nothing.

Christ, thought Josh. *If those mines don't work, I'm already dead.*

The explosion erupted against the morning sky as Josh looked over the wall. The mine had detonated, the blast shooting up into the innards of the Honda. The front wheel spun upwards, throwing the rider back. Already, the petrol tank was on fire. It would take just a moment for the fuel to react to the flame, blowing the tank and consuming the bike in a deadly fireball.

356

From every battlefield he'd ever been on, Josh knew that you saw your enemy die before you heard him. He had seen the rider spin into the air, his massive bulk now working against him. He fell heavily beside his machine, the petrol spilling from the tank and cascading over his denim trousers and his thick leather jacket. A hail of sparks was spitting out of the engine. Then Josh heard the second explosion. The wave of noise rocked him backwards. Somewhere from the middle of the inferno Josh could hear the pitiful screams of a man burning to death.

One down. Two to go.

Josh looked from behind the wall. The second bike had veered sharply to the right, the third to the left. Josh had planned the minefield precisely, taking into his calculations all the lessons he'd learned in the Army. When you were putting down mines, you placed them to destroy your enemy, sure—but you also worked out that enemy's likely escape route and laid traps for them there as well. The second biker was already learning that lesson as he rode over another mine and triggered another deadly blast. Another fireball. Another scream.

Two down, one to go.

Thick clouds of heavy black smoke were now rising. The third bike was turning in a tight circle, its driver calculating that his best chance lay in riding back the way he'd come. Josh aimed his pistol. Forty yards now separated him from the biker. He fired one bullet, aiming at the biker's spine—an accurate shot there would paralyse the man instantly. It missed, the bullet hitting the dust harmlessly. Christ, thought Josh. I need practice with this bloody gun. *I'm not going to survive many missed shots.*

The driver swerved to the left, anxious to avoid the gunfire. Mistake, pal, decided Josh with a grim smile. *You're back on hostile ground.*

As the third mine blew, the bike skidded. The Honda's front wheel was blown clean off, spinning up into the air. The rider fell from his machine, his hands still gripping the handlebars. Petrol spilled out over his body, and a shower of sparks cascaded across him as the broken and twisted bike rolled over onto him. Flames leaped up all around him, engulfing his legs and torso before flicking across the skin of his face.

'Help me,' shouted the man desperately. 'Please, somebody—I'm fucking dying here.'

Before today, Josh had only witnessed it once on the battlefield, but there were few worse sights, sounds—and smells—than those of a man burning to death. You can smell the charred flesh, like meat roasting on a spit. You can feel the heat, as the flames curl around the body. And you can hear the terrifying screams, like those of a strangled cat, getting thinner and thinner as the vocal cords slowly get burned away.

'Help me,' the man shrieked desperately, his burning hands trying to push away the bike that was lying across his body.

No way, pal.

Josh started running back towards the town. Let's see what else you can throw at us he exulted inwardly.

Another noise. Racing down the main street, Josh cast his gaze up at the ramshackle roofs of the buildings. A scratching, like that of an animal. Or a man.

'Luke,' Josh hissed towards the sheriff's office. 'You there?'

A silence. Josh could feel his heart thumping. 'Luke?' he said, louder this time.

'He's gone.'

Josh spun around. Kate was still standing at the window of the old hotel. He could hear her, but only just see her: she was in the shadow of a pair of shutters hanging loose on their hinges.

'Why didn't you bloody stop him?' shouted Josh.

'With what?' Kate yelled back.

Her voice was raw and desperate. Nothing is going as I'd planned, Josh told himself. Porter-Bell have obviously decided to kill us all. At this rate, they'll succeed.

Josh heard a scratching noise. Then the sound of a slate being broken as someone stepped on it.

There was just a split second in which to react. A man was descending from the sky. Josh threw himself sideways onto the ground and narrowly managed to avoid being crushed by the man: a two-hundred-and-fifty-pound monster, clad in denim and leather. Josh realised that his spine would have snapped the instant the creature landed on top of him.

Both of them were lying flat in the dirt. The gun had fallen out of Josh's hand, leaving it out of reach. The man grabbed out, catching hold of Josh's wounded leg. He started pulling, wrenching the bones around Josh's feet. Josh could feel pain searing up through him as the wound reopened. Blood started to leak out into the cloth of his jeans. Now a fist started to pummel Josh's side. The blows were heavy and strong, delivered with pile driving force.

Reaching into his pocket, Josh grasped one of the heavy nails that he'd taken from the hardware store. The steel was rotten and rusty with age, but still sharp at the tip. Holding it in his right hand, Josh gripped hard and sat up sharply. Concentrating his strength into his fist, his slammed the nail hard into his attacker's hand. He could feel the point piercing the skin, then grating against the bone of the knuckle. Josh pushed harder, ignoring the way that the nail was digging into the skin of his own palm. The nail forced itself through the bone, its tip emerging on the other side of the man's hand.

The man screamed in pain, letting go of Josh's foot.

Josh kicked himself free. He ran inside the abandoned hotel. 'The bombs,' shouted Josh, looking up at Kate. 'Throw the bloody bombs at him.'

He could see the fear in her eyes. She started to move but her hands were shaking.

She's frozen. The fear has got to her.

'Throw the fucking bombs,' he shouted, his lungs straining to put as much force as he could into the words.

A tear was smudging her face. He could see that her hand was shaking. She can't do it, Josh told himself. She can't bloody do it.

Josh ran forward. His attacker had struggled to his feet. The man was holding on to his hand. The nail was still sticking through it, and his blood streaked the rust on the spike. His face was covered by a biking helmet and a scarf was wrapped around his neck, but Josh could see enough of his skin to tell that he was white, not Arab.

Where the hell is Azim? *If these are Flatner's men, where the hell is Azim?*

Josh was standing two yards from the man in the dusty street. Somewhere in the distance, he could hear shouting, more motorbikes. They were now coming into town from the other side. Christ, he told himself. *They just keep coming. I need to get rid of this one before his mates arrive.*

The man was edging towards him, growling like a bear. Then he lunged forward, putting his full weight behind the blow.

Mistake, pal, thought Josh. You're over-committed.

The punch narrowly missed Josh's jaw. He danced forwards so that now he was positioned behind the man. Reaching up, he snapped both his arms into a tight coil around the monster's neck. Josh pulled with all his strength. The muscles in his arms were screaming with pain as the man struggled to free himself. At two hundred and fifty pounds, he had the strength of a wild bull. A violent belch escaped from the man's gut as Josh pulled tighter, then tighter again. His hands were scrabbling at Josh's arms and his legs were kicking backwards as he tried to loosen Josh's grip. But Josh's lock on his neck was firm, slowly cutting the supply of oxygen to his brain.

It's a McDeath for you, you bastard. Quick, nasty and cheap.

Josh had only strangled a man once before—during a mission in Afghanistan—but he knew from his training that the most dangerous moment was just before an opponent died. The oxygen switched off in the brain, yet as the victim lost

361

consciousness they knew that there was just one last chance of saving themselves, and they would throw all their remaining strength into it.

The man gave a horrific choked-off yell, then reared back, trying to use the muscles in his massive shoulders to throw Josh off.

Josh was ready for him. He tightened his arms as hard as he could, squeezing the life out of the man. He could feel a last spasm of strength surge through his adversary, then start to ebb. The man's breathing slowed, then stopped. Finally his body slumped to the ground.

Josh started looking around desperately. There was still no sign of Luke. And the remaining bikes were only three hundred yards away.

He picked up his gun from the ground and ran towards the hotel. Kate was still standing mute behind the shutters like a statue, her face pale and drawn. 'I'm sorry,' she stuttered. 'I couldn't . . . I couldn't . . .'

'You bottled it,' Josh snapped.

Immediately, he regretted having spoken roughly to her. In the heat of battle, men spoke harshly: he'd been called a million different names in a firefight and shrugged them all off in the mess later. Kate wasn't to know that: this was his territory, not hers. 'It's not your fault,' he said, quickly. 'You're not a soldier. Just take cover and try not to cause any trouble.'

He started moving up the back staircase. The wooden slats were rotten and half the banister had crumbled away. Josh ignored the danger, flinging himself upwards. He could feel the boards flaking into pieces as he trod on them.

He climbed out and crawled across the flat roof.

Ten home-made firebombs were laid out in a row. Glancing up, Josh could see the bikers advancing to the main street. The same big black Hondas, the same burly men clad in leather and helmets. The same pistols being brandished.

Serve them up a diet of death and mayhem, and they just keep coming back for more.

Josh waited, counting down the seconds. The bombs would work once and once only.

The bikes were advancing steadily, their engines roaring. The front biker was moving carefully, scrutinising the ground for stretched wires or freshly dug earth. They're checking for mines, realised Josh.

But this time the death will come down like rain from the sky.

After checking that the ground was undisturbed, the lead bike started to advance towards the corpse that was lying directly below Josh.

'Kate, take cover,' shouted Josh, aware that she was still down below.

He could see the bikers twenty feet below turning their heads up to look at him but before they could shoot Josh hurled down the first of the petrol bombs. It ignited as it hit the ground, sending a huge ball of flame shooting out. He threw down more. The bottles splintered, at first sending tiny shards of glass spraying up into the air. Then the nails packed inside the bottle spun upwards, gathering velocity as they moved outwards, forming a lethal sphere of shrapnel.

One biker was already in flames, his arms flailing desperately as he tried to extinguish the fire enveloping his body. Another was lying face down on the ground. A pair of nails had shot straight through his head, piercing his skull and sending chunks of his brain splattering across the dusty ground.

Josh ran along the length of the roof, hurling down the bombs one by one. Suddenly the street was a bedlam of explosions. Burning petrol, steel nails and glass splinters were flying everywhere. Two of the bikes exploded, sending hot oil spewing out onto the burning ground. Swirling clouds of smoke were spiralling into the sky. The noise was deafening. Josh threw himself down and gripped the side of the roof, shutting his eyes and closing his mouth to stop the fumes from choking him. *I just hope Kate has the sense to do the same,* he thought.

When he opened his eyes again, the street was a chaos of burning rubber and petrol. The bikes were mangled heaps of metal. Corpses lay strewn across the ground, but the closer Josh looked the harder it became to count the dead. Too many severed limbs were scattered around.

One man was lying on the ground. His leg had been ripped off, and blood was pulsing from the open wound. His lips were trembling as he tried to cry out in pain, but his tongue had been burnt out and no sound could escape from his mouth.

Josh dropped down from the roof and landed on the ground. He approached the wounded biker and knelt down, putting the barrel of the Wildey to the man's head. *I'm saving my ammunition, but I'm still going to put you out of your misery, pal. One warrior should always be willing to spend a bullet on another.*

He squeezed the trigger. The bullet shattered the man's skull and pulverised his brain, killing him instantly.

364

'Hold it right there,' shouted a voice. Josh looked up. Twenty yards ahead, walking towards him, he could see Flatner who was holding Luke with his arm twisted behind his back. A pistol was pressed against the side of the boy's head. Luke's head was lowered and some blood was trickling down the side of his mouth where he had taken a blow to the face.

Flatner was walking along the main street with Edward Porter at his side. He was looking at Josh, a grin playing on his face.

'Stay where you are, Josh,' said Flatner. 'This time you're mine.'

TWENTY-SEVEN

Thursday, June 18th. Morning.
Josh stood perfectly still. The fires were still burning behind him and the flames continued to lick at the corpses of the fallen bikers. He could feel the heat on his back, but despite that the blood in his veins was starting to freeze.

Flatner was still walking towards him, a cruel smile on his lips. He was holding a Glock 18 in his hand, one of the simplest, most reliable and most accurate handguns in the world, and he was pushing Luke forwards roughly.

At his side, Edward Porter was standing with his own Glock 18 held almost casually in his right hand, as if he was not used to carrying a gun. Close up, he looked much older than he had looked in any of the pictures that Josh had seen. His hair was starting to thin, and his skin was greying and blotchy. The face of a man who is rapidly ageing, decided Josh. And of a man who doesn't waste time on negotiations or compromises but cuts straight to the deal. *Or the kill.*

'Where's the woman?' said Flatner.

Josh said nothing.

Flatner glanced left and right, his stare scouring both sides of the street. Whether he felt anything about the death of six of his men a few minutes ago, Josh couldn't tell.

'Come out now, or I shoot both of them.'

There was a pause. Behind him Josh could hear the continuing sounds of burning. Then he saw Kate. She stepped from the porch of the old hotel, walking carefully through the blazing wreckage. Her face was blackened and there was sweat running down her skin. Her eyes looked tired and frightened. 'Don't hurt the boy,' she said, glancing up at Flatner. She was choking back the tears in her voice. 'We'll do whatever you say. Just don't hurt him.'

'So,' said Porter. 'Are we ready to do some business?'

'You're a bloody idiot,' said Josh angrily, looking up at the man.

Porter nodded thoughtfully. 'According to the Forbes list, I'm the ninth richest man in the world,' he replied. 'That doesn't sound like an idiot to me.'

'We'd have given you the software all along,' said Josh. 'Luke wanted his money, that's all. If you'd just given him the five million we could have done this simply and without any bloodshed.'

Porter laughed. 'You don't get to be as rich as I am by going around giving five million dollars to every two-nickel hustler who wants to blackmail the company. I'm a straightforward man. You treat me with respect, I'll treat you with respect. You try to fuck me, then I'll fuck you so hard back that you'll wish you were dead.' He glanced first at Luke, then at Josh. 'You've both tried to hustle me. Now it's payback time.'

Josh shook his head. 'It's no hustle. Luke found a flaw in your software. If he can find it so can someone else. He's performed a service for your business and he wants to be paid. Simple.'

'Then why the bombs and landmines?' said Porter.

'Why the bikers armed to the teeth?' snapped Josh.

Porter raised a hand. 'Enough of this,' he said. 'I'm a busy man. Now, I want the software—or the boy dies.'

Josh shook his head. 'Give us the money.'

'I said the boy dies.'

Josh glanced sideways. He could see Flatner jabbing the Glock harder against the side of Luke's head.

'I don't care,' said Luke fearfully. 'You already killed Ben. Kill me if you want to. I don't care.'

Flatner slapped him around the head. The blow rocked him but Luke stood his ground, and his lips stayed sealed.

'The kid's brave,' said Josh. 'You're not going to get anywhere by roughing him up.'

'Maybe we should just shoot him, then?' said Porter thoughtfully. 'No more Luke, no more problem.'

'You need him,' snapped Josh. 'Without him, the security flaw is still there. Someone else will find it.'

'I'll break them, boss,' said Flatner. 'Just give me

a few minutes to knock them about. They'll break.'

Porter raised his hand. 'We haven't got time.' He looked across at Josh. 'What are you, the kid's agent or something? You collecting ten per cent on this deal?'

'I gave him my word to protect him,' answered Josh. 'I haven't managed to hang on to much in my life, but I keep my promises.'

Suddenly and inexplicably, Porter seemed to change his mind. 'Okay, you win. Give us the software, and we'll give you the money.' He placed a black briefcase that he'd been carrying in his left hand down on the ground between them. 'It's all here.'

Josh stepped forward. He opened the case. Inside, he could see a neat stack of freshly minted fifty-dollar notes. 'There's a million in notes,' said Porter. 'The rest is in bearer bonds. You can cash them at any bank, no questions asked.'

Josh nodded. 'You happy?' he said, looking towards Luke.

'Okay,' said Luke. 'Give them the computer.'

Josh glanced at Kate. 'Get it,' he said.

Kate started walking back towards the crumbling sheriff's office. Luke had left his laptop in there. A minute later she returned, carrying the machine in her hand. She handed it across to Luke.

He knelt down on the ground. Flatner stood over him, his gun still to the boy's head. Josh knew there would be enough power in the laptop's battery to last for another hour, and its satellite connection was keeping it plugged into the internet. With a look of concentration on his face, Luke started tapping at the machine's keyboard.

'How do I know you're giving me the right

computer?' said Porter. 'How do I know it's got the software in it?'

'Name a city,' said Luke, looking across to Porter. 'Any city?'

'Name me a city, and I'll switch off the power there,' said Luke. 'Then you'll see for yourself that this is the software.'

Porter's brow furrowed. 'Austin,' he replied. 'I've always hated Austin.' He chuckled grimly to himself. 'It'll be thirty degrees there already, even at this time of the morning. They'll all be sweating like pigs when the air-conditioning gets switched off.'

Josh remained still, watching while Luke tapped away at the keyboard. A single thought was now running through his mind. Luke may get his money, but Azim hasn't shown up.

I've miscalculated. I'm done for. Even if Porter and Flatner don't kill us, if I go back to Britain without taking out Azim I'll be court-martialled for sure. *I disobeyed orders and I won't have a single argument to defend myself with.*

'You got a PDA or something?' Luke said to Porter.

Porter pulled out a small, slim case from his breast pocket. 'A Blackberry.'

'Then check one of the news sites,' said Luke. 'The power in Austin is already down. The story should be running any minute.'

Porter was staring in fascination at the tiny screen embedded in the device resting on the palm of his hand. He might be a billionaire several times over, thought Josh. But he was still an engineer at heart: the thing that fascinated him most was machines, and how they worked.

369

Porter turned the Blackberry 7290 outwards so that everybody could see the tiny screen. It showed the CNN.com website. Across the bottom of the screen, under a flashing 'Breaking News' logo, the words were clearly spelled out: 'Blackout hits Austin . . . Blackout hits Austin. Details to follow . . .'

'Okay,' said Porter. 'I believe you. Now give those poor Texans their power back before you totally bankrupt this company.'

Josh stepped forward, putting his hand down on the briefcase.

'*You* might keep your promises,' said Porter. 'But to me, words are matchsticks.' He snapped his fingers. 'I break them just like that.'

As Josh looked up he saw that Porter's pistol was pointing straight at him.

'Get away from that case,' said Porter, pronouncing the words with the kind of force that comes easily to a man holding a gun in his hand. 'Then hand over the computer.'

Josh shook his head. 'I've been jerked around once too often.'

'Put down the gun,' shouted Porter. 'And get your hands in the air. *Now.*'

If I go this time, decided Josh, so be it. Without Azim, I've nothing. *I'd rather die here than go back to Hereford and get ripped to shreds by the Ruperts for disobeying an order.*

Josh sensed how his military training just might give him the edge in this fight. With one quick movement of his hand, he pulled the Wildey from the inside of his jacket where he had been hiding it for the last ten minutes. His mind was a blur but an adrenalin-fuelled mix of anxiety, anger and

370

desperation was guiding his movements.

'You've got the safety catch on,' he barked at Porter. 'That gun's not going to kill anyone.'

Porter's gaze flicked towards his pistol. A split second of delay. Josh jabbed his gun forward, squeezing the trigger hard. The bullet knocked the Glock clean out of Porter's hand. Swiftly, Josh cocked the Wildey and squeezed its trigger again. This time the bullet struck Flatner's right hand, smashing his knuckles. His Glock fell to the ground too. Unfired.

Luke leaped forwards, unscathed. He grabbed his computer and cowered behind Josh.

'You're worth billions,' said Josh to Porter. 'Yet you're about to throw your life away for the sake of a stupid five million.'

Josh stood rock-solid and nodded at Luke to pick up the briefcase. Stepping forward, Luke gripped its handle, cradling it to his chest. Many men have died for that money, thought Josh. *Don't let go of it now*.

'Now which of you wants the next bullet?'

'I . . . I . . .' stuttered Porter.

He can order the deaths of other men, thought Josh, but he can't face it himself. Josh held the gun up, so that Porter's forehead was neatly in its sights. 'I'll finish you nice and quick,' said Josh. 'As for Flatner, I'll make *that* slow and painful.' He glanced across at Flatner. 'I owe you that much.'

'N-no,' stammered Porter, his lips quivering. 'I can give you money . . . I can . . .'

'Stand still, and take it like a bloody man,' barked Josh.

'Put the gun down.'

Josh turned around. Kate was holding her own

371

Glock. Its matt-black barrel was pointing straight at his chest.

'I said put the gun down,' she repeated.

TWENTY-EIGHT

Thursday, June 18th. Morning.
Josh looked into Kate's eyes. She was wearing the same expression he had seen nearly three weeks ago, when she had first pulled him bleeding out of the ditch. Spirit, fire and determination were the words that had flashed through his mind then, and now they seemed just as accurate.

Josh lowered the Wildey handgun to his side. His body had frozen, but his mind was calculating furiously. Of course, he told himself. You're a sodding moron, Josh. *She was working for Porter-Bell all along.*

Kate took two steps forward. She was holding the Glock straight out in front of her, her forearm steady yet relaxed, the way a trained marksman would hold himself just before an execution. 'Drop the gun, Josh,' she said, 'That's an order from your doctor.'

'Kill him, Kate,' snapped Porter.

'Who the hell *are* you?' growled Josh, looking at Kate.

'She works for me,' said Porter. 'Always has done. One of the advantages of being a billionaire. You can have a pretty big payroll.'

Josh looked at Kate again. The deception, he realised, had been perfect from start to finish. Every tender word, every moment of medical treatment, every kiss and caress—all of it had been a lie.

'Is this true?' he asked.

Kate shrugged aside the lock of red hair that had tumbled across her forehead.

'I don't know how things are on your planet, Josh,' she said. 'But on this one women don't usually start helping strange men who they find wounded in a ditch. Painful as it might be to your little soldier ego, you're not so irresistible that I took one look at you, fell in love, and decided to risk my life trying to look after you.' She chuckled. 'Only a man, and a pretty stupid one, would think that was possible.'

Kate placed the Glock closer to Josh's forehead: he could smell the grease and oil on the gun's firing mechanism.

'I took you in and took care of you because Mr Porter here paid me handsomely to do so,' she continued. 'Why? Because Luke escaped from us. Don't you remember his final words to you as he ran away? He said he'd be in touch. So we knew all along that if we were going to find him you were our best chance of doing so. So long as we had you, eventually you'd lead us to him. All I had to do was stick close, and sooner or later you'd take us to Luke. When you did so, Mr Porter would pay five million dollars. So thanks, Josh. You've made it a lucrative time. And you couldn't have played your part better if I'd scripted it myself.

'You took a nasty wound to the head,' Kate went on. 'That often causes short-term memory loss. Then I kept injecting you with mild barbiturates. You thought they were painkillers. But barbiturates cause and sustain amnesia. I didn't want your memory coming back until Luke sent you his signal.'

'And Marshall? Didn't he mind you prostituting yourself? His own daughter?'

Kate smiled. 'You're so gullible, it would almost be cute. If it wasn't about to cost you and Luke your lives.'

'He's not your father, is he?'

'Marshall? No,' answered Kate. 'My dad was in Florida playing golf the last time I saw him. Marshall's a clever operator. He ruled these wastelands. After I was charged with keeping track of you until Luke got in touch, he was the obvious man to turn to.' She was watching him intently. 'So like I said, drop that gun.'

The Wildey was resting in his palm, but Josh felt as if all the fight had been punched out of him. He'd fought like a mad dog, and it had all been for nothing. Now the game was finally played out.

Porter stepped forward, a grin lighting up his face: the fear of a few moments ago had been banished, replaced by the easy, complacent composure of a man who now knew that he could buy his way out of anything. He picked up the briefcase, holding it firmly in his hands.

'First rule of business, son,' he said, glancing towards Josh. 'Know when you're beaten. And you two boys are beaten.' Bending over, he also picked up Luke's laptop from the ground. 'I don't think we need these two any more,' he said to Kate. 'Finish them off.'

At his side, Josh could sense Luke starting to tremble. It took a man of the strongest nerves to hear with calm his own execution being discussed, and Luke was just a boy: his lips were trembling,

374

and his legs looked as if they were about to give way beneath him. I'm sorry, thought Josh. You put your trust in me again.

Kate kept the gun levelled at Josh's head. In her eyes he could see the cold, uncompromising stare of a natural-born killer.

'I'm sorry, Josh,' she said. 'In other circumstances, maybe we could have had a relationship.' She shrugged. 'But, you know, there's the money . . .'

Josh closed his eyes. The bullet was so close that he could almost feel it already, crashing through his skull, bursting through his brain, severing the membranes and nerves.

Of all the different deaths I thought fate might have planned for me, I never expected to be shot by a woman.

A sound rang out through the empty town. A shot. Josh opened his eyes again. Kate's gun was lying on the floor, blasted out of her hands. A man was walking towards them, a pistol in his hand. He was wearing aviator shades, a cowboy hat on his head that shielded him from the sun, and a white scarf wrapped around his neck. The top two buttons on his blue linen shirt were undone, revealing some greying chest hair. And his walk had the steadiness of a man used to taking command.

Josh didn't need to give the man a second glance. He'd learned to recognise him the way he might recognise his own shadow.

Azim.

Azim walked forwards steadily, emerging from the swirling clouds of black smoke that were still rising from the burnt-out motorbikes behind them.

Fifteen yards, then ten—he was drawing steadily closer to them.

'He's mine,' said Azim, indicating Josh with a brief nod.

'You take him, then,' said Kate.

Azim raised his revolver and aimed. He squeezed the trigger. As he did so, Kate made a strange, wordless sound. Then she seemed about to speak—but the blood was already foaming up through her mouth. It was spilling out across her cheeks, smearing her white skin. Her feet held steady for a second but then gave way, and her body collapsed onto the ground.

Josh saw that the bullet had struck her heart. She had been killed in an instant. Good shot, he thought. *That woman's heart is a pretty small target.*

Azim raised his gun again. He fired once, then twice. The first bullet hit Flatner in the chest, the second pulped his right eye. Blood poured down the side of his face. The second bullet to hit him had blasted a hole clean through the centre of his skull. He tilted back on his heels, trying to steady himself, then fell backwards to lie twitching briefly on the ground.

Azim had fired four bullets, Josh realised. So there were two left in the chamber. *And one of them has my name on it.*

Azim raised his gun again in a smooth arc and held it steady in his right hand. Its muzzle swung past Josh and Azim hesitated briefly, then aimed it directly at Porter's head. 'Hold it right there,' said Azim coldly. 'I'm taking that software on behalf of the British Government. If you try to resist me, you're a dead man.'

Josh had been tracking the movement of the gun.

Now he was thinking, *What kind of stunt is the bastard pulling?*

Porter was frozen, paralysed with fear. Kate was dead. Flatner was dead. His protection had been stripped away from him.

Meekly, he picked up the laptop and handed it across to Azim. From his pocket, Azim took out a blank CD-ROM, slotted it into the machine, then looked back across to Josh.

'You and I are working for the same team, Josh,' said Azim. 'As I told you earlier, I am not by nature a cruel man. There's no need for us to fight any more.'

'The same team?' said Josh. 'What the bloody hell does that mean?'

'It means you've been wrong all along,' said Azim. 'I'm a double agent, the highest-ranking British Intelligence mole inside al-Qaeda. I have been feeding information to The Firm.'

Suddenly, Josh began to understand. 'That's why they didn't finish you off in Afghanistan,' he said. 'That's why Bruton told me not to shoot you when the handover was being made with Ben and Luke.'

'Exactly,' said Azim. 'They have to protect me. I'm the best source they have.'

'Why didn't they bloody tell me?' said Josh.

'Because you're just a cog in a big machine,' said Azim. 'They can't go around telling everyone I'm a double agent. I'd be dead within minutes. And they have to let the same monkeys who are chasing my colleagues chase me as well. After all, it would be suspicious if I was the only senior al-Qaeda man who wasn't being tracked by the British or the Americans.' He looked hard at Josh. 'You see, I'm one of the most important assets Western

Intelligence has. Far more important than some ignorant squaddie.' He laughed. 'They can always get another solider. They can't find another agent like me.'

'But you tortured me. You were going to kill me,' snapped Josh. 'I don't call *that* being on the same bloody side.'

Azim smiled. 'But you'd left the team by then, Josh,' he said. 'You'd disobeyed Bruton's direct order. We had no idea who you were working for any more. And the priority was to get hold of this software. Luke turned all the lights off in London. We couldn't let that happen again. I was just doing what I had to do. Anyway . . .' Azim took the CD-ROM from the machine and slipped it into his pocket. 'Now that we have the software, our mission is closed.'

'So we destroy the computer?' said Josh.

Azim aimed his gun and blasted the laptop. At such close range, the bullet shattered the machine, leaving splinters of plastic on the ground.

'Luke's copy of the software is destroyed,' said Azim. 'It's finished. All we have to do now is execute Luke, then there will be no chance of him ever creating it again.'

The Wildey was still lying on the ground. Josh leaned down to pick it up.

'Not quite that simple,' he said and he raised the pistol, pointing it at Azim.

'I've just saved your life, Josh.'

Josh steadied his aim. His lips remained sealed, his expression focused.

'We're on the same team,' said Azim.

It was the first time that Josh had heard even a hint of nervousness in the man's voice.

'I'm on my own team.'

Josh tightened his finger on the trigger. The Wildey recoiled in his grip as the bullet exploded from its barrel. Josh cocked the gun, then squeezed the trigger again. Two bullets, he told himself. When you want to make sure you never hear from a man again, you need to put at least two bullets into him.

Azim crumpled to the floor.

It's over. At last it's over, thought Josh.

EPILOGUE

Monday, August 3rd. Afternoon.

Mark Bruton sat at the centre of the table. He was wearing uniform, but his jacket had been slipped over the back of his chair. He was flanked on either side by two sombre-faced men, both in their mid to late thirties, both with black hair. One had a blue suit and one a black suit. Both served The Firm as officers in the anti-terrorist unit, working the grey space between the Regiment and the intelligence services. Neither gave his name, nor would they at any point during the hearing. Ant and Dec, decided Josh. *It was hard to tell them apart.*

'I want you to understand something, Harding,' said Bruton. 'This isn't a court martial. Not yet. But it's a full-scale disciplinary hearing. Anything you say here may be used against you if this *does* go to a court martial. Understood?'

Josh glanced up at the officer. His expression, he reckoned, was one you only ever saw on the face of a Rupert: confident, self-righteous, and completely clueless. A 747 could land on his nose and he wouldn't bloody notice it.

'Understood,' replied Josh, deliberately inserting a pause before the next word. 'Sir.'

'And because this is a disciplinary hearing, you need to tell the truth,' continued Bruton. 'The complete truth, Harding. Otherwise things will get very nasty for you.'

'Understood.' Another pause. 'Sir.'

They were sitting in a concrete-walled room, sixteen floors beneath The Firm's Vauxhall

381

headquarters. Below the basement level, the building had a series of massively reinforced bunkers designed to survive a full-scale nuclear attack: the intelligence agencies had no intention of stopping work after such a strike. There was a series of offices, each with their own oxygen supply, designed to keep working during a biological attack. And beneath those were a layer of cells and interrogation rooms. *Once you were thrown in there, even a nuclear strike wasn't going to get you out.*

Josh had been here for nine days already, kept in solitary confinement. After shooting Azim, he'd set Porter loose. The billionaire no longer interested him. Make your own way home, Josh had told him. He took the rented Mustang and drove back towards Los Angeles, stopping at a motel overnight to shower, shave, get a decent meal and have a good night's sleep.

The next morning, while Luke disappeared quietly back to Boisdale, Josh had reported back to the consulate in LA. He had been arrested immediately. Kept overnight, he had been flown back to London on a military jet. Twelve hours in his own plane, realised Josh. Just the fuel for that trip wasn't going to leave much change out of twenty grand. It was rare that an organisation as notoriously mean as the Army treated its guests so lavishly. I must be going up in the world, he'd thought.

As the plane touched down at RAF Northolt on Sunday morning, Josh was met by six military policemen and driven straight to Vauxhall. He was taken down to a cell, and apart from the twice-daily serving of food pushed under his door that was it as far as human contact went: he heard nothing more about where he was, or how long he might be there.

Maybe they've already thrown away the key, he decided bitterly as hours stretched into days.

Now Ant said: 'You disobeyed an order. Why?'

Josh glanced up at the man. 'The order didn't make any sense.'

Ant remained expressionless. Dec smiled, and looked at Josh. 'Now, now, Mr Harding. You're a soldier. A good one. You know very well that an order is an order. We can't start negotiating which we obey and which we don't.'

'I know the rules,' said Josh. 'But when the security of the country is at stake, they don't apply any more.'

'The security of the country?' said Ant. 'Azim was the best inside agent we've managed to get inside al-Qaeda yet. He helped us foil several planned atrocities in this country. And you shot him.'

'I did my job,' said Josh.

'Your job is to obey orders,' said Ant.

'My job is to serve my country,' said Josh. 'And protect it.'

There was a silence. Josh could see the anger in all six eyes glazing at him. If the rules allowed it, they'd probably shoot me on the spot, he mused.

'Tell us what happened,' said Dec.

Josh knew that there was no point. There had already been a full written debrief describing the mission. There was nothing else to add. 'You already know.'

'Then tell us why you shot him,' said Ant.

'It was revenge, wasn't it?' interrupted Bruton. 'You were just angry at him for beating you. He pissed you off. So you shot him.'

He looked savagely at Josh. 'Admit it, Harding.

You're out of bloody control. You're not a soldier, just a bloody pub brawler. We don't need your kind.'

Both Ant and Dec glanced across at Bruton: they were silently telling him to keep his temper, but they were not disagreeing with anything that he'd said.

'If you can't explain yourself better than that, then it will be the duty of this hearing to recommend a full court martial,' said Dec stiffly. 'We'll have no other choice.'

Josh pulled a disk from his pocket: a single CD-ROM, green on one side, silver on the other. He stepped up from his chair, placing the disk on the desk. 'First take a look at this,' he said.

There was silence from all three men as they looked down at the disk. 'What is it?' asked Ant.

'Azim destroyed the computer that Luke had written the program on,' said Josh. He was standing up, looking down at all three men. 'He wanted us to believe that he'd destroyed the program that was causing all the blackouts. Before he did so, he took a copy on this disk. Now, why did he do that? So he could take it back to his al-Qaeda mates.'

'Meaning what?' said Bruton.

'Meaning that he was a *triple* agent,' snapped Josh. 'He fed you some information to make you think that you'd turned him but he was loyal to his movement. He had you guys protecting him every step of the way. That's why al-Qaeda sent him to get the software. They knew that you'd help Azim to get his hands on it.

'It was only because of me that we stopped him,' he continued, his tone turning intense. 'If it had been up to you lot, al-Qaeda would have had Luke's software by now. And the lights would be popping off all over the world every time the boys with towels on their heads felt like giving us a bit of a slapping.'

Josh paused, turning around. His face was reddening with anger as his blood pumped furiously through his veins. 'Like I said, I was just doing my job. Protecting my country.' He smiled. 'Now you do yours. If that means court-martialling me, so be it. If it means giving me a medal, so be it. I don't bloody care any more.'

He stopped, the last words left hanging in the air. He could see both Ant and Dec looking nervously at one another: this wasn't going to look good in their reports. Dec took the disk carefully in his hands. 'We'll examine this. If it's what you say it is, then I suppose that changes things.'

'And what do you want me to do?' said Josh. He paused again. 'Sir.'

'Go back to Hereford, Harding,' said Bruton. 'They can do what they like with you. I don't sodding care what happens to you.'

*   *   *

Josh could feel the breeze blowing off the Thames as he walked over Vauxhall Bridge. He paused to look down at the water streaming beneath him. It's all under the bridge, he told himself. Let it stay that way.

Darkness had already fallen. In the few days he'd been kept at The Firm, his sense of time had been shot to pieces. His nervous system was still recovering from the battering he'd taken over in

America. When he got back to base, he'd need a full medical, but he already had some sense of the damage that he'd taken. The electric shocks had left him jittery, and there was still some swelling in his chest from where the snakes had chewed him. The wounds to his leg and his neck were still painful. But I can still walk, he told himself. For now, that's enough.

It was a clear night, and the rush-hour traffic was just starting to thin out. Off to the right he could see the lights of Big Ben playing across the waters of the Thames, on the other side of the river the lights on the London Eye slowly turning. Further out, a gentle electric haze stretched out to Canary Wharf and beyond.

In a couple of days, he'd be back with the Regiment. He'd see how he felt once he was back with his mates. Maybe it was time to move on. All he wanted to do now was to get back to Emily, check that she was okay, then start to get himself back in shape.

Josh looked down again at the water. Suddenly, the lights vanished.

It took a moment for him to react. He'd noticed the reflection of the Parliament building disappearing. Josh looked up. Everything had suddenly gone black. Christ, did something fuse? he wondered. Next he looked towards the London Eye. It had stopped moving, its capsules plunged into darkness.

A blackout, thought Josh. *Another blackout.*

He looked around. Yes, the whole city had been plunged into darkness. Across the bridge the lights were out. The cars were starting to back up across the bridge, and a few yards away he could hear the screeching of tyres and the honking of horns as the vehicles tried to get around the corner without any traffic lights. Nearby, he heard a woman screaming. A couple of hundred yards away, a police siren started to whine into life. All around, people were running.

Josh glanced back towards The Firm's building, the so-called Vauxhall Gaumont. Even there the power had shut down.

'That will teach them not to mess with my man,' said a voice.

Josh spun around.

'Luke,' he shouted. 'Luke? Where are you, you little bastard?'

His eyes scanned the crowd on the bridge. People were starting to run. He could hear a woman yelling that someone had stolen her handbag, then a father shouting for his little boy.

A pale figure suddenly stepped out of the shadows. Luke was dressed in jeans and sweatshirt, with a hood pulled down partly obscuring his face. His hands were stuffed into his pockets, and there was a black canvas rucksack slung over his shoulder.

He looked up at Josh. 'That's some blackout, man,' he said, grinning.

'Christ, what have you done?' snapped Josh. 'Turn the lights back on.'

'Are they treating you okay?' said Luke. 'Because if they're not, I'm going to make them pay.'

'No worse than usual,' said Josh. 'How the hell did you know where I was?'

'It took a bit of time,' Luke admitted. 'After I got back to my mum, we banked all that money we got from Porter-Bell, then I figured we had to make

387

sure that you were okay. So we decided we'd both come to London. I always wanted to see that place on the cover of the first Clash album. And she wanted to see Abbey Road.'

'Your mum is here?'

'Well, she's in the hotel. Probably gone out to score some dope by now.' Luke grinned. 'Anyway, it took me a few hours to hack into your outfit's system. They've got some pretty good firewalls in place. But I got through. Found out they were keeping you there, then that you were being thrown out today. So I figured that if I just waited here for a bit, I'd see you soon enough. Even in the darkness.'

'You kept a copy of the software, didn't you?'

'Well, you never know when you might need it. I reckoned that if they started messing about I'd just get in touch and tell them that I'd keep shutting their country down until they let you out.'

'Well, I'm out,' said Josh firmly. 'So turn the bloody power back on. Before they send the Army out to get us.'

Luke sighed. 'I kind of like it in the dark,' he said. 'It doesn't matter who you are, what you look like or how much money you have. In a blackout we're all the same. Equal.'

Josh stepped forwards. 'Just turn it back on.'

From his pocket, Luke pulled out a PDA. He pressed a button, then fired a signal. Standing next to Josh, he leaned over the side of Vauxhall Bridge. Behind them he could hear the wail of sirens, and the sound of some police officers starting to order people to move along.

'Let there be light,' said Luke.

Up above, Josh could see the lights suddenly

388

flooding across the city. Big Ben burst into life, and the London Eye started turning again. Cars screeched to a halt as traffic lights all across London turned red simultaneously.

'You know what?' said Josh. 'Maybe you're right. Perhaps it does look better with the lights out.'

Both of them laughed loudly.

'We make a pretty good team,' said Luke.

'What the hell makes you say that?' asked Josh.

Luke tapped his PDA. 'The wars of the future will be fought as much by boys like me equipped with gadgets like this as they will by men like you with your guns and knives.'

Josh stared down at the water. The lights were beaming out across the city, the sirens had stopped, and the traffic was returning to normal.

'Maybe you're right,' said Josh. 'A couple of kids like you could probably take out a battalion of men like me. No problem.'

The crowds were starting to pack the bridge as Luke stepped back. As Josh turned around, people were starting to press into the space between them, blocking Luke from view.

'You need me, man, you just get in touch.'

'How?' snapped Josh.

'Same record, man, that will show you the way,' said Luke, laughing. '*London Calling*. But this time it's a bonus question.'

Josh looked into the crowd. 'Luke,' he shouted. 'What the hell does that mean?'

But the crowd had already closed in. And Luke had slipped away.